It is the height of the Roaring Twenties – a fresh enthusiasm for the arts, science, and exploration of the past have opened doors to a wider world, and beyond...

And yet, a dark shadow grows over the town of Arkham. Alien entities known as Ancient Ones lurk in the emptiness beyond space and time, writhing at the thresholds between worlds.

Occult rituals must be stopped and alien creatures destroyed before the Ancient Ones make our world their ruined dominion.

Only a handful of brave souls with inquisitive minds and the will to act stand against the horrors threatening to tear this world apart.

Will they prevail?

ARKHAM HORROR™

CULT *of the* SPIDER QUEEN

S A SIDOR

ACONYTE

First published by Aconyte Books in 2021

ISBN 978 1 83908 082 1

Ebook ISBN 978 1 83908 083 8

Cover art by Daniel Strange

Distributed in North America by Simon & Schuster Inc, New York, USA

Printed in the United States of America

9 8 7 6 5 4 3 2 1

ACONYTE BOOKS

An imprint of Asmodee Entertainment Ltd

Mercury House, Shipstones Business Centre

North Gate, Nottingham NG7 7FN, UK

aconytebooks.com // twitter.com/aconytebooks

1927

Attention Andy

The package was not for him. Andy never got any mail at the paper. He did not rank high enough among the reporters, and he never would, not with the kind of stories they were assigning him. He was bored and wandering down in the mailroom one sleepy, dreary Monday morning, a cup of hot coffee in his hand, lamenting this fact when he spotted a curious parcel on the mailroom's sorting table. The size itself was not remarkable. Round, flat like a box of candy. What caught his eye, besides the well-traveled look of the wrapper – khaki, rain-spotted, frayed at the edges, and tied with a dark, mildewed string – was the abundance of red stamps and the postmark.

From somewhere in Brazil? Is that what it said?

He leaned forward and rotated the box to read it better.

Heck, he was right.

Manaus, Amazonas, Brasil.

No name or street mentioned in the return address. The *Advertiser*'s address was general too, without any further direction to pass it along to a specific editor or reporter.

Just the word: ATTENTION!

And scrawled underneath that: PLEASE OPEN IMMEDIATELY! URGENT!

Hmm... that was interesting. Who in the Amazon jungle would be shipping mail to the *Arkham Advertiser* in chilly, old, gloom-capped New England, USA? He lifted the edge of it. Heavy. A cardboard box of sweets was out of the question. More like a tin case of something.

But what?

He was tempted to give it a good shake. Then he might have an idea...

"May I help you, young man?" The mailroom manager was a middle-aged gent with a sharp moustache and a bowtie that looked like a strangler tied it. His eyes bulged.

Andy startled, nearly spilling his coffee. The cub reporter had been staring so hard at the package he hadn't noticed the other man approaching. They stood on opposite sides of the cluttered table. The man looked at him frostily.

"Hi, I'm Andy Van Nortwick. I work upstairs."

No reply.

He'd been an employee of the paper for almost a year. A lot longer if you counted his time as a paperboy, biking up and down Arkham's early morning streets. Home delivery was catching on then. He tossed his bundles on porches and stoops, testing out his shortstop's arm.

"I bet you've seen me around, haven't you?" Andy tried again.

"No."

Andy glanced down, disappointed. "I'm working on blending in so I can observe others. That's what an ace reporter does. Never get in the way of the big story. I must be good at it."

"You could do better," the manager said. His eyes narrowed to slits.

Andy was about to excuse himself when a crazy idea charged into his head.

"Say, I was wondering. Long as I'm down here, do you have anything for me to carry upstairs? Save you a trip later." Andy smiled. His thumb plucked the package string. He hoped he wasn't being too obvious. But he had a sudden urge to know what was in the box.

He *needed* to know.

"I haven't finished sorting." The manager's attitude warmed. "Mondays are bad. The Saturday crew is an utter disaster. What's on the table are their leftovers. Who knows what they do besides devising ways to add to my list of chores? Today's mail hasn't even come yet."

The bell over the door rang. A uniformed man shouldering a satchel pushed inside.

"Speak of the devil. Be with you right away, Ed." The bow-tied manager turned toward the counter facing the Armitage Street public entrance of the *Advertiser* building. "'*Neither rain nor sleet nor gloom of night*', as they say. Did you know that line comes from Herodotus?"

"That old Greek must've had a postman's heart," Ed said. His cap dripped rain, and his wool uniform smelled musty. A gust of November wind rustled papers in the mailroom.

Andy shivered. Boy, he was not ready for another long cold winter stuck indoors.

He had a hunch about the Brazilian package. A quiver in his gut told him there was a hot story inside. Damned if he was going to let it go to waste. Or worse, watch it passed along to one of the hacks from upstairs, sneaking slugs of whiskey from their desk drawer bottles, chomping on putrid cigars, and treating him like a nobody.

As the other two men moved off to the other side of the mailroom, Andy snatched the pencil from behind his ear. Without a moment's hesitation, because if he thought about it too much he'd lose his nerve, he bent over the package and jotted a quick addition to the address.

So now it read: ATTENTION! ANDY VAN NORTWICK, JOURNALIST!

That's more like it, he thought.

One little worry, though.

His note didn't match up with the rest of the message, which was written in ink. But the ink was faded as if it sat roasting on a tropical dock before being tossed into the leaky cargo hold of a northward-bound freighter for a weeks-long journey trod upon by rats. Andy dipped his finger in the dregs of his coffee and smeared a drop across his name. Far from perfect. But the letters darkened. Close enough to still get noticed but not too much to cause any suspicion. He shoved the package between two piles of envelopes.

And went upstairs to wait for his big break to arrive.

2

Something More Than Curiosity

Andy shared a desk with the *Advertiser*'s best-known sportswriter. Sean "Red" Phelan had another desk among his athletically minded cronies, where they jawed about baseball, horseracing, and boxers. The desk Red shared with Andy was where he went to get away from the boys. That meant Andy had to find somewhere else to scram to whenever Red needed to meet a deadline or grab shuteye after a night out. Their desk tucked conveniently behind a pillar.

Right now, though, Andy had it to himself.

He tipped back in his chair and daydreamed.

The Amazon…

If that place didn't spell adventure, nowhere did. Andy loved the idea of jungles. Challenging yourself to survive on the knife edge between life and death in a truly wild place. Dropped into the middle of miles of impenetrable green, indistinguishable from the elemental world of the dinosaurs. A person moved forward according to their skills. And what they knew mattered more than who. Nature's awesome indifference set the only rules. You weren't subject to human whims or favoritism. He'd trade it for this stuffy office with its smoke-blue haze and backroom politics. No birdsong here but clacking typewriters.

The only river made of talk and more talk.

As a student, Andy had found escape in adventure stories. Schoolwork bored him, but he was always a reader. Haggard, Doyle, Kipling, and Burroughs. He dived into their fantasies. Ultimately, they weren't enough. He suspected it was because they wrote *fiction*. None of it was real. Paeans to empire: that quality was evident. The authors championed examples of colonial violence and ugly cultural injustices under the banner of Western progress. Elitist white men trumpeting their dominance of the globe. At what cost?

Andy was no John Reed radical. With President Coolidge deciding not to run for re-election, he didn't know who he'd vote for next year. Lots of people around Arkham, mostly the rich ones, hoped the boom years would last forever. Young Andy yearned for an authentic life experience, a journey outside Arkham, where he'd spent his whole dull life. Get away. That was the key. He wanted a broader worldview. Andy leaned forward and peeked around the pillar.

No mail cart.

His mysterious package from Manaus was stuck in transit.

He could barely keep from scouting the hallways. But he had to stay calm. Not act suspiciously. What he'd done was ethically questionable at best.

At worst...

He didn't let himself think about it. Andy wanted to make a name for himself. The *Advertiser*'s editor, Doyle Jeffries, ran a tight operation and didn't put up with rule-bending. Not from his news department. He was a muckraker through and through, a stickler for hard evidence and high standards. But it wasn't easy breaking into the circle of investigative reporters. Issue after issue, the same people got their bylines on the front page. Heck, Andy would admit he was jealous. Sure he was! He wanted in. For the longest time he was convinced Jeffries didn't even know his name. He went as far as to bet fellow reporter Minnie Klein a slice of cherry pie at Velma's that she couldn't get Jeffries to identify him after a meeting. Minnie paid for the pie.

The one time he had gotten Jeffries' undivided attention had ended in total disaster. Andy was lucky to still have a job. He shouldn't be risking blowing up his livelihood over a box he couldn't even guess the contents of. If somebody found out he doctored the address…?

Jeffries wouldn't take him back. Not the way he did seasoned staff like Rex Murphy who, despite a few major foul-ups, had the editor's respect. Andy needed to earn his way up the ladder to reach the level of a Minnie or Rex.

How could he do that with the scraps they were feeding him?

News didn't even really sell papers. Flashy sports writers like Red Phelan did. Andy wasn't about to catch any lucky breaks from the sidelines. He could feel his opportunities slipping away each week. If he didn't grab something soon…

A person had to seize their future.

He'd learned that.

What he planned to do was open the package. Carefully. Give it a good inspection. See if there was anything newsworthy. Perhaps a rumble of international intrigue that sent waves all the way to the banks of the Miskatonic. Andy had a feeling the package held something important. He knew how cliched that sounded. A reporter's hunch. It went beyond journalistic instinct. He felt an almost eerie connection. That box held his destiny. He just *knew* it.

If he ultimately decided to pass, he'd put everything back. Say it came to him by mistake.

He put his feet up and flipped through his assignment notebook. Sigh.

This week they wanted him to spill ink about the revised bus schedule to Innsmouth. A museum exhibition. Church bake sales. A burst pipe that flooded a warehouse on River Street.

Andy chucked his notebook.

Bus schedules and bake sales… leaky pipes…

How could he be expected to move up?

That box, though. That little brown box…

A headache pulsed in his temples. In the dark behind his eyes, he saw the box shifting. Imagined it coming to him. Floating.

Why was something unknown suddenly so important to him?

Is this how obsessions started? A drip, drip, drip that slowly filled your brain until there was no room for anything else. The pressure in his head grew.

The box.

The person who mailed it from Manaus obviously didn't know him. To them Andy didn't exist. To Andy they hadn't existed until this morning in the mailroom when something more than curiosity told him what to do. Write down your name, Andy. Make it yours. Steal it if you must.

Now he was able to picture them in a foggy way.

The humid air. The smell of water, mud. Two tanned hands tying the string. Bustle in the port. Noises of life. Voices. Speaking in one or more languages he didn't understand.

A rattle of coins and a pile of wrinkled bills sliding across a counter.

Licking the stamps, pressing them down on the paper.

He saw it.

Andy knew *that* sounded even more far-fetched.

But after this past summer and what he'd witnessed at the Silver

Gate Hotel he wasn't discounting anything. Certainly not the possibility of anything... uncanny.

Andy had gone to the hotel to interview a famous artist. A painter of the Surrealist movement named Alden Oakes. The hotel had burned a year earlier, and Oakes was a survivor of the horrific, deadly fire. Back in town for the Silver Gate's grand reopening. The story he told Andy over the next few hours was... peculiar. Riveting but strange. Andy wasn't sure how much to believe. But he'd unexpectedly gotten what he thought was a really good story out of it. A hot story – he wondered if he should risk the pun when he pitched it to Jeffries. If the editor in chief gave him the go-ahead, it would be the biggest piece he'd written for the *Advertiser*. They couldn't ignore him then.

Only that wasn't the end.

Andy was the last person to see Alden Oakes. Ever.

The man went missing after the interview. Vanished. Andy saw something that day in the hotel ballroom when he and the painter were alone. Or Andy thought they were alone. What he observed brought up more questions than answers. It was almost like Andy stepped into another man's dream. Or nightmare. Depending on how you interpreted things. And Andy wasn't sure. He'd changed his mind a thousand times in the past few months. The longer it receded into the past, the less certain he was. Not of the facts, but of his own perception. He wished he had another person he could check things with, a second eyewitness. Someone to validate his memories. He knew what he saw. Afterward his mind was opened to... other possibilities. This much he was convinced was true: supernatural phenomena do occur. Unexplained events *have* explanations. Some people just aren't ready to hear them.

One of those people was Andy's editor.

Doyle Jeffries.

Andy ran to the *Advertiser*'s offices that day, after a quick search of the painter's hotel room. He demanded to see Jeffries. The editor sat there staring while Andy ran through his tale, leaving nothing out. After he finished, he was breathless; his collar loose, sweat-soaked.

Jeffries made a tent of his fingers and pressed them to his lips.

"Who put you up to this?" the editor said.

Andy didn't understand. He had another one of those gut feelings. This one was like a slick ice block falling inside him. Falling and falling. He was going to be sick. He had seconds to save his career, to save himself from losing his dream of frontpage headlines and fame.

"Red Phelan," he said. His deskmate. It was the only name he conjured in that moment.

"Red?" Jeffries said, arching an eyebrow.

"Yes, sir."

Andy's face felt in flames.

Then Jeffries did the most unexpected thing. He started laughing. And didn't stop until he had tears in his eyes. "I don't go for shenanigans. You must know that about me, Anthony."

Andy Van Nortwick didn't correct his boss. Instead, he forced a smile and nodded.

"That I do," he said.

Jeffries slammed his palm on his enormous desk. Everything jumped. Andy included.

"Like a great engine a newspaper can build up heat. Things will explode, mind you. Depend on it. Unless every so often we let off a little steam. I'm not a humorless man." He removed his glasses, wiping the lenses. "Is Red here? Is he outside my door listening?" He called out. "You almost had me fooled, you redheaded, ink-stained wretch. But not quite. If you're there, you might as well come in."

Andy turned to stare at the open doorway, hoping that Red was anywhere else on earth. He prayed Red was at a ballgame. Somewhere, anywhere, but the newsroom.

His prayers were answered.

Later, Andy bought Red's future silence on the matter with a case of Canadian whiskey. Red never forgot the dubious deal they made.

"Didn't know you had it in you, kid. How about picking up a ham sandwich for me?"

Andy was reliving his brush with career self-destruction when a cough rang nearby. It was Red. Standing over him, disheveled, the sportsman blinked.

"Kid, the chair," Red said.

Jolted out of his revelry, Andy climbed away from the desk, retreating to the windowsill.

Red sat. The stogie in the corner of his mouth had gone out. He angled the chair, thumped his heels on the desk, and tipped his fedora over his face, preparing to ship off to Slumberville when the worst thing in the world happened.

The mail cart squeaked around behind the pillar.

The mailroom manager wrinkled his nose in the direction of the fragrantly reclining Red, and said to Andy, "Young man, you have an item of mail."

He held out the string-tied box from Brazil.

Awakened and alert, Red shot out his freckled hand and intercepted the delivery.

3
Curious Development

"Who do you know in Brazil?"

"Nobody," Andy said, trying to sound casual.

"Hmm, hmm, hmmm…" Red tested the weight of the box. "Heavy."

"It's probably nothing. Brazilian newspapers. I won't even be able to read them."

Andy was standing, inching closer.

"Well, nobody went to great lengths to send you nothing. Not cheap, either." Red squeezed the box with his chunky thumbs. "Why'd you suppose a stranger in a foreign land would do that? I'd be hard pressed to locate anybody who's heard of you in Arkham."

"I don't know if that's true." Andy's ears turned hot. He's trying to get your goat, he thought. Don't give him the satisfaction.

Andy picked up a pencil.

"Sure it is." Red clutched the box. His knuckles whitened. He smiled the kind of smile you see on an alligator in a sandpit at the zoo and ran his fingertip over Andy's name. Peering at the letters. Tap, tap, tap. The rumor about Red was he'd spent a couple years at

Harvard before being expelled. Intelligence shone in his bloodshot eyes. His rough persona was an act. But not the drinking. Andy smelled the bathtub gin oozing from his pores.

"Just what is it you're up to, Andy Boy?" Red said toothily.

"Me? I'm not up to anything."

Red popped a match and relit his cigar.

"You don't care if I open it?"

Before Andy could object, Red flicked open a pocketknife and sliced through the string. Two quick swipes slashed an "X" in the paper wrapper. Red skinned it back to reveal a cardboard box. He shook the lid off. Red held up the prize.

"It's a film canister," he said.

Andy was too fascinated to object. "What sort of film is it? The label's blank."

"So it is." Red touched the piece of tape that ran along the outer edge of the canister.

"Let's open it," Andy said.

"I don't think so."

"Why not?"

"Because, kid, then you really do have a box of nothing from nobody. The film in that can is exposed but not processed. If light gets at it, forget it." He tapped his ash on the floor.

Red *was* smarter than he acted. Andy's eye followed the falling ash and spotted a slip of white paper inside the box. "Look, there's a note," he said.

Red brought the paper up. "It says, 'Maude Brion is very much alive!'"

Maude Brion. The name sounded familiar, as if Andy had heard it or read it somewhere.

"You don't even know who she is. Do you, Andy Van Nortwick?" Red cocked his head.

Andy paused, trying to catch the name out of the air. *Maude Brion.*

"She's an actress," Andy said.

"That's right, boy. And what else?"

"Oh, she's that actress who went missing last year making a movie in the Amazon!"

"Give that man a prize." Red handed over the note.

Andy reread it. Just one sentence.

Maude Brion is very much alive! Well, hot damn, this was a story.

Red said, "She *is* that actress who went missing on the river. But she wasn't acting. She was directing a picture. Documentary. Looking for a long-lost rainforest god. Maybe I ought to take a break from ballgames and do an investigation. I might get a book out of it. If I asked Doyle, he'd let me take a sabbatical. Amble on south. Maybe do a little fly fishing while I'm there. Catch me a peacock bass, a mess of pacu, or the legendary pirarucu."

Andy sweated. His brain full of worry. His spirit crushed with disappointment. Until he saw Red didn't mean it. Not really. He'd done his teasing and had his fun. Red wasn't interested in leaving Arkham or the *Advertiser*'s offices. Why should he be? This was his jungle, and he was the sleepy old big cat. Red kicked his feet up. Rearranged his hat so the shade disappeared his face.

Without looking, he tossed the canister to Andy.

"Make yourself scarce. I sense a dream coming on, and the dancer in my dream says she don't want you here. Skeedaddle." Red waggled his fingers.

Andy tucked the can under his arm.

"You think there's any shot at finding Maude Brion?" he said.

"Kid, if you find anything at all, it'll be bones."

"Where can I get this developed?" Andy asked.

"Talk to Darrell Simmons. Now. Leave."

"I'm going," Andy said, smiling to himself.

"Sweet dreams, kid. I got a feeling you're gonna need 'em."

Before Andy left the newsroom, Red's snores were buzzing like a rusty saw.

4
The Forest

When the dead man visited her, his face was purple as a plum. He parted a path through the thick bush using a walking staff carved from cocobolo rosewood. Her senses were sharp, heightened, but she could not move. Despite the jungle heat, she shivered at his appearance. Because she knew this man. The staff he carried – she had bought it for him, a gift before their long journey together. She recognized the rich, darkly striped grain and the twist in its design. The man's hand – his clothes – were beyond filthy.

He stared at her but did not speak. His eyes were opaque. A milky film masked their blue.

"Can you see me?" she asked.

He must be able to see, she thought. He came to me through the forest. If he were blind …

He didn't answer.

"Can you hear me?" she said.

The man nodded.

"Good, good. Do you know who I am?"

Her heart drummed as she waited for an answer. A "no" would've added to her pain.

He nodded. *Yes.*

"I am so happy to have found you." Joy filled her, but she reminded herself to contain her reaction. She needed information from him. It was unclear how much time they would have. "I looked for you for so long. I did everything I could think of. Séances. Mediums. Where have you been?"

The man remained silent. He turned and gestured with his staff. Behind him, at the trees.

The forest.

Emerald leaves dappled with golden sun. He was in the forest. She already knew that.

"Why aren't you speaking? Have I done something to upset you?"

He shook his head, tilted it back and showed her his whiskery throat. Grossly swollen, blistered. The skin taut, its color blacker than purple. He clutched it with his fingers, grimacing.

An unknown bite. The venom had spread quickly. Nauseated, he lay in his hammock, drenched with sweat, muscles twitching. Paralyzed. Wheezing with each shallow breath he drew.

She remembered.

She would never forget the sight of him struck down and her inability to help.

"I'm so sorry this happened to you," she said. It wasn't her fault but still she felt guilty. They would never have come here if it weren't for her. The river trip attracted them both, but this spot, where they landed their boats and pitched camp, was her suggestion. She had picked it out. "Here's a proper base on dry, level ground," she said, satisfied. Then the tragedy occurred.

He was suffering terribly.

How will it all end? she wondered. Is his fate mine too?

Another pang of guilt for thinking about herself. But as she was instructed, she tried to resist any negative feelings. They had a bad effect. The energy created might even be dangerous.

Guilt is of no good to us now, she told herself. I've found him and that is a win.

In the distance, the sound of a snapping branch traveled down the green-covered hills.

They both looked up. Too far away to make out anything moving along the ground. Through a gap, a single vine was swinging gently. It might've only been a monkey. Or a bird.

Whatever it was, it was getting closer. It had crept down from the hills.

She had the feeling of being watched. Of being prey.

Maybe it was nothing, she told herself. A case of nerves. Paranoia. But she could not shake it off. The hair prickled on her neck. She'd better hurry if she wanted to find things out.

"Where did you … ?" she began to ask him.

She was standing alone. The trees, the bushes surrounding her grew still. The light faded.

"No! Don't!" she shouted into the jungle. *Not again.* "Listen! Please, come back!"

But it was too late.

The man was gone.

5
Movie Palace

"You can tell Red he was wrong. This isn't a negative. It's a 35mm print. All you need to watch it is the right projector," Darrell Simmons said.

He switched off the darkroom's red light and handed the reel back to Andy. The room smelled of vinegar. Leaving the darkness, Andy squinted as he followed Simmons to his kitchen.

Simmons was a photographer who worked for the *Advertiser*. Andy had gotten his address from the paper's office after Red Phelan mentioned him. He took a bus to Simmons's neighborhood. Knocked on the front door and caught him at home, finishing up some photos of what appeared to be rundown old houses. Head tilting sideways, Andy attempted to get a better look, but Simmons tucked the still damp photos behind his back. Andy had talked his way into the house, the mysterious film canister and Simmons's obvious curiosity doing most of the work.

"Great. So, where can I find a projector?" Andy said.

"You're in luck. I happen to have one in the basement. Care to see a picture?"

Andy smiled. "Love to," he said.

"Right this way." Simmons opened a door and led him down

an unfinished staircase. "Do me a favor and pin that sheet to the clothesline. I can do the rest. Oh, I'll need the film."

Andy set up the makeshift silver screen. Simmons wheeled in the projector on a cart.

"How'd you get your hands on a piece of machinery like that?" Andy asked.

"I write letters. You'd be surprised what I find. I'm willing to take castoffs, the unwanted. I love tinkering with gadgets old and new. I picked up this Pathé-Freres from New York after a blaze. Nitrate film is serious business. Like a celluloid firebomb. It took me some time, but I got it working. There's an old armchair in the corner. Drag it over. You can sit."

In the shadows, something gauzy and invisible tickled Andy's face. He brushed it away. Cobwebs hung from the floor joists above their heads. Basement creepy crawlies no doubt.

Simmons threaded the film, plugged in the projector's lamp. He switched off the lights. The sheet turned bright white. "I have to hand crank this French model. I'll stay here. Comfy?"

"Better than Grauman's Egyptian Theatre," Andy said, patting the dusty cushion. He was more excited than nervous, but he realized if the film turned out to be nothing, he'd feel crushed.

"Welcome to my movie palace. Ready? And… action!"

Simmons turned the crank. The white sheet came alive with moving images.

6
Maude's Party

The flickering pictures blend to tell a story.

The camera is wobbly since it is standing, along with its unseen operator, in the bow of a steamboat. Midriver currents keep things moving constantly. Waves slap the hull. The crew, mostly indigenous men, are loading gear and themselves into canoes in the water alongside the much larger boat. The camera pivots to show the stern. They have towed the skinny dugouts in a line tied behind the boat. All the dugouts are filled but one. A rope ladder hangs over the side.

The river is so large the shoreline appears surprisingly far away. Dense vegetation covers the hills. A pie-shaped section of riverbank is less overgrown. No tall trees grow there. It may be a landing area. Beyond it, the possibility of a trailhead.

JUMP CUT TO:

View from inside the empty dugout. Camera bounces. The camera operator is seated in the middle of the hand-hewn canoe. A woman climbs into the first seat. The view of the back of her head shows a frizzy, curly bob cut. A bandana keeps her hair off her neck. She stares ahead. When they hit the shallows, she is first out. Into the water. Splashing. Hauling the front end of the boat onto dry land. But not too dry. Mud everywhere. Footprints? She wears sandals. Her pantlegs are rolled. Laced-together boots are slung over her shoulder. She's done this before.

The image rocks as the camera operator goes ashore. It aims at the ground.

Yes, there are footprints in the mud on the riverbank. They lead toward the forest.

The woman charges forward with a couple of the indigenous men who are already busy swinging machetes. She has a machete too. She joins them cutting aside the brush.

The woman sees something and points. The three of them hack in that direction.

An oblong of white stone stands inside the tree line. Partially hidden but soon uncovered. The woman slices down the last barrier of vines and leafy jungle plants. She brushes the surface of the pale stone face, beckoning the camera to come in for a closer look. A carved symbol.

She turns and grins straight into the lens.

This is Maude Brion. Star of several silent films. Screenwriter of a few more. Director. Now a documentary filmmaker. We are seeing footage of her travelogue. A scenic adventure shot along the Amazon River. *Variety* magazine mentioned her departure from Hollywood. *Photoplay* gave it a full story treatment, with photos of her wearing prop shop expedition garb.

Hunt for the Spider Queen. That was the shooting title of her picture. The media reaction has run the gamut from skepticism to tongue-in-cheek enthusiasm to admiration for the boundary-breaking filmic adventurer. Mostly, they don't know what to believe. Are jungle gods real or fodder for the pulps? Maude appears as unfazed as she is determined. Curse the critics!

One legend tracks down another. That's what the *Photoplay*

story claimed. A bit of exaggeration: Maude Brion wasn't a legend yet, but she'd made a good start. No one could say exactly where she'd come from. She just appeared one day in LA. She hailed from Texas, was the gossip going around Tinseltown. Her father was an oilman, a wildcatter who'd struck it rich. But she didn't talk like a Texan, although she did ride every horse like she was stealing it. She had style. She made people nervous. A dabbler in the occult, one rumor avowed; they even hinted she belonged to a clique of Devil worshippers. She filmed a séance where a man slit his own throat. She'd only show it to if you were her friend, or if you paid a price. But you hear such stories in Hollywood.

Maude smiles at the camera.

Any person can see she has it. Magic. The camera loves her. It captures a strange energy and transfers it the movie watcher. You want to know her, what she's doing, where she's going.

Maude deflects the camera's attention. It's the white stone she wants captured.

The camera pushes in. Focuses.

The lighting isn't perfect. Too much shadow. But there's a carving etched in the rock: a round shape with multiple arms. Or are they legs? Six, seven, eight. Eight legs like an octopus.

Or... like a spider. Is this a marker? A signpost of sorts? The lines are deep. Are they old or new? It's hard to say. But it could be a clue as to the whereabouts of the Spider Queen. Maude is no archaeologist, not a scientist or expert of any kind when it comes to myths and legends.

She is a moviemaker. And she's taking her camera where no one has filmed before.

While Maude and the camera operator are studying the stone, the other men locate signs of a trailhead. Her full crew is there now, a half dozen lean men chopping away. She abandons the carving, instead plunging down the pathway which reveals itself more and more with every slash of their blades. They mount a steep, slippery climb, grabbing hold of low-hanging limbs to keep from backsliding. Eventually the terrain levels off. Behind them, the river is a lounging anaconda. Through the trees ahead, the shapes of human-made structures emerge. Buildings.

Is it a village?

No. It's a modern worksite. A plantation. The rubber companies set up stations in the rainforest. But the rubber boom is over in Brazil. Cheaper rubber can be had from Malaya. The cost of extracting rubber from the Amazon rainforest is too high. After they've drained the local resources for huge profits, the foreign business operations have pulled stakes and left the jungle.

This is a ghost plantation. Vines reach through the windows. The roofs have dark holes. Monkeys and birds pass through the openings. The interiors show a real mess. Toppled furniture. Water-damaged maps on the walls. Animal droppings litter the planks. The camera catches a not-small snake fleeing the intrusion; it moves like a bullwhip dragging down the steps and along the ground. The film is silent, but you can imagine the noise the new arrivals must be causing.

Yet there is more to discover.

Not far from the buildings, half-buried under leaves and pools of stagnant water, a pair of train tracks lay in the mud. They lead deeper into the undergrowth. Maude's party follows them.

Until the tracks end.

Abruptly.

Like a conversation cut off midsentence. The two steel ends jut up out of the muddy earth.

And no one in Maude's party is talking either. Their faces are frozen in awestruck wonder. Before them looms a second upright oblong stone covered in spider carvings. But they, and the camera, do not focus for long on the mysterious marker. Because a short distance away, housed within the shady, green cathedral of enormous trees, are the limestone ruins of a shrine.

The natural light here is poor for filming.

Yet the sight is as impressive and haunting as any old castle from a gothic novel.

Mostly silhouettes and shadows. Rubber trees stand guard around the multiple shrine structures, their trunks scarred from years of tapping. Insects dance excitedly in shafts of sunlight. Slabs of rock have crumbled to the forest floor. Plantation workers never built this place. Finding it might have contributed to their decision to get out. Because, despite the rough, intricate beauty of the arches and pillars, a sense of foreboding permeates the scene. This is a place where something bad has happened long ago. And may happen again. One cannot see the ruins and feel anything else. Yet how much of that reaction comes from a lack of knowledge about the people who made this their sanctum? For there is reverence in the placement of the ancient stone platforms, how they form a perfect ring, wearing their lichen badges and mossy cloaks – ceremonial altars erected in the smothering hot and humid, lush equatorial gloom.

The light fades.

But not before Maude records more spider renderings – on steps, altars, and pillars.

They are everywhere.

CUT TO:

Night.

Maude's party uses a lantern. They have decided for some unknown reason to remain at the shrine after dark rather than return in their canoes to the steamboat. Why did they camp there?

Perhaps the path out was too difficult to follow at night. Though this scenario seems unlikely given the short distance and the local guides familiar with navigating in the woods.

Perhaps they wanted to stay.

They've gathered on one of the shrine platforms, inside a temple-like structure with no roof. Was there once a roof constructed of plant matter that has rotted? Was it always open?

Pricks of moonlight shine above, here and there between the trees. But the party gathers around the lantern. Is it too wet to start a fire? Or do they feel building a fire here might be somehow disrespectful? The faces of the indigenous members of the party show the same uncertainty as Maude. Uncertainty, but also excitement. One of the men takes control of the camera for a brief interval. He is curious, confident. The previously unseen cameraman shows up for the first time. He appears to be an American, or at least a white person, like Maude. The cameraman and Maude are sitting on the temple floor, arm-in-arm, celebratory. They toast one another with their canteens. Singing. Laughter. Their long journey on the river has borne fruit.

All heads turn at what must be a loud sound coming from the jungle.

The cameraman takes back his camera. Pivots.

In the woods, lights flicker. The orbs float like glowing buoys on a black sea.

Coming closer.

Everyone is on their feet. Machetes in hand. They watch.

Figures dart in the woods at the edge of the shrine complex.

They're inside the ruins now. Dark shapes. The lights accompany them.

People emerge from the darkness. Men and women. Some

of them are wearing modern Western clothes. Mud-spattered. Hanging on them like rags. They are carrying torches. And...

Rifles.

Dozens of people surround Maude's party. Some stay back, are little more than pairs of eyes in the dark. Half-lit faces. The torchlight changes them, makes them seem sinister.

Others come forward.

Maude is afraid. But she drops her machete. Holds her hands up, showing she is no threat.

The people from the forest are speaking to her.

Looking puzzled, she talks back to them. How are they communicating with no translator? Are these people Americans? Or Brits? It is impossible to decipher what they are saying. One of Maude's men points up into the treetops. Maude looks but does not appear to see anything. Then the torchbearers toss their fires into the center of the ring of stone platforms.

There is a firepit there, hidden under leaf debris.

Flames leap high into the air. Higher than one would expect, illuminating into the trees.

Someone knocks the camera to the ground.

The cameraman's flailing arm enters the frame, a blurred profile of his bearded, panic-stricken face slides past the upper part of the frame. The glint of fire reflected in a pair of eyeglasses. The camera is righted again. And now it angles upward, pointing just beyond the tips of the flames. Columns of smoke. A blurry image beyond them. Firelit. Several crooked, digitate obelisks pierce the leafy treetops. Fingers spread apart, beseeching like supplicant's hands uplifted in a moment of worship. Frozen there in stone.

Are they a part of the shrine complex the expedition failed to notice in the daylight?

But how...?

A huge net stretches between the obelisks. Hard to make out. Unfocused. It sways. Trembles. The net is silver. Its thick cords are woven in an intricate pattern. More like a web.

From one corner, a black hulking mass darts out. Stops. Did it really move?

The web sways in the moonlight. Dots of moisture drip down, falling from its strands.

As back and forth it sways...

The reel ends.

7

Ink and Gold

The sound of film flapping inside the projector woke Andy from the dreamlike trance he'd been feeling, a transportation into the world of Maude Brion's moving pictures. It was only a fragment, of course, hardly more five or six minutes edited together. Yet in that time he'd left the basement of Darrell Simmons's house and walked with Maude on her never-before-seen rainforest adventure. He wondered briefly if it had all been an elaborate prank. Red Phelan and his cronies, or somebody else at the paper, mailing him the snippet of film to whet his appetite. To tease him.

Just so they might jeer at his expense.

Look at the kid! Took the bait hook, line, and sinker!

But then Andy remembered he'd chosen it for himself that morning in the mailroom. It hadn't been sent to him. This was his fate, his destiny. How could he pass up a chance like this?

Simmons switched the lights on.

"Could you run it again?" Andy said. "I'd like to take notes this time. I need to know as much as I can, if I'm going down there to look for her."

"Sure, sure," Simmons said. His voice carried a note of hesitancy.

"That really was her. Wasn't it? *Maude Brion is very much*

alive." Andy shook his head in disbelief. Was it the chill of being underground or pure excitement raising gooseflesh on his arms?

"I only saw one of her pictures," Simmons said. "But it looks like her. I read the headlines like everybody else when she didn't come back. That was, oh what, a year ago last summer. She's sort of like a female Percy Fawcett, only she's a movie director to boot."

"Who's Percy Fawcett?" Andy asked, wide-eyed.

"Famous British cartographer. Went missing in '25. Amazon expedition. Searching for an ancient lost city in uncharted territory. How much do you know about what you're getting into?"

Andy shrugged. "Not much, I guess."

"You'd better learn fast."

"I'll learn as I go." Andy was tired of hearing he was too inexperienced. How were you supposed to get experience anyway, if nobody was willing to let you take a crack at things?

"Then you won't get far. This isn't a walk around the blasted heath. The Amazon is a lot bigger, and deeper, than any Massachusetts swamp. You'll need a guide, provisions, hell you'll need a boat and diesel. And that's *after* you make the voyage to Brazil. Who's gonna pay for it?"

Andy sank back into his chair. The cushions let out a sigh.

"I haven't worked that part out yet." The photographer had a point. An expedition would cost big bucks. Andy's enthusiasm began to drain slowly away.

Simmons said, "This is proof she found something in the jungle. You should talk to Harvey Gedney." He sounded like he regretted throwing cold water on Andy's hot plans.

Andy swiveled around.

"Me? You want *me* to talk to the owner of the *Arkham Advertiser*?"

Simmons shrugged. "Who else has the cabbage to send you to South America?"

Andy thought about it. He had gambled when he wrote his name on the package. Was he ready to push all his chips in and go straight to the boss with his hand out?

"You interested in taking a trip to the jungle?" Andy said. "I could use a photographer."

"No thanks. I've got my hands full of weird happenings right here in Arkham. I don't need to go globetrotting to find more. This scoop is all yours, mac," Simmons said.

Andy wished the photographer had said yes. The prospect of asking Gedney for money was more than a bit intimidating. "I don't even know where to find Gedney," he said.

"He'll be at the Miskatonic Museum tonight. I'm scheduled to take some publicity snaps of him at the opening of a new exhibition."

Andy's face lit up. "I'm covering that story! I figured it was strictly a stuffy, mothball type of affair. Some dusty old curators would hand me all the copy I needed. But what if, instead, I stick around and mingle…. Will you point out Gedney for me? I'll take it from there."

"Sure thing. But after the shoot. That fine with you?"

"And how!" It really did feel like this story was meant to be his. "Can we watch it again?" Andy had his notepad flipped open and his pencil poised.

"The projector is ready to roll." Now infected with Andy's enthusiasm, Simmons plunged the room into darkness again. Turning the crank. Watching the steamboat passengers jerkily come to life.

Andy settled in for another trip to the ghost rubber plantation. The vine-clad ruins.

He'd ask Gedney for the money to find Maude Brion and whatever Maude had discovered about the Spider Queen. Heck, all he knew about the legend was that supposedly a goddess, or a monster, lived in the remote jungle. Either she controlled the spiders, or she was one. Maybe it was both. He wasn't sure. That black hulk swaying up between the obelisks – you couldn't make out anything, really. It might be a person in a costume. Maybe it was nothing. A hoax. But finding Maude would still be the biggest story in the country. If the *Advertiser* had an exclusive… and Andy got the byline… why, he'd be lousy with job offers from all the big city papers! He'd be on his way to the news career he always dreamed of. He'd be world famous!

Andy was the only person in the room dressed like a reporter. Another way of putting it was that the museum event was black tie. Even the catering staff looked buffed to a high-class gleam. Despite being woefully underdressed, Andy was determined to stay. He had a steely glint in his eye. Maybe that, and not his threadbare cuffs, was the reason Gedney was looking at him curiously and didn't turn away as he crossed the long, paneled room under the glow of crystal chandeliers.

"Mr Gedney, I'm proud to work for you," Andy said, sticking out his hand.

"You are?" Gedney's puzzlement showed as he shook with Andy.

"Yes, sir. I write for the *Advertiser*. And I want to talk to you about a scoop." Andy had resolved that if he was going to get fired, he might as well dive right in and get it over quickly.

"Can't it wait?" The surprise attack was working. He hadn't asked Andy straightaway who he was. A waiter offered them appetizers on a silver tray. Gedney snagged a deviled egg.

"I fear the competition will beat us to the punch," Andy said.

"We mustn't have that. Say, shouldn't you be going to your editor?"

Andy said, "It's so big we'd bring it to you eventually. I thought I'd start at the top."

Gedney nodded. It was unclear if he was interested or merely humoring Andy. Andy had a feeling that Gedney was uncomfortable with the museum crowd, and he'd just provided him an excuse to avoid the other attendees. Not that all of them paid attention to social signals. One barrel-chested man with a walrus moustache and brandy on his breath lunged over and stood himself shoulder-to-shoulder with Andy. Nodding and sipping from a cup of liquor-laced coffee.

"This is Oscar Hurley," Gedney said. "Oscar, this is ..." he paused, "Who are you?"

"Andy Van Nortwick. Reporter."

Hurley grunted as a pinniped might. His flipper-like hand clamping Andy for support.

"Andy was about to spill the beans on the *Advertiser*'s next big revelation." Gedney motioned for Andy to continue in Hurley's presence. "Oscar is tight-lipped. You needn't worry."

Hurley snorted and gave Andy's neck muscle a rough flipper-pat.

Andy wondered if Hurley would remember anything. He seemed rather ossified.

So, Andy went ahead and told them the story of Maude's reel, from jungle to screen.

Then he pitched the idea of the paper sending him on an expedition to search for Maude.

Gedney shook his head, objecting. "Helluva lot of money for a news story. Helluva lot. Even if it would be an exclusive for the paper." He was balancing a glass of icy Coca-Cola and a second deviled egg in one hand, using the other to finger wave to people across the exhibition hall. "I can't sell enough *Advertisers* to justify that kind of jaunt. It's kind of a wild-goose chase, isn't it? You've no guarantee of finding her. You don't even know who sent the film."

Andy's heart sank. Maybe Gedney was right. Andy didn't know

much. All he'd had was a glimpse of Maude among some ruins. That strange misfit crowd emerging out of the forest.

Maybe it was a fool's errand.

But was it, really?

Self-doubt and anger at not being taken seriously warred in his head. The last thing he needed was a repeat of the Alden Oakes fiasco from last summer. Andy's stubborn streak had probably hurt him as much as it helped him in life, but he'd never regretted it. He had his reporter's hunch. There *was* something there. Didn't his boss get that?

Gedney's attention shifted. He stared into a glass case behind them. Stone artifacts.

That's when Hurley chimed in, startling everyone, including himself.

"Too bad there's no gold," he said gruffly.

Andy noticed for the first time Hurley's hands were stacked with rings on every finger. Gold rings. Studded with precious gemstones. He smiled at Andy, revealing a golden canine.

Gedney looked up from the display. "Oscar is in the mining business. A real goldbug."

"But there is gold," Andy lied. "Rumors of gold, anyway. Tons of it. They say the Spider Queen hoarded yellow metal. That her temple sat atop a mine. Gods do love their golden idols."

Hurley slapped Andy on the back. "You should've started with that, my boy. You've whetted my appetite. So now feed me. Tell me more. Have you got any hard proof?"

There are moments in a person's life that punctuate their existence. Call them markers. They measure off eras. Before and after. When Andy wrote his name on the package in the mailroom that morning, he drew a mark, and now, with a flourish, he would complete it. Utterly.

"Yes," he said. "But I hesitate. What I have is too secret to be discussed in public."

He waited; the sweat turning cool along his spine. The heavy stare of Hurley melted over him. Weighing him, assessing his worth. A sparkle of wild greed was embedded in those eyes.

"Come see me in my office tomorrow afternoon," Hurley said. He reached into his vest pocket and then pressed a thick, gilt-edged business card into Andy's hand with his hot fingers.

HURLEY MINING COMPANY

Oscar M. Hurley

Founder & President

Arkham, Massachusetts

Printed along the bottom of the card was an address in the Merchant District. Appointment made, Hurley clumped off. Andy turned to thank Harvey Gedney for his time. But Gedney had drifted to the other end of the exhibition hall, his black tuxedo slipping into a chinoiserie-wallpapered corridor full of shadows. Disappointed, Andy retreated, heading for the night-lit streets. His mind was elsewhere. He had a meeting tomorrow he needed to prepare for.

He failed to notice a well-dressed woman standing nearby. Long blonde hair tucked behind her ears, so she wouldn't miss a word of the three men's conversation. She tapped the display case with a sharp, pearly fingernail. Admiring the artifacts, knowing which were fake.

She had a meeting tomorrow too.

8
Iris

"Excuse me, are you Andy Van Nortwick?"

The young man she'd overheard at the museum was holding his head in his hands. He looked up from his desk. Judging from his mussed hair, the dark under-eye circles, and the same wrinkled suit he'd worn yesterday at the museum, she guessed he hadn't been to bed. Poor thing. She'd talked her way into the building. She carried herself with confidence and was good at remembering details. A description of the young reporter assigned to the museum affair last night got her his name and desk location from a secretary. Minutes later she was striding up to him.

"I'm Andy." His voice sounded scratchy. He covered a yawn.

She clasped his fingers with her gloved hand. Firm pressure. A quick, lips-only smile.

"Glad to meet you," she said. "Is this a good place to talk?"

He peered around the pillar at the newsroom. On the other side, faces had turned, like flowers following the sun, trying to catch a glimpse from any angle. Typewriters fell silent.

"About what?" he asked.

"It's private. I know something that might help you." She pointed at him as if he were a pair of earrings she wanted to try on before deciding whether she was going to buy them.

"We should leave, then." The reporter fetched his overcoat from a wall peg.

She waited in her furs. The moment she stepped around the pillar all those curious stares fixed on her, plainly nosy in the way reporters can be. She refused to give them the satisfaction of looking back. The heels of her D'Orsay pumps clicked as she navigated between desks.

"Are you hungry?" he asked, glancing at his pocket watch.

"Famished." She wasn't. Food didn't interest her much. But she needed to get him alone.

They walked downstairs and out the door. He was leading her to the railcar diner across the street as she'd predicted he would. He'd perked up since her arrival; the cold air helped, but he was nervous, distracted by his upcoming meeting no doubt, yet curious enough to talk with her. She wondered how desperate he was feeling. His options were few. Maybe he'd already decided to tell Oscar Hurley the truth: he didn't have any proof of gold at the Spider Queen site.

Because there wasn't any.

They sat down at a table, and the waitress poured two coffees.

He hadn't asked any questions. Down in the mouth, he looked like his dog had run away. He didn't have much to sell the millionaire, except himself. And he doubted what he'd get back. But she was going to help him.

"My name is Iris Bennett Reed," she said, taking off her gloves. "I'm an anthropologist. Do you know what that is?"

Andy bit his lip and gave it a shot. "You study groups of people. Is that right?"

Iris nodded. "Cultures. I'm a professor in New York City,

although presently I'm on sabbatical. My specialty is folklore. Most recently, folklore of the Brazilian Amazon."

Andy sat up, thrusting out his chin. Suspicious. "What makes you think I'm interested?"

"Aren't you?" She stopped stirring and sipped her cup of java. It was surprisingly good.

"Well, let's say I am interested. How'd you figure that out? Are you psychic?"

"Hardly." She laughed. "I was at the museum exhibition last night. Did you see me?"

Andy shook his head. "No. I think I'd remember that."

He hadn't seen her. He was occupied with the millionaire men. But she'd noticed him. Somebody told her what to be on the lookout for. It was all part of the plan, mostly hidden from her. She only uncovered a few pieces at a time, like turns in a game. She was learning more every day.

She opened a monogrammed gold Cartier cigarette case. "Care for a smoke?"

"I'm trying to quit. They give me a sore throat."

She put a cigarette between her lips. Struck a match. "May I?"

"Go right ahead." He eyed the case as she returned it to her purse. Her diamond bracelet caught the pale November light and threw it back in glittering pieces. He seemed puzzled by her. Curious. She had that effect on some people. "You don't look like an anthropologist," he said.

"Met many, have you?" she said. They always expected her to be dowdy and wan.

He was about to say she was the first when she preempted him.

"We're not all the same." She waved out the match. "I overheard you talking…"

"You mean you were eavesdropping."

"*You* were loud. It would've been hard not to hear you, or Gedney. Especially Hurley."

He had no comeback; he was too busy digesting the bits of information she was dropping. He'd gone into a mild shock, she imagined, his brain whirring away, racing to get ahead of her. She was familiar with the feeling herself. Playing catch-up. Sifting through clues. Deducing life.

She went on. "I did pay particular attention to your conversation. You mentioned Maude Brion and the legend of the Spider Queen. And I thought, well, what a crazy coincidence."

"What coincidence?" His face screwed up. He was trying to calibrate his level of trust.

"I know her."

"You know Maude Brion?"

Iris blew smoke at the window. "The Spider Queen. I know the Spider Queen."

Andy's expression passed through phases; first confusion, then astonishment, until he landed on keen interest and stayed there. Whatever tiredness he was feeling was gone now.

"You have my attention, Professor Bennett Reed," he said. "Please, continue."

"Ever heard of Galton Reed?" Her gaze flicked at the table, a tremor rippling in her cup.

Andy shrugged. "Is he a relative of yours?"

"My husband. He was my husband. Galton is dead." She hated saying it. Putting it into words made it real. She relived it. His accident. Her loss of him. Their lives together shattered.

The waitress came and took their orders.

"I'm sorry to hear that," he said when the waitress left. "Was his passing recent? I see you still wear your wedding ring."

Most men didn't notice. Iris ignored the directness of his

comment. He was a journalist after all. A certain pushiness was to be expected. She twisted the wedding band, smiling. "I have fantastic memories." She tapped ash off her cigarette. "We worked together, side-by-side, Galton and me. He studied religious practices and ceremonies. A brilliant man. Original. His early monographs are highly regarded in the academic world."

"And his later work? What about that?" Andy said, as he buttered a roll.

Iris couldn't help but bristle. The urge to defend her partner was reflexive. This boyish reporter might be more hardheaded than he appeared. Little things caught his attention. She told herself she'd better be careful not to underestimate him. And don't get his guard up too high.

"My husband's work shifted away from indigenous religious life. He stumbled upon several artifacts that did not fit. They were mythically based. But the conclusions he drew from them were… controversial. Colleagues accused him of everything from seeking publicity to outright hoaxing. The notoriety he received was difficult for both of us. It cost Galton his job."

"Sorry, but I'm not sure I follow what you're saying," Andy said.

She wasn't surprised. Few people understood what she and Galton had to endure.

"The relics he discovered depicted spider worship. It was unconnected to any specific Amazon village or known indigenous belief system. Galton believed there were people living in the jungle who revered the spider as a ferocious and clever hunter. They devoted themselves to a Spider deity. She was their god queen. Worshipping her became the center of their lives."

"Forgive me. What's the controversy?"

Iris breathed deeply. "My husband insisted the artifacts did not originate in this world."

Andy was confused. "Where did he think they came from?"

"Another planet, perhaps. New dimensions. He wasn't certain. But not from here."

"Oh, I see," Andy said.

He gave her that look she'd seen too many times before, a mixture of pity and barely concealed awkwardness. You poor chump, it said. You got yourself hitched to the wrong man. Only you didn't find out he was goofy until it was too late. They felt humiliation on her behalf. But they were wrong about Galton. She crushed out her cigarette as their lunch arrived.

"Yes, well, the department heads at the university *didn't* see. They were embarrassed at first, then angry when Galton refused to back down. He claimed he uncovered evidence to support his theories. My judgment is not so biased that I couldn't see the damage he was doing to his career. Mine too. Galton had a temper. He could be impulsive. He said bad things to the wrong people. Words he couldn't take back. They fired him. We returned to South America one last time hoping to find definitive proof of his theories. Something scientific, undeniable."

"Amazon expeditions cost a lot of money, I'm told." Andy cut up his creamed codfish on toast and stabbed a forkful, pausing before popping it in his mouth. "How could you afford it?"

"My parents had money. I am an only child. After they died, I paid for our research with my inheritance. Plus, I was still employed at my university job in New York. It was enough."

Andy stopped eating and leaned forward. "You wouldn't want to go back, by chance? If you listened to last night's conversation, you know I need a sponsor. Gedney won't do it. Oscar Hurley said he might. *If* I promise to locate an actual gold mine while I'm there."

"I'm afraid I spent the better part of my inheritance on Galton's dreams." She tried a bite of the iceberg wedge she'd ordered. The lettuce was fresh, the Russian dressing tasty. The newsman picked a good diner. Too bad she wasn't feeling hungry. "I couldn't help you there."

"I thought I'd try. I made Hurley think I have proof of gold deposits. I don't."

"But I may have the proof you need." She pushed her plate to the side and went into her purse again. "Hold out your hand."

Andy seemed reluctant, but not very. He needed a little coaxing. Maybe a dare.

"C'mon. It's not going to bite you." She held out her cupped hands, closed like a clam.

Andy stuck out his palm.

She dropped something in. Quickly covering it before he could see.

It was heavy – what she'd put there. Small, but heavy. Warm too. Or maybe it was his hand giving off the sweaty, humid heat. He was properly curious now. Weighing it. Wondering.

She slid her fingers away.

A gold spider. About the size of an acorn. With tiny, dark red, jeweled eyes. Its two front legs were raised up as if sensing, or attacking, an unseen prey. Two sharp fangs. Andy poked at one. "Ouch!" he said, withdrawing his finger.

He stared at a drop of blood bubbling out. He sucked on it.

"You should be more careful," Iris said. "Spiders do bite."

He tilted the golden arachnid figure. It *was* fascinating. Despite the many times she'd studied it, its irresistible charm remained. Beautiful and elegant, it felt timeless, a rare, precious item that might be shown in a museum or Tiffany's window. "Turn it over. See? It's a ring."

"And this is the Spider Queen?"

"Galton thought it might be," she said. "He traded for the item not too far from Manaus. Bought it from a boatman who specialized in rubies. The boatman claimed it came from a spider shrine in the forest. It's all here, written down in Galton's journal." From inside her purse she removed a small, black notebook with a snapped elastic band that used to hold it shut but now dangled below like a fuse. "Galton kept dozens of these. For sketches and field notes. He wrote in them daily." She flipped through the unlined pages, most of them covered edge to edge with Galton's tiny, cramped handwriting. "Here we go. Be careful. The humidity gets into things and before you know it, glue is breaking down. The paper just rots. Everything starts falling apart."

She lay the notebook flat on the table, spinning it around so Andy could read it. She pinned it there like a dead butterfly. On the open page there was a pen sketch of the spider ring.

"Paid for specimen of arachnoid jewelry. Gold ring. Eight ruby eyes. Possibly worn by SQ priest or priestess???? Underside inscription. No known language. Robbed from the altar proximate to…" Andy stopped reading. "What's this say? I can't make out these next words."

She cocked her head to decipher her husband's inky scrawl.

"*Interdimensional gateway?* I told you Galton had unique hypotheses." Iris blinked at him and snatched the journal back. Only a taste. She needed to keep him interested, make him want to know more. That was a natural trait in most journalists, the desire to find things out. If he wanted something from her, then she had a better chance of getting what she wanted from him. "The important thing is you can show this to Oscar Hurley. The spider and this notebook which corroborates its significance. He'll go for it. Couldn't resist."

"You'll let me have this?" Andy turned over the spider to examine the odd carved marks.

"To borrow. I'll wait outside while you have your big man meeting with Hurley."

Andy thought about her offerings. "It doesn't really prove there's gold in the ground."

"Who cares? *If* Hurley gives you the money… and after he sees this, he will."

"I don't know. I mean, if I get to the Amazon, how will I know what to do next?"

Andy wanted this enterprise to work so badly, but instead of charging ahead, he was clearly starting to see how it might go awry. Losing his nerve. He wasn't used to dealing with people on Oscar Hurley's level. They were different. They were rich. He was probably wondering if he could close the deal, convincing Hurley to back him. He'd fudged the bit about the gold, and his white lie had him feeling on shaky ground. She needed to stop him from thinking negatively. He had to be confident. Confidence would sell the expedition to Hurley. He'd believe it if Andy believed it. And Andy needed a push to make it over the top. Well, she'd give him that push.

"Listen," she said. "Show me the film you got from Manaus. I'll look for clues. I can go with you, Andy. We'll find Maude Brion and her crew. I can discover the shrine. I know I can. I've never been there, but Galton and I were so close before he got sick. So, let's go back. You and me." Iris hoped she hadn't overplayed her hand. She didn't have the resources to launch a full-scale expedition on her own. Yet something was calling to her. She had to make this trip.

"I can't make any guarantees…" Andy started.

"I'll pay my own way." Iris lifted the spider ring from his hand and placed it on the table between them. "Together, we can do this. Tell Hurley you talked to an authority on the subject. That's me. I said I'd accompany you. If he says no, what have you lost except your shot at the biggest adventure story of the century? But if he says yes…"

Andy was nodding. A grin spread across his face.

"I'll do it! We'll do it!" Andy suddenly grew serious. "Hey, tell me why you want to go there. I need to know the whole truth. What is it you want from this proposed journey?"

"It's where I left Galton five years ago. Dying in a hammock in the rainforest. He was too weak to leave camp. There's was nothing to be done, no saving him. He told me to go. I owe it to his memory to finish what we started. This is my work too. I'm just as devoted as he was." What she said was true. Maybe she hadn't told Andy the whole truth. But that didn't matter to her right now. Galton felt so close to her. It was as if he were sitting there in the diner with them.

"That's a better reason than anything I could dream up," Andy said. He checked his pocket watch and rose from his chair. "Now to visit our new old friend, Mr Oscar Hurley."

"One last thing," Iris said, seizing Andy's arm, dragging him down. "We need to hire an expert guide. The best we can find. This is not negotiable. Without a guide we are doomed."

"I thought you were going to be our guide?" Andy sounded amazed.

She shook her head and went searching for her gold case and another cigarette. "I'm an academic with extensive field experience, true. But I'm no expert in the bush. If Galton's death proved anything to me, it was the necessity of hiring someone whose job is the team's survival."

"Heck, I wouldn't know where to start looking." Andy, exasperated, swept his arm out.

"Don't worry. I know the perfect person. She took part in a salon discussion at the museum this week. She's still in town. If you're lucky, you will get to her before she heads off on another dig. But you need to act fast. This one, she doesn't stay put for long."

Andy's mouth was open, but no words came out.

"You look surprised. Is it because she's a woman?" Iris let the question hang. "Her talk at the exhibition. Did you go? No, but I did. She told a tale of high-altitude Himalayan adventure. It was fantastic. Thrilling. Far more intriguing than anything her male counterparts presented."

Andy said, "The Himalayas? Isn't that about as far from the Amazon as you can get?"

"You'd be surprised. Things are not always where you'd expect to find them. And nothing is as close to a person as their dreams. Therefore, we will dream first. And go second. She will make sure we come home in one piece. A most excellent plan. Don't you agree?"

"I do. Who is this woman whose hands I'm putting my life into?" Andy said.

"Ursula Downs," Iris said, striking a match.

Before she lit her tobacco, she held the flame over the gold band. Moving it slowly back and forth until the skin of the spider took on a luxurious glow. Andy and Iris both leaned closer.

The jeweled eyes glistened as if they possessed life.

And a distant intelligence.

9
Ursula & Jake

"When do we leave?" Ursula Downs asked the young reporter.

At the other end of the office, Jake Williams's eyes grew wide. Jake was her loyal partner in expeditionary adventures. There was no one she knew better or trusted more with her life.

She shot him a glance that said, *Be quiet. I know what I'm doing.*

Luckily, Jake was sitting in a beaten leather chair off in the corner, observing the conversation and absently spinning a globe. The reporter, seated right across from Ursula and her desk covered with maps, hadn't read any significance in her look. Her nonverbal communication was enough to keep Jake quiet. Their guest was none the wiser. She hoped to keep it that way.

"As soon as possible," Andy said. "I'm prepared to leave at a moment's notice."

"A small housekeeping matter, Mr Van Nortwick–" she said.

"Call me Andy," he said, looking eager and impossibly fresh-faced.

"Tell me, Andy, how will Mr Hurley be paying us?"

"Is cash acceptable?"

"Cash? Oh, very much so." Ursula willed herself not to look directly at Jake. But on the edge of her vision, she spotted him vigorously nodding his head. She could hardly believe their good fortune. What archaeologist didn't fantasize about funding? She didn't pinch herself, because if this was all a dream she wanted it to last. "We'll expect our full guiding fee up front. An account needs to be set up for miscellaneous costs. I must have access to it without anyone glancing over my shoulder or second-guessing my decisions. Of course, we'll need cash on hand to buy supplies as soon as we land in Manaus, to hire local workers, pay the boat pilot and crew, etc. Money will need to cross palms to guarantee everything runs smoothly. Port officials and governmental inspectors can derail an expedition if they are not kept happy. Is this agreeable?"

"Absolutely." Andy peeked over at Jake to include him, although it was clear that Ursula was the one negotiating this deal. It was her name and title on the office door. "Mr Hurley was explicit. We will have all the resources necessary for our mission to succeed."

"Hurrah for Mr Hurley," Jake said.

Ursula curled her lip at him. She hoped if Andy saw her, he mistook it for a smile.

"About our *mission*, Andy, how would you define it? Its primary goal, I mean."

"Oh, I thought that was obvious. We're going to find Maude Brion."

"But Mr Hurley's interest is not in Miss Brion. Is it?" Ursula asked, pointedly. She had some knowledge of Oscar Hurley's reputation. She was skeptical about his motives. He didn't seem the type to care about motion picture productions or missing female directors.

Andy fidgeted in his chair. "No, not precisely. He's in the mining business."

"I'm aware of Hurley Mining. Not specifically their operations in Brazil, but in Africa. He is not a model of ethical business practices, shall we say? His companies have no regard for the wreckage they do to the landscape, the ancient archaeological heritage, or the people for that matter. How am I to square his evilness with my being a scientist and a decent human being?"

Ursula folded her hands and awaited his reply. If the reporter told her an obvious lie, she was ready to pull the plug. Funds or no funds, she wouldn't sell out her principles.

Andy's attitude changed. His cheery boy scout demeanor fell away. "Hurley thinks there's gold down there. If we see any while we're looking for Maude, he wants to know about it." His voice sounded mature, savvier. Not quite a babe in the woods. "That's the extent of it."

"Why does Hurley think there's gold, Andy?" Ursula said, raising a dark eyebrow.

"Because I told him there might be. I showed him an artifact, a gold spider ring from the area I want us to search. I have a field journal that suggests there could be more. If artifacts in the area are made of gold, where'd it come from? I handed him the pieces. But he put them together, drawing his own conclusions. My interest is in Maude Brion. I'm no geologist, I assure you."

"And I'm not a prospector. This will not be a gold hunt. El Dorado doesn't make my list of things I want to see before I die. Because El Dorado doesn't exist, Andy. While I might take Hurley's coins, I'm not devoting any energy to exploiting the Amazon. I'll help you look for Maude Brion. Jake and I will keep you safe. That's as far as we go. The only reason I'm still talking to you is because I've spent a lot of time in this part of the rainforest. There's gold to be had on that great river, but you're unlikely to find any where we're headed. Just so we're clear."

"As a mountain stream," Andy said. "Help me find Maude. I'll worry about Hurley."

Ursula was satisfied. At least for now. She smiled and stood up.

Andy stood too. They shook hands.

Jake joined them. He was a head taller than Andy. His dark hair and stubble struck a sharp contrast to the reporter's baby face. Where Andy was young and smooth, Jake was lean, weathered. His nose bent, not without a certain charm. A few scars creased his profile, and the dark wrinkles around his eyes revealed an amused disposition and an earned sense of wariness.

"When can we see the film?" he asked.

"I can set it up for tonight," Andy said.

"Peachy," Jake said.

"I'd like you to bring that spider ring and the field journal too," Ursula said. "This isn't the first time I've heard about the legend of the Spider Queen. But it's the only thing that sounds remotely credible. I'm excited to get started."

Andy said he'd call when the reel was ready for showing. Then he departed.

"Shall I pop some champagne?" Jake said.

Ursula had walked Andy to the door. She shut it, resting her back against the dark oak.

"Can you believe what they're paying us?" Ursula did pinch her arm now. "Well, I'm not dreaming. We're getting more than my last three grants put together. I about fell out of my chair when he accepted the number that I threw at him. I could hardly keep myself from shouting, *What!* It's phenomenal, though, just phenomenal."

"It's not his money," Jake said. "This Hurley fella must have so much dough he burns hundred-dollar bills instead of birch logs in his fireplace." Jake thumped the office's radiator.

"Hurley's certainly done enough dirty deals to deserve one done on him. Do you realize the good we can accomplish with his extra cash? I can finance my digs for the next ten years."

"Let's not get carried away. Dollars are like ghosts. Touch them and they disappear."

"All right. If not ten years, then five. I won't know where to start."

"Back to Tibet? Looking for Leng?" he said.

Ursula had gotten back from her Himalayan holiday less than a month ago. She couldn't stop talking about it to Jake. She'd gone alone. Ursula spent most of her time riding horses and visiting with generous nomads on the Himalaya high pasture. She practiced the Tibetan language during the day and slept in a yak-hair tent under a multitude of stars at night. The trip hadn't been part of her professional research, although learning new things wasn't work for Ursula. She also did it for fun. She might've been the first American woman to visit the forbidden city of Lhasa, had she not refused to violate the holy site by entering in disguise. She'd left that fact out of her presentation at the museum: *Dreaming of the Leng Plateau. Tibetan Stone Fragments.*

The chance to visit Lhasa had been an unexpected bonus anyway. She felt no regrets.

Curiously, the stories about Leng didn't come from anyone she'd met in Tibet. It was on the Nepal side of the mountains someone brought it up. In the market. A British wool trader.

He also dealt in rare antiquities, or so he said.

"Would you like to see?" he asked. She was doubtful. Something about his oily manner exuded unscrupulousness. When she hesitated to reply, he turned and walked back into his tent.

She followed him.

Inside the tent was gloomy. It smelled of sheep. The trader's breath stank of chhaang. He sat down on a three-legged stool and pulled one out for her. Then he produced a wooden mug of the fermented barley wine and offered her a sip through his straw, which she declined. He took a long one himself. Gasping, he bent over and dug into a satchel, coming out with a bundle wrapped in green canvas. When he unrolled it on the ground, she saw the wrapping had several deep pockets. From inside these, he withdrew three oblong stones, each about the size of a small loaf of bread, the same baked color, too. She squatted for a better look. He unhooked a lantern from an iron nail in the tentpole, so she might examine the specimens in a stronger light.

"Here, take it. I can't bring the stones outside. I don't need thieves," he said.

More likely, the stones were stolen from a monastery. He didn't want any trouble.

"What are these?" Ursula said.

"Leng stones. Ever heard of the Leng Plateau? That's where they're from. Very unique. Ancient and visionary. Thousands of years old, tens of thousands. Who can tell? You won't find anything like them anywhere else in the bazaar. Another buyer is interested. He'll be here soon."

She was skeptical. "What's this writing? I don't recognize it."

"Old Tibetan," he said, erupting with an airy hiccup. "Mystical qualities. Potent."

The trader went back to his straw and mug. Slumping, he seemed bored. Or drunk.

Ursula wasn't kidding when she said she didn't know the writing. It was strange. It didn't resemble any Old Tibetan she'd ever seen. Two of the stones were covered with meticulously carved characters. The third stone had writing on the top half. The bottom depicted a monstrous creature, multi-limbed, with possible wings and other whiplike appendages. It was unnerving.

"Are you in a spending mood, miss?" he said. "I haven't got time to waste."

She doubted if they were Tibetan. Perhaps a poor job of fakery.

That's why the writing made no sense. Forged or not, when viewed together the triptych delivered a most eerie effect.

And that creature...

"Dear woman! Are you buying, or not?" He raised his voice but not his sluggish body.

She was not. Although somewhat intrigued by the oddity, she was going to leave.

Until...

A market boy poked his head in the tent and told the trader someone wanted to talk.

"That's my other buyer." He kicked his stool aside and squeezed past her. "He's here."

"Let him buy it, then," Ursula said. She was tired of his bullying salesman patter.

"You'll be sorry. Mark my words. Once in a lifetime opportunity..." he grumbled.

He went out of the tent, probably to discuss a possible wool sale.

Ursula took the opportunity to snap a few quick photos with her Vest Pocket Kodak camera. She kneeled on the cold ground, turned up the lantern's flickering flame. It would do.

Click, click, click.

Jake snapped his fingers.

Ursula reemerged from her Himalayan reverie. She tucked loose strands of her long brown hair behind her ears.

"Boy, today has knocked you for a loop," he said.

"Stop. I was only remembering. Daydreaming."

"Tibet again?" Jake smiled a bit too smugly for Ursula's taste.

She refused to give him satisfaction. "As a matter of fact, I was thinking about Manaus. A return to the rainforest has my blood pumping. We've got work to do," she said. "We'd better get cracking. I can't wait to see that film of Andy's. It's intriguing if it's really her. I mean Maude Brion! Can you imagine if we found her alive? Everybody would talk about *that* discovery."

She slapped Jake collegially on the shoulder. Probably harder than she should have.

"I know you won't want to hear this." His voice had that tone. And she guessed what was coming next. "But are we sure this is a good idea? It's that I just had a bad, weird feeling, like cold fingers grabbing at my neck while Andy was talking. We're rushing in, Ursula. I hope you know what you're doing. What *we're* doing. That's all I'm going to say."

Jake's protectiveness was simultaneously endearing and annoying, she thought.

"Stop worrying. It's a boat trip. A bit of jungle walking and making sure the tourists don't wander off and get lost." She crossed the tiny office, picked up a magnifying glass, and started inspecting her maps. "More sightseeing than anything else, most likely."

"Most likely," Jake said.

She didn't bother to look up and check if he was being serious.

10
She Creeps

She found him this time. He was hunched over a small, smoldering fire. The threads of rising white smoke transfixed him. He reached out and passed his fingers through the vapors. His cocobolo walking staff leaned against the trunk of a nearby rubber tree. A tapper had sliced the tree bark with a knife in a downward slanting spiral; the small cup that collected the latex that spilled out hung there, crookedly. It had been there a long time. The tree bark was healed.

The man looked better than when she encountered him last. His face wasn't horribly purple. The swelling in his neck reduced to normal. Yet he did not look anything like a well person. His skin appeared stretched shiny at his cheekbones, as if a tight stocking had been pulled over his skull. Violet-black lines branched from under his jaw up the side of his face like a dead vine. He was so skinny: a pale scarecrow. He didn't seem to notice her presence. She walked up slowly, not wanting to frighten him away again. A terrible stench permeated the forest. Her heart ached when she realized she was smelling him, his sour fever sweat.

"She walks. She creeps. She creeps," he said.

Was he talking about her?

No.

His fingers twitched, acting out a movement as he spoke to himself, or to someone he saw but she couldn't. He was almost singing the words rather than saying them. It reminded her of something that didn't belong here. A classroom activity: children chanting a nursery rhyme.

"Slowly, so slowly. At first you wouldn't know. She's moving. She's coming. Wherever will you go?" His fingerplay grew more emphatic, his voice louder. "There she is. Here she is. How far, then so close. Your heart, it beats. Puff, puff you breathe. She knows. Oh, she knows."

"Galton, can you hear me?" Iris asked him.

Her husband turned his head toward her and nodded.

His eyes.

They weren't right. They were all white, like latex bleeding from a rubber tree.

"I've found you, my darling," she said. "I've longed to hear your voice again."

"She walks. She creeps. She creeps," he said. He sucked his hollow cheeks in and out.

"Who does, Galton?"

He pointed a skeletal finger toward the forest.

"She does," he said.

Through the green tangle of vegetation Iris detected a darker shape looming. What she had first taken for the old stalks of decaying plants were legs. Tall, angular, covered with light tawny hairs, and bent inward like a tent frame that had collapsed on itself but still stood. At the center of this jumble: a body became visible to her through the latticework of viridescent leaves.

Whatever it was, it was plump.

Round and ripe like a giant walking grape. Belly settled two feet off the ground.

It was especially hard to grow fat if you were eating in the Amazon. Unless you found food everywhere you looked. Either you weren't picky about meals or… killing came easy for you.

It wasn't breathing. No air pumping. Didn't move an inch.

What the hell are you? she wondered.

Thicker than a jaguar. Jaguars had always been the killer she'd feared the most in the Amazon wild. This thing looked heavier even than a tapir which grew to over five hundred pounds.

It was more like the size of an African river hippo. She'd seen one once on a safari. Thousands of pounds. The deadliest animal in Africa. Could crunch you up like sugar candy.

Iris only had a partial view of her stalker. The stillness made it worse, like a jack-in-the-box ready to spring. She could almost hear that tinny *plink-plink-plink* music playing when you give the toy handle a turn…

God! Get it over with! If you're going to jump, then jump already…

She felt eyes on her but couldn't see them. Fear shot through her nerves. Galton's quiet muttering to himself made it almost intolerable. She wanted to scream but didn't dare.

The thing in the bush. Where was its face?

What kind of a face was she looking for? Did it even have a face? A chilly sizzle jerked through her body.

With certainty she knew it was watching her. More dreadful, she felt its icy assessment.

I'm only food to it.

"Who goes there?" she said suddenly.

Absurdity! She sounded ridiculous to herself. Was she supposed to be a military guard or something? Who asks a creature a question like that? But damn if she couldn't feel it pondering.

"Slowly, so slowly. At first you wouldn't know. She's moving. She's coming. Wherever will you go? There she is. Here she is. How far, then so close. Your heart it beats. Puff, puff you breathe. She knows. Oh, she knows." Galton's fingertips touched one off another as he rotated his wrists back and forth while repeating his singsong lines. Only this time he sounded numbed.

The Itsy-Bitsy Spider. That's what his chant reminded her of.

Down came the rain.

As soon as she thought those words, raindrops began to fall. A downpour.

"Galton, I'm afraid." She tried to snap him out of his entrancement.

He waved the smoke from the fire toward the crouching figure in the bushes. Floating wisps of white.

Iris stepped hesitantly toward the dwindling flames.

The rainy deluge put them out.

Galton shot up his hand, motioning for her to stop.

She did. Her eyes searched the jungle maze, but she could not find any trace of the giant beast she was sure was pursuing her. Galton seemed unfazed. Iris strode past him in the rain.

She wanted his walking staff, a weapon to protect herself from an ambush.

But she was too late.

Leaves exploded into the air. The smell of torn vegetation. A loud crashing like a team of horses bursting through a waterfall of rain. Torn earth. Green, wet. A windy rush of movement…

The thing grabbed her adroitly around her middle. It didn't thrash her around or tear at her, didn't break her neck like a big cat would. No, it spun her. Round and round. It didn't really feel like an animal attacking her. It was more like she'd fallen into a thoughtless machinery that crushed, bound, and blinded. Vised at her torso, her legs were tied close together, and her arms were pinned to her sides. A gauzy, suffocating mask quickly encased her head. She had no space.

In a flash, she could barely breathe.

"She creeps. She creeps. She leaps. She leaps!" Galton cried out.

Iris didn't see him anymore. Had he been helping her attacker? Her struggles were muffled and went unheeded. Iris opened her mouth to scream, but the precise creature gripped her so firmly she was unable to produce any noise whatsoever.

I'm dying, she thought. Panic set in. A claustrophobic pressure that grew unbearable. Her greatest desire was to thrash her arms and legs about wildly and twist her head back and forth while screaming, screaming... but none of this was possible. It was a kind of instant madness.

These are my last moments. This is how it ends for me...

Iris sat up in her bed.

She was panting. Her hands balled into fists at her side. She unclamped them. Sweaty fingers, pink moons where she'd dug her nails into her palms. Under the blanket, the bedsheet braided between her legs. She kicked free, blinking at her sun-filled bedroom. A bright, cold morning view. Frost on rooftops. Smoke unwound like yarn from the neighbor's chimney pipes.

There'd been no mosquitos in the forest. She and Galton standing there, right before the rain started. His puny fire wouldn't have discouraged mosquitos. That should have tipped her off. A clue to where she'd been. The reality of things. Because there were always mosquitos in the jungle. Except when that jungle was a place you traveled to in your mind while you were asleep and dreaming.

A dream. But not only a dream. A dream plus more. She had found Galton; they talked.

It was progress.

She also saw what was with him in the dream forest.

A monster. It had glossy black eyes. She counted them after it seized her.

Eight eyes. The same number as it had legs.

A beautiful symmetry. Despite her terror she admired that quality.

She lifted the field notebook from her nightstand, writing everything down before she forgot it.

11

Voyage of Doubts

Everything went quickly in the following days.

Andy felt like he'd been caught up in a gigantic whirlwind. Oscar Hurley gave Andy, and therefore Ursula and Jake, the funding he had promised in his quest to acquire the golden profits he might strip from the earth. It had been easy to convince him. Though Iris's contributions oiled the hinges, Hurley's greed was the thing that slammed the deal closed. Andy didn't feel too guilty about fooling the millionaire. Ursula and Jake made plans. They purchased the equipment and provisions it made sense to transport; they would buy everything else in Brazil once they reached the port of Manaus. The group booked passage, along with Iris who paid for her own ticket, on a voyage out of New York. First-class cabins all around. Ursula insisted they keep their expedition team small, which she said gave them the best chance of survival and success. Four was a solid number. They would hire a boat and a pilot in Manaus. Ursula knew a few tried-and-true captains from her previous explorations. They'd need dependable helpers to haul gear and run the canoes once they left the big boat to investigate shallower waters and narrow tributaries. A great deal of their trek would be on water, not land.

This revelation surprised Andy.

They were, the four of them, sitting in deckchairs, bundled against the brisk salt air, enjoying unseasonably mild weather aboard the luxury ocean liner. Andy had never traveled anywhere first class. He was getting used to the creature comforts. He didn't mind the idea of a few days hiking in nature, but just thinking about the confines of a canoe gave him leg cramps.

"You mean we won't be getting out of the boats and walking?" he said.

"The rainy season will be underway. There is always rain in the rainforest. Now is the flooded season. Maude's party went missing two summers ago. They left in July, a dry month. Different conditions. Lower water levels, more trails. If she's still down there, and alive, she'll be on higher ground." Ursula advised them to pack light. "The good news is our boat can explore deeper into the jungle. Using canoes, we'll have access to places not reachable in drier months. The bad news is that trails will be harder to come by and tougher to navigate. There will be mud. Prepare yourself to be wet, day after day. Keep your feet as dry as possible. Mosquitos are omnipresent. You will have to get used to them. Sickness is a real risk. Malaria, dysentery, odd fevers and infections. I won't even mention snakebites, or what will happen if you get one."

"Why? What will happen?" Andy asked, stiffening with alarm. He hadn't considered the details of traveling in a remote and dangerous landscape. He'd been too thrilled to leave Arkham.

Jake shook his head, running a finger across his throat. He closed his eyes, tongue out.

"Maybe it's better to stay in the boat," Andy said.

"We'll get out when have a good reason," Ursula said. "I've studied the maps. And with all the background materials you dug up on Maude Brion's journey, I've made a logical guess where to start looking. It won't be easy. A year and a half is a long time to be missing. The forest will have swallowed up most, if not all signs of their passing. Witnesses are unlikely. If we're downright lucky, we may spot their steamboat, or its wreckage, which is the largest piece of evidence we–"

"The shrine to the Spider Queen is our best option," Iris interjected.

A foamy wake tailed behind the ship. The bright afternoon sun beamed through ropes, cables, and wires – casting a network of shadows. Most of the other passengers were inside fantasizing about Rio de Janeiro's tropical warmth. But their vessel had yet to pass the southern shore of Cape May, New Jersey.

"What do you mean, Iris?" Ursula said. She and Iris had yet to become friends.

Iris had recommended Ursula for the expedition leader, while remaining frosty and distant toward her within their group. Perhaps the anthropologist wasn't used to working with anyone other than her husband. Andy still had hopes that the chill between them might thaw.

"We should try to locate the shrine. The film showed us Maude at the shrine. Someone sent it to the *Advertiser*, obviously intending people to go searching. The message is clear. If you want to find Maude Brion, first find the Spider Queen." Iris was smoking in dark sunglasses, her hair wrapped in a silver turban. It would've been easy to mistake her for a famous film actress.

"No one's ever been able to prove if the Spider Queen exists. Those ruins on the reel may not even be a sacred site dedicated to her. Granted, they are unusual. Rumors of them would be worth following up." Ursula waited for Iris to expand upon her point, attempting to draw her out.

Iris merely shrugged, which frustrated Ursula who seemed to invite a friendly challenge.

Andy broke the tension. "Are we going near where Percy Fawcett disappeared?"

Ursula shook her head. "He was searching for his lost city of 'Z' in the Mato Grosso. The flooding down there would be extreme. It's south of where we're headed." The archaeologist pulled a map from inside her coat and unfolded it, pinning it to her knee to keep it from flying away. "We're going here." She pointed to a spot on the map. Andy eagerly left his chair to see it.

"Not much else around it is there?" he asked.

"Nothing you'll find on a map," Jake said. "People have lived there for who knows how long. We don't even know what we don't know. Uncharted isn't the same as uninhabited."

"Are they dangerous?" Andy asked. "The people who live there."

"Are we?" Iris said.

Andy couldn't tell if she was joking. Her lenses glared like stars.

"We will need to be respectful. It's their neighborhoods we're visiting." Ursula refolded the map. "The pilot will know better than we do. Safety is my top priority. Avoid unwanted contact. We aren't there to cause harm. But those who came before us did plenty of damage."

"Do we have guns?" Andy asked. "In case we encounter, I don't know, a serious threat?"

"We do," Jake said. "It isn't our plan to lead with weaponry. They're a last resort."

"Weapons won't help you. Not the kind you're talking about," Iris said.

After uttering her cryptic comment, she left their company, claiming the sun had given her a headache. She wanted to lie down before dinner. She was the picture of elegance in a red dress and a blue fox shawl. Andy had a hard time imagining her roughing it in the rainforest. But what did he know? He'd never been camping in his life, let alone on a wilderness expedition. How would life change once they were in the bush? Ursula made it sound rough, but Iris had lived in the Amazon too. She didn't seem overly bothered about what they were facing. Or maybe she was just better at hiding things. They each had their own style of tackling the mission.

"She's a strange one. Isn't she?" Ursula said, after Iris was out of earshot.

She got up and went over to the rail. The wind caught her long brown hair. Jake and Andy followed. She was watching Iris retreat through the glass enclosed Promenade Deck. Waves might rock the boat but not Iris.

"Do you mean who packs a fur wrap when headed to the jungle?" Andy said.

Ursula swiveled back. "It's not her clothes that intrigue me. It's her reason for coming."

She had objected to bringing Iris on the mission. Ursula wanted to keep the team as small as possible. Fewer people, less potential for problems. She didn't know Iris, but she'd heard of Galton Reed. She knew that Iris and Galton had a disastrous last journey together. She worried about taking Iris into the remote wilderness again. What memories would it bring back? Would Iris hold up if events took a sudden bad turn? But Andy insisted. He felt the need to defend her inclusion. "She's an expert on the local legends. Iris and her husband searched for the Spider Queen. He died out there. She wants to finish what they started. I admire her resilience."

"Did she tell you how he died?" Jake asked. He had a bag of peanuts he offered around.

"Not specifically. A sickness. He was too weak to move. He told her to go."

"I can't picture a man convincing her to do anything she didn't want to do," Ursula said.

"Hard to believe. I've only heard rumors of such things," Jake said, shaking his head.

"Quiet, you." She jabbed him in the ribs.

Andy knew Ursula and Jake were partners in exploration. It was obvious they were also friends who'd been through a few tight spots together. Being with them gave him a feeling of confidence. But he was also envious of their closeness, constantly aware he was an outsider.

"If you're worried about her, don't be," Andy said. "She suggested I hire you, in fact."

"I'm not worried about her." Ursula paused. She took a handful of nuts, shelling them, eating them one by one, tossing her shells overboard where seagulls dived at the empty husks. Determined, the gulls flew closer to the rail. "Her husband had quite a reputation," she said.

The water was dark, hypnotic. It made Andy dizzy to stare at it passing swiftly below.

"Galton? She said he was… outside the mainstream with his speculations. A driven, unconventional thinker. A real genius, though," he said. "Is that what you learned about him?"

"Not precisely."

"What then?"

"That he was pompous. Misanthropic. A paranoiac. The jungle made him worse."

Jake crumpled the bag, shoving it in his pocket. The sun dropped low; the sea was gray.

The seagulls lost interest. The wind shifted and it grew raw, tasting like metal, or winter. Andy suddenly felt like a man who had crawled too far out on a limb and heard wood cracking.

"I don't know what he was," Andy said, finally. "We'll never know, I guess."

"That is a good thing." Jake slapped the rail. "I, for one, am ready for dinner. Shall we?"

He and Ursula started back to their cabins to change their clothes.

"I'll join you in the dining room," Andy said. "I want a cigarette."

Jakes hugged himself, rubbing his arms. "Don't stay too long. You'll catch cold."

"He's a big boy. He knows when it's time to come inside," Ursula said.

Andy couldn't help but smile. Finally, someone was treating him as if were an adult and not a fledgling journalist. He saw himself as plenty capable, even if he was barely out of his teens.

He pulled out his cigarettes. It took three matches to get one lit. The first inhalation provoked a coughing fit. He really should chuck them. Hiking in the rainforest when your lungs hurt wasn't good. But he needed to think; a smoke helped him do that. Or being alone did.

Andy had felt sympathy for Iris. Now he wasn't certain how to feel. Ursula had him wondering. It was going to be a long time at sea, doubting things. He trusted Iris and Ursula to help him find Maude or figure out what happened to her. He had a lot riding on this story. Gedney talked Doyle Jeffries into giving him a leave of absence to pursue his Amazon scoop. The big boss called the shots. Andy couldn't tell how Jeffries felt about letting him go. He gave him the news in person but tersely. Did he resent that Andy bypassed him? Was he angry?

Red Phelan needled him the day he left. "Don't worry, Andy boy, this job wasn't great."

"I'm coming back, Red," he'd said.

"Sure you are, kiddo. Sure you are." Red cackled. "You're irreplaceable!"

If Andy didn't fire off the story of the year, he figured he'd find himself fired for good.

Please be alive, Maude, he thought. Let there be a Spider Queen too. Make it all be true.

Find her, he told himself, and you'll be golden. It's that simple. You and your friends might well be the ones to do it. Only forward from now on, no second guesses, and no retreating.

Go out into that jungle and find her, pal.

12
Two Lives

Jake was glad when they arrived in Manaus. He'd traveled to the Amazon with Ursula on several occasions, each of them fraught with risks and dangers, but he'd always felt excitement more than anything else. This time was different. At first, he didn't know how to name the sensation. But now he did. He was filled with an awful, gnawing *dread*. It ate away his enthusiasm, replacing it with a persistent unease. He failed to pinpoint its origin. Although, like the Amazon River, it had a source. From that source his fears flowed freely. It made him restless. Agitation buzzed inside him. He tried to write it off as the aftereffects of a monotonous sea voyage. "Nothing beats the ocean for repetition," he told Andy, when the reporter paced the ship complaining of boredom.

But that wasn't it.

Jake hadn't shared his worries with Ursula, because he didn't want to burden her with more concerns than she already had. An expedition was a major enterprise, complex and multifaceted. This one had come together faster than anything they'd attempted before. The flavor of it was strange in a way he couldn't describe. Not that strangeness was new to them. They'd shared a host of inexplicable experiences, including the last time they came through Manaus, searching for the Jaci uaruá, the enchanted lake, and the location of the legendary Plague Stone. It took Ursula hours of library research, and a few daring climbing maneuvers in the storm-thrashed jungle canopy. But they'd found what they were looking for.

Only to have it stolen away.

That was in the past now. Irretrievable but unforgotten. The sting still hurt.

It was one of the reasons a return to Manaus seemed like an invitation to misfortune.

Jake didn't bring the subject up. The same way he wasn't talking about his nagging sense of doom, of disaster approaching, or rather, drawing them in like a magnet. He didn't only worry about what might happen to Ursula. He worried about himself. He took a beating on these trips. He felt guilty, even a bit selfish, thinking like this. While he could afford to focus on supporting her, Ursula was the team leader and had to consider everyone as her responsibility.

Jake had to admit he'd grown fond of Andy. He was like a little brother you looked out for, and you were happy to do it. Iris was the tricky one. She was smart and experienced but hard to read. She'd brought them in on the project, then acted like they were somehow blocking her. As if she wanted to be the leader. Yet in other moments, she could be funny and charming. It was like she was two people. Or maybe he hadn't gotten to know her well enough. They'd certainly have a chance soon. Nothing brought you together like an expedition. There was also the money to think about. He and Ursula were raking in a bundle from Hurley. So, Jake clammed up.

Maybe it was in his head.

Or he was getting older and thinking too much.

He couldn't shake it. That fact bothered him as much as anything, its stickiness.

There was no good way to raise an alarm. Ursula simply did not respond well to being looked after or restricted. He liked that about her as an exploration partner. And as a friend. It was what made her a groundbreaking field archaeologist. She went where she was told not to go by the powers that be and did the things people told her were impossible. She relished proving her detractors wrong. Her unapologetic brashness served her well, as it did every area of study to which she applied her considerable talents. She was the most courageous person Jake had ever known. She could also be exceedingly stubborn. She freely admitted this.

Although, at times, if Jake were being honest, Ursula's urge to defy societal, particularly *manmade* boundaries led them into hostile territory. They ran into situations that were difficult to escape. Enemies appeared, then multiplied. They got themselves into trouble. Ursula, so familiar with roadblocks and opponents, had come to expect these conflicts as inevitable. While Jake tried his best to steer around obstacles, she went right over the top. She didn't need a guardian, she often told him. He agreed. She was right. But he didn't have her nerve. He worried. He got tired of battling. It wasn't in his personality. Couldn't they do things the easy way, occasionally? He knew the answer, so he never bothered asking. It wasn't their choice to make.

Was it?

Something near the end of their ocean voyage particularly bothered him.

It involved Iris and what he saw her doing one night in the ship's smoking room.

The interior might've belonged to an elegant club. Potted palms.

Heavy, buttoned leather chairs, oak paneling, brass lamps emitting a low, cozy richness. Even a tiled fireplace, crackling.

Men *only* was the custom. But it was late. Half a dozen old boys were gathered around drinking French brandy and smoking pipes or cigars. The rules governing the waking hours were relaxed. Not knowing why, Jake stopped outside the doorway, skirting the moonlight, listening.

Then he saw Iris sitting in the middle of the group.

"Is this an example of Freudian nonsense?" a heavily bearded man asked her.

Iris drew on her cigarette. The men waited. Despite the hour, no one appeared sleepy.

"It has nothing to do with Dr Freud, or his symbolism. I am not interpreting dreams."

"What are you doing, then?" said a gold-spectacled man.

"I am aware of the dream state while I dream. I direct my actions. Simply put, I live a second kind of life while I sleep. With training and practice, you may do the same."

"How often does this happen?" The question came from a man with pencil moustache.

"Nightly, Mr Norton," she said.

"Hogwash. I don't believe you." The spectacled man gestured with his empty snifter.

"Fortunately, your belief has no bearing on my abilities or the truth of my statement."

"She's got you there, Douglas," said Norton, amused. He relit his pipe.

Iris continued, "Who is to say my dreaming life is less real? I may have two lives, or I may live one life divided between two worlds. One while I am awake, the other while I sleep. There is nothing I do in the so-called real world that I cannot do in the other. But the reverse is not true. My dreaming life is far more fantastical and vivid than here. I fly! I experience domains that are impossible to visit otherwise. Outside this planet, or within. I am an explorer in dreams. This is nothing new. It is chronicled across many cultures, dating back to ancient times."

"You're talking about astral projection?" said a fourth man with a shiny bald head.

"I don't call it that. My spirit or soul – my self – leaves my body, this is true. I travel. I see things. All of which I can remember upon waking. I keep a daily record of my dreamlife."

"Amazing. Do you behave the same way in the dreamworld as you do here?"

"Not always, Mr Norton. I might visit, say, an event in my past, or perhaps even the future. I communicate with people who are in faraway places. I even talk with the dead."

"Necromancy!" Douglas shouted, as another brandy was delivered to him on a silver tray.

"Again, gentlemen, your labels hold no interest for me. I'm telling you that this reality," she tapped her knuckles on the table, "is not the only one. But it is late, and our conversation has tired me so… time for bed." She finished the last of her brandy and rose from her chair.

All the men stood to bid her goodnight.

"Sleep well," she said to the group, holding out her hand.

She was wearing a gold ring – the Spider Queen artifact – on one of her fingers.

The yellow metal sparkled; its ruby red eyes winking maliciously in the firelight.

One by one, the men bowed and kissed her hand in farewell.

"Perhaps we will meet on the astral plane," Norton said, touching his moustache.

"You are more of a dreamer than I," Iris answered back to his warm amusement.

Before she reached the threshold, Jake secreted himself between two stacks of deckchairs. She passed without noticing him. He felt a bit foolish hiding like a child playing games. Yet he was happy to see her go. Jake never recalled his dreams when he woke in the morning. If you asked him, he'd say he didn't dream. His whole life he had found discussions of dreams to be disturbing, almost as if people were talking about interacting with the supernatural.

He needed to tell Ursula about tonight. About Iris's nighttime dream activities. For the woman appeared to believe what she had relayed to the men in the smoking room. Jake feared she was more than enigmatic. She harbored grand delusions. Telepathy? Talking to the dead? Who knew what other arcane notions she adhered to? She questioned the very nature of reality.

In the light of the next morning he felt less sure. It wasn't really anything to brood about. Silly dreams. Iris was eccentric like her dead husband. Weren't they all odd ducks on this wild Amazon excursion? Watching mysterious films and chasing after vanished Hollywood directors among lost ruins devoted to an obscure spider goddess worshipped by her band of cultists? Ursula once chided Jake saying she wanted to see more bravery and less vigilance out of him.

With that in mind, he decided to keep his worries to himself.

13
Manaus

Ursula hadn't forgotten the intense heat of the jungle, but the oppressive humidity retained the ability to surprise. It lay upon the port city like a bloated leech sucking the energy out of everything that moved. The air possessed a liquid quality, unseen but nonetheless perceived. Wading replaced walking. A languid torpor not only surrounded you; it filled you up. You became aware of the effort necessary to breathe, the stale sweat drenching your khakis and the lucky bandana you always wore around your neck. There was no escape. Colors were different, like brushstrokes of fresh paint on a canvas. Everything was still wet, still subject to alterations. Chaos, turmoil, the flux of life. She supposed it existed everywhere. Only here it was obvious. You couldn't detach yourself from what was happening around you. You were in the soup whether you wanted to be or not.

This feeling of submergence she was experiencing couldn't be attributed to the weather alone. You got used to weather. Your body adjusted to a new climate. In time your mind did too. Creatures, human and otherwise, adapted. Or they perished. No, there was another atmospheric change that needed to be accounted for. Just as omnipresent, equally daunting. Perhaps more so. What was worse, it might become permanent or intensify in strength. Ursula could afford to ignore it no longer. For an aura of doom had descended upon their group.

She couldn't put her finger on its source. And she didn't like that. Every expedition took on an identity. Personalities in the group mingled to form a whole new organism. But in this case that logic didn't apply. The individuals were, as far as she could tell, positive. Although rushed, she and Jake were confident about their journey. They might not find Maude Brion. It was a shot in the dark from the get-go. They almost certainly wouldn't come across any gold deposits. Everyone on the team knew the improbability of hitting upon an accidental motherlode. And young Andy was giddy about writing his adventure story, making a name for himself. Ursula hoped he'd do it, even if they couldn't promise they'd walk up to Maude filming footage of the Spider Queen and her followers inside a vine-clad shrine.

That left Iris. If there was another presence contaminating their group, it had come in with her, like a parasite hitching a ride. Could it be this presence somehow emanated disaster?

Ursula felt guilty about being suspicious of the other woman on the team. As Andy had said, Iris was an expert on the Spider Queen legend. She'd been here before. She had earned her place to go back with them. She'd provided the evidence that convinced Hurley to fund the project. She had her husband's field journals, containing hand-drawn maps and sketches as well as detailed descriptions of land-marks and oral accounts of indigenous encounters with the Queen.

So why did she make Ursula wary?

Ursula wasn't sure. She had decided to reach out to Iris before they launched on the river. If it proved to be nothing, all the better. If something needed to be sorted, then they'd sort it now.

•••

They docked in Manaus shortly after dawn. The day already felt steamy. Manaus, like all ports, existed just this side of absolute pandemonium. Men everywhere, loading and unloading, a few basking in the wavy heat like lizards on stones. Women sold food and clothing. Children ran chattering like clouds of birds seeming to burst in one place, scatter, and reemerge loudly. Signs of commerce, an undercurrent of illicit products for sale, the pungency of humans, animals, food, and sour bilgewater. The team walked down the ramp, waiting for their baggage.

Andy squinted at the sandy brown waters lapping at the dock pilings. He swatted away a squadron of mosquitos swirling around his face. But he was beaming. His adventure had begun. Ursula envied him the excitement of launching on a first expedition. He'd never forget this trip.

Sharp-eyed Jake was checking to see that no one walked away with their gear.

Thieves thrived in liminal spaces. Disorientation favored the predatory type.

Iris sat on her bag studying a tattered field journal, hardly bothering to look around.

Ursula scanned the dock, thrilled to be taking in the sights and sounds, until she saw him.

"You've got to be joking," she said. "Tell me that isn't who I think it is."

Strolling toward them, gripping a bottle of German lager, came a man in a Panama hat. He didn't match the surroundings. It was as if he'd been added on top, his form printed on a sheet of glass laid over the scene, the glass sliding along as he got closer. An optical illusion.

"What is he doing here?" Jake asked. He looked as if he'd swallowed a juicy bug.

"I don't know," Ursula said. "I can tell by that smirk he sees us."

Andy turned to study the man in the immaculate white suit. "Friend of yours?"

"Not by a mile," Jake said.

Andy stepped aside as stevedores began to pile up their provision boxes.

Before Ursula or Jake could say more, the man spoke out in a smooth, preppy voice.

"Imagine! Just imagine my meeting you two here. What *are* the odds?"

"Ashley Loot, my favorite talking fish belly. What's there to steal in Manaus?" Jake said.

The man extended his hand to Andy who shook it, tentatively.

"Ashley Lott Jr," he said. "Glad to make your acquaintance. Jake is funny. Isn't he?"

Ursula noticed Andy wincing. It wasn't because Ashley had a hard grip. It was because touching Ashley tended to make a person recoil. Andy wiped his fingers discreetly on his pants.

Ashley appeared as if he had stepped out of a tailor's shop. Not a speck of dirt on him, cleanly shaven, smelling of peppermint and a lemony splash of Penhaligon's Blenheim Bouquet.

"Another hot one." He removed his hat, fanning himself. "Ursula, you seem tense."

"Not at all," she lied. "Getting used to being on land. When did you arrive, Ashley?"

Ashley leaned sideways, gazing around Ursula to study Iris, who was still reading.

Ursula shifted to block him. "Been in town long?"

"We tied up yesterday. You didn't miss anything. It was raining. The river is high for the season. Who's this charming blonde? I don't believe we've met." His mouth did something to imitate a human smile. He bent toward Iris. Ursula noted his golden hair was already thinning on top. For ears he had small pink snail shells. His eyes, rising to meet hers, were rancid gray.

Ursula was pleased to see Iris ignoring him. Deadpan, the anthropologist turned pages.

Ashley drained his beer, casually tossing the empty bottle in the water. "Well, it's swell that we've found our paths crisscrossing again. History repeats itself. Fate, some would say."

"Or bad luck," Jake replied.

"Ah, but for whom? Not me, I assure you. My time in the Amazon is always profitable."

Ursula held her tongue. Silence often proved to be an adequate antidote to Ashley.

Its taste, however, was bitter.

"Are you an archaeologist too?" The reporter spoke directly to their rival.

"I think of myself as a student of antiquity." Ashley's mock humility was laughable.

Ursula rolled her eyes. The corner of her mouth twisted dubiously at his false modesty.

"What are you hoping to learn with this visit?" Andy said.

Ashley rocked on his heels, then poked his white gaiter-covered boot at a piece of rope.

"Oh, this and that. To be honest, I'm not doing my own research this time out. A batch of European geologists have hired me to guide them around. They have no idea what they're doing unless it's rocks and minerals. I'm to usher them through this forbidding green maze."

"Geologists?" Andy sounded suspicious. His journalistic hackles lifted in alarm.

Rightly so, Ursula thought. Ashley was up to something shady. Because he *always* was.

"Those poor geologists. They have no idea what they're in for," Jake said.

"I know," Ashley laughed. "They think there's gold out there. *Pffft…* it'll be like mining in Hell, I told them. What precious metals you may discover aren't going to be worth it. But do they listen to *moi*?" He shook his head. A glistening line of perspiration silvered his upper lip.

Then came the question Ursula had been expecting from the moment she saw him.

"Where are you off to on your little excursion?" Ashley faked an offhand attitude.

For the first time, Iris glanced up from her book, her attention riveted on Ursula's reply.

"That's private information," Ursula said. "Although I wouldn't tell you even if I could."

"Not working for yourself either, then." Ashley rubbed his chin, mulling what she said.

My, oh my, how she loathed this man.

Ashley clapped his hands together, a moist smacking that roiled her stomach.

"We are alike, then. You're working for hire, the same as I am. How utterly amusing."

Ursula was ready to end this conversation. The team had too much work to do.

Ashley mused, "*Who* are you working for? That's the key question, isn't it? No use guessing. Because you won't tell me if I get the answer right or not."

"You're right about that," she said.

Ashley tutted. "I only hope it's not Oscar Hurley paying you."

It took infinite discipline for Ursula not to look around at the others on her team. She hoped they were doing better at hiding signs of recognition. She knew she was likely failing. It didn't surprise her that Ashley would know of Hurley. Unsavory types often swam in the same waters. But Ashley's name-dropping smelled of a form of intelligence gathering. He was letting her know that he knew things he shouldn't, hoping to rattle her into inadvertently oversharing.

"If it is Hurley," Ashley went on, "you should know something. He'd better get his gold, or he'll take his revenge. A pound of gold or a pound of flesh. You know what he did to the last crew he sent down here when they returned empty-handed? He fed their hands to the piranhas."

"Look, pal, if you don't shut your trap–" Jake started.

Ursula cut him off. "Enjoy the jungle, Ashley. I hope your geologists stay safe."

"Thank you, Ursula. I'd love to catch up with you before we get back to Arkham. Until we meet again. Goodbye Andy. Goodbye Jake." He took a bow. "And goodbye to you, mystery blonde who is so interested in reading her book." Ashley Lott popped on his Panama hat, turned, and strolled away. Owing to an innate repellency, he didn't need to worry about the fog of bloodthirsty mosquitos pestering the others. The little flies let him to go by without a moment of harassment.

14
Bananas & Guns

Rain pocked the sandy, milky river. A drizzle became a deluge, the torrent settled into a steady driving beat as watery nails pounded the ground, turning dirt into mud and brown puddles. A turbulent stream flowed quickly down the street where suppliers sold various goods to sailors.

Andy and Jake went searching for a pilot and crew. Ursula had given Jake the names of captains she'd hired in the past. He had an inventory of necessities they needed to stock up on.

But they'd run into problems besides the rain.

Ducking under the awning of a fruit seller's stall, Jake consulted his waterlogged list.

Andy didn't bother trying to dry off. His clothes were saturated, his soggy toes squishing inside his boots. He wiped his wet face with a damp hand. The rain fell. White noise masked the market sounds. Andy had difficulty hearing things. It made him feel edgy. The fruit seller wanted to sell him a bunch of bananas. But Andy didn't speak any Portuguese.

"Are bananas on our list?" he asked Jake. He was smiling, nodding at the seller.

"We can buy some," Jake said, distractedly.

Andy motioned at the seller. "Yes, I'm interested. I'd like some of these." He pointed.

"He wants to know how many, I think," Jake said.

"As many as you like. Did you see those men boarding that first boat we went to?"

All they'd seen were boats. Fishing boats. Boats hauling market goods. How could you see, really? The rain screened off the world. There were people out there moving in it furtively.

Dashing and splashing.

"Can't say I noticed them," Andy said. His senses felt overwhelmed.

"I did. That was Ashley Lott's boat, the one he's hired. It's the nicest boat, with the top captain. He's bought up twice the helpers he needs and cleared out everything but the most basic supplies. You'd think he was feeding an army." Jake chewed on his pencil as he looked outward.

"Well, this fella has plenty of bananas."

Jake pointed his pencil at the river. "If those men were geologists, then I'm a toucan."

"Can I have some money?" Andy said to Jake. He held up three fingers to the fruit seller who picked up a stalk as thick around as Andy's wrist. It held many banana bunches and looked to weigh about a hundred pounds. The man grabbed for a second stalk.

"Oh, no that's too many. Isn't that too many, Jake?"

"You know what I think? Those ruffians look more like soldiers. Like mercenaries."

Sighing, Andy hoisted the first banana stalk on his shoulder. He wasn't really listening to Jake's speculations. "Just one." He held up one finger. "Three is too many. One, please."

The seller took the money from his hand.

Arkham Horror

"Now why would Ashley be in Manaus with a boatload of gunman? I don't like it. We must go back and tell Ursula. Ashley has brought in a gang. Soldiers of fortune. Say, you must really love bananas! What are we going to do with all of them? Bake a banana cream pie?"

Andy had a look of panic. He was collapsing under the weight of the fruit on his back.

"Don't worry, pal. I'll take one of those off your hands." Jake got their change from the seller and hoisted up the second stalk. "Let's get back before the flooding really starts."

They trudged off.

Ursula and Iris were having tea under a tarp, keeping their supplies secure amid the hubbub.

Ursula updated Jake and Andy when they returned. "Great news. I met Marcos Lima buying dried fish in the market. I hired him on the spot. He's got a couple of canoeists who know their way around the tributaries. They grew up in a village upriver. What're you doing with all those bananas?"

"Making pie?" Jake said. "Marcos is a fine pilot. We're lucky to have him. I was getting worried we wouldn't find a proper boatman. Ashley's been busy. Wait until you hear this."

Jake filled in the two women about the guns for hire he'd spotted on Ashley's boat. Andy wasn't sure what to make of it. Ashley Lott didn't seem like much of a threat to him. But mercenaries were another matter. He'd been more worried about mosquitos, tropical diseases, and natural predators. Soldiers hadn't made his list of dangers. Until now.

"That man is unspeakable," Ursula said. "I wouldn't put it past him to plan a coup."

"He's always seemed more a graverobber than a strongman," Jake said, peeling a banana.

"If he's a graverobber, the spirits will deal with him," Iris said.

Ursula frowned. "Spirits? I didn't take you for a believer in ghosts."

Iris sipped her tea. "In many ways, the dead have more to teach us than the living. It's a matter of establishing a clear channel of communication. How do we reach them? Through artifacts and writings, the bits they've left behind? Certainly. But there might be a more direct method of making contact. If Dr Lott is looking to pillage sacred resting places along the Amazon, he'll need better than a few hired gunmen for protection. Powerful forces look after the dead. And the dead attract entities, good and bad, who aren't afraid of bullets, or men…"

She reached into her pocket and brought out the gold spider relic. She slipped the ring on and stroked its smooth, round abdomen.

"The Queen, for example," she said, "fears no man. She is a huntress of the forest. She lives in dreams too. Her powers are not bound by societal rules. She weaves her own world."

"I thought she was just a big spider. Wouldn't a big shoe kill her?" Andy joked. He hadn't decided what to believe about the legend. He'd read what he could find. And listened to Iris and Ursula talking. But in his mind, she remained a misty collage of words and images. Was she a goddess? A spider? Or a goddess who looked like a spider? Or, at different times, all three?

Iris stared at him, unamused.

"It is men who tremble at the awesome spectacle of the Spider Queen," she said. "Not the other way around. If you are lucky enough to meet her, you'll see what power is."

"You talk as if you think she's real," Ursula said.

"She is… if a person knows the proper way to meet her. Not everyone sees the Queen."

"Do you mean real in the same way this rain is real?" Andy said. "Or these bananas?"

"Tell me, Andy, what is more real? This place or the dreams that brought you to it?"

Andy could see her point. If he hadn't grabbed the package in the mailroom and initiated a search for Maude and her story, none of them would be here sitting under a tarp in the rain. His ambition, and Ursula's and Jake's, led them to this moment, Iris too. Their dreams became real.

"When you say there are more direct ways of contacting the dead, are you speaking of mediumship? Because I don't find that mediums hold up under scientific scrutiny," Ursula said.

"Perhaps you visited the wrong seer," Iris said.

"I didn't visit any seer. I'm simply saying–"

A lean man with large, leathery hands, and a black captain's hat, stepped under the tarp.

"Marcos!" Jake said as he greeted the newcomer with a hearty handshake.

"Olá! Jake, you look older and wetter than the last time I saw you," Marcos said.

"But not as old as that rusting hulk of yours. Has she sunk yet?"

"That rusting hulk is good enough to ferry you. She has the finest pilot on the river."

"So humble," Jake kidded him.

"No humble man ever made a good river captain. I am stopping to tell you that you are welcome to come aboard my rusting boat. My men will help carry your things. These are good men. The best." Marcos held back the flap. Two younger men stepped underneath. Andy guessed they were around his age. "Davi and Thiago are brothers raised on the river. They know the waters as well as they know each other."

Marcos spoke to the men in their language. They nodded in understanding but kept quiet. Although they were friendly, they acted cautiously in front of the expeditioners. Through a warm drizzle, the seven of them carried the gear and supplies out to where the steamboat was tied.

One thing was for certain. It was not the prettiest ship on the river.

Andy had thought Jake was exaggerating when he called it a "rusting scrap hulk" , but it was hard to tell what kept the vessel afloat. Andy had seen better looking shipwrecks washed up on the shores of Cape Cod after a Nor'easter. Her paint peeled; the corroded red metal felt rough as sand. The idea of starting the engine, depending on it to run them upriver, seemed... charitable.

"Don't be fooled by her looks," Marcos said, clapping Andy on the back.

But the words of encouragement only made his doubts stronger. If Ursula didn't seem so calm, he would've scrambled back on land. Instead, he stowed his bags below. His bed was a hammock. They all had hammocks. Jake tried his out, swinging, as the ropes creaked and squeaked.

"Cozy like a bug," Jake said with a wry smile.

But Andy saw him test the hooks screwed into the wall before he climbed in the netting.

A loud rumble proved the engines did indeed run.

The sensation of being in forward motion. A sudden test of one's balance. Warm breezes blowing through the open portholes. The thud of ropes hitting the deck above. Sailors moving about.

Their voyage was underway.

Marcos called down the cabin steps. They were passing the Encontro das Águas, the Meeting of the Waters, where the tea-stained Rio Negro from the north – steeped in dead plant matter –

and the silty, chocolate milk-colored Rio Solimões met, running side-by-side for a few miles, their currents refusing to mix. The expedition would go east, following the pale Solimões, or Amazon, as the world outside of Brazil commonly knew it.

"Let's get a photo of us with the waters in the background," Ursula said. "Hurry!"

She had a small camera in hand. They rushed up the steps and headed to the bow. Thick air. Rich, earthy smells reminded Andy of spreading mulch in his mother's garden. Smoke belched from the old smokestack into a clearing sky. The brothers trod around the hot deck, securing things. The steamboat picked up pace, as land glided past. With fewer and fewer buildings.

The trees took over.

"Everyone, stand together now. Closer. Marcos, will you take our picture?"

Ursula joined the group. Iris was happiest of all, smiling, her face positively aglow.

Davi and Thiago were watching, smiling. Davi steered the boat for Marcos.

"Ready?" Marcos said. "One, two, three!" He clicked the button. "I think it worked."

Manaus diminished behind them. Fewer boats floated on the river. An old man waved.

Ahead, the jungle – impassive, wild, rank – welcomed them silently inside.

15
Magus

That first night they slept on Marcos's boat Iris had her most vivid encounter yet with Galton.

He wasn't sick!

She could tell that straight away, even before he emerged fully from the bush. She watched his face hovering amid a patch of river ferns. His intense, rather stern gaze taking in a troop of golden tamarins snacking on crickets. His right eye was crystalline blue and bright as a steely marble. As he turned away from the treetops, she noticed the left eye, blinded, white as paste. But it didn't seem to slow him down. He tromped through the forest like he lived there. Which of course he did now.

Galton stepped into a patch of yellow sunlight. She waited to call out to him. He was so fit. In his adolescence he'd been a star athlete. A swimmer. He'd played football, too. Good enough to do both sports in college. Physical feats came easy to him. And he'd always been handsome, more handsome than his father who'd had a reputation as a cad and had never been faithful to any woman. But Galton was different. He loved his mother as only an only child could. From her he learned affection, kindness, and love. His father gave him his focus. His ill temperament too came from the paternal side. But Galton wasn't like his father, Iris thought. He loved her. He was loyal to her alone among women. Well, except for the Spider Queen. And she wasn't a woman. Was she?

Galton walked out in front of an enormous display of pink orchids in bloom. Bees buzzed drunkenly from flower to flower. The sound was hypnotic.

Iris couldn't resist any longer.

"Galton! Here! I'm here!"

She waved.

He seemed alarmed.

She hadn't noticed, but now she could see he was wearing that horrible magician's robe he'd picked out at a theatre costume shop in Manhattan. A cheap velvet thing, black on the outside, with a blood-red inner lining. He'd been so excited when he found it hanging on a secondhand rack. He called her over to show her the silver-threaded symbols – swords, wands, cups, and pentacles – stitched gaudily across its back. The clasp was an ouroboros made of tin.

"Can you imagine me in this?" he asked, sounding like a boy.

She dared not burst his enthusiasm.

"Try it on. Let's see how you look."

She was hoping once he saw himself he'd reconsider making the purchase.

The opposite was true. He slipped it over his shoulders and twirled in the mirror.

"It's perfect," he said. "Just perfect."

He paid the cashier, and they left. Iris assumed it vanished into the back of his closet.

She could hardly believe it when he brought the robe out of his bag at the jungle camp.

"Why did you bring that?" she sneered, and might've even laughed as she said it.

He acted hurt, stomping off, not returning until after dark. Wearing it.

After all this time in the forest, it had grown thin in spots. Light shone through. Moths, or something, had eaten out a few holes. He wore it as though it was the most precious garment in the world. He recognized her. That was the good news. And when he spoke, he sounded whole.

"Iris, how did you get here?"

"I'm dreaming, darling," she said. "You won't believe this, but I'm here, in the Amazon."

"Where?" He sounded suspicious, angry at hearing the news this way. Sensing deceit.

"On a steamboat on the river. We've just left Manaus. We're… I'm coming to the place where you are. Where we last parted." She dared not bring up his death. She did not know if his spirit realized he had crossed over into another land beyond the place of the living.

"You are?" Now his voice showed a hint of interest. His eyes – his good eye – glinted.

"I'm on an expedition to find the Spider Queen. And there's this woman director."

"You mean Maude Brion?" he said, to Iris's amazement.

"Why, yes. How do you know about her?" Was Maude dead too? Were they together on that plane of existence? Iris had so many questions. She was sure the Amazon held the answers.

"She's here with me. With us. She's come to the shrine. The Queen is here," he said.

"The Queen?" Iris wasn't sure he was telling the truth. He could be such a prankster, although now he appeared serious. Judging his state of mind was more art than science.

"Yes, I've brought the Queen here. To us. From the other dimension. I've used… magic."

He pulled nervously at the tattered edges of the robe. And she knew then that he'd been aware of how silly she'd always found him in it. She felt awful for that, as if she'd somehow belittled the most vulnerable, secret part of him.

"Your magic helped you find the Spider Queen. That's excellent," she said.

"I said it brought her here from the other dimension. I did it. No one else. It was me."

He'd always been sensitive about his achievements. Feeling he never got full credit for his work. After he'd gone to college, his father died. The family discovered he'd lost most of their money on reckless investments. They were suddenly poor. The shock and heartbreak killed his mother. Or so Galton believed. He never forgave his father. He and his mother had been cheated. After he graduated, attempting to establish his career as a scientist, the thing he hated most was having to beg for money. He'd rage, "I'm a charity case now! A pitiable thing, subject to the whims of my inferiors!" These rages preceded his bleakest moods, where he lifted his head from the gloom only long enough to curse his fortune, his father's carelessness. Galton became obsessed with his vanished youth. All the things he would never get back. Time. Money. Or things he never had. Support and fatherly love. When he did receive funding for a project, it always had a way of running out before it produced results. "Cheated once again," he'd say, with a bitter grunt. Never getting credit for his work. Overlooked. Undercut by authority at every single turn.

He retreated into magic and dreams. Magic was the route back to his rightful status.

Iris chose her words precisely. "I'm happy magic has brought the success you were due."

"Overdue," he snapped back.

"Yes, of course. That's a better way to put things."

Galton came closer. He moved with swiftness. Her breath quickened in fright. He was unpredictable. There were moments when he lost his grip of himself and lashed out at the world.

He laid his hand upon hers.

"I've missed you, Iris. You are so special to me." He kissed her cheek, almost shyly, as if they weren't husband and wife but new lovers. Two strangers who barely knew one another.

This was a dream. Iris was aware of that. Her husband was dead.

This was all she had left of him, a connection through her dreams to a place where the dead wandered. At least she had that. Galton still existed. They could be together in a fashion. She was aware of his manipulations, his need for any kind of control whenever he failed at handling his own volatile moods. The emotions she was experiencing were real too, as in life.

She wanted to help him.

She loved him.

Together they were strong. And good.

"I missed you too," she said.

"Then let me show you how to find me," he said.

16
The Margay

In the pink flush of dawn, Ursula was surprised to see Iris talking with the two boatman brothers near the ship's stern, using a mix of Portuguese and an indigenous language she didn't recognize. She went over to them. Iris was sharing her American cigarettes. A soothing breeze carried the traces of smoke away and blew backward the bugs and diesel fumes. The soft early light was pleasant; the air in front of the boat smelled astringently clean. Yet this scene of them in conversation made her feel queasy. She couldn't put her finger on it exactly, just the nagging suspicion that Iris had hidden motives.

"What's going on?" Ursula asked, not liking the accusatory tone of her own question.

Iris smiled. "Why, we're only talking. Are we not allowed to talk aboard ship?"

"No, no, of course not. I'm a bit stunned. That's all."

"That they speak Portuguese, or that I know their language? I am an anthropologist."

"Yes, you're right. It's my fault. You conducted research not far from here, didn't you?"

Iris nodded. "For the better part of a decade I collected oral folklore. I had to learn to communicate with the people I interviewed. Like these young men, for example. We're not using the language their family spoke but another they picked up after they moved to Manaus. Would you like to talk to them? I can translate." Iris was being a good teammate. So why was Ursula feeling such a reluctance to extend her trust to the woman? She decided to try and do better.

"I would love the opportunity to speak with them. My Portuguese is a little rusty." That wasn't quite true. Ursula only wanted to Iris to think it so. *You really are resistant to confiding in her, aren't you?* She castigated herself but made no attempt to correct her white lie.

Iris patted the wood cargo hatch beside her. "Have a seat. Davi and Thiago speak Portuguese. They went to a Jesuit missionary school. That's when they got their new names. In their home village, they were called differently. We've been using Tupi to talk just now. I think I'm doing pretty well despite my time away." She asked the brothers a question. They both smiled and nodded. "There, you see. I must've had good teachers. We understand each other."

"What have you been discussing?" Ursula asked, hoping to sound casual.

"A little family history. I asked them how they came to be boatmen." Iris told the men that Ursula had the same curiosity she did. Where did they come from? How did they learn their skills working and guiding on the river? What brought them to their jobs helping Marcos?

The men talked the way close siblings do. Davi started and Thiago would pick up the thread. They related their story together, each lending support to what his brother had said. The men spoke rapidly, yet chose their words with precision, being careful to be perceived correctly.

"They say their father was a fisherman," Iris said. "The best in their village. He loved nothing more than to be in his canoe on the river. He hunted all the famous fish. The arapaima, payara, and peacock bass. Many times, he would venture far from home. It was extremely dangerous. There are numerous indigenous groups who live on the river. Some get along. Others do not. A few are openly hostile to outsiders. They don't like strangers, viewing them as threats and potential invaders. Who can blame them after what colonization has brought? Disease, theft of their lands, religious oppression. A man traveling alone far from his home village risks being shot by an arrow, or even killed if he's caught in the wrong place. Their mother would tell their father to stick closer to his own people. She was a leader in the village, but their father refused to heed her advice. He liked to travel by himself in his boat, to chase fish and search for new places he'd never visited before. He'd been that way since he was a small boy."

"A born explorer. Tell them we're like him. We go where others tell us not to."

Iris translated, pointing to herself and Ursula, two American women heading up the Amazon to search for another countrywoman who'd gone missing looking for something more.

The brothers nodded. Thiago, on the right, bent his arm to show them his ropy muscle.

Iris said, "His father was physically strong. Very brave. The bravest man in the village. He was first on the water. No one would argue this fact. But he was always apart, even when he hunted or fished in groups with the other men. His eyes showed he was thinking of going away on another trip. Sometimes he would paddle far, without getting tired, not thinking about how long it would take him to get back, only thinking about the fish he might catch, or the strange new things he might see. He would stay out all night in the darkness on his boat. Not sleeping, but watching, always watching. In the village, they called him *the margay*. That's a small solitary jungle cat, like an ocelot, that hunts at night in the trees. Big eyes. He told his boys that with his big eyes he saw monsters in the shadows. He said this to the other men too. Creatures lurked after dark that never appeared in the daylight. Other bizarre things lived deeper in the jungle, up the tributaries."

Davi pointed to a narrow stream pouring into the main channel they were on. He turned his wrist like a screw to indicate the twisting path of the water disappearing into the thick foliage.

Iris continued translating, "He would see them when he was out looking for a fresh pond to fish in. Monsters. Crawling up out of holes in the ground. They made him afraid. He worried they might follow him back to his village and kill the people. But still he kept going out, farther and farther each time. Once, when he was away on an excursion, a fever arrived in the village. Many people got sick. They laid down, too weak to stand. Unable to eat or drink. Everything they ate rushed back out. Their bellies hurt as if an animal ate at them from inside."

Thiago clutched his stomach as if he were experiencing the same pain. Then he pinched his forearm and rubbed his hand back and forth. Davi nodded in agreement.

"Their skin turned red," Iris said. "They started to die. Within days, half the village was dying or dead. Their mother's sisters died. Then their mother got sick. By the time their father returned, she was dying. Their father felt bad that he had been fishing while the fever destroyed his village. But the mother told him, no. This was good. She told him to take her sons and go away from this place, because she did not want them to suffer the way she was.

This was the last thing she said. He put the boys in his canoe and fled. For days they hid in the forest. They were careful never to be seen riding in their boat, covering themselves with leaves and branches so they looked like floating debris. Eventually they came to Manaus. Months afterward, their father went home to see who was still alive. When he got there, all was quiet. The people were gone. Even the dead. Searching for survivors, he saw a giant web hanging in the trees. Like a spiderweb but big enough that all the people of the village would have fit in it. Their father, who was the bravest of men, felt his bones shaking. So, he left."

Ursula's flesh prickled. She had no doubt the brothers were telling the truth. "Are they afraid to go searching for the Spider Queen?" she asked.

Iris relayed her question. The brothers answered without hesitation.

"They are brave like their father. He taught them how to watch and not be seen."

"Where is your father now?" Ursula asked.

"They say they don't know," Iris answered. "He went out fishing one day and never returned. They found his boat, his things. He wasn't there. This happened a couple of years ago."

"Tell them I'm sorry to hear about their father's passing."

The brothers both shook their heads. Their faces revealed more resignation than grief.

"They say he is still fishing on the river. Looking for a new place to catch big arapaima."

Marcos called for the men. He needed their assistance.

"There's a bad stretch coming up," he said to Iris and Ursula. "They must stand in the bow to guide me through the fast water. We don't want to crack up out here. Long swim back."

Ursula and Iris followed Marcos into the pilot house. They asked if he knew anything about his mates' missing father. His eyes were locked on the white water churning ahead.

"When people go missing by the river," he began, "you hear talk of huge snakes. Anacondas. Or maybe caimans that got them. They fell overboard, and the piranhas enjoyed a tasty meal. People drown. That's the truth. The river brings life, but she's a killer too. This jungle doesn't preserve its dead. It eats them. Too many hungry things live in the forest. Bones and blood make good fertilizer. Now, I'm sorry, but I can't talk. I have to steer."

His calloused hand caressed the ship's worn wheel.

"Thank you," Ursula said. "Tell your crew they've been most helpful."

Belowdecks the men were just waking up, swaying in their hammocks as the boat dipped and swerved like a Coney Island roller coaster. Water gushed at the portholes, wetting the floor.

"What's happening?" Andy said, groggy. His hair stood spiked as if he'd been electrified.

"Oh, we're going through a set of rapids," Ursula said.

"Rapids!"

"They're small," she said. She was having a bit of fun with the newcomer.

They tilted hard to port, then harder to starboard. The rear end kicked around, threatening to spin sideways. Ursula grabbed onto a pole. She'd ridden rough waters before.

Iris wrapped her arm through her hammock ropes.

"Is this dangerous?" Andy was awake now. Panic would do that to a man.

"Only if we go over on our side." Ursula suppressed a laugh. "Or flip."

"Or crack up. Remember, Marcos said something about that," Iris added cheerily.

Andy was buttoning his shirt. Pulling on his boots. "I don't much like water. You know?"

"Why would a person who doesn't like water take a river cruise?" Iris asked.

"Not prudent." Ursula tsked. "Boots off unless you want to sink. Less clothing is better."

"I wholly agree," Iris said. "Right to the bottom you'd go. Like an anchor. Spalooosh…!"

Andy unbuttoned his shirt, shucking out of the sleeves. He stripped off his undershirt as well. "I had no plans to be in the water. That's what the boat's for, I thought. The boat goes in the water. I go in the boat," he said. "See, I wasn't going to tell you this. But I can't swim."

Ursula cringed inwardly at the news. She'd have to keep a closer eye on Andy than she planned.

Their path straightened. The dips were levelling off. Soon they were running as smoothly as if they'd been set down on a pair of steel rails cutting through a farmer's wheatfield.

Ursula grabbed the toe of Andy's boot, the one he'd managed to put on… the wrong foot.

"I thought you wanted adventure?" She shook his foot.

"Adventure? Yes. Drowning? No," he said, good humor returning. "Hey, that's just me."

Jake yawned, hopping out of his sailor's bed. "I second your opinion, Andy. Hear, hear."

Andy looked up to him and smiled meekly.

"You can't swim a stroke?" Jake asked.

"Not even the doggy paddle," Andy said.

Back to business, Ursula dug into her bag, dragging out a cardboard tube. From the tube she extracted her map of the area. "I want to show you where we're heading," she said. "It will take four days, weather notwithstanding, to reach our first destination."

"I have another recommendation," Iris said, "from an impeccable source."

"Oh, really?" Ursula said. She made no attempt to hide her astonishment this time. *Who is running this show? Looks like I'll need to make things clear once and for all*, she thought.

As Iris snatched the map cleanly out of her hands.

17
Dream Followers

"Here. This is where we'll leave the main river. Not in four days, but two. Then one more day, taking this left fork to a tributary running parallel to the branch marked. Our path isn't on the map." Iris had Ursula's chart spread out on a hinged table that unfolded from the bulkhead. Now that they had passed through the rapids, the boat was riding steady on the river. Iris felt a surge of energy welling up inside of her. It seemed to come from nowhere. Its force surprised her.

"This is unacceptable. You're not the leader of the expedition. I ought to have Marcos run you back to Manaus," Ursula said. "Give me back my map." She snatched away her plans.

Iris leaned over the empty table. Calm, self-assured. Unruffled by the sudden argument. It was as if she were merely a witness to her own actions. Words were coming out of her mouth, but she felt tamped down inside of herself. The sensation was more baffling than frightening.

"I'm not trying to take over anything, Ursula. Really, I'm not. We're dependent on you to get us to the shrine safely. But I know where to look. Don't you see? Last time, Galton and I were so close to finding the Queen. I dreamed of Galton last night. He showed me where to go."

"Your dead husband spoke to you in a dream?" Ursula asked.

Jake was looking curiously at Iris, waiting for her answer.

"Yes, that's right. He talks to me from the beyond. I don't expect you to understand. Our bond in life was exceptionally strong. Death could not destroy it. Look, I'm trying to help you, if only you'll let me. Galton is too. You're being stubborn. Not listening to what I have to say…"

"I am stubborn. I need to be. You're only proving the reason why."

"Galton told me what to look for. The signs. How to find the location of the shrine."

"In a dream?" Andy said.

His attitude displayed more curiosity than the others'. He would be the easiest to win over. Still young, his ideas about the world had yet to harden like concrete. His mind was open.

"Yes, in a dream." Iris turned defiantly to Ursula. "It's how we communicate."

"That's preposterous," Ursula said. "It's unscientific to boot. You should be ashamed."

Iris straightened, pointing her finger at Ursula. She wasn't the type who pointed her finger at people. She always hated when Galton did it to her. Yet here she was. "You're rigid. Unwilling to hear anything that doesn't fit the model you were taught. But there are other ways. The people who live here in the rainforest take dreams seriously. They draw no line between the physical and spirit worlds. Dating back to ancient times, many cultures regarded dreams and their meaning with the deepest reverence. You act as if my perspective is new. Dreams play a key role in many religions. But you'll never be convinced. Will you? Unless you experience it yourself. You don't even realize the wonders you're missing. What a dull existence it must be, seeing life through eyes half-shut." Iris slammed her hand on the table and made herself jump.

Ursula waited a beat to make certain the lecture had finished.

"Nonetheless," the explorer said, in a voice rocksteady. "We will follow my plan."

Iris felt heat in her cheeks. Her brain filled with emotions that felt volatile and foreign. Rage. Superiority. Her fists clenched. She wanted to battle these people more than sway them.

"Now, wait just a minute," Andy said. "Let's think about this."

Ursula swiveled toward him. She hadn't expected him to speak up for her. No one had.

Least of all Andy, by the look on his face.

Iris brightened. The explosive tension in her ebbed for the moment. She might've found the ally she needed to aid her in this debate. She fought to calm herself. To listen before talking.

"What's the harm in hearing Iris's theory?" he asked. "I, for one, am interested to know what Galton had to say." Andy reached into his bag, pulling out his reporter's spiral pad. Curiosity was his business, after all. Iris could see his angle. The logic was simple. Galton's spirit visited her in a dream. That made great copy. Readers would eat it up. Even more so if the details panned out and proved to be critical in tracking down the missing filmmaker and the Queen. She needed an ally no matter what the reason was.

Jake said, "Andy, the point is that Ursula is in charge."

Ursula shot Jake an angry look. Apparently, she didn't want his help.

"If Andy wants to hear from Iris, we won't stop him. He brought us into this project. It's his prerogative to listen to all sides regarding the search. Even if those sides are not equally valid." She turned to the anthropologist. "Tell us about your dream, Iris. Let's have the facts."

The way she said "facts" left no doubt she was expecting nothing of the sort.

Iris didn't hesitate to present her vision. Words rushed out of her almost faster than she could think them. It was a giddy feeling. Thoughts bombarded her. She proudly told them of Galton's assistance, of precisely what happened in her latest jaunt into the dream realm. Part of her couldn't wait to talk about it. Well, most of it. She had to throttle the words back. Let them out in short bursts. A strange ticklish feeling ran over her, as if she were being touched by invisible threads. Her body twitched in little involuntary spasms she hoped no one would notice.

"I saw Galton in the forest. He says Maude Brion is there. She's at the shrine."

"What! When were you planning on sharing the news?" Andy shouted, scribbling wildly.

"Just now. That's what I am trying to do. I knew I'd face a certain… skepticism."

Ursula shook her head. "Heaven knows why."

"Anyway," Iris continued. "There's an abandoned rubber plantation. It's high up the bank from the river. On a hilltop. Beyond the buildings, Galton showed me train tracks under water."

"You are telling us what we already saw in the film. The one sent to Andy," Ursula said.

Andy winced as if he'd been pinched.

Iris wondered what that meant. She had a flash of insight, as if she could peek into his mind for the briefest glimpse. Had he obtained the film by less than virtuous means?

Baby-faced Andy was full of tricks, wasn't he?

She went on, "Galton walked me to the water's edge. He pointed out landmarks. A section of trees blown over in a thunderstorm. We'll see them from our boat."

"There must be a thousand downed trees we've passed already," Jake said, incredulous.

"But in the middle of this blowdown, there's a stone marker. Like the ones in her movie. It's unmissable. On the beach, Galton drew me a map. I copied it." She retrieved a notebook from her pocket. "See? I made this as soon as I woke. Before I forgot."

"I don't remember seeing you sketching in our dark cabin," Ursula said.

"You were still asleep. I had enough light from the porthole."

Iris passed the notebook to Andy who glanced at the pencil lines before handing them to Ursula. Jake leaned over her shoulder. Despite their doubts, they scrutinized her cartography.

"Galton drew this?" Jake asked.

Iris nodded. "With the end of his walking stick, in the mud."

At the top of the page, the Meeting of the Waters was clearly depicted.

Ursula ran a finger down a thick line.

"This is where we are now," she said.

"The tributary we need to follow is the same one Galton and I used before. I know I can find it. That tributary feeds into a lake. The blowdown is on the western shore of the lake. If you stand at the shrine site, through a gap in the sloping canopy, you can see the stone."

"Maude's movie showed them anchored on a river," Andy said. "Not a lake."

Before Iris could address his concern, Ursula said, "Maude left in July of '26. It was the dry season." Ursula compared Iris's hand-drawn symbols with her own map. "Flooding would turn that wide part of river into a lake. What's this?"

Iris came closer, peering at her own sketch.

Ursula pointed to a dark circle in a thicket of stick-figure trees.

"That's a cave of some sort," Iris said. "Galton says the Spider Queen lives there."

"A cave?" Jake asked.

"Quite hidden under the canopy. Made of iron ore. If you don't know where to look, you'd never find it. I'm not sure if it's completely natural. He didn't tell me. But he showed me the outside of it, the entrance. There were tailings on the ground. Hundreds of them."

"Tailings?" Andy said.

"She means it's likely a mine. They're drilling samples. Rock cores prospectors take to look for whatever might lie beneath the surface," Ursula was sounding intrigued, if still dubious.

"Where there's iron ore, there might be gold," Jake said. "The two are found together."

"Gold? This gets better by the second. Those are specific features Galton pointed out to her," Andy said. "Aren't they? I mean, if we can find this standing stone in the blowdown and these tailings outside of an iron cave, or mine, then we know we're in the right spot. Yes?"

Iris nodded. "I will find it. Galton died less than a mile from the place he revealed to me. We were so close," she said. "I really can't believe it."

"I'm having a hard time as well," Ursula chimed in. Her mind resisted the dream vision.

But Iris heard a wavering in her voice. A threadlike crack of doubt.

"How far is it?" Andy asked. "From where we are now?"

"As I said, two days to the tributary. One down the fork until we reach the lake," Iris said.

"So, three days from now we could be sitting with Maude, looking into that cave or up at that web – whatever it is – waiting for the Spider Queen to make her appearance. I say we do it." Andy's enthusiasm was infectious. Jake smiled at him.

Ursula handed the notebook back to Iris.

"I'll admit that what you say is tantalizing. But there are old rubber stations all over this area. When the boom ended, they couldn't pull out fast enough. The rest is… vague. Sorry, but I remain unconvinced."

"Where were you going to have us go?" Andy asked. "Are the odds any better?"

Ursula said, "According to my research, Maude was secretive about the specifics of her destination. She didn't want anyone with a bigger name and better funding to beat her to the punch. But we know she told her producer she had a tip. Start out westward. Use an American guide, a Texan, living in Manaus. He'd seen something… unusual. I know who that guide is."

Iris quickly added, "Then you must also know the Texan is a notorious teller of tall tales. A drunkard who fought with Maude from the minute she arrived. He was conning her. She figured it out. They clashed over money. He tried to back out in Manaus before they launched. Bullying her to keep his fee. She threatened to shoot him." Iris couldn't help but smile at Maude's negotiating tactics. "So, instead, he took her out on the river. That first night, he stole a canoe. Dumped the bulk of their provisions overboard. He left her not too far from Manaus. Figuring it would teach her a lesson. Except Maude went ahead with a handful of locals to run her boats. Fishermen saw them, warned them to turn back. She said they would, in a week's time. That's how long they had until their maize and manioc ran out. But they never returned…"

"Who told you this?" Andy asked.

"I still have contacts in Manaus," Iris said.

"Dream contacts?" Ursula said.

Iris felt rage boiling up in her again. Usually, she had a better grip on her emotions. It was always Galton flying off the handle at people. She was the one who had to keep him calm. When he was feeling agreeable, he referred to her as his "regulator" . Other times he accused her bitterly of being "cold" .

"Contacts," Iris repeated, leaving it at that. She swallowed the venom in her mouth.

"They were one day into the trip. Three on her own. Then…" Andy was doing the math.

"They found something on the last day. Before they were going to turn back," Iris said.

"The Spider Queen," Andy said.

His gaze was out-of-focus, glassy, as if he were viewing the past, or perhaps the future.

Iris felt herself smiling wide. She touched her cheeks. They felt numb. *Why am I acting so oddly?* Was it the pressure of having to persuade the team to switch plans? No, not only that.

She willed herself to go on.

"They found it despite the odds. I won't go as far as saying '*by accident*.' But luck was on her side," Iris said. "Maude Brion, and her crew, made the discovery of a lifetime."

"Pure speculation," Ursula said. "Apparently her luck hasn't held out, has it?"

"Everything works." Andy started pacing. "Maude used this very route!"

"I asked that Texan where he left Maude. Right around here was his answer," Iris said.

She switched her stare from Andy to the porthole. A slice of brown water, green shore.

Iris believed in her plan. She believed in Galton. She would go there to prove him right.

Andy looked out, his eyes growing big in excitement.

He began to mutter, "We gotta go… we gotta go…"

"Iris, why are you only telling us this now?" Ursula said. "It's awfully convenient. The mysterious Texan… why keep him a secret? I would've liked to speak to him."

"I didn't know I needed your permission."

Ursula replied, "When *did* you speak to him?"

"While you were in the fish market hiring Marcos. I visited a tavern where the Texan is known to spend his days. I paid him for his information."

"Or for his lies," Ursula said. "You said he's a conman."

"We won't know," Iris said, "unless we go and find out."

Iris had an answer for every one of Ursula's objections. She couldn't tell if it was helping or infuriating her.

But Iris had won over Andy. He was sold on the idea.

"We can't pass this up. We owe it to Oscar Hurley. I owe it to the *Advertiser*'s readers."

"Hold it right there, Andy," Ursula said. "Understand something. You hired me to look for a missing person. You're hoping for a great story. Hurley hired you to find gold. There's a good chance we won't get either if we follow Iris's flimsy dream."

"You're wrong," Iris interjected.

"Noted." Ursula turned to Andy. "I'm advising you to stick to the plans we drew up in Arkham. But if you decide you want to follow Iris's map, I'll do it. It's your call."

Jake looked shocked.

Iris couldn't believe it either. She was giving in. They would listen to Galton!

Andy thought for a minute. Finally, he said, "Let's follow the dream."

18
Not Here To Play It Safe

Andy and Iris stayed in the cabin so he could hear a fleshed-out version of her dream. He wanted to take notes for his article, which he felt might grow into a full-length book. Ursula took both maps, hers and the hand-drawn sketch Iris tore from her notebook, depicting Galton's mud tracings. Jake accompanied Ursula up top to tell Marcos about the change in plans, and also so gauge his opinion on it. Jake agreed that was a good idea.

"This part here where she says to go? It's no good," Marcos said, eyeing the chart.

"No good because you can't get the boat through?" Ursula asked.

"Maybe we can go if the water is deep. The water's been flowing down from the mountains and it's raining. Probably we're good." Marcos scratched his scruffy chin. "Why it's not so good is because of the reputation. That's a bad place."

Jake sipped from his canteen. The day was getting hot. The jungle steamed like a bath.

"What kind of a bad place?" Jake felt a crawly feeling shifting around inside him.

"In there? Boats get lost. People too." Marcos shook his head.

"How can they get lost? It's a short tributary that runs into a lake," Ursula said.

Marcos shrugged. Sweat rivulets ran down his face. His shirt was soaked. He removed his black captain's hat and wiped his brow. "They get lost. Crews disappear. No fish either. I don't know. I never went all the way to the lake."

"But you've been there in the flooding season?" Ursula said.

Marcos nodded. "Not for a long time. Never that far." He sounded discouraging. As if he didn't want to talk about it anymore. It might've been his imagination, but Jake thought Marcos was avoiding eye contact. As if he wished they would go away and forget their new plans.

"Will you take us?" Jake asked, wishing the captain would outright refuse.

Marcos took his time considering. "If that's where you want me to take you, I'll take you," he said. "You want to go? Sure. We go." He almost sounded angry with them. Fed up.

Jake grew alarmed at his tone. The mixture of warning and defeat.

"If it's deep enough, we can get down that uncharted fork?" Ursula pointed to the spot. Her concerns were practical, logistical. Identify obstacle. Overcome obstacle. Proceed to goal.

Marcos didn't look at the paper. He didn't look at them either. He watched the water.

"Yes. But that doesn't make it a good idea."

"Iris? The other woman with us? She says she's been there," Ursula said.

"She's been?" Marcos was taken aback. "And she wants to go back?" He shook his head. "People are strange. What happened when she went? Huh? Anything unlucky?"

"Her husband died," Jake said.

The wind had stopped. The mosquitos swarmed them. Marcos scratched his whiskers. He slapped a bug. A splat of blood on his cheek. Jake couldn't help staring at the red smear.

"So, you'll take us there?" Ursula repeated the question. She needed confirmation.

"I'll take you. If the river is where I think, we'll clear it. Too shallow, too narrow… we have the canoes. I'll wait for you to come back. I stay on my boat. You go with them."

He pointed at the brothers with his chin. They were out of the sun. Sitting in a wedge of shade until they were needed again. Davi was dozing. Thiago's eyes looked alert in the dimness.

After rechecking the maps, Ursula and Jake went to the bow.

Once they were alone, Jake said, "I should've told you earlier. I heard Iris in the smoking room on the ocean liner. Talking about her dream life. How it was as real as the waking world."

"It doesn't matter," Ursula said. "She's put it in the open for us now."

"Why are you going along with this?" Jake asked.

"Because if we don't, Andy will always wonder 'What if?'"

"That's not enough of a reason," Jake said.

He knew Ursula well enough to know she didn't make a habit of explaining herself. Or her decisions. But he was going to insist. She saw that.

So, she told him.

"This isn't my expedition, Jake. I'm heading it, but I have no stake in what we find. If we make it home safely, I'm happy. I want the money. We need it for our work. Being down here, I'm eager to return to my research. Money buys us freedom. No donors to satisfy. No museum board on our backs. Freedom." She gestured to the jungle. "Maude Brion is probably long gone. The Spider Queen is a myth. The only thing we're going to find at that spooky lake is mosquitos. After we take Andy there we've done our job. He can tell that to his boss. Then we do what we want. Our reward is independence. That's a trade-off I'll make. If I give in to them here, I'll earn their trust should bigger matters arise. We're better off. The group functions more efficiently."

Jake nodded, trying to follow her reasoning. "So, you don't think there's an old rubber plantation?"

"On the contrary," Ursula said, "I'm pretty certain there is."

"What? I don't understand." It was so bright he was finding it hard to keep his eyes open.

"I've heard rumors. Stories about a haunted rubber operation in these parts."

"Haunted? Now you sound like Iris." A headache hit him like a nail pounding into the center of his forehead. He rubbed his temples but that did nothing. Except maybe made it worse.

Ursula shrugged. "Haunted. Cursed. I heard people got sick. They had weird accidents."

"At this plantation on the lake?" Jake was feeling more than a physical discomfort. He grew uneasy. Panicky. It was crazy how quickly it overcame him. He had this ridiculously strong urge to leap off the boat. To get away, get away… He mustered his will to resist it. He gripped railing. Hot metal. The pain on his palms distracted him, for the moment.

"I don't know. But I think so. It was supposed to be there somewhere," she said.

"Are we making a mistake?" Maybe he was getting a little seasick. Dizzy. Nauseated.

"Who knows? Look, if I thought we'd be in absolute danger, more danger than is normal for these parts, I'd say, 'No' and stick to my guns. Truth is, I don't know where to look for Maude Brion.

No one does. But I don't want to miss out because we played it safe. I don't want Andy to miss out on his big story. I don't want to miss finding Maude if she's alive. And I don't want to miss seeing whatever it is people are calling the Spider Queen," she admitted.

"We go forward, then." Jake couldn't open his eyes. Slits. She was a blur. He thumbed at the sweat and tears. He turned away. To the shining water. But he couldn't look at it.

"We go forward. I'm not here to play it safe, Jake. I play to win. Our chances are better if I get everyone to play together. Second-guessing can get us killed. I need to build their trust."

"I'm with you." He meant it. He wiped his face with his shirt. Sick. He felt sick.

"I know." She clapped him on the back.

Maybe I'd be better if I got out of the sun, he thought. Drink a few sips of water and climb back into my hammock until this feeling passes. The somatic changes afflicted his mood as much as his body. Mind fuzz. He was having trouble putting thoughts together. He'd just have to wait the thing out. It was probably nothing. Fatigue from traveling. A bug he picked up.

"And there's another thing," she said.

"What's that?" He hoped Ursula didn't notice his distress. He stumbled a little. Paused.

The last thing they needed was him out of commission.

"I know Ashley Lott is never going to end up at that lake. He'd never find it."

"Makes the whole thing worthwhile." Jake might've laughed if he didn't feel so awful.

"It does, partner," she said. "It truly, truly does. Ashley imagines he's this big-time…"

Jake didn't hear anymore after that. Because he was falling… falling…

He felt something soft catch him. Pulling him in close. But it wasn't trying to save him.

It was eating him.

19
The Part of the Dream She Didn't Say Out Loud

Iris left out some of the dream of Galton when she told the others about the map in the mud. She left it out again when Andy asked her for more details. There are some secrets between a husband and wife no one else needs to know. Privacies.

Nothing she'd said was an outright lie. Galton did show her things. How to find him.

And Maude Brion.

And the Spider Queen.

What Iris didn't say was about the magic. Galton in his gaudy robe covered in symbols.

Galton crawling around in the grass. In the dirt. Bending himself into bizarre shapes. It caught her off guard when he did that. She found it… disturbing. And she was Galton's wife. What would these people think? They didn't know him. Didn't know he was brilliant.

So, she kept it.

A secret.

The thing with his legs was peculiar. How did he learn to be so flexible? And his arms seemed to elongate until they were the same length as his legs. It was like he had four legs, not two. Down in the grass, poised. His body taut as a piano string. Head tilted up. Unblinking gaze. No expression on his face, but his mouth moving and uttering strings of words she'd never heard. It frightened her to see him this way. But he was communicating, using his body to contact… well, she didn't know what. His contortions had purpose. The words he spoke bothered her more. Not a language, she thought at first. Gibberish. A tumbling expulsion of sounds. But the longer she listened, the more she doubted herself. If it was a language, where did he learn it? Not in the rainforest. She knew most of the languages in the area they were going. Not that she could understand them all, but she knew the kinds of sounds people made when they spoke. Galton was making noises that didn't seem, well… human.

He crept on the ground.

He skittered.

Now, of course, this was happening within her dream. In dreams impossible things become possible. Yet Iris had a suspicion that he was doing this ritual in the real world. If it wasn't happening right in the moment with the two of them together, then Galton was skimming along the forest floor somewhere else in time, the dim past or the unknown future, while she was sleeping on a steamboat in the here and now. It made Iris feel very confused.

In any case, he showed her his ritualistic moves in front of the iron cave. Or goldmine. Whatever it was. She didn't know. He hadn't told her. Hadn't said anything *human*. Not once he got himself twisted up. His robe dragged behind him, until, somehow, he flipped it onto his back. He looked plump with velvety cloth piled on him. He looked just like…

A big spider.

Before this little act of his he told why he must do it.

"It keeps the Queen in her lair," he said.

"Like a magic spell?" Iris said.

He nodded. "I do it. To summon her. And then I contain her. With my magic."

Galton was proud of his accomplishments. It was contagious. She couldn't help smiling.

"He was a beautiful man once," she told Andy when he asked her to describe Galton. "Whip-smart, rugged. I wanted us to be closer. No luck. Part of him was out of reach. By me, by anyone. He has this fascination with his family's golden past. I was never convinced it was true. Their perfection, I mean. He's the only member of his family who didn't die years ago. I met a man at a party in Boston who grew up in the same neighborhood as Galton. He said the Reeds were remarkable for being so *unremarkable*. That's not how Galton recalled it. We lived and worked side by side every day. Yet he'd feel far off. Lost in dreams. Not always good ones."

Andy jotted it on his pad.

"Was he close to his family?" Andy asked.

"Close? I wouldn't say that. I never met them, you see. But Galton was obsessed with his past. Dreams of a childhood mansion, gardens, sailing. Exploring. Was any of it ever real? Oh, I don't know the extent of what was and wasn't. It was real enough for him. He lived in his mind."

Andy looked at her like he had another question he wanted to ask but didn't.

Iris remembered the last time she and Galton traveled on the Amazon together. He had refused to hire a steamboat. He wanted to take canoes the whole way in. Riding with the *indios,* as the Portuguese referred to the indigenous peoples. "You know, Iris, sometimes I can't tell whether I'm dreaming or awake. Isn't that funny?" He'd bought some peculiar tobacco from a man who unloaded boats in Manaus. And he'd been smoking it in his pipe at the front of the canoe the whole trip in. He always experimented with various concoctions he said "to help him sleep better. Deeper". But she knew he liked it for other reasons than enhancing his dream states. He mixed his potions with magic. "Oiling the hinges on the doors to other dimensions," he'd say. Although she never partook, she also didn't object to his mind-altering experiments. He was only ever happy when he pushed boundaries. Be they personal, intellectual, or perceptual.

After they'd lived in the jungle for a while, he tried brewing teas from local plants and even some poisons, in minuscule doses, derived from cane toads or other creatures, as defensive measures. He thought they'd give him revelations. Mostly, they made him sick or unpredictable. Iris recalled a bad time near the end of their encampment. He ingested a toad secretion which caused horrific distorted visions and extreme anxiety. He whacked the vegetation with his stick.

"This jungle is filthy. Shameless! Degeneration wherever you look. See!" He pointed into a dip in the forest, a lush glade teeming with life. Iris saw nothing unusual there. Deep green plants and colorful birds flitting about. "I sense it around me. I'm awash in it, Iris. Are you telling me this decadence won't seep into my mind? Already I'm absorbing its corruption."

Iris told none of this to Andy. What good would it do, sowing doubts in their group?

She also withheld that Galton eventually found his perfect tonic. Spider venom.

He'd let spiders bite him. To see what would happen. He only told her afterward. He could be so reckless. It might've easily killed him. Yet he thrilled at the chances he took.

"Here I am! Alive! Alive!" he exclaimed. "Better than ever!"

Such a boy he was. His exuberance vexed as much as it charmed her.

Iris and Andy were interrupted when Marcos's men carried Jake down to his hammock.

"What happened?" Andy asked. He was shocked to see Jake limp and pale.

"He fainted," Ursula said. "I think he's coming to now. Give me water."

Iris passed her a canteen.

Ursula tilted it up to Jake's lips. He drank a small swallow.

"Is it the heat?" Iris asked.

She knew it wasn't. She'd given him a little taste of venom. Just a drop, mixed with a potion Galton taught her to brew from rainforest plants he collected. She rubbed it around the rim of Jake's canteen; put it there while everyone was sleeping. Served him right for spying on her from outside the doorway of the men's smoking room the other night aboard their ocean cruise. Did he think she couldn't see him hiding among the deckchairs? Silly boy. Anyway, she was only testing dosages. Part getting even and part experimentation.

She'd been shocked by her actions even as she carried them out. *What am I doing? Is this really me?* As she carefully applied the drops, using the brown bottle Galton kept in their tent before she left him to die alone at their camp along the river. He'd milked the spider himself and would add a drop or two to his pot as it boiled. Experimenting. He said it made his mouth tingle. Sped up his heart.

Her heart was pounding now.

The cruel rashness of what she'd done was horrifying and exhilarating. She hadn't felt like herself lately. Less and less since Galton died. Returning to the forest intensified her feelings of ambiguity. In her grieving she felt she'd lost more of herself than of her departed husband. All those years with him… something must've rubbed off. There were times now when she caught herself acting like Galton. Thinking the same way. The force of his personality overshadowed her. *Why worry now? What's done is done*, said a voice in her head. Dabbling with poisons had never killed Galton. He'd been bitten. Spider venom needed to hit the bloodstream directly for the most potent effect. The spider had to inject you. You couldn't sneak it from her like a thief.

Jake looked like a strong man. He must've had a small cut or cold sore in his mouth.

He was already perking up after his drink of water. See? She hadn't harmed him.

"What happened?" he asked.

"You fainted," Ursula said. "How're you feeling now?"

"Foolish," Jake answered. "My tongue is numb on one side. I bit it the other day chewing gum. More water." He swished the liquid around in his mouth.

Ah, his tongue! So, that was it.

Ursula gave him the canteen. "You haven't swallowed any insects, have you?"

Jake shook his head. "Not as far as I know."

"It was probably the heat. Your body has to adjust," Iris said.

Ursula gave her a skeptical look. "Jake and I have been to the jungle many times. Hiking for days, hacking with a machete through thick brush. He's never fainted before."

"I feel fine. And I've never been farther south than Philadelphia," Andy said.

Everyone stared at him.

"Well, really. I haven't," he said.

Jake sat up. "I'm feeling better. You know the oddest thing

happened while I was blacking out. I had this sensation I'd gotten tangled up in this web. I couldn't free myself."

Ursula laughed; she picked up something – gray, slack, and shapeless – off the floor, where the brothers had dropped it after they'd worked to extricate Jake's arm from its snarls.

"Here's your culprit. You landed in the bait nets," she said.

"Me, a dumb minnow," Jake said. "That must've been it."

Iris smiled at him coolly.

Ursula was watching her. What was she looking at? Always drilling at her with her eyes.

"It must be traumatizing for you, Iris," she said.

"What?"

"Seeing someone fall suddenly ill. Struck down, as it were."

I've poisoned the wrong person, Iris thought. Next time I'll get it right. Just you wait.

"You mean because of Galton. I hadn't thought of it, honestly. His case was different."

"Different how?" Andy asked.

Ursula said, "Yes, how did he die? I don't want to pry if it makes you–"

"He was bitten by a spider. On the neck." Iris stepped toward Ursula, reaching out, tapping her polished fingernail sharply against the side of Ursula's throat. "Near the jugular vein. The venom worked slowly to kill him. But the disabling effects were apparent immediately. A neurotoxin. Likely from a Phoneutria specimen. But we never saw it."

She removed her hand from Ursula's throat. Pink marks from her fingers lingered.

"Phoneutria?" Andy asked, pencil poised. He scratched his head instead.

Ursula said, "A Brazilian wandering spider, or 'banana' spider as they're sometimes called. As their name suggests, the species is prone to exploring. They like to hide in the daylight hours and come out at night to hunt. Unlucky fruit workers find them stowed away in banana crates. Their bite is painful. The term 'Phoneutria' comes from the Greek. It means *murderess*."

"Galton had the typical symptoms," Iris said. "Knifing pain. Tremors. Cramping. He couldn't stop sweating. He saw things that weren't there. Before long he couldn't walk. Have you ever seen an adult man drool? He swelled up. Couldn't breathe except with great effort." She lit a cigarette.

Andy paused his scribbling. "How terrible. My God, Iris. I'm so sorry that happened."

"Thank you, Andy." Her expression softened at his recognition of her pain.

"What was he doing when he was bitten?" Ursula persisted.

The tip of Iris's cigarette reddened. She let out a stream of smoke that found the porthole.

"He was practicing magic."

"What sort of magic?" Ursula asked.

Iris shrugged. "He was off by himself. He came stumbling back into camp. I knew something horrible had happened. His face looked… I just knew. He told me he'd been bitten. He'd been lying prostrate on the ground. Worshipping. Calling on gods. Galton had developed an interest in contacting other dimensions. He wanted to unlock gateways. To see the beyond."

"Were these indigenous rituals?" Andy said.

"No. Not at all. He'd read about them in some moldy old book he'd brought here."

"Do you remember the title of the book?" Ursula pressed.

The women locked eyes. Neither of them spoke for what felt like an eternity.

Finally, Iris said, "I don't recall a title. He burned it. Or threw it in the river."

"Which was it? Burned, or drowned it?" Ursula said. "Surely you must know."

"He burned it first then kicked it in the river. What does it matter?" Her voice grew edgy.

"It doesn't," Ursula admitted. She had rattled Iris, and she knew it. That smug smile. Trying to get her angry. To make her explode. Well, she wasn't going to give her the satisfaction. Iris was angry with herself for temporarily losing control. She'd fight to regain it. She'd win.

"I stayed out of my husband's magical pursuits. They were his passion. Not mine."

"But you didn't object?" Ursula said. "Why? Because you thought they were harmless?"

"No, because they were his. I respected Galton's privacy."

"What happened to him at the end?" Ursula asked.

"It took a long time for Galton to die. I stayed by his side. He knew his fate. He asked me to go. I like to imagine that he was thinking clearly, but by that point he was hallucinating. He called out to invisible creatures. He spoke in a made-up language. He was raving. Then he grew very quiet. After that he told me to leave. To get away because he couldn't save me when *they* came through."

Andy paused his jotting.

"Who? Who was coming through?" he asked.

Iris gestured vaguely with her cigarette. The smoke moved in swirls. "Things."

"Things?" Andy said.

"Things. Gods. Creatures from another dimension. I don't know their names, Andy."

"So, that's when you left," Ursula said. "You never saw him again. Except in dreams."

Iris ignored the slight against her dream communications with Galton.

"Yes. I went home and grieved my partner. End of story."

Not quite, though, Iris thought. I didn't go before I saw something ripping apart in the forest. The air shimmering. Torn like a sheet of silk sliced with a razor. She'd been walking away toward her canoe and the men who would row her out. Galton was chanting. He sounded so hoarse, like he'd gargled broken glass. He was shouting. She couldn't help but turn around.

That's when she saw it.

The rip in the world. Its fizzy edges scintillating as if were stitched with silver sequins. The surrounding jungle wavered: a blurry, green velvet curtain stirred by a gusting wind. Inside the rip was thick empty black. Perfect stillness. A void.

Then it came through.

The tip of something crooked and living touched the ground. Lightly. Testing.

Pressing down.

Finding its footing. Filling up the doorway Galton had opened with his magic.

Iris ran.

20
The Lefthanded Fork

The next two days of their journey went smoothly. It rained. Not constantly but on and off. The hot sun loomed between the clouds. The river was high, Andy thought, by the look of things. It climbed up trees, so their upper branches now reached for the boat. Monkeys and birds chattered. Dabs of color were usually animals on the move, alert. They watched them pass. Curious at the sight of people and diesel-powered monsters that belched smoke and blew a piercing whistle when the captain pulled the cord.

Marcos had grown sullen since they altered their course. The two brothers stayed clear of him. They talked to Iris, and sometimes Ursula. They didn't seem nervous, and that made Andy feel better. He stared at the water, wondering how deep it was. He tried not to think about falling in. About the predatory inhabitants lurking in the opaque depths. Marcos pointed out a caiman sunning itself on a stone. It looked like a dinosaur, its lineage so ancient it was almost alien. Although this place was its home. Andy was the outside invader.

"Right on schedule," Iris said, coming up from behind, startling him from his sightseeing stupor. The sun was setting. Thunderclouds moved in. Gray paint poured into a bucket of orange.

She clutched a map in her hand. Andy was seated in the bow, hoping to catch a breeze.

Iris inched beside him as she pointed out a bend in the shoreline.

"That's our lefthanded fork." She turned to the pilot house, waving to signal them.

Ursula and Marcos were in there huddled over a map.

The boat veered across the river, making the turn into the tributary.

Iris looked happy. Andy felt good for her, and glad she'd come with them. He wasn't sure how much stock he put in gut feelings when all was said and done, but he had a strong feeling that they were going to find something big. He'd look back on this for the rest of his life.

"Iris, can I ask you something personal?"

She twisted her lips quizzically, then said, "Go for it, Andy. Shoot."

"Are you hoping to – what happens if… if you find Galton's remains?"

She squeezed his arm. "Don't worry about me. I can handle Galton, dead or alive."

"You wouldn't try to bring him back?" The wind shifted, rattling the leaves in the trees.

"And bury him in Boston?" She shook her head. "He was never at home there. Galton lived in the past a lot when I met him. We lived together for a while in these wild places. But his real home was his dreams. After one of his visions, he told me, 'I have important information. They will take me to a city I built though I cannot remember doing so. I will be honored as a god for beyond time'. He didn't talk about me tagging along. He belongs wherever he is. That's his destiny. I was glad to be together for the time we had. We still talk. But I have my own life too."

"I've never felt about anyone the way you feel about Galton," Andy said. He didn't know what it was like to fall in love with someone, or to lose them tragically. Grief sometimes caused people to do things others found strange. Who was he to question how Iris grieved for her mate?

"He was a smart man. A good man, too. People had a hard time seeing it. But I saw it. I never felt more alive than when we were together. Before things broke him. Even then."

"Aren't you sad?" Andy said. "Being here, I mean." He squinted as raindrops hit him.

"Oh, Andy. Everyone's sad. Don't you know that?"

The boat left the main river. The horizon turned the yellowing purple of an old bruise.

It started raining harder. Lightning flashed like exposed wires. Thunder rumbled.

"Does this fork have a name?" Andy pulled a tarp over his head, sharing it with Iris.

"I don't think so. Not a colonialist name. The groups that live here likely have a word."

The waterway narrowed. Trees closed in on both sides. After the big water it felt secret. There were no other boats around. None had passed them in a day. The surface of the water shattered as the sky opened. But the rain did nothing to relieve the heat. It was warm, like tears.

It was that night after the downpour that they noticed the lights glowing in the forest.

Andy commented about the lack of wildlife on the riverbanks.

"Where did all the monkeys go?" he said.

"Maybe there's a jaguar around." Jake was cutting dried fish and offered Andy some.

"No thanks. I don't mean this spot. Since we turned down the fork, the animals have gotten scarce. Not just the monkeys, but the birds too. I can't think of any time we haven't had bird racket. But listen now. Nothing. Only the damned mosquitos." He scratched a fresh bite.

"Look, there on the shore," Ursula said. "What are those?"

Andy stared. Jake had given him a pair of binoculars to study the fauna. He spied the area Ursula indicated. "Little green lights along the ground. They look like… like…"

"Mushrooms," Iris said. "I've never seen any bioluminescent fungi in this jungle."

"All over the place. See? On both sides of the river. Marcos? Have you seen this before?"

"No," the pilot said. He said something to Thiago who went to the rail for a better look.

The young boatman turned and spoke to his captain.

Marcos said, "He says he doesn't know what it is."

More and more patterns of blue green appeared on the banks as the dark deepened.

"It's just foxfire," Jake said, sounding unconvinced.

He joined Thiago at the rail. Andy stayed back. The odd lights in the dark disturbed him, despite the fact they appeared to pose no threat. Ursula walked the length of the ship searching with the binoculars she'd taken from Andy. Iris sat by the moth-covered lantern with Davi, smoking to keep the mosquitos at bay.

A loud crash exploded from the banks near Jake and Thiago. Both men jumped backward, away from cracking tree branches and thrashed leaves. Everyone heard a coughing noise. Human sounding. Clatter of hooves. The quick flash of yellow-red eyes that disappeared.

Andy's pulse pounded in his ears. His sweat turning cool as

glass beads. Everyone else seemed more curious than frightened, so he did his best to follow suit.

"That was big," Jake said. "Whatever it was."

The commotion was moving away from them. Deeper into the rainforest.

Davi, sitting with Iris, said something to her in a quiet voice. He dragged his fingers down his forehead, nose, and lips. His expression was flat, his eyelids closed but fluttering.

"He says it looked like a horse." Iris pitched her cigarette over the side: a comet, arcing.

"A horse? How could he see anything?" Jake said. "I was standing right there. I didn't."

"He has good eyes. Like his father," Iris said.

"He said it looked like a horse with no face," Ursula said. "Isn't that right, Iris?"

"Yes. That's correct." Iris was smirking in the lamplight.

"What the hell does that mean?" Andy said. "A horse with no face." He searched the shore in vain for clues. But it was impossible. Why were they so close to the bank?

The boat had lanterns hanging on long poles stuck out at the sides, illuminating the water.

They didn't help. Sinuous shadow forms shifted below the thinnest veneer of the water's surface. Some broke the plane completely, if briefly – gray-black or green-tinged – weedy, slimy tongue-like humps that dived quickly under again, accompanied by a smack or wooden plonk.

Once there came an awful series of gurglingly wet gulps.

"It's too dark to see anything," Jake said. "Except what you imagine."

Andy noticed he didn't go back to the rail. There were trees laying in the water. Slithering ripples weaved between the angled

Arkham Horror

half-sunken trunks. Insects awhirl in the light haloes. That eerie blue-green luminescence unnerved him. Although it was strangely fascinating.

Marcos steered the boat, saying nothing.

21

The Prize

"You want to look? Go ahead. I'm telling you the boat's gone," the sniper, a wiry American the other men called Toothpick, looked up from his telescopic gunsight. "Ain't nobody home."

"I'll take you up on your offer." Ashley Lott suspected the mercenary thought he would back down. Ashley had handled arms before. He'd hunted pheasant with his mother's family on a trip to England. He remembered what he wore: a flat cap, heavy tweeds, and wellies.

"Have at it. Keep your finger off the trigger. Drop my weapon in the drink, you're going in to get it."

Toothpick stepped away from the bow. He held out his Springfield rifle. The sniper sported bushy black eyebrows and a dimple nicked in his chin. Ashley had found him among the least threatening of the soldiers he'd been assigned to accompany, despite his raptorial keenness.

"How do I do it?" Ashley asked.

"Look in the tube."

"Right, of course." Ashley took the rifle and carefully braced one hand underneath it, pressing his shoulder into the butt. He leaned forward, shutting one eye, peering with the other.

Toothpick was correct. Captain Marcos's boat was no longer ahead. How disappointing.

"Well. Where do you think they went?" Ashley asked, handing the rifle back.

"Your guess is good as mine. Turned off somewhere. Probably yesterday. 'Fore it got too dark. The river was bendy back there. We sure ain't seen a lick of 'em since sunup."

"What do you propose we do?"

"Turn back."

Ashley stroked his freshly shaved jaw. He pretended to consider various factors.

"I've decided we will turn back. Tell the captain. I will inform our men," Ashley said.

"Men don't need to know. Unless there's something for them to do."

Ashley deflated. "Don't you think they'll be curious why we're turning around?"

"Only if there's something for them to do." Toothpick bit a plug of chewing tobacco.

"Keep an eye out," Ashley said.

"What?"

"That's what they can do. Keep an eye out for the boat. It gives them purpose." Ashley was surprised Toothpick was able to lead, having so little insight into the psychology of men.

"Go on and tell 'em if you want." Toothpick went to talk to the captain.

Ashley took the steps down to where the men lounged, checking his appearance in a mirror he'd hung from a nail outside his cabin. People responded to leaders who were flawless. Attitude played a bigger role than substance. He couldn't imagine how anyone would follow Ursula Downs. While she was certainly attractive in a rough, tomboyish way that appealed to some men, how could a person have confidence in her abilities? At best she was potential wife material for a third-rate academic who needed caring for while toiling in the field. A welcome distraction from the oppressive heat and pressures of work. Did they really think they would be safe with her as a guide? Heavens! How could a woman even protect herself in this untamable wilderness? Why, the sight of her would imperil the whole group if say, a cannibal, or even a simple warrior decided to steal her for fun. Sheer recklessness.

No. They were fools. Trusting in a woman to negotiate the plethora of tropical dangers.

And now these soldiers of fortune had lost her. How does one do that? Lose a boat on a river? There are only two basic directions. The tributaries, of course. That was the answer. He'd seen the maps. Captain Marcos had likely been hitting a bottle of rum and made a wrong turn.

They'd find Ursula's trail again.

And follow.

As ordered.

When the time came, if Ursula and her party happened to luck into locating that frivolous silent film star – Maude Something – who had gotten herself tangled up in the jungle, then Ashley would step in. His men would rescue her. He really couldn't care less about that. Maude Something was probably dead. Or worse.

No, what Ashley cared about was the Spider Queen. He wanted her. So did his boss. That's why he'd hired Ashley and shared intelligence about this mission. The Spider Queen would make Ashley more famous than he already was. She would seal his stellar reputation.

Before Ashley gathered the men together to hear the news of their turnaround, he climbed the ladder down into the cargo hold. At the bottom – oh, the stink of this hellhole – he held a handkerchief sprinkled with Penhaligon's to his nose. He lit a lantern and studied the tool he'd brought with him to accomplish his mission. It wasn't put together yet. The men would do that.

But an imaginative person could piece together what it was. Locks, chains, and all.

A stout ten-foot cube constructed of steel bars as thick around as his thumbs. Inescapable.

Ashley Lott was going to catch the Spider Queen.

Alive.

Even if she turned out to be just woman sized, who knew what she'd be capable of?

He'd put her in this steel cage to be safe. Then he'd bring her back to civilization and place her on display. For educational reasons. In the name of science. And if he made a handsome profit…? Cream does rise to the top. They would set forth on a multi-city US tour.

No! No! Think bigger, Ashley!

Ashley tried to shake one of the disassembled barred walls but couldn't budge it an inch.

Once this Amazon business was over, she would be his prize. He'd take her everywhere.

For all the world to see. The entire world!

Presenting: The Legendary Dr Ashley Lotts's Spider Queen!

22
O Lago

The morning light did little to calm the sense of disquiet among the shipmates as they followed the lefthanded tributary on its meandering path through the jungle. Marcos had kept the boat moving all through the night, switching hands at the wheel with Thiago and Davi. Ursula slept fitfully, awaking with the impression she'd spent the last few hours tormented by nightmares. Yet she remembered nothing of them except the lingering taste of fear.

She tied back her hair and wetted her bandana, draping it around her neck.

The heat had grown worse. There was no wind. On either shore, the bush smoldered as if from an invisible fire. When Ursula stretched her arm toward the bank, she detected a rise in temperature at her fingertips. A pulsing warmth. The steam-bath air was laborious to breathe. She moved sluggishly. Every minor action required extra effort. She was tired although she'd only just left her hammock. Sleep's restorative powers were nowhere in evidence.

Ursula yawned, her involuntary cry the solitary song in that long green riparian corridor.

Thiago piloted the boat. He nodded a good morning. His face

glistened; damp black hairs were pasted to his head. He'd stripped off his shirt to cool off.

Ursula felt slicked in her own perspiration. Her stale field clothes chafed at raw skin. Using her fluency in Portuguese – no secret now – she asked Thiago, "Where is the captain?"

Thiago hooked his thumb to the stern. The captain had been awake all night, he said.

A trail of smoke trickled from under a bamboo canopy. With it came the pleasant smell of a woodfire. Marcos sat beside a kettle grill, poking a broken-handled gaff at a coffee pot. The coffee aroma was pungent. She hoped a cup might revive her. Although from the looks of him, it hadn't done much for Marcos. His bloodshot eyes glared at the sticks charring in the grill. Sallow skin sagged on his face like a melting mask. Inside the V of his unbuttoned shirt his naked chest had turned the color of fried bacon. He offered her no greeting.

"Is this your special brew?" Ursula asked, taking a seat on the bench beside him. How could he stand being so close to the fire? Why did he look like a man forsaken by the world?

Unlike Thiago's glowing sheen, Marcos's appearance was as dry as an ancient tortoise. His cracked lips parted. The tip of his tongue stuck out, a dusty pink nub.

"I cannot close my eyes," he said, blinking slowly.

Ursula wasn't certain she'd heard him correctly, but before she could ask, he continued.

"I shut them. But I don't go anywhere. I stay right here."

He pointed at the deck between his rough bare feet.

"Insomnia?"

"What?" Flies were crawling in his hair. He either didn't notice or didn't care.

"You can't sleep?" She fought the urge to swat the flies. Instead, her fingers combed through her own hair. Something was clearly wrong with him. But what? And how bad was it?

Marcos shook his head. "I drive. I watch. No sleep."

The coffee was boiling. He ignored it.

Ursula wondered if he was ill. "Maybe you should go below. We can anchor while you try and rest. We'll take the canoes out. Do a bit of exploring."

Marcos's eyes widened. He turned to face her. "Go ashore?"

Ursula grabbed a rag and took the pot off the coals. She filled a tin cup. Marcos's fragility appeared both mental and physical. Saying the wrong thing might aggravate him.

"We don't have to. We can just paddle around. If you've been running all night, we should be ahead of schedule. Is the lake coming up soon?" She looked at the toffee river in the channel. The water was not wide but passable. The view revealed no farther than the next bend.

"We should be there," he said. "*Onde fica o lago*? Where's the lake? I don't know. A little more." The backs of the captain's hands twitched. He gasped like a landed fish. His knee bounced to a fast tempo only he could hear. No, he was not well. She worried about him. If heat was the issue, they might be able to help him. But if it were something else… an unknown…

There were no sounds on the river. Which was strange. Not a bird. Not a monkey. No frogs or frolicking otters. Nothing splashed or dared to take a drink from the banks. The leaves didn't rustle for there was no living creature to disturb them. The trees seemed posed, dull as waxworks. Ursula had never known the Amazon to be so quiet for this long.

It was as if the forest had stopped talking.

The engine chugged. The steamboat plowed forward. Its paddles churned along.

Davi appeared, his brow creased in worry. About his captain? Or all of them on board?

"Is everything good, Davi?" Ursula asked. "Any problem with the boat?"

"The boat is fine." He was staring at Marcos.

"Will you help the captain to his bunk? He needs some water. He's not feeling well."

She went to Marcos. Those flies. She flicked them away and gripped his upper arm. Davi seized his other side. They stood him up. Marcos's arm felt like a log baking in the sun. "Wait," she said. Dipping her bandana in the river, she removed the captain's hat, squeezing the wet cloth over his head. "To cool you down," she told him. But he did not say anything back.

Heatstroke, she thought. That's the likeliest thing. But Marcos was used to this weather. He'd gotten this way some time during the night. It made no sense. At least he was semi-lucid.

Davi walked him to the top of the steps.

Marcos stared ahead. Like he's sleepwalking, she thought. Or drugged.

"I shut my eyes. I am still here." Marcos accepted the canteen Davi offered him. His throat jerked as he guzzled it down. "All night I drive the boat," he said, after wiping his lips.

"Drop anchor. We're taking the canoes," Ursula said to Davi. "How are you feeling?"

"I am well." Davi seemed less nervous now that the captain was up and about.

"And you?" she asked Thiago.

"I feel like I always feel," he said.

"Good."

Marcos was smiling at Ursula. At least he was the only person affected.

She gazed at the bubbling river. "Do you think an anchor will hold here?"

"It will hold," Thiago said.

"You're all going to die," Marcos said, still smiling. "Me, you, them. Everybody dies."

He said this in English. The brothers didn't understand. Ursula decided not to translate.

Marcos looked at the flooded zone. "Where is *o lago*?"

He chuckled dryly.

"Take care, my captain," she said to Marcos. Then to Davi, "Find me if he gets worse."

Davi nodded. At the wheel, Thiago watched his brother descending the steps. Davi turned, said something to him in Tupi. Thiago steered the boat to a sandbar in the middle of the river. The water would be shallower there. A good place to anchor. The current didn't look bad.

Davi took the captain down.

Ursula followed.

Belowdecks the others were dressed and ready for the day's activities.

"Have we reached the lake?" Iris asked.

"Not yet. Marcos isn't feeling like himself," Ursula said. "We'll monitor it."

"Sick?" Jake said, raising his eyebrow.

"I'm not sure. He's going to rest. Too long in the sun maybe. I really don't know."

"The sun's only just come up," Iris said, matter-of-factly.

"I've told the brothers to drop anchor. We'll take the canoes out." Ursula checked the gear in her bag. "Bring water. It's steamy. I don't want people dropping like flies." *Those flies.*

"We're going on land?" Andy asked, both excited and slightly trepidatious.

"I don't plan on leaving the canoes. We can explore into the flooded zone. Through the trees where the steamboat can't fit. The jungle is oddly quiet. I'm wondering if there's activity."

"Human activity?" Iris asked, her voice chipper as a bird's.

"Perhaps."

"I'll bring the rifle just in case," Jake said.

"Aren't humans what we're looking for?" Andy said. "Why do we need a gun?"

Jake said, "It's for our protection. Don't worry. I won't shoot anyone."

"Don't shoot *me*," Andy said. "How will I break this story if I'm dead?"

Iris laughed. Too loudly. She was wearing a wide-brimmed hat, tall snakeproof boots.

Did she already know they were going on a scouting mission today?

Iris turned toward the wall, slipping the gold spider ring on her finger. Rubbing it.

Ursula frowned. The relic was too conspicuous to hide. What was her game?

Iris flashed the arachnid relic with the dazzling ruby eyes around the cabin. Andy and Jake said nothing. Didn't they notice? Could they be that oblivious? Ursula shook her head.

"Anything might be lurking in the forest," she said. "We won't venture out of sight of the boat. And we won't be gone long. It's relatively safe. I'll ask one of the brothers to guide us."

Thiago went with them.

Both brothers lowered the canoes into the water. Jake and Andy climbed in the first boat. Ursula and Iris took the second. Thiago would paddle alone. He would take the lead. They'd follow. A short, easy trip. It was early morning when they launched. The whole day lay ahead.

Davi watched from the sandbar, waving farewell.
The rainforest had yet to break its eerie silence.

23
Crystal Clear

Jake followed Thiago as he weaved between the trees. The water was high. Weeks ago, the branches soaking their tips would've arched overhead, supporting toucans and marmosets, sloths, howler monkeys, scarlet macaws. Now their heights were truncated by the rising flood. Bushy crowns hovered inches above the surface like a man's walrus moustache touching the top of his beer foam. The tallest, oldest trees still soared. The scene reminded Jake of mangrove swamps he'd visited in Louisiana during his itinerant youth. Except there were no Cajuns or alligators haunting the murky lanes of these spooky, legend-laden, backwater swamps.

No signs of life, in fact. It was eerie. This zone should've been teeming with animals.

The vegetation was thriving. Shafts of light penetrated a lush emerald cathedral. Multitudinous leaves filtered sunbeams like shards of green-stained glass.

"It's really beautiful," Andy said from the front seat. "I'm awestruck."

"I couldn't agree more," Jake said. Yet he couldn't shake his nagging sense of unease.

Thiago paddled ahead. With little apparent effort, he had pulled away six boat lengths.

"I've dreamed of this," Andy said.

Jake's neck hairs prickled. "You dreamed?"

"Of coming to a place like this." Andy nodded. "Since I was a boy. That's when I first read about jungles. Riding on the big paddleboat is fine, don't get me wrong. But going in this way feels authentic. I wish I'd learned to swim." Andy peered carefully over the side. He stuck his paddle in to measure. Down it plunged to his wrist without touching anything. Undulations distorted his reflection: a boardwalk funhouse mirror. "How deep do you think it is?"

"Hard to tell. We can't see bottom."

"What do you mean 'can't see bottom'?" Andy said. "I see it. Well, I see down."

Jake looked and startled. The water was crystal clear. Visibility to ten feet at least. Maybe deeper. That was strange. He'd expected to find zero clarity, as chocolatey-brown and silty as the Rio Solimões. It would be unusual enough to find blackwater, those tea-stained waters full of acidic tannins prevalent in the Rio Negro to the north. This gin-like clarity seemed impossible. In the sunniest patches he was amazed to observe drowned plants, delicate fronds and leaves broadly beckoning, serpentine tendrils tossed about limply in warm, liquid motion.

He turned to share their findings with Ursula.

But he couldn't locate her. He pivoted around, spying over his other shoulder. Then he stopped paddling, drifting as he scanned the waterscape for the other canoe.

They had to be here.

Yet not a trace of Ursula and Iris.

"Why are we stopping? Thiago's leaving us in the proverbial dust," Andy said.

"I'm looking for Ursula." Where could they have gone? In five minutes? His previous disquietude shifted into a higher gear. Not panic. Jake prided himself on being coolheaded. But a creeping dread encircled him.

"Ursula!" Jake cried out. "Ursula! Where are you?"

He and Andy waited. But no reply came. It was easy to get confused in a flooded area. Everything started to look similar. Landmarks disappeared. A thousand paths unraveled on all sides. If you looked only forward, when you turned back after your wake vanished there was no way to know where you'd been. No breadcrumb trails. Jake wiped his forehead with his shirt.

"Ursula!"

"I don't see the boat," Andy said.

"Obviously, Andy. That's why I'm shouting for her."

"No. The big boat. Marcos and Davi. Weren't we going to stay in sight of them?"

"They're right over…" Jake peered into the middle distance. "They should be there." He pointed with his dripping paddle. "We've been going straight." He swung his puzzled gaze from side to side. Acid trickled up from his gut. "It must be an optical illusion. Light reflections. The sun's playing tricks on us." He slowly turned their canoe around.

"Where's Thiago?" Panic lodged in Andy's voice. "He *was* over there."

Jake spun back. He dipped his paddle, rotating the canoe again. "He's probably pushed on a bit. These shadows are darker than they seem. He'll realize it soon and come back."

"Thiago!" Andy shouted. Twisting, he yelled out to the trees, "Ursula! Iris!"

"Keep calm," Jake said, although his heart was racing. It was simple. They'd wait. The river current wasn't moving them in the backwater areas. It was easy to stay put. The big steamboat on the tributary couldn't be more than one or two hundred yards behind them.

Where was Ursula?

24
True Believer

Ursula cocked her head.

"Do you hear something?" she said.

"No. Isn't that peculiar? I've never had this happen before. All the time Galton and I spent in the jungle, exploring the river, gathering folktales. I can't imagine it being so hushed. Not in the daytime." Iris rode in the bow. Her enormous hat nodded like a heavy blossom.

Without looking back, she was aware of Ursula's stare. That's how it felt to Ursula. When she reached around to adjust her hat, her fingers wriggled. The gold spider glinted.

"What was Galton up to out here?" Ursula said.

"Sorry?"

"You and your husband. You weren't only studying folklore."

"We weren't? You could've fooled me. I worked day and night collecting data."

"Galton changed somehow, didn't he? He might've begun researching evidence of a mythical goddess. At some point that stopped. He became a true believer. Is that it?"

Iris didn't turn. Her shirt stood stark white against the jungle's green. The sun dappled the river like hundreds of golden trinkets shimmering from below.

"Galton found a way to open portals to other dimensions using dreams and magic."

"I have my doubts." Ursula talked to the back of Iris's head: a faceless blot.

"Do you?" Iris's voice took on a dreamy, singsong quality. "Galton said he could see them, you know. Other 'Dreamlands' where fantastic cities stood. He visited many times."

"What did he find in the cities? The Spider Queen? *She's real* – is that what you want me to believe? Where's the evidence? Did he use sorcery to call her from Planet X or something?"

"Not from Planet X," Iris tutted. "By the way, while you've been busy interrogating me," she swiveled, asking with a sly smile, "where did Jake and the boy reporter disappear to?"

Ursula lifted her head. She'd been so busy focusing on Iris, she'd lost track of Andy and Jake. It shouldn't have been hard to follow them. She cursed herself silently for a rare lapse in her attention, as she continued to hunt in vain for the smallest clue of their canoe or its passage.

Finding none.

25
White Flag

"The rubber tappers employed brutal forms of violence against the indigenous populations," Jake said. "It was horrific. Whole villages ravaged by disease and bullets. It's no wonder the people fought back. They knew the rainforest. Ways to move without being seen or heard. Mimicry. How to blend in for stealth. They valued harmony with the natural world."

The two men had been sitting in their canoe for a long time, hoping to spot another boat. Their talk had turned to the cruel history of rubber operations and their exploitative practices. Andy had wondered what the chances were that they might run into anyone near the old station.

Jake thought it unlikely.

"Shouldn't you hide that rifle anyway? We wouldn't want to provoke someone watching us." Andy checked the forest for human shapes. It was useless. He'd never pick them out if they were here. He wondered if finding another person might be the help they needed. Or maybe not.

"The rush for 'black gold' has made this place more hostile for everyone. The rubber boom is bust. I'm not sure white people deserve any more chances. Not here. However, we could run into a jaguar or an anaconda. What about Ashley's band of mercenaries? The rifle may give us our best chance to escape. It's my job to keep you alive… but I'll keep the gun out of sight."

The landscape was imbued with threat. If the forest didn't get you, hostile humans would. Clouds massed above the canopy. The rays of sunlight vanished. Palpable darkness spread. They'd been waiting hours, so it seemed. Andy's watch had stopped. Jake didn't have a watch. He had a compass. But it was malfunctioning. The needle circled round, bouncing like a nervous terrier, refusing to settle. Jake wondered if there was a strong magnetic force in the vicinity. But not even an iron ore deposit would make the compass act so wildly.

Andy didn't like how he was feeling observed.

Jake must have felt it too.

"We've waited long enough, Andy. I can make a good guess about the direction of Marcos's boat. It's not far. Ursula might've gone back after they couldn't find us."

No matter where Andy searched, he saw only trees looming in water.

"Why can't we hear them? They'd shout, wouldn't they? Or blow the boat whistle?"

Darker now.

Jake said, "Disorientation leads to confusion which leads to panic, and that is the surest route to a premature death. Keep calm. Plan. Act. That's what Ursula taught me."

"Thiago was ahead of us," Andy said. "He'd come this way to get back. Where is he?"

"Do you have a handkerchief?"

From his pocket, Andy extracted a monogrammed linen square. "My mother gave me this as a gift after the *Advertiser* hired me. Thought it would add a touch of class. If she only knew."

"Excellent!"

Jake snatched the handkerchief. Before Andy could object, he started tearing it into strips with his knife.

"Hey!" Andy protested.

"We need a marker. A flag we can spot from a distance. Would your mother approve of you being saved?"

"Go on. It's too late now." Andy waved at him.

Jake hung one of the white linen strips on the end of a branch above their canoe.

"This marks where we've been," he said.

Andy glumly surveyed the tree branch adorned with his shredded hanky.

"White. Easy to pick out." Jake shook the limb. "We'll keep it at our six o'clock. See?"

"The steamboat is at twelve?" Andy perked up, pointing to where he thought the river was. A lock of damp hair fell in his eyes. His head felt hot, almost feverish.

"By my logic, yes," Jake said. "Now we proceed fifty yards or thereabouts. Always keeping our marker in sight behind us."

"If we don't see the boat?"

"We come back to the flag. Try another direction. Spokes on a wheel. From one of those spokes, we should see Marcos and Davi or one of the other canoes. Sound good?" Jake asked.

"The bee's knees."

For the first time in hours Andy's spirits lifted.

26
New Galton

"How can it be getting dark? It must be a thunderstorm," Iris said. "Did you see lightning?"

"Maybe I saw a flicker above the trees. But it's curious," Ursula said.

"No thunder."

"Exactly."

More bright flashes without thunder. One. Two. The air crackled with electricity, making their hair stand on end. No rain. A hot metallic smell surrounded them. Iris's teeth ached.

And it kept getting darker. The farthest trees disappeared. Their visible world shrank.

"I am here, my dearest," said a whisper in her ear.

Iris had her matches in hand, a cigarette between her lips; the lit match cupped, its petal-like flame wavering as it illuminated her heart-shaped face. "Pardon, what did you say?"

"I didn't say anything," Ursula dug into her field pack. "Ah! Here it is. I knew I had one. Light this, please." She passed a candle to Iris who – after lighting her smoke – lit the wick.

"Good idea," Iris said. "Before you know it, we'll be in total darkness."

The spider's ruby eyes sparkled with mischief. Did she feel it vibrating on her finger?

"The light is going to draw mosquitos. But we have no choice. I don't want to paddle in the dark," Ursula said. "We're lost as it is. There's no sense in denying it."

"There are no mosquitos. Haven't you noticed? Everything feels strange here." A little tremor ran through Iris. Her hands were shaking slightly, she noticed. Too many cigarettes and not enough food? Perhaps. But it felt like more than that. She didn't know what though.

The two women sat flummoxed in their canoe. They had tried navigating out of the forest, but the flooded terrain was endless. The canopy grew solid above them. Last tufts of gray sky vanished. Silence felt close by, as if it were a living thing. Ursula had been paddling, counting her strokes between the ribbony trunks of giant kapok trees. On each tree she carved a number at eye level. *1, 2, 3* .... They had not passed the same tree twice, despite attempting to double back. Once, when they thought they'd found one of their markings – number *4* – the women were puzzled to see the symbol had turned white, weathered, and greatly aged, as if it had been carved decades before. They decided it couldn't be *their* 4.

"Someone else had the same idea." Ursula hardly sounded convinced.

What were the odds? Iris thought. Carving numbers here? Infinitesimally small.

As the final traces of natural light seeped away, a palpable pressure increased. It felt as if a hidden powerful sinister force, now activated, had shifted its malevolent attention toward them.

"Behold me," it said.

That voice. She heard it again. Not a whisper this time, but the same voice. Deep, bold sounding. Iris recognized it this time. She couldn't believe it. But she knew it just the same.

Beside the last kapok tree, several feet above the inky river, floated Galton.

His arms spread wide in welcome. His gaudy cloak obscuring his face. A silver halo formed around him.

Iris's breath caught in her throat. He was there… he really was there. *Galton.*

She was awake! In her dreams last night, he told he'd come to her if she got them off the boat. Now he was here! She wasn't sure how he did it. But he did. Just as he had promised her.

She pinched herself hard on the forearm. A shot of pain radiated. This was no dream.

Galton…

He looked peculiar… His flesh glowed the same blue green as the mushrooms they'd seen on the riverbanks. His teeth… well, his gums must have receded, because his teeth were longer than Iris remembered. They were the only part of his face she could really see. But it was him.

His voice. Harsher than she'd remembered, doomier. More formidable.

She had almost forgotten how he sounded.

But him. Yes, it was him. Had to be. She knew in her heart Galton's spirit was there.

He grinned hellishly at her, rubbing his hands as if he were washing something off, or maybe smearing something in. His curling fingernails clicked together. It sounded like rats in an attic.

His floating made her dizzy. Her stomach felt like a wet, cold, floppy fish.

How was he doing this? What was wrong with him? He shouldn't frighten her. Maybe it was the light. Or the darkness. Something that wasn't his fault that made things look worse. Whatever it was made him glow like foxfire. A color from space, a dreamworld color.

She should've been overjoyed at meeting him while awake. Instead, she was confused.

"It's magic, my dear. My magic." He drifted away from the kapok tree over the glassy pools of obsidian water. His stars and symbols – stitched so crookedly into that moth-eaten, cheap costume – scintillated and danced. They were spinning free, making a slow orbit in the air.

Why wasn't Ursula saying anything? Why wasn't she screaming?

Because despite Galton being the love of her life, Iris felt like screaming her head off.

Or maybe because of that.

This wasn't the Galton she knew; he'd been just a man in the end – a brilliant, exciting, and extremely flawed man. A real, whole person, her partner in all ways for years. *Her love.*

How had she left him to die in the jungle alone, in such terrible pain? Her worst mistake.

She did it because he had asked her to. Because she was frightened of what had happened to him. He'd crossed a forbidden threshold and called something out of the depths from beyond.

Why did he need to go there? Wasn't their life good enough? Iris thought it was.

This new Galton emitted icy coldness. At the sight of him she tasted bitter ashes; her sour stomach lurched. Her mouth burned with sick. He was both her husband and not her husband. Divided. Doubled. Monstrous. Her mind could not reconcile the awful, foul twoness of him.

"Am I dreaming?" Iris wanted to pretend this wasn't happening. Not like this.

"What?" Ursula said.

"You will be seeing things. Things few living humans have ever seen," Galton said.

"I don't want to," Iris said to her husband. His voice buzzed like a terrible, angry hive.

"Yessss," he said. "They are coming through. She crosses... crossessssss with them..."

"I don't want to see it! Get away from me!"

"Iris, what are talking about? You don't want to see what?" Ursula said. "Look at me. Is there something wrong? Please, look at me." She leaned forward and touched Iris's shoulder.

But Iris ignored her and kept looking at Galton. How could she look away? It was impossible. This was a trick. It couldn't be Galton. Something was using him. Possessing him.

It was wearing him like a glove.

He was its puppet.

Ursula swiveled her head to the forest. She took the candle away from Iris and stuck it out into the dark where Galton floated with his buzzing voice, his glowing flesh, and his long teeth, grinning. "There's nothing there," Ursula said. "I can't see anything at all."

Iris wasn't sure if Ursula was talking to her, or to herself. Maybe a little of each.

"Go away. I don't like this dream, Galton. Make it stop," Iris pleaded.

"Thisss is no dream... Thisss issssss... Behold, the gateway is held open. I opened it!"

"Snap out of it, Iris!" Ursula yelled. "You're hallucinating."

The candle snuffed out.

At the last moment Galton reached for them and extinguished it between his fingers.

In the black, something huge jumped into the water in front of them. *Gulummppp!*

"Stop it! Galton! Make it go back!" Iris froze in the dark. "I can't take this. I can't…"

Galton was gone. She didn't see it happen, but she knew it was true. As the candle went out, he disappeared. Ursula was fumbling with her pack. "Iris! Matches! Give me your matches!"

Meanwhile, the huge thing splashed in the water. A great spray of heavy droplets rained over the canoe. Slaps hit the water. Flat, hollow, booming crashes that blew dank, fetid, watery gusts at the canoe, rocking it, wobbling them in the tarry darkness where there was no way to tell up from down. One of the blasts knocked Iris's hat off. She was afraid of falling in the water.

"There! Look at its eyes!"

Iris pointed – she might've laughed if she didn't think how utterly, absolutely mad she would sound, as she was gesturing in the undivided dark. Trying to keep a shred of sanity. To survive. To live through this. Ursula couldn't see her. But Iris could see them – "There! Its eyes are pink! My God, they're the most hideously repugnant shade of pink…"

The huge thing was getting out of the water. It was clambering up one of the kapok trees. Sloshing. Drippy. Its body was drizzling great volumes, like a collection of sodden mopheads draining all at once…

A snap-sizzle as Ursula lighted a match – she must've discovered some in her pack. Illuminated by the matchlight, she looked wet and scared. Her eyes bugged out as she scoured the darkness for monsters. That small circle of candlelight was more than enough. It revealed the huge thing clinging to the ribboned trunk of the nearest kapok, a tree so thick around that if the two women hugged it, their hands wouldn't have touched. Yet this black, coarsely furred beast encircled the trunk easily. Muscular, gigantic. It had stout, barrel-sized forearms: each arm splitting at its terminus into two paws the size of park benches. Four fat paws and two clawed feet dug deeply into the tree, keeping the abominable creature from slipping back into the water. Though the worst part was its mouth. The jaws divided its head… *but vertically*… fangs as slick and yellow as hot buttered corn. Bulbous goggle-like pink eyes jutted from the bifurcated head…

The monster's legs flexed.

It's going to jump! Iris thought. At us! The canoe will smash to splinters. We'll be drowned. Our bodies crushed. Who knows what those fangs will do to us before we die…?

The monster made horrible clownish faces at them from the edge of the shadows.

Then its head tilted the way dogs sometimes do when they pick up a curious sound.

Ursula grabbed Iris roughly. "Get down!"

She pushed Iris into the bottom of the canoe and laid on top of her. Iris sensed rather than saw something leaping over them. Sharp, hard objects – its hooves? – clipped the nose of the canoe, nearly upending the boat. Oh no, she didn't want to fall in that water.

It wasn't the hairy creature jumping on them, because the hairy creature was on the other side. This new monster pushed off their canoe to pounce on the hairy thing!

"Stay down!" Ursula said. "Cover your eyes. Don't look!"

But she did look. An unspeakable fight ensued between the creatures. The hairy one beat its attacker against the tree, and the other one – the hopper – gave out a wounded, guttural sigh. More of the hoppers arrived on the scene. Hunting in a pack, Iris thought, judging by the guttural explosions that ensued from two directions, converging on the spot where the hideous beast clung to the kapok tree. Harsh coughs barked out across the swamp.

The coughs sounded exactly like the noise they'd heard from the shoreline the night before.

A filthy, repulsive battle was taking place at the base of that ancient and battered tree. The rip of rending flesh, the stink of blood, filled the air. Iris didn't know which creatures to root for. Did one victor portend better for their own fate? Or were the loathsome beasts fighting to see who would eat them? She laughed at that.

How unseemly of her.

As swiftly as the unclean war of these grotesque beasts had begun, it was finished.

Ursula and Iris lay in the canoe. Quiet, unmoving. Wondering…

"They're gone," Ursula said at long last.

"Where to? I didn't hear them swim away."

They sat up. Ursula had blown out her candle to avoid drawing the monsters' attention. Iris helped her to light the wick for a third time. It took their combined courage to lift the candle in their co-joined hands. Higher, higher they raised the flickering flame…

Iris held her breath.

The water was empty. The unnatural night grew still again. And silent.

"They've vanished," Iris said softly.

Slowly, the atmosphere around the canoe grayed. Iris saw tall shapes hunching over them. Trees, only trees. Vines. A hump of land where delicate ferns grew. Spade-like leaves emerged around them in exquisite detail. The water shone like undisturbed pools of mercury…

Ursula blew the candle out. They didn't need it anymore.

Daylight had returned.

27
The Margay Comes Back

Thiago paddled in the forever twilight. Not brightening like a new day, not turning into night. The other canoes were gone. The river – gone too. This place was nowhere in the world.

Thiago wondered if, somehow, he had died. *Is this my final journey?* he was thinking when the front of his canoe struck land with a violent jolt. The canoe rode up the mud and stuck.

That's when he saw his father.

Standing in the bushes. His eyes shone like smoky oval stones polished in the river.

He was peeking out from between leaves. His skin looked smooth, covered in muddy streaks that had dried and cracked. Clumps of dirt hung in his hair. He stared at Thiago.

Thiago could not speak. He wanted to, but when he opened his mouth, no sounds came.

Why was he seeing this? What did it mean? He had no answers, only questions.

His father had been digging in the ground when Thiago interrupted him.

Why is my father so short? he thought, until he saw that his father was standing in a hole.

He wore no clothing. His flesh had turned the colors of rotting meat, wrinkly, sunken and soft, like fallen fruits even animals wouldn't eat. His shoulders slumped. Bones poked like sticks sliding under his skin. He looked hungry. His strong, brave father had never looked this way.

Was it him?

Thiago was able to speak. He called his father's name in the language of his people.

But his father said nothing back.

He only stared at him without even blinking his sad eyes.

"Father, am I dead?" Thiago asked. But he did not get out of the canoe.

If this was his father, why didn't he talk to him? Thiago did not want to see him like this. He wanted him on the river in a boat or fishing for arapaima. Not a starving, silent man.

From somewhere near his father came a sound: "*Mee-mmeepp. Meeep. Meepmeepme…*"

It was not a sound he father ever made. Not a people sound.

His father's face did not change. The sounds continued. Thiago watched as his father turned his head but not his eyes and made a quiet meeping noise back down into the hole where he stood. Then Thiago knew that this hole was a burrow of some kind that went deeper into the earth and that his father was not alone but there were others farther down in that muddy hole and they were talking in a language Thiago had never heard before and did not want to hear again.

Not for as long as he lived.

Because now he knew he was not dead. He was alive and he had to flee from here.

His heart drummed loudly in his chest. He dug his paddle in the mud and pushed off. But the canoe was too high on the bank and did not budge. Instead, his paddle sunk in. This muddy thing he had mistaken for his father, when it turned its head, Thiago saw it now had a muzzle like a dog's and it was a grubby, foul-smelling thing that came out of the ground. A pile of picked-clean bones heaped at its feet. A human head sat atop the pile. It still had hair and torn skin, one cloudy eye, and the thing with the dog face had dug it up. Thiago knew this was its food.

He stepped out of the canoe. Shouting at the dead-eater to get back. *Stay away from me.*

The dead-eater crouched low, watching him fight to get his canoe off into the water. Its eyes were big. On its forehead grew a patch of white mold as big as a man's thumbprint.

Finally, Thiago pried his canoe loose from the mud; shoving it back into the rippling twilit waters. He jumped in, paddling fast, putting distance between himself and this thing he was ashamed to think he'd mistaken for being his father because his good, laughing father did not live in a hole in the ground with others and make meeping sounds and dig up bodies in the forest.

His father did not eat the dead.

28
Half an Hour

Marcos had his binoculars out. He was leaning against the railing looking for Ursula or for Jake. Neither of their canoes had returned from their short day excursion. Scouting the nearby area for signs of what? He wasn't sure. He knew that after they left his boat he started feeling better immediately. Something had happened to him during the night. He couldn't remember it all.

Monsters.

Strange nightmares. Creatures on the shore. He heard them coughing, crashing through the bush. He knew what they were doing. Hunting. The sound of animals being run down, torn apart. At one point he saw something swimming ahead of the boat. Staying away from the banks. A giant "S" gliding with its nose out of the water. A green anaconda, its head the size of a cow's, a length of ten, no, twelve meters. The biggest snake Marcos had ever seen.

It's afraid, he thought. This killer snake won't go on land, and it's moving out of here as fast as possible in the middle of the night. What would scare a snake that size? Nothing.

As least nothing Marcos knew.

He didn't want to know more, either.

Then he was feeling like he was having a bad fever. The kind that come with dreams.

Then nothing. A blank in his memories. Later, it was morning. He got the coffee pot on the coals thinking he'd feel better with food and drink in him. His head was like it wasn't attached to his body. He thought it might go up in the sky like a balloon and he'd be lost then.

Float away.

He recalled Ursula talking to him. She had worry in her eyes. Davi helped him.

While he was lying in his hammock, he heard them taking the canoes, putting them into the water. He wanted to tell them "Stop!" but he couldn't move. Then he heard something else. It was crazy music. Flutes and trumpets. How far away? Music carried far on the water. Cymbals clashed. Did the others hear this music? Why were they getting in the canoes if they heard it? He didn't know this music. But he hated it. Marcos remembered going to the big opera house in Manaus to listen to the orchestra. Famous singers from Europe. He didn't like that either. It was too much of everything. But it was better than this music of flutes and cymbals. His body, his nerves, twitched in time with the appalling song he couldn't stop hearing even when he plugged his fingers in his ears. The song was in the river, vibrating the trees, the plants, the mud. Staining everything. Contaminating it. Making it rotten and foul. Sick. It made him hurt inside.

Then the canoes left.

And Marcos was feeling much better.

He got up and went to see Davi.

"Where's Thiago?" Marcos asked him. He scratched his belly. He was hungry now. He felt like himself again. He could think. He wasn't losing himself, floating away on dream songs.

"He's with the others," Davi said, gesturing, looking drawn.

"Huh," Marcos said. That was bad. He didn't need Davi worried too. He was worrying enough for all the crew and guests. *Bah*, he thought. Why did I ever agree to take them here?

The lake. The swampy lagoon where bad things happened. Where was it?

Ghost stories. Monster stories. That's what he'd heard about this place. But sailors and fishermen were known to be liars. Maybe there was good fishing there instead. A secret treasure.

Bah!

The stories were real.

Thiago and the rest were out there. But they weren't all gone long.

Then Thiago came paddling back. Alone. Looking like he'd seen a ghost. Or a monster. Davi helped him as he sprang into the boat. They left the canoe bobbing in the river.

"Where are the others?" Marcos asked. "Don't tell me you left them."

Thiago said he got lost. He didn't see the canoes after they entered the flooded forest.

"You were lost?" Marcos said.

Thiago nodded. He was telling his brother something in their old language, talking so fast Marcos couldn't make heads or tails of what he said. Davi yelled at his brother, "No… no, no, no…" and he shoved Thiago away. He looked hot with anger at him.

"What's with you two?" Marcos asked.

It was about their father. That much he'd understood. Their father and other dead people.

They were upset, on the verge of tears. Thiago's trip into the forest disturbed them.

"Stop fighting. We must search for our passengers."

The brothers didn't refuse. But they didn't climb into the canoe either. Marcos fetched his binoculars. The three of them scanned the part of the rainforest where the canoes had entered.

"There," Marcos said after a few minutes. "It's Ursula and the other woman. Iris."

The women paddled out from the shadows, not far off, returning to the steamboat's side.

Marcos and the brothers got the women aboard. Ursula was excited, agitated.

Iris was quiet.

"Where is Jake? Andy?" Ursula glanced about the deck.

Marcos looked sheepish. "Thiago lost them. They are not back."

Ursula turned to the jungle. "We've got to look for them."

"It is only a short while. They will come," Marcos said.

"It's been hours," Ursula said. "We must do something. I'll go if you won't."

Marcos was confused.

Ursula eyed him and his crew suspiciously. "What aren't you telling me?"

"It is less than half an hour since you left. Jake cannot be far. I'll blow the whistle."

Ursula stood there, stunned. Unable to process the disjunction in time.

"Half an hour?" Iris sounded incredulous. She'd sunk onto a bench, smoking, shivering. "We were out there for half an hour?" She laughed: a hollow, disbelieving eruption. "Ho, ho, boy… thirty minutes…" She laughed, coughed. Shut her eyes. Rocking on the bench.

"That's impossible," Ursula said. "We entered that jungle before the thunderstorm came. It feels as though we'd been gone for an entire day."

"We had no storm." Marcos was puzzled. "Look at the sun in the sky. It is still morning."

29
Bundles

Jake was pulling on a branch, studying the tip. Finally, he let it go. The limb whipped back across the water, skimming the surface. He held a broken twig and a moldy knot of material.

Andy twisted around to watch him.

"How could that be our flag?" the reporter said. It was the voice he imagined using to question crooked Arkham politicians caught with their hands stuck in the proverbial cookie jar. It demanded a clearer explanation for murky events. Andy yearned for a bit of clarity now.

Jake picked at the brittle threads. Their texture was slippery; they smelled wet, mulchy.

"I don't know," he said. "But this *is* our tree."

"C'mon, it can't be ours. That stringy mess is probably something left behind by rubber tappers. Or surveyors. How about the men who built the Devil's Railroad? They're the ones."

Jake shook his head. "The Madeira-Mamoré Railroad is a thousand miles from here. Besides, this area's too close to the river for any rail system. If you haven't noticed, everything is currently underwater." Jake examined the knot with his knife. "It's certainly weird." Separating the fragile degraded material, he frowned. He chewed at his lower lip as he regarded its inner secret. Finished, he passed the scrap to Andy.

Andy recognized the raised design immediately.

ANV

Andy's mouth fell open. "The stitching… it's my monogram." His head ached trying to make sense of it. He felt like a dupe at a magic show, peeling an orange to discover his playing card hidden inside. The silky, smirking magician bowing. The audience clapping their approval.

Jake got the canoe moving. "I tied that knot. Why it looks the way it does, I can't…"

"But how? It's rotted." Andy held the piece up to the fractured sunlight.

The discolored cloth disintegrated in his fingers. He flicked the greasy fragments overboard, swirling his hands in the water to get them clean. The material had come from the earth and now it was going back, reclaimed by the rainforest. But that wasn't possible. Not this way. How could his cotton handkerchief decompose in such a brief time? He didn't want to ask Jake. Every answer Andy could imagine was only going to make him feel worse hearing it said aloud. Had they been in the flooded forest much… *much* longer than they'd thought? Still, it wouldn't be long enough to decay things. They'd have starved before that. Or perhaps their canoe entered a time warp? HG Wells territory, the stuff of fantasy.

Was the jungle itself attacking them? Pure paranoia. Andy had settled on the opinion that the jungle was indifferent to him, which was terrifying enough. The jungle didn't care about you. You were not taken into consideration. Your god didn't live here. You had no influence. No worth. Except as a meal or parasitic host. You didn't belong. So whatever happened to you was your own damned fault for coming here in the first place. Who did you think you were? A better person than Percy Fawcett and Maude Brion? You weren't. At best, you were a fool. At worst, a doomed egoist. And what was happening to Jake and Andy, exactly? What powers held sway over their slim boat adrift in this primeval green infinity? The solution might be simple. He and Jake had gone mad together.

"What's next?" Andy said, doing his best not to sound discouraged.

"I'm thinking of shimmying up one of these trees for a look around," Jake said.

Jake was nearly at the top of the seventy-foot-tall palm tree, when Andy, down in the canoe, heard him cry out. Andy could see him up in the devilishly tangled canopy. He wasn't moving.

"Jake?"

No response.

"Is everything fine?" Andy yelled.

Maybe Jake was tired. Or having second thoughts. A bout of vertigo?

"Lost your nerve, eh?" Andy kidded him. "Don't worry. If you fall, I'll catch you."

The lush shadows swallowed his attempt at a joke.

Jake's silence bewildered and perturbed him.

It made him feel small, alone, and vulnerable.

Jake remained frozen, neither going up nor coming down. He'd grown as mute as this maze they were in. Andy stared, hoping the explorer might signal him that he was safe. A finger wag would do. Anything. It was frustrating. And Andy was feeling increasingly nervous.

"Hello, Jake! Say something!"

Jake didn't so much as twitch. He might've been part of the tree.

Andy had watched Jake go up the palm. It seemed straightforward enough. Hand over hand, step by step, a vertical walk. He could follow him. He'd been an enthusiastic tree climber in his youth, famous throughout his neighborhood for chasing up sycamores, maples, and chestnuts. Never palm trees, of course. And he'd had no cause to worry about venomous snakes in New England. Be bold, he told himself. This is your adventure. Don't wait for a hero.

Be one instead.

"Jake, I'm coming up. Hold on. I'll be there in two shakes of a lamb's tail."

Again, no reply. Andy ignored the chill in his blood.

He untied his boots, tucked them in the bow. Shucked off his socks, stuffed them inside his boots. He stood, seizing hold of the tree, and looked up. Oh, it was awfully tall, wasn't it?

Well, here we go. Live and learn. Take the bull by the horns. Stop the cliches and go.

If I fall, I fall in water.

The sound of my body slamming back to earth will summon every predator in the forest. So, let's not fall. *"How about it, kid?"* as Red Phelan would say. *"Think you got what it takes?"*

I'll prove that I do, Andy thought. Prove it to all the doubters. I'm ready for this.

Andy set out.

Jake had made the climb look easy, cupping his hands around the backside of the trunk and walking up the scaly bark. Putting one foot after the other. Before he'd stalled out. Turned into a mute statue. Andy took things more slowly. He was deliberate, establishing a solid rhythm. Wrapping his hands. Bracing his feet. Up, up, up. See you at the top. Adjusting his weight as he rose higher into the humid green canopy. The first thirty feet were no problem. His confidence soared. You're doing it! He was going to save Jake! Now that'll have to go into the big story.

Then Andy made the mistake of looking down.

At the shrinking canoe.

Like a toy boat it bobbed on the pitchy waters. Dizziness. The world atilt under him. Dabs of sun dancing. A slight head spin overtook him. Nothing drastic. But his foot slipped. His fingertips scraped painfully along the rough bark. His back twisted, making him wince.

Yet he caught himself in time. Avoiding the plunge.

Only now he was thinking too much.

His rhythm turned into a series of false starts and jarring stops. At fifty feet, he was concentrating hard on not falling. So hard that he failed to notice Jake right above him.

Jake's shadow blocked out a slice of sun. Andy sensed a bounce vibrating in the trunk.

That's when he finally tipped his head skyward.

Jake was coming back down. Quickly.

Andy felt instant relief. He wouldn't have to go all the way to the top.

Maybe Jake's cry had been one of joy. Had he seen Marcos's steamboat? Was that why he stopped so suddenly? Was he returning with good news of how stupid their whole ordeal had been? How easy it was going to be resolving their dilemma? Had Jake been so focused on figuring out their precise path home that he didn't answer when Andy called up to him?

"Safety is right over there. You won't believe how close, Andy."

That's what Andy imagined him saying.

What he dreamed of.

But it was not what came to be.

Prompted by an impending collision that would send them both plummeting, Andy yelled, "Whoa! Easy there, Jake."

Jake startled. Losing his balance. For a horrific moment, Andy saw him flailing wildly, his right arm wheeling around in empty air. His right leg kicking out at nothing, nothing… Jake's head snapped down, revealing gritted teeth and a look of absolute panic.

Then he regained control.

Jake bowed his head. Blowing out a long breath.

Squeezing his eyes shut as sweat streamed off him.

"You're in an awful hurry," Andy said. "You almost took us both out of the picture."

Andy grinned up at Jake. He spotted something past him, hanging in the highest part of the canopy, tucked up between the branches. They looked like bundles. A cache of some sorts?

"Holy moly! What're those things?" he asked.

Jake continued his retreat until he was on top of Andy. Andy could've bitten his leg if he tried. Jake, bending in close, said in a rough whisper, "Go down. Be quiet. Don't look up."

Andy was irked by the lack of information. Always taking orders. Do this. Move there.

But he did as he was told. The worse of their ordeal seemed to have passed. But Jake was jumpy. Andy couldn't help but feel that other unnamed obstacles remained. Why didn't Jake just tell him what was going on? He could handle the news. He was a newsman, after all.

Walking down wasn't as easy as going up had been.

But before long they'd made it back into the canoe.

Andy put his boots on. Making a point of not asking. Like he didn't want to know more.

Except he did. It was his nature.

"All right, Jake," he said, red-faced, brushing his raw hands on his filthy pants. "You answer me. What the hell is going on? What'd you see in the trees? What're those bundles?"

"Danger," Jake said. "Gotta get away from here. Fast."

Andy waited for more. Jake was busy paddling backward, turning the canoe around. Launching them in another direction. He kept scanning the shadow-haunted canopy. What's Jake looking for? Andy thought. Why isn't he telling me? Andy was fed up with being treated like a junior member of the team. He was the reason they were all here. He had hired them. He wasn't some lackey. They owed him more than that. "We've been in danger since we climbed into these canoes. Even before that. It started when we landed in Manaus. You know what? Come to think of it, I feel like I've been in danger since the moment I laid eyes on that cursed film reel in the *Arkham Advertiser*'s mailroom. I stole it, you know. It was never addressed to me. I was looking for a way out, a way up. So, I lied. Get it now? I put myself in danger because I can deal with it. I'm not a boy clerk who fetches your coffee and sandwiches."

"Andy," Jake whispered again. "I discovered something in the canopy." He paddled.

"I know. Danger. What is it? What could be worse that what I've gone through today?"

"Bodies. Inside those bundles? There are dead bodies. Dozens." The color drained from Jake's face. He looked ten years older than when he'd clambered his way up the palm tree trunk. "They're wrapped up tight and suspended in sacks. I touched one. It was sticky like glue."

Andy was stunned by what he was hearing. He had questions. He always had questions.

"Not animal bodies? You mean people. You found dead people hanging in the trees?"

He wished he'd taken a better look for himself. Could Jake be mistaken? Were there really corpses hanging in the treetops?

"Most were only bones," Jake said. "Picked clean. Others had skin and hair."

Andy's voice dropped to a whisper. His eyes shot up to the branches. They didn't seem high enough now. Every shadow was a bundle to him. "You're sure they were dead?"

Jake nodded. "They're encased in those tough fibrous sacks. Webs, I think. Like when a spider envelops its kill. But the size... chewed up... digested. Parts missing. Most of the meat gone. The juices sucked out. They looked inhuman. But they were human. I saw their faces."

"Maybe they were old. They could've been up there for years. Decades even," Andy said.

Jake shook his head. "I don't think so. A couple of the workers smelled... fresh."

"Workers? How do you know they were workers? You said most were skeletons."

"Feet," Jake said. "They wore boots. Whatever is eating them doesn't eat their boots."

30
Another Baker

Iris felt shaken. Belowdecks she collected her thoughts, deciding what to do next. Her plans were shattered. Her nerves: a frazzled mess. Everything thrown into disarray. This wasn't what she had hoped to do on this trip to the Amazon. Following Galton in her dreams. Yes, she wanted to do that. Letting him guide her. What did she think would happen? She didn't know. Not really. She only knew she wanted to feel close to Galton. He was dead in this world, but alive in the Dreamlands, as he called them. So, she pushed forward. Searching. She couldn't say what for. An alternative to her grief, something other than gray sadness day after day. There was no bringing him back. Maybe she thought that by returning to the scene of his horrible death she would be able to commune with his lost soul. Tell him she was sorry she wasn't by his side at the end. Her guilt never left her. It must've been awful dying how he did. Alone in the wilderness. Feeling extreme pain without relief. Then the endless darkness. Perhaps there was a way to bridge the gulf between life and whatever lay beyond. Conquer time.

Oh, it sounded foolish if she said it out loud. The pipe dreams of a stricken widow. But some part of Galton still existed. She knew that absolutely. She saw him, felt him, heard him. On that dreaming plane they touched again. They were together. Leaving the Dreamlands, opening her eyes to the blue wash of a new dawn, plunged a dagger in her heart each day. Yet knowing that at night she might find Galton kept her going through the dreary daylight hours. Sleep was her ticket to escape, a substitute realm where she learned mysterious, important things. She didn't know how it worked. But a dream told her to go to the Miskatonic Museum that evening when Andy first met with the owner of the *Advertiser* and that rich drunkard, Oscar Hurley. The dream whisperer indicated she should stand by a certain display case at a specific time and keep her ears open. So, she did. It was like a game. A fun challenge. Figuring out what she was supposed to do, never knowing where it might lead. Though she didn't recognize it at the time, she was now sure Galton was the one communicating with her. He wanted her to come to Brazil. The jungle. This river. Of that much she was certain; he'd made it plain. But what she saw in the flooded zone was terrifying. She worried she was going insane. Were those actual monsters? When her dreams seemed real, she liked it. But when real life turned into a waking nightmare…

Returning to the steamboat, she felt as if she had awakened from a years-long slumber.

What had she turned into during that trance-like interim? She wasn't herself anymore.

Who was in control?

She was *poisoning* people. All because Galton asked her to in her dreams. It was absurd. She would end up in jail. Or worse. What if she killed someone? A real person?

She almost had, twice. Iris Bennett Reed. Pioneering New York anthropologist.

Murderess.

How could she live with herself then?

Iris had trusted Galton from the very beginning. It defined their relationship since the day they first met. It was one of the reasons why she loved him. A sunny autumn day in Manhattan. The crunch of dead leaves underfoot. The damp fishy smell of the Hudson River masked by a breeze that tasted of winter. He'd been sitting on a bench in Riverside Park, facing the flow of cold, steely water, eating an apple. She'd found it funny, or maybe *he* was funny. Odd in a city full of odd folk: he took such a methodical approach to polishing off that Stayman Winesap, small precise bite by small precise bite, as if he'd measured them out beforehand, rotating the fruit with his black-gloved fingertips, holding the apple firmly, his arm stiff, wrist cocked, his teeth sinking in – round and round – consuming every fiber, pips too, until there was nothing left but a stem, which he tossed aside casually after he was finished. Full of self-satisfaction.

She picked up her bicycle. Rode to him. She stopped, laid her cycle down in the dying, crispy, yellow-brown grass. When he failed to do anything, staring past her at the river, she lifted the books from her basket and stood squarely in front of him, resting the stack on her round hip.

"You taught him a lesson," Iris said.

Alarmed, he looked up at her. Sea gray eyes. In them were beautiful mornings, afternoon storms, private midnights. He had good bones, a certain class of person might say. Structure. A regal setting for those lovely, changeable eyes. Their colors shifted with his mood.

As they did now. Deep blue rising to the surface. Thundercloud iron dissipating as the storm passed. "Pardon?" he said in a clipped tone. He pulled at the tassels of his purple scarf.

I've made him nervous. The autumn air wasn't the only thing giving a blush to his cheeks.

"Your apple. I was watching you eat it. From the other bench over there."

He turned his head swiftly like a predatory bird.

"That bench?"

"Yes, that's the one," she said. "I was reading. I got bored. Then I spotted you."

"I didn't notice."

"Care if I join you?" Before he said anything she dropped onto the bench with her armload of books. He slid away. She moved closer. "Thanks for making room."

He considered what she had said – the entirety of their encounter – before responding.

"You're welcome. I have more apples. They're Winesaps." He held out a paper sack. She shook her head. No thanks. He set the sack down, rolled it closed. "Are you a Barnard student?"

"I graduated last year. I'm studying with Professor Boaz at Columbia."

He tilted his head to inspect the spines of her books. "Anthropology?"

He didn't act surprised that a woman would attempt such things. She liked that. Nodded.

"As am I," he said. He thrust out his gloved hand, then took it back, removed his glove, and held it toward her again. "Galton Reed. I'm glad to make your acquaintance, ah, Miss…?"

"Iris Bennett."

His grasp was toasty. He had these big, lovely hands. Long-boned, smooth knuckles, piping veins – not ugly like a pair of meat hooks. You could feel how physically strong he was despite his awkward bookish manner. She immediately felt as if they had known each other for years. It made no logical sense. Instantly, she trusted him. And she knew he trusted her too. No matter what might happen to them – and she knew there was going to be a "*them*" – they would always be able to count on each other. Two against the world. Those outside of their relationship remained skeptical, even puzzled at the news they were together. Galton was cold and standoffish, her friends said. *But not with me.* He imposed and was argumentative. *We enjoy our share of intellectual jousting, to be sure. But he's respectful of my opinions. He makes me think. I make him do likewise, he admits.* Iris knew Galton had vulnerabilities, quite a few of them, and to keep himself feeling safe, he put up a shield, battling with people before they might object to his bold statements. Iris knew she would have to protect him. She wanted to. He would die for her without hesitation. Because he loved her. It started that day on the bench. "I find him frightening," a friend confided to her over tea and cucumber sandwiches. "Aren't you afraid?"

No, not a bit.

And she hadn't been.

Until today. That floating, toothsome, mad-looking Galton terrified her.

In some bizarre way she'd become closer to Galton after leaving him in the jungle to perish. Her dream life with him, fragmentary and hallucinatory as it was, became intensely real. She felt as though she knew him from the inside out, that he had access to all her deepest thoughts and emotions without either of them having to speak a word. Yet when he introduced her to those creatures… that was asking too much. How could he want his lover to meet horrors?

She felt cut off, suddenly, as if a thick ice wall had fallen between them.

Am I going crazy? Why didn't Ursula see him too? My husband. My dear, dead husband.

In her dream last night, he told her they were going to take the canoes into the flooded zone. He needed her help. His magic was strong, and the steamboat was near the liminal space that bordered the gateway. He wanted them off the big boat. He'd take care of the rest. That book of his had spells in it, incantations, combinations of words, that, if chanted correctly, blurred realities. The group needed preparations before meeting the Queen. Their minds had to be softened. Kneaded like bread dough so that later they would rise and become something else.

"You're baking their brains?" She was feeling sort of evil. Enjoying the sweet rush.

He laughed. "That's a good way of putting things. Magic is the yeast. I'm the baker."

"What am I?" she said.

"You're the baker's assistant," he said.

She frowned. "I don't like that. I should be my own separate thing. Equal."

"It's only a metaphor. Say you're another baker. We're baking a cake together. How's that?"

"I've never been much for the kitchen. Why can't we go straight to the lake?" she asked.

"I told you. They aren't ready for it. It won't work unless they believe. A closed mind kills the magic. I want you to find Maude and the Queen. But it takes magic. You need me." He passed her a gourd. She drank from it. Not sweet. Vegetal. Fermented. She preferred champagne.

"What's this? It tastes perfectly awful. Blech."

"Something I made. Give the boat captain a wee nip of my venom cordial. I'll put a spell on him inside his dreams. Remember, too much venom will kill him. We don't want that yet."

"I know. I tried it on Jake. He didn't die. I know what I'm doing. Well, mostly."

"Who's Jake? The young one?"

"No. Jake is Ursula's righthand man. A stalwart, loyal companion type of fellow."

"Ah. It doesn't matter. None of them do." Galton used his walking stick to part the bushes. "The Queen's in there. Waiting. Soon the world will know her. She's a god, you know. I'm giving the world to her as a sacrifice. She'll be happy with me then. Appreciative, I think."

"What am I going to do again?" The drink made Iris drowsy, her limbs loose and oiled.

Drunk. I'm a little drunk. In a dream.

"You're bringing the Queen what she needs for now. Maude is going to shoot a motion picture. She'll show the planet what's coming just over the horizon. It's such a fortuitous set of circumstances. You and I, we can be together again. A new world is dawning. We will be the first to see it. I'll show you a sample after you get them into the canoes. I'll help. I can put ideas in their heads. They won't know it's me. But the captain must stop at the correct place. I don't want him mucking things up. He knows the river too well. They'll listen to him. You fix that."

"I will," she said. "I never want this dream to end." She slid into his arms. Relaxed.

Galton was murmuring in her ear in an unfamiliar language. Welsh? No, it wasn't Welsh. It had an ancient quality. Too garbled. Harsh. No music in it. Is it extinct? she wondered.

Dead words doomed to tripping on a modern tongue. Where had Galton picked it up?

He kept talking.

And she slept.

31
Death Chandeliers

Jake spotted more of the body bundles hanging, not high in the canopy, but just above the water ahead of them. The web ropes swayed despite no wind blowing. He didn't like the look of it.

Why were they moving?

"Are those what I think they are?" Andy said.

"They're the same as the others I found."

"Why aren't they up there with the rest?"

"I don't know." Jake gave them a wide berth. But soon they were floating through another low hanging cluster. They looked like Christmas ornaments. The sticky webs sparkled icily like tinsel and glass where the sunlight hit. You'd find them beautiful if you didn't know what they contained. As the canoe passed through the hanging forest of bundles – there was no avoiding them now – Jake couldn't help but peer through the gauzy encasements to make out the grisly decomposing contents. Bones mostly. Like the canopy sacks. One body per. A skull pressed against the gluey netting. Vacant eye sockets staring at Jake head-on. Fleshless jaws gaping as if it were having a good laugh at them.

No, not laughing. Screaming.

He told himself not to look but couldn't help it. Shredded

clothing. Khakis and linen. Scuffed, mud-caked boots. So, not native. More forest workers. None of these bodies had any hair or skin. Strangely, there was no insect activity, only a bit of fungal growth. He guessed they might be older. They didn't stink. Whatever snacked on them had finished with its leftovers.

"Jeez, there are so many," Andy said. "Do you think whatever made them… the thing that caught and bound them up… fed on them… it probably lives alone? I mean, there's only one of those web-spinning things wandering around here we need to worry about. Right?"

Jake shrugged. "Hard to say. Most spiders are solitary."

"That's what did this, then? A giant solitary spider?"

"It's my best guess," Jake said. "A creature unknown to modern science. A new species."

"Great. I can put that in my book if I don't end up inside one of these," Andy said, pointing with the end of his paddle as they passed a sack with a leg bone sticking out, dipping its toes in the river. He trembled, racked by a shiver despite the soupy heat.

Jake smiled grimly. Andy was holding up for now. But Jake didn't know how long it would last. Keep calm. Plan. Act. Ursula's survival lesson kept him going. If they got lucky, they wouldn't encounter the spinner of these macabre food baskets. It had to be one huge arachnid, given the amount of cached sustenance. And it lived close by.

"Hey, look!" Andy said. "That one's empty."

He was pointing to a sack dangling loosely over a patch of river glowing in the sun. Like a golden pool in the middle of a void: its reflection created a second sun, shining and bright.

"You see anything in the water there?" Jake asked.

Andy half-stood in the bow. "Nope. The light penetrates far down. It's creepy."

"I'll paddle closer. Be careful."

"Sure thing," Andy said. "What am I looking for?" He gripped the edge of the boat.

"Anything abnormal."

Andy snorted.

"You're kidding, right? Each one of these death chandeliers is a coffin. This is a cemetery we're rowing through. Everything qualifies as abnormal."

"Stay alert. Pay attention to things that move."

"Things that move. Will do." Andy stood taller. The canoe glided between the sagging stuffed bundles, steering toward the golden circle where the single empty web-sack drooped from the treetops like a pendulous string of snot. It was disgusting *and* fascinating.

"If this is her food, wouldn't our spider keep it hidden? Out of reach?" Andy asked.

"You'd think so," Jake said. "Unless…"

"Unless what?" Andy glanced over his shoulder at the grizzled explorer.

"Unless it's a trap," Jake said. "Luring in the curious. Distracting them until it strikes."

Both men gazed around them in every direction. Jake licked his salty, parched lips.

"You've got that rifle ready?" Andy asked.

Jake laid the weapon across his lap. He stowed the paddle in the bottom of the canoe as they drifted up to the golden circle. Jake shaded his eyes. Looking up. High above them was a circular gap in the canopy. It almost looked pruned. Bright sunlight poured straight down.

"Remember. Aim for the eight-legged thing." Andy stared up at the dazzling light.

"It must be noon," Jake said. "Sun's right above. No clouds. That hole… it could be a door. If the spider crawls on top of the canopy, that would provide quick access in and out."

Andy gulped. He reached for the glittery pouch of webbing. Grabbing hold. Pulling the torn bag toward him into the narrow bow. The canoe veered on an angle. Entering the circle.

"Careful…" Jake lifted the rifle. He felt taut as a guitar string and hoped he didn't snap.

"Eww… you're right about it being sticky. The cords are tough, but it's like they're coated in clear honey." Andy wiped his hand on his pants. Tendrils of adhesive stretched from his thigh to his palm. His fingers gummed together. He forced them apart using his other hand. He touched the thick cable that ran up into the shadowy branches overhead. "This cable isn't sticky. But it's strong as hell. Like an anchor rope. The sack looks like it's been cut. The fibers are slashed cleanly in a line." Andy reached out farther over the side to investigate.

"Watch yourself," Jake said.

"Honestly, I don't think I could let go of this even if I tried–"

A surge of water hit Jake in the face. His eyes closed involuntarily. He spat out the water that splashed into his open mouth. He was soaked. He pawed at his eyes to dry them.

When he opened them again, the bow was empty – Andy was gone.

Jake scrambled into the bow seat, peering over the side. He aimed the rifle at the water. But there was nothing except a rippling gold reflection where Andy fell in.

Something thumped against the underside of the canoe. A solid bang he heard and felt.

Then another noise. A slow, raggedy scraping trailed off to the starboard side.

After that, nothing.

Jake checked the perimeter of the boat. Prepared to fire at anything not human.

"Andy!"

The young reporter couldn't swim. There was no telling how deep the water was. Deep enough to drown. He'd gone right down like a lead weight. No sign of him.

Jake debated jumping in. If this was an ambush, then Andy was being held underwater. On purpose. Whatever had him wanted to drown him. The spider – if that's what it was – had been lying in wait. Clever, disciplined. A huntress. It needed Jake to get in the river too, where it would latch onto an ankle or wrist, yanking him below the surface to certain death. Keep calm. Plan. Act. The rifle would be useless, even if he could manage getting off a shot through the chains of bubbles and rising panic. What were the odds of accuracy? Would one bullet do the job? They'd both likely be dead in a few minutes. The spider would bundle them and feast later.

If only he had a flashlight, he could point the beam into the depths. Locate his enemy. Shooting from the boat… If he took a clean, steady shot… he had the slightest advantage.

The water was settling. The crystal-clear depths came into focus. Nothing.

Jake crawled from one end of the dugout to the other, trying to glimpse signs of Andy.

An explosive clamor from behind the canoe. Thrashing. The turbulence nearly sent Jake tumbling backward into the flooded zone. He sat down hard in the bottom of the canoe, hitting his tailbone. Pain bolted up his spine. He lay like a turtle on his shell. Legs pumping in the air.

"Argghh…" he grunted in frustration. He rolled on his side, turned himself upright.

Just in time.

A wet hand shot up over the side. Dirty fingers clawing in desperation.

They hooked the edge of the canoe, trying to haul up into the boat. The hand became an arm, crooked at the elbow. Grappling for purchase. The canoe rocked. Dangerously close to flipping over. Hollow thuds as the man overboard pummeled the hull attempting to climb inside.

On his knees, Jake rushed to help.

"Hold on!" he shouted.

He dropped the rifle and clutched the arm with both hands. Pulled. Leaning over, he seized a fistful of shirt. His other hand fastened to the belt of the man's pants. Dragging the struggling swimmer to safety. No way he was letting go.

"Easy, pal. I'm here. I got you, Andy."

And he came up over the side, coughing water, gasping for air.

Long hair, a beard. Sunburnt skin. His clothes torn to shreds. No boots.

It wasn't Andy.

Jake let go. Sat back, stunned. He scrambled away from the stranger until he ran out boat.

The man had leaves of river grass streaming off his body. A stout stick poked out of his pocket. He locked his bloodshot eyes on Jake. He spit out a mouthful of river and blood.

And he started to rise.

Jake twisted. Where was the rifle?

He fumbled for it blindly. As the man put a viselike grip on his leg, Jake's fingers closed around the rifle stock. When he brought it around, he was surprised to see not a firearm but his canoe paddle. It would have to do. He swung it toward the man's jaw, hoping to connect.

"No!" The man knocked the paddle away.

Jake's hand was slippery. The paddle sailed out of the boat.

It splashed in the river.

"Get off me," Jake said. Without much room to fight, he kicked the man in the shin.

The man growled in anguish, clasping his own leg this time.

I must throw him out, Jake thought. The canoe rocked heavily.

The man was quickly on his feet. Advancing. He had the heavy stick in his right hand.

Jake might've been able to shoulder him in his torso like a linebacker and send him flying. But as he prepared to launch, the pain in his spine returned, stabbing him with a vengeance. The agony speared him. He teetered, clenching his lower back.

A grimace contorted the man's wild-eyed face.

He raised the stick, as if he were ready to crack Jake's skull.

That was the very sound Jake heard: a *whump* of wood hitting bone.

Followed by a blunt sigh.

Only he felt nothing. Instead, he watched the man's chin jerk sideways. A spray of water left his hair. His eyes rolled, showing their whites. He fell stiffly, headfirst, into Jake's lap.

Knocked out cold.

Standing where the man had been a second before – like a doppelgänger – was Andy. Like Lou Gehrig smacking a homerun, he held Jake's paddle tight in his two fists.

A look of triumph, mixed with pure amazement, blazed across his waterlogged mug.

32

An Intelligence

It watched the men fighting in the boat. High above them, peering down through the entrance to where it had been storing its food since it last escaped. They would be easy to kill. But it wasn't hungry. It needed to learn. In order to survive. So, instead of killing, it watched. And learned.

It knew the difference between a stick and a stick that blew out fire and pieces that hurt when they hit and went inside its body. Men had shot it before. The pieces didn't kill it. But they were better to avoid. Two of these men came floating on half an old tree. Lots of men did this.

The other man was the one who escaped. The one it caught two suns ago.

He broke out of the web before it could eat him. No matter.

It tied him here in the sunlight to see if others would come.

Two did come, and it was watching all three of them now.

Days, it went out walking under the sky. Looking for a better place. A quiet, dark one. It didn't need the place yet. But soon, soon. It went exploring. Under the ground. That was good. Behind a small waterfall it discovered a spot. Cool, hidden. Tunnels were good for hiding and killing. A thin crack in the rock, a crevice. It could squeeze through, turn, and see out. Watch.

That was the place it would go next. In the rock, through the waterfall. But not yet.

It crept. It observed. Patience was perhaps its greatest strength. A patient hunter often slept with a full belly and many offspring. That was life. Purpose. To go on while others failed.

The voice sometimes pushing inside its head was a man's voice. Where the voice came from, it now knew. It found him. None of these. Another. Like a moth he was. It hated the man's voice. Especially when it went where it was not wanted. Bothering. Fluttering about. Dancing and humming. Buzzing his mouth like fat bees in a hive. But the man had some power. Strange.

It would have to be cautious. It would kill him. Later.

Like the slow, clumsy three fighting below. Future food. They did not know how to battle. Its ways were not confined to brute force alone. Time taught it so much. To spin, to eat, to survive longer than its rivals. These were the measures of greatest importance. No more to learn today from the fumbling men. They never saw it watching them. Food cannot maintain alertness.

That is why food is food.

And it is it.

With no more to learn, it crawled away. Feeling the sun, the trees, the coming rain.

33
Anything Stronger

"How does this sound?"

Andy read from his notebook:

"The light dims. We are deeper still. Lost in this morass. A blackhearted gloom descends upon us, literally and spiritually. In these circumstances one's will goes woefully slack. Thoughts of death in various guises populate the weakened mind, springing open like jack-in-the-boxes, jarring already eroded nerves, adding hopelessness to the layers of our extravagant despair..."

"It's a tad too..." Jake started, pausing as he searched for the right word.

"Too rich?" Andy asked, his pencil poised above the page.

"I'd say so. Just a tad."

Andy started scratching out lines.

Ursula sat beside the man tied up in the hammock. He'd blinked several times and mumbled unintelligible phrases, but he didn't wake. Andy hadn't managed to kill him. But he'd given him a goose egg on the back of his head and probably a concussion. The man had no identification. Ursula took advantage of his unconscious state to investigate his mouth. He had fillings, even a gold one. And there was a pair of cracked spectacles buttoned in his shirt pocket.

After their interlude, lost in the flooded zone, and their jarring confrontation with the mystery man, Jake and Andy had found their way back to the steamboat. Much like Ursula and Iris.

Ursula was relieved everyone made it. The sight of Jake paddling toward them went a long way to restoring her calm. It filled her with pure happiness. Jake was alive. Despite the circumstances, her constant, reliable companion had reached safety once again.

They took the raggedy man aboard. After a brief reunion, the expeditioners, along with Marcos and his crew, tried to figure out who he might be. They agreed that whoever he was, he'd already proven himself dangerous and unpredictable. So, they tied him up. And waited.

"I was reaching for the empty sack when he snatched at my ankle," Andy told them. "I never saw him do it. Only felt his hand. Then I was in the river. We struggled. I was glad he wasn't a giant spider, but who the heck was he? I didn't give it much thought because, after all, I was drowning. Next thing I knew he was away from me. Boy, I sank fast. My foot touched bottom, so I kicked off. It was automatic. Well, it couldn't be *that* deep because I could see the light still. But it didn't matter. I can't swim. I came up for a breath and went down under again. And wouldn't you know it, I was standing on the sturdy limb of a sunken tree. Half out of the drink. Alive. There was the canoe right in front of me. I saw the man there getting ready to coldcock Jake. I stuck out my hands. 'Hey, what's this?' I said. 'Why, it's our canoe paddle floating around.' I used it to pull the canoe to me, and I flopped in. I thought they'd notice me right off. But they were busy with their donnybrook. That guy was ready to bop Jake on the head with his homemade billy club when I caught him with the flat side of my paddle. End of story."

"It was a thing of beauty," Jake said.

"A thing of beauty." Andy wrote the phrase on his notepad.

The man moaned.

Ursula said, "Give me water. Quickly."

Jake handed her his canteen.

She twisted off the lid and sprinkled a few drops on the man's face.

His eyes opened wide. In sheer terror.

"We aren't going to harm you," she said. "You're aboard a ship. Do you understand?"

The man nodded. He looked like he didn't believe her.

Ursula held out the canteen. "Thirsty? Would you like a drink of water?"

The man nodded again. Vigorously.

She put the flask to his lips and supported his head as he tilted it forward.

He guzzled, trying to upend the canteen. Water dribbled down his chin. He coughed.

"Slow down." She returned the container to Jake. "That's enough for now."

The others gathered around the hammock. The man looked from face to face, searching.

"Doesn't he look kind of familiar?" Andy asked.

Jake cocked his head, rubbing at his whiskery chin. He snapped his fingers. "I know!"

"Yeah," Andy said. "Who is he?"

"He's the guy we fought in the canoe!"

Andy slugged him in the shoulder.

Jake smiled at him like he was the little brother he never had. Except he did have brothers, three in fact, but none of them talked to him anymore. His travels had taken him far from home. He told Ursula he had nothing in common with his family these days. They were uncurious people, suspicious of the world. They'd rather shoot off a toe than meet a new idea.

Andy had changed. He looked more confident. Ursula hoped it wasn't overconfidence.

"I'm being serious," Andy said. "I've seen this fella somewhere before."

Ursula thought of something. She snatched the spectacles off the table and put them on the man. He didn't seem to mind, though there was no way to stop her if he did. Ursula imagined the cracked lenses might make him look a bit less rough. While there, she flattened down his untamed locks, picking out a twig. Standing back, she was sorely disappointed in the results.

However, the alteration provided the clue Andy needed to solve the puzzle.

"That's Maude Brion's cameraman! From the reel. I know it's him," he said.

The man showed no reaction.

"Are you who he says you are?" Ursula asked.

Andy stepped forward. "I don't need confirmation. It's him. I'm positive." He bent over the man, who was still bound in the hammock, his attitude drifting somewhere between petrified and catatonic. "I'm going to loosen your bonds. Listen. We are not your enemy. We've come here to find you. To find Maude. I'm a reporter. My name is Andy Van Nortwick. I work at the *Arkham Advertiser*. I received a film canister showing Maude, and you, in the shrine of the Spider Queen. At least that's what it looked like. That's why we're here. To rescue you."

Andy untied the man's wrists. Jake stood prepared to subdue him if necessary.

It was not necessary.

"My name is Gerald Hopkins," the man said, rubbing his wrists.

He had a slow Southern drawl. He looked at Andy. "I'm the one who mailed that reel of footage to Arkham. But I'm afraid you all are too late. Maude is long gone."

The man stuck out his lower lip, a caricature of sadness. Shade passed over his mood.

Andy looked simultaneously excited and crushed. His expression passed through a range of emotions. Joy, defeat, and confusion were among them. He seemed unable to speak as well.

Ursula did her best to hide her amazement. Firstly, she wasn't sure if she believed the man. Secondly, she needed time to figure out what it meant for them if this was Maude's associate. Her brain was speeding along. She took over the questioning.

"Why did you attack Andy and Jake?" she asked Hopkins. Her voice had steel in it.

"I didn't. You must forgive me," Hopkins pleaded. "I had to escape that hellish place."

He began coughing again.

Ursula reached for the canteen.

"Do you have anything stronger? Whiskey?" he said, pulling at his beard.

Iris opened her bag, retrieving a silver flask which she tossed to the hammock.

He caught it in midair. Uncapping the bottle with shaking hands, he drank several swallows.

"Hit the spot?" Iris asked.

"Most assuredly." The man wiped his mouth and uttered a faint burp.

"Where did you come from?" Jake said. "In that swamp, we didn't see you."

"I hid. Underwater. In the grasses." Hopkins patted his empty pocket. "I had a hollow palm stem. It's a flute, you know. But I used it as a breathing tube. My fingers plugged the holes." He smiled. "I kept myself submerged so she wouldn't find me. I was too afraid to swim."

"Who wouldn't find you?" Ursula asked.

The question appeared to strike Hopkins as ridiculous. Or too obvious. He hesitated, until he saw they were being serious. He seemed to reassess them.

"The Spider Queen," he said in a hushed voice.

The steamboat's cabin grew quieter. The pause gave Hopkins a chance to sip more.

Ursula put a hand over his and eased the flask away from his open lips.

"I need you sober."

Hopkins reluctantly let her have the whiskey, with the promise of another drink after his debriefing. Ursula wanted to know everything. How he got to Manaus to mail the reel. Why he was back on the river tributary at this remote locale. What happened to Maude's expedition? Who, or what, was the Spider Queen? How did he get into his predicament in the flooded zone?

Hopkins swung gently side to side in the hammock. The motion soothed him.

He stared off at a porthole as he spoke.

"I left the shrine at night. I took a boat that belonged to the old rubber plantation. I'd found it dragged off in the bushes behind the bunkhouse. It looked seaworthy. Anyway, no one knew I had it. I took the reel of film and the boat. I was sure I'd die, lost out there. But I got lucky. A fishing boat found me. That first morning, I think. Or afternoon. In Manaus, I sent the film to Arkham."

"Why Arkham?" Andy said. "Why the *Advertiser*?"

"I've heard stories," Hopkins said. "I thought Arkham might be the one place in the world where someone would believe what we'd discovered in the jungle. The *Advertiser* was the only paper I knew. Maude had a few issues in her luggage. She's the one who told me about the city, come to think of it. Well, I knew we needed to get the story out. I never dreamed anyone would come to help us. That's why I tried to go back to the shrine. I couldn't leave her. Not after all we'd been through together. Even if she had changed, she was still my friend."

Tears filled the cameraman's eyes. His lip trembled. He bit a knuckle, choking back sobs.

"Why didn't she leave with you? When you found the boat?" Ursula asked.

"Oh, she didn't want to go. It was a dream come true for her."

Hopkins started to giggle. He stuffed his fingers in his mouth, sucking on them like a child. Ursula thought it was the most disturbing sound she'd ever heard. That wet gurgle.

The man did not seem… mentally balanced. Which might have been an understatement.

Ursula needed answers while he was still somewhat lucid.

"What happened to Maude's expedition? Where did it go wrong?"

"Go wrong? It didn't. We found the shrine. We shot our film. Filled up the reels. It was glorious and mad… completely, utterly mad… I met many oddities… impossible to describe…"

He trailed off. Slurped his fingers. His eyes traveled from the porthole to the flask.

"What did you meet?" Andy asked.

A light lip-smacking noise. "Might I have the tiniest sip?" Hopkins asked the reporter.

Ursula said, "Not yet. Answer our questions and I'll give you the whole bottle. Now go on."

Hopkins returned his gaze to the porthole, which was filling up with shadows. Thunder rumbled. Wind hummed in the boat lines. Marcos, Davi, and Thiago left to check things on deck.

"Let me ask. Do you all believe in gods?" Hopkins said, after they were gone.

"What does that have to do with anything?" Jake said.

"It has everything to do with everything." Hopkins grinned a ghastly, jaundiced grin.

Before anyone could pepper him with more queries, he continued.

"As I said, we found the shrine. Her lot of devotees. The Queen arrived much later."

"Who is she?" Ursula asked.

Hopkins threw up his hands, wiggling his fingers in the air. Whistling weirdly through his teeth. "I cannot tell you that. But she tried to kill me when I went back for Maude. I never got there. Not all the way to the shrine. I was lost. And she nabbed me out of my boat at night. Trundled me off and trussed me up. Hung me like a trophy, or a side of beef. I was as good as a dead cow. Or better yet, a hog. I watched her eat. She'd do it delicately. But I could hear. Gulp, gulp. Like a lady at an ice cream shop drinking melted milkshakes through a straw. And she chewed too. Not ladylike at all when she did that. You ever witnessed a starving dog dispose of a rat in an alley? I had my Buck knife. Lucky me. Enough wiggle room to slice myself free. It took hours. I dropped into the water. I was sure she'd hear and come back to, well… finish me…"

The giggles started up.

"Sorry," he said, regaining his composure. "I'd only gotten out of the web right before you arrived. I didn't mean to scare you. Truly, I am sorry. I wasn't sure you were real. Not even when I knocked you in the river. But thank you for saving my life. I owe you all my gratitude."

"Can you show us where the shrine is?" Iris asked.

Hopkins shook his head. "I'm lost. I told you that."

"Let me get this straight," Andy said. "The Spider Queen is a giant spider?"

"Very much so." Giggle, giggle. "She is a queen. A god-queen. Queen-god. There is no question." Hopkins stuck his thumb in his mouth and sucked at it like a lollipop. His whole hand was wet. With his other hand he twirled a lock of his snarled and foul-smelling hair.

"I'm not sure he can take much more of this," Jake said. "Maybe we need a break?"

"One question," Andy said. "Gerald, how did Maude die?"

His thumb came out with a loud pop. "Die? Oh my, my, no… she didn't die." He shook his head, swinging the hammock, his eyes like wet stones. Smooth, dull, and moist.

"She's there now," he said. "She's with the Queen."

Then he laid back, unwilling to speak another word even after he got his promised drink.

34

The Hopkins Interview

In the past few hours, I have learned much from our new arrival. Initially, he was reluctant to speak. Persuasion that we meant him no harm, and a handy flask of bourbon whiskey, loosened his tongue. But only briefly. He slept for twelve hours. Post breakfast, during which he ate heartily, I attempted to once more engage him in conversation. To my delight, Gerald Hopkins proved talkative and utterly fascinating. I credit myself for taking a private approach, as I suspect an audience brings out his nervous condition, which is always in evidence, though sometimes only lurks beneath the surface. Unfortunately, on other occasions, Hopkins appears to be teetering on the edge of a complete mental breakdown. Hysteria, paranoia, bizarre hallucinations – these are but a few of the hallmarks of his illness that manifested while we conversed. But I am no doctor. I simply did my best to keep him calm and get his story.

We stayed belowdecks for our interview. Hopkins currently resides in my hammock. I spent last night sleeping on the deck with the crewmen. Our captain has grown silent. His former jovial demeanor is absent. The weather has turned sour and rainy, and I hope he will recover his enthusiasm when the sun breaks through the clouds again. Alas, the rain offers no relief from the steam-room level of heat which wraps around my head like a barber's hot towel. The river is like a corrugated sheet of hot, rain-pummeled steel. I keep telling myself our plight is temporary.

I will not bother with any details extraneous to the expedition. Hopkins is a slow talker, as many Southerners are, and although intriguing, many of his verbal meanderings took us far from the present surroundings and the odd predicament he finds himself in – and ourselves too!

I will relate this much for the sake of proper background. Hopkins met Maude Brion some seven years ago. She was an actress at the time. He was a photographer, writer, and aspiring filmmaker. They struck up a friendship at a party. It seems that both had an attraction to bizarre characters and esoteric subjects of all sorts. The party thrower owned a bookstore that specialized in rare and extremely old books dealing with topics that strayed far from the realm of straightlaced society. Neither Hopkins nor Maude had money to buy the books under discussion. But the social gathering offered other stimulating benefits. Maude met a motion picture producer. This meeting led to an audition. Maude had no ride to her audition. Gerald offered to drive. She ended up not getting the part. But the producer hired Gerald to fill in for an assistant who had quit that morning. One thing led to another, and Maude and Hopkins ended up making four motion pictures together. Maude found she was better at calling the shots behind the camera. Gerald's artistic eye and technical skills made him a natural for handling the mechanics and logistics of photography.

Neither could find interesting work on the comedy/drama side of the business. But when Maude hustled the opportunity to shoot a short scenic in the Mojave Desert, they found their niche. Maude wanted to film real-life adventures. Her desire was to take the audience on a trip to a mysterious, far-flung locale they had never visited. To show them what they were missing. She didn't want run-of-the-mill scripts that amounted to little more than stage plays on celluloid.

Instead, she wanted grandeur and awe. To make people's hearts race and jaws drop.

Discovery. Revelation. To film the dream palace filled with real people and places.

"That's why the Spider Queen legend was a perfect fit. It offered everything wrapped up in a gorgeous package no one had filmed before. We'd be famous. We only had to hitch our wagon to a legend already out there. It was too good to be true. But true it was. She had a map, a genuine fresh lead, and by the gods, she went out and scraped together the funding. Don't ask me where she got it. She wouldn't tell me. But somebody else was interested in the Spider Queen. They gave Maude the dough to see if she was real. I wouldn't be surprised if that old bookseller had something to do with it. What a spooky charmer. He claimed to have visited other worlds.

"Things fell apart fast when we got to Manaus," Hopkins said.

He told me about the unscrupulous guide who tried to cheat them. How he stranded them on the river to get back at Maude for standing up to his shenanigans.

"A real swindler. But she wouldn't give him the satisfaction of standing on the dock watching us crawl back into port emptyhanded. She insisted we go on until the supplies ran out. She could read a map. We had a few of the crew who stuck with us, just to see what would happen, I think. Good men. They're all dead now."

Hopkins didn't explain. When I pushed for more information, he told me he had a headache. I think that might've been it for our talk, if I hadn't bribed him with another bottle of hooch that Iris had stowed away. Where did she hide all the booze? What kind of party was she planning? No matter. The liquor helped me keep Hopkins talking. Rain poured outside the portholes, sizzling, like bacon frying in a skillet. Hot as a kitchen too, in our confined cabin.

Hopkins's story didn't follow in a line. It came to me in pieces of varying size and shape.

He claimed he knew about the strange creatures some of us had seen in our exploration of the flooded zone. "Those ones you heard coughing are called ghasts. Sickening-looking things, with legs like a kangaroo. The light kills them. You only need to worry about ghasts at night. Not very smart and they hunt in packs, usually. They'll eat anything. Yellowy eyes and excellent sense of smell. Faces like a noseless man. Filthy ugly things they are. Diseased mouths. Hooves like a horse."

He broke off without any explanation of how he came to possess this knowledge.

I made no judgment listening to him talk about the creatures.

I didn't want him to stop spinning yarns.

"That big, hairy thing they were fighting was a gug. Gugs. They're quiet for as big as they are. Anyway, they fight with the ghasts. Each of them will eat the other if given the chance, or so I've been told."

"Who told you?" I asked.

He only smiled. He tapped a finger to the side of his head. And turned an invisible key between his lips. His skin was a terrible yellow-orange hue that seemed baked in by the sun.

"You don't need to tell me anything you don't want to," I said. "It's up to you."

"You think I don't know that?" he replied. "Momma didn't raise no dummies."

I waited to see if he'd say more to me. I was afraid pushing him would lead nowhere.

Eventually, he went on. "I hate to tell your buddies working the boat. They came down here with the captain, asking me about a sighting one of the young ones had. Haven't they told you? No? It was a creature that looked like their father. It probably was him. Only he's turned into a ghoul. Dead-eater. Some of them go greenish. They live underground. Where the bodies are." Hopkins wiggled his eyebrows. "Slumping around. Dog-faced. Sad. Wouldn't you be? Don't tell them I told you. Skin like rubber. Makes a person sorrowful to think a loved one would become one of their kind, don't it, though?"

"Why are we seeing these things? I've never encountered anything like it before."

"Oh, my boy, that's because you've never been this close to the Dreamlands. Maybe when you sleep you are. But you don't know it. Or you avoid it. Or you can't remember. But only a few dreamers realize what the Dreamlands are. That's changing. He's thrown the gate wide."

"Who has?" I asked.

"There's a gap in our worlds, son. That's where the Spider Queen climbed through."

He crawled his hand along the wall beside the hammock. Tappety-tap-tap.

"Someone opened the gate and let her in?" I asked. "That's what you're telling me?"

He nodded. "He thinks he controls her. But he doesn't. Not likely. No, sir, not likely."

"Who does?"

He ignored my question. "She's going to make a bridge, and then this will all be gone. You, me, them upstairs. The whole world's going to collapse. People aren't in charge, son. Not by a long shot." His own statements seemed to catch him off guard. He shook his head.

I asked him to tell me more about the Dreamlands and the one who opened the gate.

"I'm so very, very tired. Let me rest my eyes some. We'll talk later. How about that?"

I agreed to let him rest for a while. Said I'd come back to him and his story.

Only we never talked later.

And by midnight he was off the boat. Lost again. We had much bigger problems by then.

But I'm getting ahead of myself.

35
Blue Flash

The two women stood in the bow, surveying the river. Marcos ordered the anchor up. Its chain rattled against the hull. Davi, sullen, stayed close to his brother. And Thiago scanned the forest through the falling rain. Hoping to see his father again. Or perhaps it was the opposite wish which compelled him to keep searching the shores for a fleeting glimpse.

"I'm having the boat turned around. This expedition is over. The risk is too high," Ursula said. She wore binoculars around her neck. Wiping the lenses dry, she brought them up to her eyes. The boat turned slowly in the channel, wake churning tan, she drifted sideways, precarious for an interval before Marcos and his men managed to swing her around and point her nose back the way she'd come. Once more centered in the middle of the tributary, he opened the engine up.

Full speed ahead. No stopping unless it was necessary. They'd be back in three days.

Four, at the most.

But everyone was leery of predicting time since their experiences of the last day and a half in the flooded zone. The jungle's aspect remained as it had been for most of the journey, yet every tree, each dripping wet plant seemed alien and strange. The rain flicked the leaves like a million green switches. Lightning branched across the leaden sky. Glowing as if it were hot, twisted metal, then fading to dull grayness. Thunder rumbled so you felt it in your guts.

Iris nodded. The rain pelted the hood of her jacket. Every time she tried lighting her cigarette, the wind, or a raindrop, put it out. Disgusted, she threw the damp butt in the water.

"I agree," she said. "It's not too late. We must turn back while we can."

This trip had been a mistake. Whatever debt, or loyalty, she owed her dead husband – this wasn't any method of repayment. She'd been reckless. Outright devious. And for that she felt a sense of guilt which compounded the complex emotions that came with her profound grief. Galton wasn't in this world anymore. She would never find him here. She would have to use other methods. Seances, meditation, guided dreams – she wasn't sure. But not this. This was vile.

"When we take Hopkins back, people will listen. Andy will have his story, even if it's less than he hoped for. Perhaps there will be another chance to return. With more people, better resources. I think the shrine is still a worthwhile goal. And an attainable one," Ursula said.

"I'm never coming back here," Iris said.

She meant it.

Suddenly the engine reduced power. The women lurched at the change of speed.

Marcos called from the wheelhouse.

"There! Look!"

The women glanced back at him to see where he was pointing.

Straight ahead.

Iris squinted into the rain blowing in their faces. It was warm, like tears.

The river channel grew wider.

Then the shore on both sides of the steamboat pulled back rapidly.

"It's the lagoon," Ursula said.

"But… we've turned around." Iris could not deny what she was seeing, though it defied logic. The peace she'd felt within herself about the expedition returning was gone.

They entered a large spoon-shaped pool of stagnant-looking water, which quickly expanded to a width greater than anything they had navigated on their journey. The far end of the lagoon was invisible behind a veil of rain. But it couldn't be close. They might as well have entered an ocean bay, the view was so great, and equally barren of other ships, or any life.

Ursula looked at the captain.

"You must've passed through the lagoon that night when you felt ill," she said.

Marcos was emphatic. "No. No, I was awake. I would have remembered."

He idled the engine.

The ship bobbed on the water. Unrelenting rain pounded down on them.

"It's so big," Iris said. "I never recall anywhere on the river looking like this."

"This is nowhere on the river," Marcos said. "It's witchery."

He said something to the brothers who looked more tense than at any previous time.

They answered him. Their attitude was guarded; they spoke in soft whispers.

"What did they say?" Ursula asked. She sounded like she was hoping for reassurances.

"This is a spirit place," Iris said before Marcos. "They have never visited here before."

Jake had been asleep under a tarp. He kicked off his sheet, rain dribbling down his face.

"Where are we? It looks like we're out fishing in Michigan. On Lake Superior," he said. He appeared as dumbfounded as if he'd woken up on the far side of the moon.

"Drop the anchor," Ursula said. "Let's see how deep it is."

Marcos ordered the anchor down. The chain unspooled and unspooled. It hit the end of its length with a clanking jolt. "That's all the chain I have. It's not touching bottom. We drift."

The rain changed to a misty spray. It tasted bitter. The smell of the air was like a campfire that had recently gone out. In the distance: light bursts. Iris guessed it was lightning, but the flashes were almost at the water level. Such a bright white, they were nearly blue. They hurt if you looked for too long in their direction, despite their distance and the murky vapor surrounding the boat.

"What are those?" Jake asked. "It's like bombs going off."

"I've never seen anything like it," Iris said.

The flashes repeated. They made no sound. No shockwave hit.

The frequency of the spectacular blue-white light bursts grew, as did their intensity.

"They're getting closer," Jake said. "Look, there's more to the port side."

"And the starboard," Iris said. It was difficult to tell the new flashes from their afterimages which lingered even if she closed her eyes or looked away. She blinked and covered her face. She rubbed her eyes but that only made it worse.

"Marcos, turn around," Ursula said. Fear was evident in her words. "Get us out of here."

The anchor clattered back up.

Andy came on deck. Notepad in hand. He stood astounded at the alteration of the landscape. "Where'd the jungle go?"

Marcos drove the boat in a big semicircle. Davi stood on top of the wheelhouse. Thiago ran from port to starboard, scouring the water for submerged obstacles. They all could see the wake trailing behind them. Rows of waves fanning out. When Marcos reached the point where the river had connected to the lagoon, he increased speed, to take them back into the channel.

Except there was no channel.

Only more water. More mist. Thicker, like fog now. A rich, creamy fog.

And those cursed blue flashes on every side. Undimmed. Closing in on them.

"Are they other boats?" Andy asked.

"I don't think so," Marcos said. "Too fast. I hear no engines. Listen." He turned their motor off.

The silence roared at them.

When he tried to turn the engines back on, they failed. He shouted at Thiago. Thiago unscrewed a cap on one of the diesels and peered inside. He said something back to Marcos who swore and slammed his hand on the wheel. "We have fuel. It isn't the damned fuel." He inspected the cap, sniffing at the reservoir. Davi jumped down. The three did what they could to get the boat going again. They weren't moving. Just sitting there.

The blue lights were approaching.

Getting closer. Brighter.

"They look like stars," Andy said.

Iris felt a bone chill the heat did nothing to diminish. Were

Galton's monsters coming back? Was a glowing puppet-Galton going to float across the water toward her?

She ran belowdecks.

"What do you know about this?" she asked Hopkins, sitting awake in the hammock.

"I know nothing," Hopkins said.

"What are these blue flashes? Where is this place?"

"Blue flashes?" he said. "That's a bad sign. They typically presage occurrences."

"Occurrences of what?"

"One never can tell," he said. "I've met your husband, you know. Galton Reed? That's his name, isn't it? He had a photo of you. You're quite a beautiful woman."

"What are you talking about? How could you know Galton? He's dead."

"I know him from the Dreamlands," Hopkins said. "We were very close."

"You dreamed of him. That's what you mean? If you know him, tell me something about how he looks." She was sure Hopkins was playing some cruel game with her. Lying. But why? Galton would never interact with someone like Hopkins, in the Dreamlands or anywhere else.

"He's blind in one eye. Since the spider bite, he said. But he sees the other world in that eye. Likes to wear that gaudy bathrobe. He'd make a good button man, a real killer, your hubby. So frosty with those ice-blue peepers. His gaze curdled white with eight-legged poison. Brrr…"

Hopkins shivered. He was grinning at her. Racked with tremors, unstable to keep still.

She thought he was playing with her, but his trembling didn't subside.

"Get me up on deck. I'm wobbly, but I need fresh air," he said.

She loathed touching him, but the man had caught her off guard with his mention of Galton. He looked like a hospital patient. She wondered if he was dying. If his brain was fevered. He felt hot to the touch. But weren't they all soaking in a steam bath?

Hopkins took the steps with care, watching his bare feet, which Iris noticed were yellow and shiny as polished horn, the nails hooked like talons. The man has gargoyle feet, she thought.

"Will you look at this fog!" he exclaimed. "Isn't it outlandish?"

He cackled and coughed, until she sat him on a bench to catch his breath.

The blue light flashes were repeating faster. Blinding explosions of sapphire radiance.

They didn't seem to affect him, although the others kept their faces down for protection.

Hopkins stared straight out at them.

"There's a boat coming!" he cried out. "A big one."

Iris presumed it was a hallucination, but when she looked up, shielding her gaze with one hand in case another flash might mar her vison, she was astonished to see the fog dissipating with great swiftness, as if were being sucked away into the trees by some giant creatures inhaling smoke. And yes, those were trees. The shore materialized again as the vaporous cloud cleared.

Iris saw no boat coming.

Their paddleboat was, indeed, in a large lagoon. But the river pond was of normal proportions for this section of river in the rainy season. Its previous vastness must've been an optical illusion. The others standing on deck appeared spellbound by the transforming landscape.

Davi was the first of the expeditioners to spot the black boat in the distance.

Confirming what Hopkins had stated. Hopkins was still excited, yipping like a small dog.

The boat was alarmingly near and moving fast.

It must've been concealed in the misty fog. That was the logical explanation for its sudden appearance. Besides being notable for its peculiar dark color, its shape was… unique.

Certainly alien to this region. An ancient style, perhaps. An uncommon sight to be sure.

Owing to the fact it did not run by mechanical engine but many unseen rowers.

36
Galley

Hopkins grew agitated. The proximity of the black boat brought about a tremendous body quake and a stream of uninterrupted mumbling. His brow furrowed. He shook his fist in the direction of the vessel. True, it was not well suited for river navigation, but that alone seemed inadequate in causing him such vexation.

Ursula noted the size of the ship was nearly double their own boat. Long and narrow, it rode near the surface of the lagoon and sported a pair of masts. Its sails were furled. Many oars on either side gave the vessel a centipedal appearance. The oars, like every inch of the ship, were painted a deadly coal black.

No sailors appeared on deck. Nor did anyone emerge after several minutes of waiting.

Marcos asked Ursula what she wanted him to do.

"Nothing for the moment," she said. She knew too little about it to be afraid. "I am curious. Give me a chance to indulge my interest in this oddity. Do you recognize its design?"

"I do not," he said. "It is most bizarre."

"I'll venture a guess based on her looks. And my books." Ursula boosted herself on top of the wheelhouse, where Davi had been a short while ago, attempting to direct them out of the misty fog. "She's a galley. Egyptian, maybe. More at home on the Mediterranean. And about two thousand years too late to the scene. I've studied replicas and old wrecks, but only in museums."

"I wouldn't know," Marcos said. "I'm only a riverman from Brazil. She isn't from here."

Ursula craned her neck, taking in as much of the anachronistic vessel as she could.

"Can you circle around? I'd like a better look at her. My, she's sinister to behold. See her three rows of oarsmen? That's called a trireme. I'll bet she's fast. A touch more Phoenician than Egyptian come to think of it. But that's not quite right either. There are Greek and Roman influences. A puzzler. They were warships. Good for ramming. Used for trading too, often slaves. Does that evil practice still go on here?"

Marcos said, "Decades ago, certainly. Today there are tales of villages being raided. People kidnapped in the night. I assume most reports are mistakes. Groups decide to go inland for food or safety. The rubber boom made slaves of the natives. Fifteen, ten years ago, you saw it. Many crimes took place, unspeakable abuse and violence. I've seen the scars and heard stories during my time on this river. In these remote areas, who knows? Even now it might exist."

He talked while the brothers drove the paddleboat around the strangely barren ship. It had restarted with ease.

Their discomfort was obvious. It was a bad harbinger.

"Hello in the black ship!" Ursula called out, repeating her greeting in several languages.

No reply. No sign of any person. The oars remained motionless.

Iris had corralled Hopkins. Andy was helping her, attempting to calm the cameraman, when unexpectedly the sickly fellow broke loose from their grips and sprinted toward the stern. With a nimbleness one might've thought impossible for a person so physically depleted, he evaded the outstretched arm of Thiago and launched himself like a college halfback sensing the goal line. Up and over the rail he went. He must have executed his dive with skill, for there was hardly any splash at all announcing he had entered the water. The emergence of his head and shoulders, twenty yards away, swimming the American crawl, proved he had. His intention was to reach the nearest shore. In order to do so as quickly as possible, he kicked up a flurry.

"Hopkins! Get back here!" Andy shouted.

Jake grabbed a canoe and, along with Andy, lowered it in the water. They climbed inside, trailing the cameraman, who continued to display uncommon speed and determination in his watery escape.

Hopkins struggled up the muddy bank without a glance toward his pursuers. His bare feet slapped the mucky soil. Ducking vines, he vanished into the rainforest.

Jake and Andy hit the shore soon after. Andy remained with the boat, dragging it to level ground, while Jake chased Hopkins up the squishy, soggy slope.

Ursula and Iris took turns with the binoculars, watching for developments. Hopkins was a walking trove of information. The cost of losing him was incalculable. His judgment was also impaired. She hoped Jake would catch him. The bush was thick with dangers and places to hide.

Marcos touched Ursula's sleeve, causing her to jump.

"Sorry. The sun is setting in less than an hour. What do you want me to do?" He twisted an oily rag, glancing over his shoulder at the other ship.

"We can't go without Hopkins," she said.

Marcos pressed his lips together. Clearly, he did not agree.

"Give Jake more time," she said. "He'll either find him or he won't. Soon we'll know."

"I don't like this foul thing adrift like a ghost ship. I want to leave. It will be dark."

"I understand. But they've made no threats. We don't know if anyone's on board. She may be deserted. We'll stay until all our party is here. I'm not leaving anyone behind."

"She didn't row herself, Dr Downs," Marcos said with gruff annoyance.

He's not doing well, Ursula thought. That galley causes him much anxiety. We're all feeling under pressure. She felt it too. The black boat was foreboding. But she wouldn't run.

"Bring us into shore. Put space between us and the ship. Anchor there," she said, pointing to a strip of rocky beach.

Marcos did as she requested. But he was not happy about it.

The sun had set. Pink light melted into the trees. Violet to purple. Night fell.

Andy came for Ursula in the canoe. The mosquitos had made a triumphant return. Andy was covered with red bites. He scratched his swollen face and neck. Ursula waved at the clouds of bloodsuckers. Jake had yet to reemerge from the thick of the forest.

"What do we do?" Andy asked after he'd paddled her to shore. "Do we go after them?"

She shook her head. "It's dark. Help me build a bonfire. We've got this little clearing among the rocks that's hospitable for now, as long as it doesn't start raining again."

"I don't think there's dry wood," Andy said, kicking at the trampled grass.

"We've got diesel. I'll dig up something dry on board for kindling."

Paddling back to the boat, she found a few old newspapers and a pair of broken paddles.

"If nothing else, a reporter's work is fit for fire-starting," Andy joked upon her return.

They got the paper and paddles lit. Pitched a couple of tarp lean-tos to keep dry. The smoke held the bugs at bay. It would prevent most predators from drawing near to them, too.

When Ursula went back for fire materials, Iris joined her, bringing a pair of lanterns.

The lagoon became a black wedge on a black mirror. Marcos, Davi, and Thiago huddled on the boat, talking. They had refused to step ashore. It had been two hours since Jake followed Hopkins into the jungle.

"Jake knows what he's doing. He's an excellent tracker," Ursula said.

"He'll see our fire." Andy tried to sound optimistic. "He can smell the smoke."

"Did you happen to smell anything from the black galley?" Iris asked.

Firelight flickered, illuminating her as she talked with them. She wore the spider ring.

"I didn't notice." Andy brushed away a large moth from his chin.

Ursula shrugged, not wanting to dwell on factors contributing to the sense of gloom.

"It stinks," Iris said. "Take a good whiff when we get close again. It's like rotten meat."

Andy rubbed his hands together as if he were chilled. But the fire and jungle were warm.

The moon tumbled like a bone rolling across the tablecloth of the midnight sky. Stars were spilled salt. The wind shifted. Waves lapped the shore. The flames crackled: an open oven.

Ursula smelled it. There was no denying the tang of spoiled flesh charring over hot coals.

A scream pierced the air.

It didn't come from the direction of the black ship.

It was from the opposite side. The forest. Not far off. It sounded human.

"That was a man," Iris said flatly.

"It wasn't Jake," Ursula said.

"How can you tell?" Andy asked. The look of expectation in his eyes made her ache.

"It wasn't him," was all she said back. Screams sounded alike, she knew. But she pushed the idea out of her mind that Jake might be in pain, that he might be screaming in terror or for her help.

They couldn't go into the jungle in the dark. She had to trust Jake to keep himself alive.

Aboard the steamboat, the trio of shipmates huddled around the glow of their lantern.

Their light moved. Swinging briefly.

Before it went out.

"Hey, where did it go?" Andy said. "The boat light … they turned down their lantern."

"Might've run out kerosene," Ursula said. "Don't always presume the worst."

"I don't," he said.

He carried his lamp to check on the canoe they'd used to ferry back and forth. There was a long stretch of rocky shallows between them and the steamboat. Marcos had dropped anchor fifty yards offshore, as close as it could get without risking a scraping bottom and hull damage.

The steamboat engines started up.

"What's he doing? Marcos is firing up the motor!"

"Marcos!" Ursula called out. She walked toward the water's edge. "Marcos! Hello!"

She raised her lantern in time to see another canoe separating from their boat. Coming toward her. Something must've happened. Signals from the galley? He was coming to tell them.

The canoe bumped into the muddy bank. She took hold of the bow. Pulling.

"I was worried…"

The canoe was empty. There were two paddles neatly crossed in the center. A sack of food, some cans, and three corked bottles of fresh water. A knife and a hatchet. Jake's rifle. Their personal bags.

The engines' growl grew louder. The anchor chain thumped and rattled.

No, no, no…

She thought about jumping in the canoe and racing after them. But it would be no use. She'd never catch up. The steamboat's big engines chugged away, belching gray clouds that smeared into the jet sky, obscuring sight of the moon hanging overhead.

Iris and Andy joined her.

Together they watched helplessly as their guides motored away.

When the diesel haze disappeared, the moon returned. Full, heavy. Pocked and scarred as an ancient relic unearthed from the mud. A sharp disk of bone, round as a dish. Empty.

The black galley waited. For what? For them?

They went back to the fire to add wood.

37
The Bite

"We're as good as dead," Andy said. He poked a stick into the fire and batted away a moth.

"Nonsense," Ursula replied. She didn't sound as convincing as Andy would've hoped.

"Ursula's right," Iris said. "We have provisions. We're on the river. People have lived here for millennia, and they will for millennia more."

"But which people?" Andy said. "Us?"

"Yes, us," Ursula said. "We will make it. It's only a question of how."

"And when," Andy said. "I don't plan on growing old in the Amazon."

"Be careful you don't die young here instead," Iris said, her voice swelling with angry emotion. "You wanted the adventure of a lifetime. Well, now you have it."

The heaviness of her comment landed full weight. He couldn't deny the truth. He'd asked for this. Gamed and manipulated his way into it. Now he had to deal with the consequences. The panic of seeing Marcos's rusty boat pulling away led to a sinking despair.

The engines growing quieter and quieter. But that was finished too. It was eerily silent, pitch black except near the fire.

At least he wasn't alone.

These two women had been here before. They were experts. That gave him someone to pin his hopes on. He might not be able to solve this. But they surely could. He nodded to himself. "Right. What do we do?" he asked them.

"In the morning, I'm going out to that black galley," Ursula said.

"I don't know about that," Iris replied.

"We need to know who they are," Ursula said. "Maybe they'll help us. They might be as afraid of us as we are of them."

"They're cannibals," Iris said. "That boat has come here from another time, another place. A very bad place. Look at it. The only thing they'll help you do is fill their bellies."

Andy was back to panicking. He hadn't thought seriously of being eaten.

"Don't you recognize the smell of burning human flesh?" Iris said.

"How would I?" Andy said. "This is the first time I've left Arkham in my life."

"Don't be sure they aren't eating people there too," Iris said. "Making sacrifices."

"What? Are you saying–"

"None of this talk is helping," Ursula interrupted. "Focus on the facts."

Suddenly, she alerted to a snapping coming from in the bush. The rustle of leaves.

Audible breathing. Getting louder.

Ursula reached into the canoe for the hatchet.

Terrified, Andy snatched up a paddle.

Iris looked on impassively.

"Who goes there?" Ursula called in a loud voice.

Iris hadn't taken up a weapon. She made no move to defend herself. She only watched. Does she want to die? Andy wondered. Is this part of some personal suicide pact she's made?

A figure approached the fire. Tall, loping through the foot-stomped mud.

"Jake!" Ursula shouted. She dropped her hatchet and rushed forward to her partner.

She threw her arms around him and brought him over to the light.

Jake.

He had scratches on his face and arms. Begrimed with mud. But alive and well.

"I couldn't find Hopkins," he said.

"That's all right," Ursula said.

Andy clapped his back. His despair turned to exhilaration. "You found us. We have a bit of bad news, though."

"Marcos and his crew are gone. I saw the steamboat pass by on the river. It's my fault. I thought for a minute you might've all left me behind. Then I saw flames through the trees. I heard voices." He smiled, embarrassed, and turned from the firelight.

Ursula watched him. She said nothing. But Andy could see she was glad Jake was safe.

Andy passed one of the water bottles to Jake. He uncorked it, drank. Judiciously.

"We were talking about what we're going to do next," Andy said. "Planning."

"We can't go into the jungle." Jake pounded the cork back in the bottle.

"Because it's night?" Andy said. "Marcos sent us a care package. Your rifle."

Jake said, "The rifle isn't going to help."

"You saw something," Iris said. "What did you see? Who?"

Ursula stared at him in the flickering Halloween oranges and shadows. A campfire story, Andy thought. This would be the proper time, except we're living out the horror others imagine.

"What is it, Jake?" Ursula said.

"I didn't come back for so long because I was hiding. Under a log. I don't know what I saw exactly. It came down out of the trees. Went right for Hopkins. Too fast. Never saw anything move like that. It took him in a rush. It was a big…." He paused. "A blur."

"We heard a scream," Iris said.

Jake nodded. "Hopkins knew. I saw his face in the moonlight. He'd given up by then."

"When Galton and I were collecting legends, the people spoke of the Spider Queen," Iris said. "Not as a real spider in this world. But as a spirit, a god spirit, in the dreamworld. She hunted people in their dreams. She was something to be feared. But she couldn't hurt you when you were awake." She leaned into the fire. The gold ring – it couldn't have moved, Andy thought. Even slightly.

"Sounds like she hurt Hopkins," he said. "He'd seen her before, too. Not in his dreams either. Jake and I found those bodies bundled up hanging in webs from the treetops. She's real."

"Galton thought the Spider Queen masked another more powerful god. Atlach-Nacha. She has power over all spiders. She lives far from here, but she spins in the underworld. Her web connects places that people think are unconnected. She lives in the cold, in mountains. Underground. She lives in dreams. The Dreamlands. People say the god wears a human face."

Iris crouched on the ground; her features were lit by the flames. Her body bunched. Arms, legs curled tight. Her hair created a halo around her head. Her skin was smooth as an egg.

"Did Galton think he'd made contact with Atlach-Nacha?" Ursula asked.

"I don't know. But she knows failure. Spinning, she has power."

"Galton knew failure too. He tried to meet her. That's what he was doing?" Ursula said.

"When he died, he said a spider bit him. I never saw the spider. But I remember the bite."

"What's hunting in that jungle is real. Andy's right. Hopkins was too. It's no dream," Jake said.

"She's a huge spider god with a human face. Sorcerers can speak to her if they know the words to use. If they go to the sacred places at the correct times. That's what Galton told me," Iris said. "He wanted to share in her power. He said he had spells that would control her."

Iris rocked on the grass. She shut her eyes. Fading out, as if she'd fallen in a trance.

"We can't leave here going through the forest," Jake repeated. "That thing is out there."

Ursula nodded. "That's why I'm planning to board the black galley. Check it out. See what's inside."

"When?" he asked.

"In the morning," Andy said. He'd experienced enough excitement for one day. Or one life. "Everything will look better after a good night's sleep. You'll see. Off to bed, I say."

"We'll build the fire bigger," Jake said. "I don't think the spider will go near it."

"What about what Iris said? This Atlach-Nacha. Are gods afraid of fire? I don't think I could deal with anything that resembles what she was talking about. Not tonight." Andy was exhausted. His mind overloaded with thoughts, fears, and extreme fatigue.

"I don't know what to make of the legends," Ursula said. "Our most pressing need is to get away from here. I'll go to the ship right now. Before it gets light. It's better to scout in the dark. Easier to hide. In and out. Fast and agile. Like a thief in the night. That's the best way."

"I don't know…" Jake said.

"It's not up to you," Ursula said. "I'm taking a canoe. Jake, you're in charge. You have the other canoe if something happens. Three can fit. I'm only doing reconnaissance. I'll be back before you know it. That galley is a key to things. I feel it, trust me."

Andy gazed at the black wedge sitting there in the moonlight and shuddered.

Burning flesh…

Then he looked to the forest and thought about the spider that ate Hopkins.

He wouldn't be getting any sleep tonight.

38
Finest Rubies

Ursula paddled out to the galley. A gentle night breeze rippled the lagoon. She glided up to the hulking ship. The question of how to climb aboard was settled for her. A rope ladder hung off the side. She hadn't noticed that before when they'd circumnavigated the galley. But there it was.

Black ropes, black steps.

She reached up and pulled herself onto the first step.

The canoe immediately began to drift away. She had no way of tethering it.

"Curses," she muttered.

She tried catching the edge of the bow with the toe of her boot, but it was too late. Waves took it. At least it was being blown back to Jake and the others. Their fire danced in the darkness.

Ursula climbed higher.

She peeked over the deck rail. It was as deserted as she had observed earlier.

Like a panther she crept along the quarterdeck boards searching for a way below. The skylights were closed. When she tried the doors, they didn't budge. Bolted from inside. From the chimney in the forecastle wafted the putrid odors Iris had mentioned. They were stronger here. No visible smoke, but Ursula smelled the unwholesome, meaty stew suggestive of pig farms and slaughterhouses; a fatty, woodsy barbeque mingled with flyspecked old blood. She did her best not to gag and covered her nose and mouth with her bandana.

Midships gaped a passageway leading down. The moonlight poured silver on the top wooden steps. Farther down, a thick, velvety darkness flooded the space.

Ursula crawled over to the gap and listened. All was quiet. No sailors talking. No sounds of snoring and sleepy nighttime grumbles. That same smoky odor of spoiled meat wafted up, tainting the stale air of confinement. Maybe the ship was empty. But living creatures had been kept down there for a time. Long enough to leave their bouquet. Were they there still?

She didn't dare to strike a match. But she was debating with herself the risks of venturing below to see what she might *feel* when the mellifluous voice of an unseen observer spoke up.

"Permission to come aboard granted," it said. Followed by a warm, low chuckle.

Ursula tensed and turned, struggling to locate the source of the laughter.

She detected nothing. Until the crumb of a pipe bowl glowed red, and the plump attributes of a man's smirking face were illuminated. She'd mistaken him for a coil of cable but jumped when he moved. He touched a thin taper to his pipe bowl and with the flame lit a lamp on a small, folding table. He sat in a similarly styled chair beside the table, looking relaxed and settled. A second matching chair was arranged across from him. But he smoked alone.

"Join me, please. I am bored, and the night begs for conversation."

His eyes crinkled merrily. Cheeks like a squirrel, she thought, stuffed with stolen nuts.

Ursula approached. Her hand covered the knife on her belt.

"I mean you no harm," the man said. "I am a merchant, not a warrior."

"Both have the potential for danger," Ursula said.

Another chuckle. His neck rolls expanded like a frog's. He clamped down on the pipe stem. "Bravo for canniness." He hooked the leg of the unoccupied chair and slid it out to her.

Ursula turned the chair to face him, head on. Putting the table between them.

She sat.

"Who are you?" she said.

"A dealer of jewels, traveler by trade. Sailor by necessity."

"Turn up your lamp so I may see my new acquaintance in a better light."

The man's pudgy fingers twisted a thumbscrew on the base of the lamp. The circle of yellow radiance spread around them. He was rotund, his cheeks scarred with pockmarks. His eyebrows spread over his brow like a pair of crow's wings, shiny, black, and waggling above his intelligent eyes. Atop his head he wore a sort of cloth cap wrapping, all of one continuous piece, fashioned in a style which produced dual mounds upon his head.

He grinned at her. "Join me for a drink? I'd offer you moon-wine, but I am out. I have something better. My private store. From the homeland. It is as delicious as it is stimulating,"

The brightened lamp revealed an oddly rough, red bottle on the table.

And two goblets.

"You were expecting a guest, I see," Ursula said. *Moon-wine? What was moon-wine?*

"Where I come from it is customary to always put out another cup. In hopes an old friend may drop by. Or a new one. Please, enjoy a taste. It is bad luck to refuse. But do as you please."

He lifted the rough red bottle, pouring a small amount of liquid into the cup.

"Are you alone on this big black galley?" Nothing about this encounter was as she had expected. Where was the night watch? Why was everything locked? The so-called merchant would've looked more at home in a port tavern. "Where are your shipmates?"

He laughed cordially, holding out the cup with his sausage fingers. His cuff hung loose.

"They row all day. It makes them tired," he said.

Ursula took the cup. "And silent."

He ignored her comment. "You are noticing this extraordinary bottle, yes? It's a ruby. That is my business. I trade in the finest rubies known. Look at that size. Remarkable, no?" He tilted the bottle in front of the lamp's flame. The reds – cherries, grapes, and plums – blazed.

"I don't know much about rubies or rare foreign wines."

"That is unfortunate. Pleasure is the business of life. Or it should be." He executed a sinful smile. A pencil-thin oval of fine black whiskers ringed his ample mouth.

Ursula swirled her wine but did not drink. "My friends and I are stranded on the bank."

"I saw your fire. To be honest, I was going to help. But…" He didn't bother looking at the shoreline fire where the others were waiting for her. They both knew where it was.

"But what?"

"Frankly, I thought you might be vicious bandits. A merchant guards his wares. The paddleboat left the lagoon in a hurry. Without you."

It was Ursula's turn to ignore him. "Where did you learn English? You speak it well."

"A merchant must familiarize himself with the language of all his customers."

"You sell to Americans?"

"I sell to anyone with gold in their pockets." Absently, he patted his round stomach. He dressed well. He wasn't the one rowing this ship; that was obvious. Silky, shimmery in body and dress, he worked with his words. She pictured him weighing gems on a scale. Keeping a ledger.

"Is gold all you accept for payment?" She was careful to watch the layers of his reaction.

That corrupt twist of lip, the knowing, sly sharing of an unearned camaraderie: a born salesman he was. Drawing you close. Offering easy favors. But never without a price.

"Is there more than gold? I hadn't noticed." He filled his cup and drained it off quickly. Then he refilled it, sniffed, sipped. "You haven't sampled my wine. Its taste is like going home."

Ursula put the glass to her lips. Fruity. Like a cat she touched it with her tongue.

The wine was not too sweet. If someone had served it to her elsewhere, would she have drunk it? Yes, most likely. And yet…

"How can I be of assistance?" he said.

Ursula was keenly aware of how utterly artificial and bizarre this meeting was. Surely, she'd been watched from afar. They'd prepared for her. The ladder, the chair and cup.

The greeter with his unctuous, yet persistent manner.

Was he only a trader? How much did it matter who he was if he might transport them to safety? The ancient-looking ship was odd. But what were their options? She was tired of playing games. They needed help. A ride. It wasn't asking much. So, she asked. "We are headed for Manaus," she said. "Will you take us there?"

His beetle eyes glittered like wet black ink. He pulled on his pipe; the bowl reddened.

"I might, I might," he said.

"We can't pay you until we reach the port. There I can wire for funds."

The man shook his head. "I don't want gold from you. In fact, I would refuse. Well, probably I would." A conspiratorial snicker. Let's make a deal, it said. Everything's on the table.

"What's your price?" she asked him. "Name it. Within reason, of course."

He looked abashed. "Price? Drink your wine. Share the moonlight with me. That's all."

Ursula investigated the goblet. It was only wine. And no more than a swallow. Still.

She gave him back the goblet. And took his.

"I'll finish yours," she said. There was a thimbleful, or two, swirling at the bottom. She drank it down in a gulp. And plopped the cup on the table.

There. Not bad. Quite flavorful. She wiped her lips with the back of her hand.

"We can pick up my friends before the channel," she said, feeling a rush of dizziness.

Was the boat moving? It was like the onset of seasickness she was feeling. A twinge.

"Your friends aren't going with us," the man answered. Or so she thought she heard.

Her vision filled with the same coal darkness as the ship's color. A void opened somewhere behind her, though it felt like it was inside her too. A chasm without sides or bottom.

Darkly, backward, Ursula fell in.

39
What Would Ursula Do?

Jake had been gazing back and forth between their dwindling fire and the black galley when a sudden flash of blue light swelled outward, growing fast, looking fragile as a soap bubble, aswirl with strands of cosmic colors constantly in motion, like squiggly liquid paint crawling over the ship. And then it burst. The dome disappeared. The lagoon sparkled under cold moonlight.

But the galley, like the dome, had vanished.

"Oh, no. Not again," Andy said, rushing to the water's edge.

Jake heard the rhythmic splashing of oars echoing from the river channel. The noise was far off and fading rapidly into the distance. It was dark out, and the jungle loomed darker still than the mud banks and the shining flood zone waters. He watched an empty canoe adrift on the wavelets. He knew it was the one Ursula had taken to investigate the galley.

"What do we do, Jake?" Andy asked. "They've gone. And taken Ursula with them."

With Ursula missing, and likely in grave danger, Jake felt paralyzed. He wasn't normally the one calling the shots. And, even if trouble were a regular, if not constant, companion on the expeditions he took with Ursula, he never had to be the one in charge. It just wasn't his job.

He didn't make hard calls. Except now he had to. And quickly. He weighed his options.

Andy was a greenhorn and, although capable, more of a liability than an asset.

Jake didn't trust Iris. Despite her experience and expertise, he hesitated to rely on her.

She was lying next to the flames, asleep.

What now? he thought. What is our best course of action? What would Ursula do?

"I'm going after her," Jake said.

"You're what? And leave the two of us here? Alone?" Andy sounded exasperated. The poor guy had experienced his fair share of the bizarre over the last couple of days, including a physical attack, near drowning, abandonment in the wilderness – not once but twice – and now he was being told that Jake intended to drop him at the forest's edge with a giant jungle spider prowling nearby and a half-lucid, grief-stricken widow as his sole ally if things went south.

"We'll be fine," Iris said, sitting up and staring into the fire.

"No," Andy said. "I do not concur."

"I must go alone," Jake said. "And I must go now. You'll slow me down, Andy."

"You don't even know where the galley went. It was another blue flash. What does that mean, eh? She could be anywhere. You going to use the canoe and leave us traveling on foot?"

"I'll swim out to Ursula's canoe and take it," Jake said.

"And we're to go in the other? Where exactly? I don't have a map. I couldn't follow one through this maze of tributaries if I did. I can't even swim!" Andy shrieked and stomped his foot on the mushy bank.

"I had a dream," Iris said.

"Oh, that's fantastic," Andy said.

"I know where the standing white stone is. Galton showed me. I can take us to the rubber plantation. We'll find help there. Maude. The shrine. There's a group of followers. Hopkins wasn't far off, but he went the wrong way.

"Jake, you go after Ursula. Andy and I will paddle to the shrine and wait." Iris stood, dusting the ashes off her khakis. She fumbled for a cigarette.

"I'm not going anywhere with her," Andy said.

Jake wasn't sure what to do. Andy was right about the galley. He'd heard rowers in the channel, but he'd never catch up unless they stopped. If he left his team waiting here, the spider would get them. They'd die like Hopkins. He couldn't do that.

"Iris, what did Galton show you precisely?" he asked. He was desperate to rely on her.

Iris took the cigarette from her lips, exhaling a stream of smoke. "The white stone from the film. It's across the lagoon. The other side. Right over there." She pointed into the darkness.

Andy changed tack. "She's been right before. Let's all go and check. If the rubber plantation is there, then maybe they know about the black galley, whose ship it is, where it might be headed. Jake, we need you more than Ursula does. She's an expert at survival. I'm an amateur. I'll haul my own load. Do what I'm told. More than ready to take risks. But give me a fighting chance."

Iris went over to the canoe and rummaged around. She came back with the binoculars. Scoping the opposite shore, she proclaimed. "I can see it. The stone. Have a look for yourself,"

She passed the glasses to Jake.

He saw... something in the moonlight... an indistinct,

lumpen blur. Possibly the stone, but it wasn't clear. Jake stood, contemplating his choices. The galley was getting farther away…

Andy grabbed the binocs. "Oh, you're right, Iris. She's on the trail now. Maude's over there, isn't she? You can see the hill rising behind. It's like Hopkins's film. The whole setup."

Wishful thinking, Andy. Jake took the glasses back and turned them to the channel.

"You don't even know if they went that way," Andy said. "That ship was unnatural."

Jake felt torn. He'd never *not* put Ursula at the top of his list of concerns. But now he had other responsibilities to consider. Not only Andy and Iris, but Maude. And a historic discovery.

If she were in his place, what *would* Ursula do?

"I've made my mind up. I'll go with you to investigate if that is the standing stone. Either way, you're safer over there than on this side. Get in the canoe. We'll fetch the other one and tow it to the bank. Iris, keep a bead on our target. Andy, help me launch."

The three entered the lagoon.

By the time they found the stone, it was getting light.

40
Leeches

Her brain was muzzy, full of fog. Iris was still afraid of Galton. Nothing had changed her mind. She wanted to help her team get back to Manaus. With Ursula kidnapped, what were their chances? Not only of finding Maude Brion, but of surviving? She'd put on a brave face for Andy's sake. But the Amazon didn't forgive mistakes. They'd made too many. The Spider Queen was out there feeding. She'd snatched up Hopkins and killed him. She'd get them too. This was her terrain. If she were a god, what could they do?

They could pay her tribute. Make a sacrifice.

They could die. By offering up a life they might save others. It was nothing new under the sun. Cultures practiced sacrifice for as long recorded history. Gods seemed to approve.

She'd told them the truth about Galton visiting her in her dream by the fire.

He did visit.

Apologetic, his head hanging down. In shame? Galton didn't feel shame, not for the things he did himself, only for the things done to him that he failed to prevent. Or avenge. He'd left the robe out of sight and come to her calmly with his walking staff swishing through the tall, whispering grasses. Calling out her name. Announcing himself, his imminent arrival. No surprises this time. Peaceful. He looked like a college boy again. Stripped to the waist. Fit and healthy. He was carrying a garland of orchids. He wasn't floating with those horror show teeth and beastly talons. Galton walked up to her and placed the garland around her neck.

"My queen," he said, kissing her cheek. A peck. Almost shy. Despite her anger, her heart ached to see him restored to the way he was in better days. But she wouldn't give in that easily.

His face felt hot as he drew near.

"What do you want from me? Get away," she said. "I'm tired of your lies. Let me be."

He stepped back. Offended.

"I never lied, Iris. Maybe I didn't share the whole story, but I never once lied. You weren't ready to know everything. I didn't want you feeling overwhelmed. This is gigantic. There absolutely couldn't be bigger news. The universe is ending, Iris. Atlach-Nacha will build the bridge. Nothing will ever be the same. I'm not playing humble when I say you did it."

"What do you mean I did it?" she asked. She looked at him suspiciously. He deserved that much, didn't he? For scaring her. His one eye was opaque. Purple, vine-like scars marred his cheek. Oh, poor Galton. Otherwise, he looked better. Revitalized. A new man. He'd get these surges of energy that appeared out of nowhere. His attitude reversed overnight. Suddenly, no dreams were too big. No goal unreachable. It was infectious. His zestful spirit lifted you too. Like a great rushing wind, signaling dramatic weather ahead. High seas. Sometimes storms.

Could she live in her dreams with a man like this? In life she had done so for many years.

Galton said, "You've made it. The rubber plantation is across the water. If it were daylight, you'd see the white stone, upright like a sentinel. Maude's there. The Queen's devotees. It's all so close. Because of you. When you wake, take the others there. I'll do the rest. It'll be easy." He pointed where she should stand to look for the stone. Where to land the boat.

Iris sat in the front of the canoe now. What was she doing? She had no clear idea. Galton was guiding her. Maybe Jake and Andy would figure things out at the plantation. They wanted to find the Spider Queen. She'd help them do that. But Galton was talking apocalyptically. She wished she knew the right thing to do. She didn't. Andy behind her, paddling hard. Jake steered.

"There," she said. "Take us in to shore. I see a good spot."

The men paddled to the mud. The canoe slid right in. They were careful of hitting rocks in the morning twilight. They towed the second canoe without problems. The three of them climbed out and stowed the canoes behind the stilt legs of a walking palm. Thunder rumbled like boulders rolling down a mountainside. Far away. No lightning visible in the sky. It would rain.

The river was going to keep rising.

Iris went first. She slashed through the grasses with a machete Marcos packed.

The stone was where Galton said it would be. Iris touched the carving, hard to make out in the dimness. She felt the grooves. Eight legs. Round body. A spider. This was the marker.

Entering the Queendom of the Spider Queen. A claim and a warning.

Jake had a lantern. The sun started peeking over the horizon. Colors bled back into the world. He'd slung his rifle over his shoulder. Iris could tell he was worried. About them, about Ursula. What might they encounter on this anonymous shore?

"It's the white stone all right," Andy said. "By God it is. Iris, I'm sorry I doubted you."

"It doesn't matter," she said.

"Thank you for saying that." Andy placed a sweaty hand on her arm as he glanced into the bush. "If I recall, the trailhead should be..." he started.

"Right this way." Iris didn't wait for Jake, who was inspecting the stone's inscriptions.

She hacked at the grasses. Ahead of them, a pathway opened, a steep trail zigzagging up the hillside. Even in the half-light, it was hard to miss. Human-made. Recently used. There were footprints. Boot prints. Holes poked in the mud where a climber had jammed a stick down for balance and leverage, spearing the vegetation-draped slope. People were living here.

"C'mon, Jake," Andy called over his shoulder. He turned to Iris. "I wish we had Ursula's camera. I'd like to record this for my book. If I get too excited, I'll miss things."

"Maude has a camera," Iris said.

"She's really here, isn't she? We're going to find her today. I can feel it."

Jake caught up with them. "First things first. If we reach the old plantation... and the shrine... if there are people there, we ask about the black boat. We see if they know anything. If it's safe, we form a search party. Failing that, I'll go look for her alone. You two can make camp. I wish Hopkins had been more coherent. He might've led us to Maude."

"If Maude hasn't been able to find her way back, I doubt she can help us," Andy said.

Iris slowed.

"She may not want to go," she said. "Have you thought of that?" She seized dangling vines, branches, dragging herself upward.

Dawn was breaking. Light streamed through the trees. But it didn't penetrate far. Fog hung in the air like damp smoke. The trail was slippery, difficult. Iris and Andy were out of breath. Jake, a more practiced hiker, passed them, taking over the lead.

"Why in the world would Maude stay here?" Andy asked. "I can see visiting, but…"

"Hopkins said it was 'a dream come true for her'," Jake said. He thwacked at a limb.

"Nothing explains love. When you find it, you don't ever want to leave," Iris said.

"She's in love with the jungle?" Andy said, shaking his head.

"Or something she's discovered here." Iris stopped. "Hold up, Jake. I see something."

Jake paused in his chopping. "What is it? Where?"

She cupped his shoulder and pulled him down to her sight line.

"Through the branches. Slanting there – it's a structure of some kind," she said.

Jake followed the tip of her pointing finger.

"Is that a roof? Or a leaning wall? Yes, I see it now. It isn't natural. Let's go."

He began carving a new trail. Soon they discovered a second path, a "V" forking off from the one they'd been following. They were running now, like children. All three of them.

"It's the rubber plantation," Andy said. "Or what's left of it. What a shambles…"

He jogged up onto the steps of the large, flat, single-story building. Iris caught up. The roof was collapsed in sections on the floor. The jungle had begun to refill the rooms with plant life, like a green waterfall pouring over the top of the walls. The furniture they'd seen previously on film was buried now. They made out vague shapes – a chair, filing cabinets with their drawers pulled out – smothered in greenery. They paused on the threshold.

"Remember that whip-thick snake from the reel," Jake said, as she was about to step in.

But Iris hadn't noticed any birds or monkeys. Maybe the snakes were gone too.

Still, she didn't feel brave enough to wade into the hip-deep foliage and test her theory.

Instead, she left Jake to poke around. She had other things she wanted to see.

Andy stood in the center of the station, taking it all in.

"Jake, Andy, come here!" Iris called. "Quickly."

Despite having witnessed – or previewed – aspects of this scene with her husband in her dream, Iris's heart was pounding. She too had searched for years for the legendary Spider Queen. She'd made it the subject of her studies, painstakingly gathered myth-like tales and first-person oral accounts, attempting to pinpoint the remains of a hidden shrine, perhaps even an active temple of ritual worship. Tracing rumors of relics, sorting through broken fragments, tossing out the frauds and hoaxes, cataloguing the best artifacts she and Galton had collected. They hoped to find definitive evidence, hard, scientific documentation of a ceremonial site created by true believers to honor a jungle goddess. A goddess unconnected to any known indigenous group. Not a native religion but a fervent local obsession that defied the limits of modern categorization.

Iris stood beside a lane of stagnant water. Gooey muck. Two rust-red iron railings protruding from the soggy jade pudding like a pair of demonic fingers. They represented the defeat of humanity at the hands of Mother Nature. She'd swallowed them. Spit out the red bones.

"It's the old rail lines," she said. "And that over there… is the second white stone."

Like a hulking naked man, the stone squatted beside the lane. Spider carvings covered it. No mosses or lichen blotched their message. The marks were as plain as if they'd been scrubbed.

The forest mists had not abated, though the sun was rising fast. Golden light burned tunnels through the vapor. A big space yawned before them like a cavern. Ahead lay mystery.

"The shrine should be in there," Andy said. "It's only a few yards."

He took a small step. Hesitated. Started going again.

"Wait," Jake said.

Andy paused. He looked relieved that Jake had called him back.

"We go together. Side by side," Jake said.

Iris nodded.

They linked arms.

Their boots squelched in the mud. Sloshing along the watery lane, they proceeded.

In the dream, Galton never showed her the shrine. Iris swallowed, a dry click. Warm brown ooze topped her boots, encased her ankles in mud. Putrid water fouled her calves. She thought of leeches. Their bladed, sucking mouths. Iris marched through it. Jake and Andy too. All their eyes remained fixed on the swirling, pale fog. Searching. Fearing. Hoping for miracles.

Through the blurry morning haze, ill-defined shapes began to emerge.

"My God," Andy said. "It's real. It's actually real." His pace quickened.

Iris broke free from the men. She tore ahead.

She was careful to avoid stepping on any of the fallen slabs of cut rock. She didn't want to harm anything at the site. She ran up into the ruins. The Shrine of the Spider Queen. The steps were swept. Vines trimmed back. It was old, obviously. Ancient. But someone was taking care of the place. Maude's film revealed rough, deteriorated conditions. But there had been attempts at preservation since the filming took place. Iris touched a pillar. Chisel marks. Grit on her fingers.

Fresh carvings? She examined a pictograph. Two figures: spider and human. The moon above them: a sharp crescent. The human figure was positioned higher, uplifted. Arms spread.

In the spider's jaws.

It was all too much to comprehend, like stepping into a dream and waking to find it real.

Jake walked the perimeter of the largest structure, tightening his circle, eyes returning to the treetops, his head swiveling around. He hadn't unslung the rifle. Not yet. He rejoined Iris.

"It's incredible," he said.

Andy spun around, his arms wide apart. "I can't believe we did it! It's here. We're here."

"But no one else is," Jake said.

"It's still early. Maybe they don't sleep in the shrine. It's like a church, right?" Andy knelt on stone tiles, running his palm over a meshed network of intricate design. "A huge web."

Scraping from the back of the shrine. Purposeful. As if the mover wanted them to hear.

It came from behind a raised table that might be an altar. Heavy stone slabs.

They turned at the sound. Watching. Something was moving around. Bipedal.

It was dark. The most shadowy part of the shrine. The surrounding walls survived intact.

A shadow grew taller. It shuffled. Footsteps, and a tick-tick-tick knocking on the tiles.

"Is that a person?" Andy whispered. "Is somebody back there? Spying on us?"

Jake was too stunned to think about using his weapon. He observed the shadow.

Gliding.

"It is a person," Andy said. He ducked his head, then walked off quickly to one side.

"Andy," Jake said through his teeth. "Get back here."

Iris couldn't move. The shadow was slim. Not too tall. It moved with confidence in the dark, as if it was familiar with this place. Comfortable being there without a light. Did it have long hair? Was that the flowing shape of a dress? Would Maude have brought dresses to the jungle? Andy disappeared around one of the pillars. He reemerged. Closer to the shadow person.

"Are you Maude Brion?" Andy said in a loud, clear voice. "We come from America. I'm a reporter. I work for the *Arkham Advertiser*. Gerald Hopkins sent a film to me. Of this place."

Jake took Iris's elbow, pulled her behind a rubble pile. "Get himself killed," he muttered.

"Maude? Is that you?" Andy and the shadow stood only a few feet apart.

Iris tugged out of Jake's grasp and ran to Andy. He's only a kid, she thought.

Too young to die.

The darkness parted like a curtain. A green-tinted curtain made of dank, sickly perfumed air. She stood at Andy's side. They were both breathing heavily. The warm air felt thick as cream. It tasted like dead flowers. Funerals. Andy stopped talking; his mouth hanging open.

His face paled.

He stared at the person in front of the altar. Iris stared too.

It wasn't Maude Brion.
It was Galton.

41
A Locked Cabin

Ursula awoke with the worst headache she'd had in years. The last time it was like this, champagne was to blame. It happened after a night at the Miskatonic Museum. Full of disappointments, the gala where she had been prepared to accept the honor of joining the Miskatonic chapter of the Archaeological Institute of America, proved to be a disaster. The biggest risk that night should've been boredom. A museum event populated by the sorts that attend museum events. But no, it was much worse. She hadn't been honored. She'd been insulted. Doubly so. They neglected to induct her, and instead they initiated Ashley Lott in her place. To top it off, she'd had a fabulous discovery, a rare artifact, stolen from her display case during the festivities. Jake managed to smuggle a couple of bottles of contraband champagne into the gathering for a planned celebration with a few colleagues and friends.

She sat up the next morning convinced her skull was about to split. Crying would've been appropriate. But she didn't.

Sitting up in a bunk now, she was experiencing quite the same sensations. Dry mouth. A terrible aftertaste on her tongue. Where was she? It took a minute for the memories – what memories there were – to flood back. The black galley. Drinking peculiar wine poured from a giant ruby.

Then blankness. A chasm without bottom or sides, or apparently, memories.

Ursula did an inventory of her person. Headache aside, she felt normal. Alert. Her back was stiff, but the bed was too soft for her preference. Silky orange bedding pulled neatly at the corners, as if a maid had just made it up. She'd slept on top of the blanket, arms at her sides like a graveyard sculpture. Her outline drawn in wrinkles. The room bounced lightly. The galley was in motion and meeting waves. She felt a touch seasick; her stomach wobbled, perhaps from the drink, but they were moving at a good clip. She finished checking herself. No blood or bruises. Nothing taken. Fully dressed, she still had her boots on. Laced, double-knotted the way she always tied them. The cabin offered no mirror. She was ready to leave.

Ursula got off the bed and went to the cabin door.

Locked.

She tried shaking the handle. Kicking at it. But it wouldn't budge. No one came to see what the racket was about, either. They didn't hear her. Or they didn't care. She sat down on the floor.

She retied her ponytail while looking around for a weapon. Something to break the door handle. The room must've been interior to the ship. There were no windows. For a ship's cabin it was spacious. There was a desk (empty) and a chair (bolted down). She opened the little set of black doors beside the desk and was surprised to find a small library. None of the volumes were written in any language she knew, but the words looked naggingly familiar, as if she'd seen them once before. In another book? The texts were bound in uncommon skins, softer than cowhide.

One of them displayed diagrams of our solar system. But it was a work of fiction, depicting hordes of toad-like beings on wharves, playing flutes and marching through strange villages of windowless cottages and white fungal forests, over hills to a far, fantastic city.

Another contained hand-drawn sketches of gemstones. Prices listed in the margins.

So, her poisoner was perhaps not lying about being a trader of precious stones.

Among his other interests, who knew? The odds they were unwholesome seemed particularly strong. Poisoning, kidnapping, imprisonment. He was no follower of the law.

She checked her belt. Her knife was still there. She hadn't been chained or put in restraints. Well, if he came back, she'd see if he bled ruby red. In the meantime, she worked the tip of her knife along the side of the handle. It had no visible lock. Nowhere to put a key. If it was bolted, then the mechanism was mounted outside, which was, to say the least, unusual. She tried to find the bar by feel, but the gap along the door was tight. She whittled away wood, prying out splinters. She couldn't see anything. The wood was hard. She'd given herself a blister.

There came a knock from the other side.

"Yes?" Ursula said.

"May I come in?"

She readied the knife. Oh, most definitely, she thought. But you will never leave again.

"You may enter," she said.

The door did not open.

"You aren't planning to stab me with your knife, are you?" the voice asked.

"No."

But still, the door did not open. Ursula waited.

"You cannot escape the ship. I want you to know this. Even if you were to wound me and find your way to the deck. Escape is impossible. Attacking me would only result in your being bound and housed in bleaker quarters. You would not like this downgrade, I assure you," he said.

She was certain that the voice talking to her through the door belonged to her poisoner.

"I'm not going to stab you," she said. "Come in already, if you're going to."

He opened the door.

Ursula lunged with her knife, swinging it downward with great force at his chest. Alarmed, her poisoner and kidnapper – who were one and the same – leaned back and barely avoided catching the blade in a vital location. As his good luck, and her bad luck, would have it, the guard of the knife stuck in the hole slashed through his loose garments. Using two hands, he grabbed her wrist and, twisting deftly with his thumb pressed into the joint, he immobilized her hand and caused Ursula to release her grip on the knife, which clattered off. She winced in pain.

"You said you wouldn't stab me," he uttered in amazement. His nostrils flared.

"I'm not good at telling the truth," Ursula said. "You know how that is."

"You're angry about me taking you from your friends. I see. Not everyone can tolerate the wine from my country. I apologize. But it is business. Nothing personal. I'm a merchant."

He did not give her back her arm. But he lessened the pressure, and the pain vanished.

"Let go of my wrist," Ursula said. She tried to stomp his foot. But his shoe, and indeed his whole foot, was oddly short and rounded like a horse's hoof. In any case, she missed.

But he howled, nonetheless. In outrage, it seemed. Her behavior flummoxed him.

"Why do you keep doing this?" the man asked, tossing the swathed humps on his head like a pair of bull's horns. "I am only talking to you. I have no weapon. Yet you resist violently."

"Let me go, then. Take me to the shore and drop me off. I don't wish to be here."

"I can't do that," he said.

"Why not?"

"Because you are, not unlike my finest rubies… promised to a client. My patron."

"Do I understand correctly? I am taken captive. That is clear. And you have sold me?" Offense was too mild a term for what she felt. Outrage. Shock. Disgust. A mix of these.

"In a manner of speaking, yes. Come with me on deck, and I will explain. Aren't you curious? Don't you want to learn the facts of your journey, and with them, your destination?"

Ursula retrieved her knife from the floor and sheathed it.

The merchant was not foolish enough to interfere.

42
Webs

Iris staggered. Andy caught her and helped her stumble to a half-crumbled wall. She trembled but could not tear her eyes away from the man who had come from behind the stone altar. He wore his hair long, swept back like a prince or a wizard, Andy thought, although he'd never met either to his knowledge. The man used a walking staff of striped wood. Purple scars traced over a quarter of his face. One eye was like a steely blue ball rolled in milk. Iris slid off the wall. Andy lowered her gently to the floor of the shrine. He kept his hand between her head and the tiles. The man looked concerned. Andy noticed him clutching at the frayed edges of his cape.

"Is she feeling all right?" the man asked. But he made no move to come closer.

"She's fainted," Andy said.

"Hmm. I've never known her to do that before. It must be a shock to her senses."

"Never known her?" Andy asked, confused.

"Iris is my wife," the man said.

"You're Galton? But she said you were dead," Andy said. Alive! It was a jolt to his system, and he'd never known Galton. He couldn't imagine what Iris was going through. Clearly, she believed Galton was dead and speaking to her in dreams. But he wasn't. All this time he was here in the jungle.

Iris's eyelids fluttered.

"Are you going to help her?" Andy asked her husband.

"She's coming around," Galton said. "Iris is a tough cookie. The air grows thick around the shrine at times. Ah, look." He waved the head of his staff at the forest, the leaves shaking as if his gesture gave them animation. "The others are coming. They were sleeping at the mine."

Galton moved off, smiling. He twirled his cape and called out a cheerful greeting.

"What's he talking about?" Jake crept up to Andy and Iris.

Iris had revived, but she was unable to speak. Jake offered her his canteen.

Andy peeked over the wall. There was a group walking up from another trail in the shade.

"There must be a dozen people. Maybe more. Could he really be Galton?" Andy said.

"It's him," Iris said. Andy didn't think she sounded completely thrilled at the idea her husband had survived. It hasn't sunk in, he thought. Five years mourning a man who isn't dead.

"You must feel as though you're dreaming," Andy said.

"But this is real," she said, gripping his forearm fiercely. "Isn't it?"

Andy nodded. "As real as anything I've ever lived through. Galton must have an amazing story. I must talk to him. What an exclusive." Andy saw Iris watching Galton talk. "After you two catch up, of course. Reunited at last. Say, there's an angle. Our river adventure is turning out to be better than I imagined. Here they come. There's a whole slew of them."

Andy left Iris and Jake inside the shrine and rushed to meet the newcomers. He noticed none of the people who emerged from the forest resembled the indigenous tribespeople he'd observed on this trip. They matched the Portuguese-speaking Brazilian workers from Manaus, dressed in modern clothing, though raggedy and threadbare. A remarkable number of European-looking members made up this ragtag troupe. Pale skins, blue-eyed blonds, freckled redheads; their number was composed entirely of middle-aged and younger men. Where were the women and kids? Andy's heart tripped. Where was Maude Brion? He decided to wait and see.

"Mr Reed! What's the first thing you want the world to know? I need a quote."

"That's *Doctor* Reed," the caped professor replied, spinning around, enjoying the attention. His cape was a patchwork of suns and moons and repaired holes sewn shut. He smirked at Andy. Galton's face was twitching, as if invisible wires tugged at the skin.

"Tell the world… are you ready?" he said, waiting for Andy to get his pencil and pad.

Andy wondered if the man continued to suffer symptoms from his bite.

"Shoot, Dr Reed. I'm ready to go."

The others gathered around the professor, as if they were adoring students he'd invited to attend a lecture on the green lawn of some prestigious university. They hung on his words. "Say to them: your dreams are too small. New dreams will come to burst your minds."

Those gathered around him laughed. They were infused with a secret mirth. Their faces froze in expressions of bliss. It was as if they'd heard the joke before, but the retelling gave them pleasure. Andy wrote down what the professor said. It didn't seem very profound to him. But what did he know?

"Dr Reed, who are these people? How did they get here? Why do you live in the forest?"

Galton tilted his chin toward the rising sun, grimacing. Twitch, twitch.

"These are profound questions, young man. Where am I to begin?" He shuffled his feet.

"How come you didn't you die?" It was Iris asking him. She'd come from the shrine.

"My darling, you are awake." Galton stepped toward her. "I am so happy."

She backed away as one would from a dangerous animal in a pen.

"How? I saw you on the threshold of death. You were raving. Fevered. You couldn't breathe. I watched life leaving your body. There was no coming back from that. I smelled it."

"Behold me now." Galton stepped forward and gathered her in his arms.

Iris recoiled as he embraced her.

"Feel me. My muscles are strong. I am alive, I live. Not dead," he said. "Reborn."

Reluctant at first, she acquiesced. Then she was hugging him back, in tears, finally accepting him. "It is you," she said. "I missed you more than anything. I wanted to die. To be with you."

"I have dreamed of this day. When we would be together again." He kissed her.

"You were in my dreams... I dreamed we talked, but I never knew if it was really true..."

"Everything is true here." Galton swept his arm out wide. "These are the ones who saved me. The devotees of the Spider Queen. They found me in our camp. Like you remember, I was badly off. They had medicine. Antidote for the toxin coursing in my veins. They knew a cure."

The devotees ducked their heads modestly. Reverently, they folded their hands and bowed at Galton, murmuring praise, denying their role in saving his life. Andy heard American English, Spanish, and Italian accents. He wasn't good with languages. Hadn't spent any significant time outside of Arkham. But he knew the sounds of the immigrants who lived there. Nothing fits, he thought. How did these people end up together in the most remote wilderness in the world? And they just happened upon Galton dying in his hammock? It strained credulity.

The hot sunlight burned off the last traces of fog.

As the mists evaporated, the gauzy aura surrounding the shrine remained in place.

They're webs, Andy realized. He wished again for a camera.

The shrine was covered in spiderwebs. Like spun glass they glittered. Dew diamonds dripped from their cords. Beautiful, so delicate in appearance, but strong, designed with purpose, webs served both as shelter and a trap for prey. Time and rainforest weather eroded this temple. But the spiders rebuilt it. Through half-closed eyes, he saw the silent glorious wholeness.

"Where is Maude Brion?" Andy asked. "Is she here? Because that would take the cake."

Galton curled his arm around Iris's waist. She was still in a daze, but she stayed by Galton's side.

"Maude is at the mine. She is tending to the Queen," he said. "You'll meet her soon."

"The Spider Queen is here?" Andy said. "Gosh, I mean, that's the cat's meow."

The devotees dropped to their knees and began to chant a low, susurrating, insect hum.

"The Queen is sacred. All knees bend at the mention of her name," Galton said.

Then he knelt too. His cape spread out like a pair of velvet wings as he pulled Iris down.

What do I do? Andy wondered. He'd gone from feeling about as great as he ever had to getting a bad case of the heebie-jeebies. Nothing felt right. Stand or kneel? He didn't want to cause any offense. But he wasn't a worshipper of any old rainforest goddess. Frankly, the sight of the shrine enshrouded in thousands, maybe millions, of webs, had him creeped out. It reminded him of the bundles hanging from the treetops. The corpses. Where were all those spiders? Were they venomous? What did they eat? Thinking about them, he felt itchy all over. Hey, this was the story of a lifetime, but did he need to kneel for it? *I'm out of my element.*

He looked to Jake's example for the proper etiquette, but Jake was nowhere to be found.

43
Goldmine

While Andy was busy interviewing Galton, Jake took the opportunity to follow another trail leading from the back of the shrine complex. All his inner alarm bells were ringing. Galton had the air of a snake oil salesman who'd fallen for his own con game. As Jake suspected, the trails intersected throughout the site. Soon he was on the same track the devotees had come up. He spotted them at the crest of the hill, backlit by the morning sun streaming through the trees. They were singing or praying. Jake kept low and took the track down. It was more rock than mud, and planks were laid over the wettest spots to give surer footing. They'd hacked a green tunnel through the bush.

He wanted to know where they'd come up from. Galton had mentioned a mine.

A goldmine? Oscar Hurley would find that too perfect. Jake hadn't spotted any gold yet.

The path descended the slope. The canopy was thicker here, the jungle floor dark as nightfall. But the trail was easy to follow. It revealed signs of heavy daily traffic.

Ahead of him the track climbed again. It had to. Because there was a cliff rising like a plateau amid the lush landscape. That's where the mine must be, he thought. He heard the rush of water, the thunderous sound of a falling stream beating against rocks and a pool. There it was, winking at him through the trees. Shiny water. Emerging from the bush tunnel, at the pool's edge, he saw bright fish darting in the shallows, foam afloat on the surface, eddies and swirls; the water ran clear. Those must've been logs resting at the bottom in a jumble like bones. Jars, broken relics, and faces glaring up at him like drowned swimmers. Sculpted humans or gods, he couldn't tell which, but the same color stone used at the shrine. This must be their garbage dump.

A waterfall sent up a spray drifting on the breeze, enveloping him.

It felt good. Refreshing in the sticky heat. He closed his eyes, relishing its coolness. When he opened them again, he studied the path, how it terminated and fanned out into an angular clearing, the earth trampled flat, stubby tree stumps showing where a section of forest had been cut, a regular campsite. Lean-tos, hammocks, sleeping rolls spread on the ground. A firepit. Jake got the prickly sensation he was being watched. He looked for pairs of eyes. The forest seemed everywhere alive here. Not dead quiet as before on the river. Teeming. He heard birds, saw their vivid feathers flitting in the treetops. And monkeys, always curious, hopped branch to branch, lowering themselves to check him out. Maybe they were the ones making him feel seen. They screeched and hollered. Underneath the jungle noise, he detected something else. Rhythmic, almost mechanical-sounding, a click-whir that fluttered continuously.

It was coming from the rock wall near the waterfall. He went to see. It was a compulsion.

Explore. Discover. Curiosity was essential to him. As a kid he was the one to go first.

It was a mine.

Tool marks evident on the rocks, a hump of rubble piled nearby. Chunky wood beams framed the entry like the door to a subterranean dungeon. Dragon's lair. Sealed off, apparently. Crisscrossed boards nailed over the mouth. Heavy stones dug up, levered from the ground, and rolled in front of the opening. Grooves, scuff marks scarred the soft soil. This plugging of the access was a recent addition. Some of it at least. They really wanted to keep people out. Finger paintings covered the face of the rock around the opening. The boards and the bigger boulders had them too. A manic, crude graffiti of nonsense words – at least he could make no sense of the scribblings. The images were easier to interpret. Spiders, slathered in purple and blue, daubs of ocher and white. Red was the dominant color. But not for the spider paintings. Red was for humans. Stick figures. It didn't take an expert archaeologist – although Jake qualified – to figure out what the paintings depicted. The human stick figures were dead. Or dying. They stretched out under the spiders' long jointed legs, torn apart, or lay stacked like cordwood. Mostly they were bundled up in hanging sacks, waiting to be devoured. Red droplets drizzled everywhere. The strange thing was it didn't look like a scene of gruesome horror. This wasn't a massacre.

Not from the point of view of the artists who drew it.

It was a celebration.

A spider-killing-humans party. Everybody invited. The mural over the mine entrance captured an atmosphere of chaotic glee. Had this happened? Jake wondered. His stomach was roiled by the scene. Was this a record of the past? Or future yet to come?

Whir-click, whir-click.

That fluttering sound was louder here. Was it from inside the mine?

Jake crawled over the rocks to the nailed boards. They were from the rubber station up the hill. He saw torn corners of maps still pinned to the wood. What was the purpose of having a goldmine if you were going to shutter it? Jake put his ear to the panels.

Listening.

Nothing.

Whir-click, whir-click, whir-click.

It was coming from behind him. The sound bounced off the wood. But its source...

He turned around and saw her then.

Shorter than he imagined she would be. Insectile legs. He saw a cold black eye glittering in the leaves. A tuft of dark hairs. She was good at keeping still, he'd give her that. It took a real set of nerves to sit there and watch as a stranger walked down the trail, exploring, as he had done. To know he was looking for something. Maybe her? And to do nothing but roll film.

That's what she was doing, he realized. She was filming him.

"Maude Brion, I presume," Jake said.

The fluttering *whir-click* stopped abruptly. The wooden bug legs of the camera tripod had blended in with the stems and vines. That glittering black eye was the lens of a Bell & Howell.

It swiveled.

The petite woman behind the camera stepped out where he could see her.

"I'm Maude. Who're you?" she said.

She had brown curly hair, brown eyes, lots of freckles. A clean-cut jawline set hard.

"Jake Williams." He couldn't believe they'd found her alive. Even in the rough and tumble of the Amazon she looked like a star. He felt like he was the one who needed a bath and a shave.

"Never heard of you. You in pictures?" She braced her hands on her hips, legs apart.

"Now I am. You were shooting me that whole time, right? Since I showed on the trail."

"I thought you might be important. Are you?"

"I don't think of myself that way," Jake said.

"Too bad. Everybody ought to think they're important. Why are you here?"

"I came looking for you," he said.

"Mission accomplished. Here I am. You'd better step away from the gateway. The mine."

"Why?" he asked, glancing over his shoulder.

"I'll tell you later. After we're acquainted. Let's go back first. You said you're here looking for me. Why? Doesn't make sense. How'd you find me? I'm not even sure where I am."

She looks robust, Jake thought. Her speech is quick; she's even impatient with me.

"Which do you want first, the why or the how?"

"You pick."

"Hopkins sent a film reel to Arkham–" Jake started to say.

"Hopkins? My Hopkins? Is he here? I thought he was dead. Drowned in the river."

"I'm afraid he is dead. But only yesterday. Before that, weeks ago, he mailed a film canister from Manaus to a newspaper in Arkham, and well, long story short, somebody saw the film and got curious. The 'how' is a longer story. There's an expedition out to find you. We're here. I'm not alone. The rest of my party, most of them, are up at the shrine with Galton."

Maude's expression grew stern. "That's my film. Hopkins had no right to mail it to anybody. He is – was – a great cameraman. But he's lousy at business. You say he's dead? What happened? I liked that guy. He didn't drown, made it as far as Manaus, but then died anyway?"

"A giant spider killed him," Jake said. "I saw it happen."

She had no quick reply to that. Whatever she was feeling she kept it private.

"You said, 'most of them'. Did others in your party die? Like Hopkins did?"

"No. My friend, our leader, Ursula Downs – I think she got kidnapped by a black ship."

"Oh, one of those. I know about the black ships. You're right. Your friend has been kidnapped. Those guys with the funny hats? The ones on the boats selling rubies? Men of Leng, they're called. They traffic in more than rocks and gold coins. Slavers. We were hiding from them yesterday. We used to have triple the number of people living here at the shrine until they started raiding us. Twice they took folks. They roped in the gullible ones down at the lagoon. Second time they came ashore at twilight and tried to surprise us. They got a surprise too. We had us a little jungle tussle. But a few more of our people got themselves taken. You didn't see the rowers, did you?" She waited for him to answer. Expectant. A curious energy churned in her.

"I didn't see anyone at all," Jake said. "The black galley looked abandoned."

His worst worries about Ursula were more than confirmed. She was in the hands of the lowest kind of culprits. The desire to locate her was more urgent than ever.

"Nobody sees the rowers. I'd love to catch them with my camera. Though I suppose I've already shot enough footage to last four or five pictures. Hopkins told you I needed rescuing?"

"Hopkins didn't say much that made sense. He seemed… imaginative. And rather lost."

"That's Hopkins for you. I hate to hear he met a bad end. I'll miss him. But I thought he was dead already, so it's not like I haven't processed things. Considering the matter of my guilt."

Jake felt surprised. "Your guilt?"

"I forced him to come here. He wasn't keen on the idea. We ran into troubles."

She gazed off, and finally came close enough to extend her hand.

Jake shook it. Firm, dry. Never broke eye contact. She pulled him down, inches from her.

"Hopkins ever mention moon beasts?" Her hair stood tall, a frizzy nest in the humidity.

"Moon beasts? No," he said. "He told our reporter about gugs, ghasts, and, ah, ghouls."

"No moon beasts. Huh. Maybe it's better not to know." Maude strode back to her camera.

"So, you're a film star." Jake decided not to ask about moon beasts for now. He had too many things to sort already.

"Film director. Was a star. Small one. Didn't take to it. Stand here. Say this, do that. I like giving orders. Set up my own shots. Never got very far listening to what other people said."

She was finished shooting. She folded the tripod, carrying the camera under a lean-to.

"I need your help," Jake said.

She laughed. "My help? Jake, I'm in no position to help anybody on God's green earth."

"My friend who was taken by the Men of Leng–"

"Nothing we can do for her, I'm afraid." Maude shook her head. "Forget about it."

"Ursula can take care of herself. She's familiar with danger. And she knows something about Leng," Jake said. "What's confusing is that Leng is supposed to be on the other side of the world. In

China. Or Tibet. She saw these Leng tablets in the Himalayas. It's a legendary place."

"She visited the Himalayas? I'd love to go there someday. This much I can tell you. Legend or not, Men of Leng are on that boat. I don't know where it goes or how it gets there. But Leng is one of the stops. Funny place, I bet. The black boat takes people. It never brings anybody back." She toweled off her Bell & Howell. "This is a 2709," she said, proudly. "Same as Chaplin uses. I could've bought a nice house with what it cost. The jungle's hell on equipment. Hell on everything and everyone. The damp heat – it's bad for cinematic machinery, let me tell you. And celluloid film is like gasoline. I can't keep it anywhere near the firepit. If it's not water, it's fire."

"I only want to know how to follow the black galley," Jake said.

"Go to sleep," Maude said.

Jake frowned. "What does sleep have to do with pursuing a ship. Where's it going?"

"You wouldn't believe me if I told you."

He was frustrated with her dodging answers. He'd demand straight talk. No more games.

Voices. An echo filled the grotto of wet rocks around the waterfall. It was Galton and the devotees of the Spider Queen marching down the path. Andy and Iris walked with them.

"There's our missing visitor," Galton shouted, jovially. He jabbed his staff in the air. "I told you he wouldn't get far. Maude has snared him." He chuckled and drove the group forward like a sheepdog. "You've discovered my treasure. I'll have no choice but to kill you now."

"Maude Brion! Holy Moly! Today is one for the books. My book. I need to talk to you, Miss Brion. You're the reason we're down here. I'm your biggest fan, Andy Van Nortwick, of the *Arkham*

Advertiser." Andy shouldered through the loitering devotees and stuck out his hand.

Maude shook it. "I love to meet a fan. Never had one stalk me this far afield."

"We haven't been formally introduced," Jake said to Galton, who he disliked immediately. The feeling came by instinct more than anything. Jake trusted his instincts.

"You are Jake Williams. You come from Arkham. Your partner is Ursula Downs who is missing. Stolen by the hoodlums in the black ships." Galton split off from his clan. "You are loyal to a fault. Brave. There is no doubt. But leadership is new to you. How am I doing?"

Jake said, "On target." The presumption of the resurrected anthropologist goaded him.

"Iris told me all about you."

"I'd have thought you had more pressing things to talk about. After being separated."

Jake gritted his teeth. Whatever skepticism he felt toward Iris went double for her husband. He gave off charlatan vibrations; his bravura oozed chicanery.

"We picked up where we left off. It is as though we've never been apart."

"How charming," Jake said.

"We are two of the lucky ones. Joined at the heart," Galton said.

With his left hand he covered his breast, and with his other hand he touched his wife.

44
Upright Worms

It watched through the waterfall. The man who trapped it reached out for his mate.

It hated the man and his voice and his sorcerous trickery. Lured here. She'd been lured here to this place, this crack behind the waterfall, thinking it was a perfect place for what she had to do. Her time was coming, the time to lay her future. Her little ones. He tricked her. Lured her here and made her senses confused. It was a trap. He forced her to sleep. She fought it until she couldn't. When she woke again, the wood blocked her in. They put something against the wood outside. She couldn't push her way out. Trapped. She was angry. But the crack behind the waterfall was real, and she put her eyes to it. She would kill this man. Kill all of them. They put her here. They tried to control her. Stupid creatures. She would eat them. They would feed her. Her and her babies. She would drink their juice, chew them. Grind their bones and suck the sweet red marrow. They were no match, no rival. Look how many of them it took to snare her. Without his magic, what was he? She knew bigger magic. Gods laugh at the magic men do. Food for the gods they are and no more.

What fools they were. This man especially. He was dumber than a moth. Slower.

That was why she was so angry. To be tricked by a fool. She hated him.

With her fangs she picked the loose rocks lining the crack under the waterfall. Hard rocks. But she could make them move. Jiggling. With patience and time, she'd free herself. She could squeeze through anything. So flat. So clever. How did they think she got here, to this world?

Through a crack.

A tiny gap.

She was curious and hungry and an explorer by her nature. She crawled in.

To see what she might see. No one led her here. She led herself. Alone.

Then the man with the voice that slammed into her head – unwanted – thought he did it on his own. Imagine that. On his *own*. The gods had little use for such as this. He was a morsel. Amusing for a short while, then not. What did he spin? Did he make little ones? Could he hunt or show patience and make himself still as stone? Could he creep in the night like a sigh of wind?

What good was he? This mind intruder. This annoyance. This small, tedious, weak man.

He was food. Simple, slow. Food stuck onto bones like skewers. Worm-soft.

So proud it could walk. It couldn't even fly or hop! It had no shell to break. Nothing!

She loosened another avalanche of gravel. It slid down between her legs, under her. There was a small mound growing there already. She pressed one of her eyes tight to the crack.

Did they notice? Did they hear her coming?

Did they?

The clumsy bags of pulp and juice waddled up the hill making noise. Upright worms.

See the food walk! Listen to the racket they make as they go. Begging to be eaten.

With her fangs she worked the rocks loose.

One by one.

45
Switcheroo

"You say it's a warship? For what reasons do you draw this conclusion?" Ashley Lott was having trouble keeping his nondominant eye closed while peering through the sniper's scope. They'd been wandering, looking for Marcos's paddleboat for forever, it seemed. He was fatigued. Now they finally saw a boat. Only to discover it was not the one they wanted. Disappointment!

"I draw this conclusion by the evil look of her and the fact she's bearing down on us at a rate of speed that'll split us in two," Toothpick said in his inimitable laconic style.

"What do you suggest we do?" Ashley didn't like the sound of *split us in two*.

"Take evasive action." Toothpick had reclaimed his sniper rifle and continued his watch.

"By all means evade, then." Ashley backed away from the bow, crying out, "Evade!"

Swiftly, they drew up parallel to the nearest bank. The curious soldiers of fortune lined the deck to observe the sleek black galley ripping past them, heading in the opposite direction. Their guns were at the ready. They even had a cannon, about which they had neglected to inform Ashley. But he was comforted to see it pointed at the marauding vessel that had appeared out of nowhere.

"She's mighty peculiar," Toothpick said. "Want me to take a potshot at her?"

He put his sights on the mass of the ship.

Ashley was aghast at the suggestion. "No! She's none of our business. We don't need distractions. We're having an infernally hard time finding that rust bucket paddleboat. Who knew there were so many tributaries? Besides, why stir up a wasp's nest? They might be friendlies for all we know."

"They ain't friendlies." Toothpick spit his trademark pacifier into the water.

He replaced it with a fresh-from-the-box duplicate.

The steamboat rocked in the wake of the galley. Ashley clamped his hand on the rail.

"They row awfully well, don't they?" he said.

"Uh huh." Toothpick traced the ship departing in the purple dusk. "Whoa. Looky there."

Ashley stared, but the channel was harboring too many shadows, and his eyesight wasn't what it used to be. In his younger days he could make out the prettiest girls from a huge distance.

"Is that two people at the stern?" he said, craning.

"Yep. And one of them you know."

"Give me the gun tube before it's too late," Ashley said. "Who is it? Who?"

He pressed the rifle stock to his cheek.

"I can't see the ship at all," he complained.

Toothpick lifted the end of the rifle higher.

Ashley felt his mouth go dry as a mummy's nose. "It can't be. Is this switcheroo supposed to throw us off the scent? That's Ursula! Follow her immediately, Toothpick."

"We can't catch up. They're too speedy. She's practically flying."

"They'll beat us to wherever it is they're going! What if she already has the Spider Queen on board? Not to mention untold treasure. Gold! She might have a bellyful of riches in her hold."

He raised the rifle as if he was preparing to throw it overboard in a fit of vexation.

"Don't. You'll dive for it. Remember?"

Ashley passed the weapon to its owner. Instead, he tossed his sun umbrella into the river. As if it were the carcass of a strangled bird, it was borne away by the current. "I don't think of her as Damned Miss Downs for nothing. Oh, she's a perfidious opponent." An idea sprung into Ashley's suggestible mind. "Two can play at that game. Fire the cannon. Do it, Toothpick. We may not be able to get close enough to board her. Or even to follow on her heels. But she will know that she has awakened our fury!"

"I thought we were supposed to be trailing her quietly. So she doesn't know we're here."

"I don't care. Fire, fire, fire away!"

46
A Toast

They were standing off the port side, in the stern and out of the wind, when Ursula noticed through the blur of passing landscape the unmistakable shape of a steamboat tucked under the eaves of the trees overhanging the river. There were men on deck aiming rifles and pistols.

"Who are they?" she asked the ruby merchant.

"It doesn't matter. At our speeds, it is as if we travel on another, higher plane."

He smirked, too smugly for Ursula's taste, and rather prematurely, as it turned out.

But in the moment, he continued. "A merchant trades in many things. We do not choose the masters we serve. More often they choose us. It is their appetites we must feed. Believe me, it is a burdensome chore. I am but a link in a long chain, a cog in a wheel. A pawn, not a king."

Ursula leaned out past the edge. The merchant didn't try to stop her. Diving overboard at their tremendous rate of travel would've broken her body *before* she drowned. She had never been aboard a ship that sailed so fast. It was unnatural, especially for one powered by humans.

She mentioned this.

"Who says we are powered by humans?" He leered at her. Massaging his whiskers.

"The rowers. Are they not men like you?"

"Like me?" he laughed. "I cannot comment. My masters would not like me talking."

He brought up the subject of his masters repeatedly. It irked Ursula. He talked of his bosses as if their existence justified any action he took, however immoral or unjust.

"That's no excuse," she said. "Blaming those above you for what you do. *You* drugged me. I would like to see you hanged by your fat neck. Your small feet kicking until they stop."

He peered at his shoes, but only briefly. "Look what a terrible fight you put up when your blood is clean. I did it as a matter of easing tension. Simplification. We often drug captures. It's common practice. There are older, more barbaric means. Take my word when I tell you this was better for all parties. Chipped rubies offend the eye. I wanted to keep you safe and undamaged." He glanced at her knife in its scabbard. "My own self too. I had little choice in the matter. Well, it's of no use persuading you that my reasons for last night were sound. All is in the past now."

Ursula scoffed. "More excuses. I reject them."

"But it's true. Plans to obtain other… goods… proved difficult. My day had been frustrating and long. Time wasted. Where do the hours go? Then you showed up. You came to *me*. I took it as an omen. A sign of better fortunes to come. That's a compliment, by the way."

"You lost your slaves? And you nabbed me instead, as a consolation prize? No thanks."

"What kind of prize will you turn out to be, I wonder. A cursed one? Not my problem."

As soon as he made this comment, there came the roar of a cannon. The cannon ball, launched with a fiery belch of smoke from the steamboat, snapped the rearmost mast of the galley and ruptured through a corner of the midnight deck boards into the mysterious hollows below, causing the merchant to react violently. Ursula thought of leaping off the galley in the chaos. But the risk was too great. The odds of injury or death too high. The merchant stalked about, clopping on the deck boards. He flushed, his knuckles bulging. "Oh, they have made a fatal error. Those men we passed. My masters will not tolerate such open hostility." The black galley slowed. The rowers lifted their paddles. "See? What did I tell you?"

With great skill the unseen drivers of the ebon vessel reversed direction.

"We'd better go to the cabin," he said. "There are bound to be bullets."

He was correct.

The flying bullets did nothing to discourage the galley rowers from their lethal goal.

Ursula, confined belowdecks with the merchant, didn't see what happened. However, she felt the sudden impact. Heard the terrible screech of metal and an explosion of wood shattering.

The screams of men also penetrated the hull.

"They're dead idiots now," the merchant said, shaking his head. "For what? A fireworks display? My masters are cruel. Do you understand what I protect you from? They show no mercy. Their decisions are unappealable. They relish doling out harsh punishment. Would you like a drink? I'm having one." He produced a ruddy bottle from the folds of his silks.

"You're kidding, right?" Ursula tapped her knife.

"I drink alone." He sipped from the uncorked ruby. "To the dead cannoneers."

He raised the hollow, multifaceted gem. In the lamplight his hand and face turned bloody.

She pictured in her mind the wreckage in their wake and did not join him in his toast.

47

Green Forever

Galton and his group were eager to give the new arrivals a tour around the shrine complex. They were proud of their hard work, sprucing up the tiles and inscriptions, hauling out the debris – dried brown plants, bones – trimming back the constant encroachment of living forest.

"Pruned within reason," an Englishman named Bradley said, dusting a stone with a rag. "The jungle's not our enemy. Life-giver to multitudes. The Queen's chosen home."

"The Spider Queen visits the shrine?" Andy asked. "Does she approve?"

"I should hope so," Bradley said gruffly.

"You've seen her then? She comes here on a regular basis, eh? Is it every night?" Andy wanted to know how long he was expected to wait to catch a glimpse of a legend. A goddess. None of her devotees seemed frightened of her.

"Would you ask a Catholic priest if God visits his church?" Galton said. He was a teacher prodding his student to think along new lines. Instructive in manner, charitable in the sharing of his bountiful wisdom.

"I might," Andy said. "I've seen some things that make me

question who's running the show. Are we weak, erring creatures in the hands of an angry god? Or are we loved? I believe in the supernatural. But is that only a term we use to explain events we don't yet understand?"

"Ah, you're getting somewhere. Why do we presume we're smarter than our ancestors? Religion crops up in every garden of this paradisical planet. Do Europeans have the market cornered on spirituality? I think not. There's more spirit evident in a wild acre of the Amazon than in the whole of so-called civilized continents." Galton picked a red, cherry-sized fruit from a nearby bush and pierced its skin with his teeth. He sucked out the juice. "Want to try one?"

Andy said, "What's it called?"

"Camu-camu." Galton plucked one and tossed it to him.

Andy bit. His lips puckered. "Ugh… could use a little sugar," he said.

"You get used to it. Life isn't meant to be sweet."

"Sometimes it is, darling," Iris said. She'd remained close to Galton as they roamed the site. That was to be expected, Andy thought. He'd been lost, and now he was found. Alive and well. Living in a place where she'd left him for dead. It must've been like visiting a cemetery and seeing your loved ones having a picnic on the gravestones. She hadn't said much. Soaking in the atmosphere. Adjusting her reality to the newfound circumstances, he guessed.

"Do you have a bigger boat I might use?" Jake asked. He'd grown increasingly impatient with the group's slow response to forming a search party. They had to go after Ursula's kidnappers. Uneasy, fidgety, he was ready to set off on his own.

Andy kept him within sight. He didn't want him going before they talked.

"The boats are smashed. No good," said the gray-haired Italian.

A chemist from Rome with a broad face and an intense stare. "After Hopkins go, he take the last good boat we have."

"Didn't you come here in a paddleboat, Maude? What happened to it?" Jake said.

"There was a bad storm. Our paddleboat rests at the bottom of the lagoon, whatever hasn't washed away in the current. We dragged our dugouts to higher ground, but the Men of Leng chopped holes in them. They ended up firewood." She had tagged along with Jake.

"I'll go in our canoe, then," Jake said.

Andy lingered nearby in a spot of shade. Galton and the others reclined in the shrine.

Maude pulled Jake aside. "I know she's your friend. But it's really no use. I'm sorry."

Andy was close enough he could hear their conversation. He never felt guilty about eavesdropping. What journalist does? He flicked his eyes on a frustrated Jake.

"I can't give up. I must do something. I'd love to explore this discovery and meet the so-called Spider Queen. But I can't. Not with Ursula in danger. Do you have any food I can take?"

"Certainly, we'll pack a crate. Federico!" she called to the Italian, "Are there any more of those crabs we ate last night? What about figs? The salted fish, too. And nuts."

Federico went to fetch the leftovers.

"At least you won't starve," she said to Jake.

He said, "Maude, come with me. You must be eager to get away. Galton obviously oversees things. Hasn't that been difficult?" Jake was being careful, reading her attitude. Andy could see how difficult it was for them to talk here in the open, so close to Galton and the others. It was a dicey situation. But going off to hide would look worse and raise more suspicion.

"Galton has Iris now. That might make things better," she said.

"You're the only woman in this camp," Jake said. "Were there others?"

"The Queen protects her own," Maude said. "She keeps her favorites. We accept that."

"I've seen what the Queen does. On the tributary, we paddled through a hanging garden of web bundles. Dozens of dead bodies. Did they all come from this plantation?"

Maude shook her head. "I don't know. It's been confusing for me since I arrived. My mind… I don't sleep well. Hopkins said we were being poisoned. He didn't get along with Galton. I don't know. Galton has survived out here for years. He adapted. But there's something wrong…" She walked with Jake away from the shrine complex, toward the old plantation buildings. No one stopped them. But Galton was watching. Andy trailed after them, pretending to gaze at the shrine from afar. He ducked into the trees, the shadows.

"Where are you two going?" Galton said. "I heard a jaguar growl this morning."

"I've got my rifle," Jake said, tapping the gun slung over his shoulder.

"We're looking at the river," Maude said. "Jake's worried about the Men of Leng."

"Those jackals," Galton said. "Fire a shot in the air if you see any ships."

Galton waved his fingers and went back to his discourse with the devotees.

Jake moved off to the forest trail; the sunken rails stuck up like a pair of thrusting horns. He and Maude passed into the ghost plantation. Andy kept following. It was eerie. The smell of death hung over the place. The trail to the river was right there. They started going down.

Maude glanced backward, trying to conceal her worry. She didn't see Andy. He didn't want to run and startle them, or to draw any more attention from Galton. After they'd descended a few steps, Jake paused. He put his hands lightly on Maude's shoulders.

Andy spied them through the trees.

They weren't too far off. Their words were faint but intelligible.

"Galton's not concerned about the Men of Leng," Jake said. "Or a jaguar. Will he let me leave?"

"I don't know. Probably. He's unpredictable." She turned to look again. Squinting.

Andy lifted his hand. But he was too slow. She was facing Jake.

"Why have you stayed?" Jake said to her. "You must've shot all the film you needed."

Maude peered at the horizon through a gap overlooking the water. Andy looked there too. Under a blaze of sun, the green treetops were like broccoli heads, shades of green varied from chartreuse to emerald to muddy crocodile. The green went on and on, endless. A green forever. She shrugged and said something to Jake that Andy couldn't quite hear. Andy stared down, trying to decide where to put his foot on his next step. The leaves were slippery, the ground steep. He reached up, grabbing a branch to steady himself.

Maude's voice rose. "You're sure Hopkins is dead? The spider. You saw her?"

"With my own eyes. Was Hopkins right about Galton? What have you seen, Maude?"

At that moment, the branch Andy was holding cracked. It came loose in his hand. He was rolling, flat on his backside, sliding in a rush of leaves and mud. Scrabbling for a handhold.

"Andy?" Jake caught him by the collar. Saving him from a rough tumble downhill.

"Sorry, I–"

"Were you listening to our conversation?" Maude said, flustered.

"Guilty as charged," Andy admitted. "I'm nosy, I know. I had the best intentions. I need to talk to you. You're taking off without me. What can I do with Galton here? Listen, I've got a bad feeling. It's getting worse after what I heard you say. What's going on? They're crazy, aren't they? That look in their eyes. Glassy, far-off. Like they're drunk or hypnotized. I don't know about you, Maude. You might be different. But I've got to be honest. I don't want to stay here one more minute. If you're leaving, take me. Iris won't split without Galton. I'm ready to vamoose. I've got enough to write about." Andy brushed the leaves out of his hair. "Spiders!"

"They're only leaves," Maude said, as she picked a stem from the top of his head.

"No. Down there. Climbing the path. There must be thousands of them. Look!"

Andy turned Maude around.

They both screamed.

48
River of Spiders

Jake raised the rifle. It was futile. Bullets would be no good. Andy had been right, there were thousands, maybe millions, of spiders of every species. The largest species were the easiest to spot – Goliaths, tarantulas, giant fishing and banana spiders – all crawling up the trail from the river. It looked like water flowing backward uphill, a river of spiders rising, flooding the track.

"Run," Jake said.

"Go back to the shrine," Maude added. "Watch your step. Be careful not to trip."

Andy grappled with a vine. It rebounded, nearly flinging him into a freefall.

Maude grabbed him by the belt. His arms spiraled in the air. She pulled him to safety.

Jake took hold of him too, then slingshotted the reporter forward to the front of the trio. Andy hugged the roots exposed on the hillside. His chin laid in the mud. He breathed wet earth.

"Don't stop. They're faster than they look," Jake said.

Andy scrambled, fighting the slippery ground. Clawing the soil. Throwing back clods.

Maude mounted past him.

"C'mon," she said. "Keep going."

Andy tore up a handful of slick pipe-thin stems, stripping them of their leaves. With his other hand he clung to the snarls of a thorny shrub, ignoring the punctures afflicting his palms and fingers. Blood added to the greasy instability of his grip. But he was stubborn. Kicking out footholds from the sloppy reddish clay. Pushing with his legs, he ascended. Clambering as he grimaced. He chanced another look at the progress of the spiders. They seemed much closer.

"I'll try to slow them down," Jake said.

"How?" Andy called out as he topped the steep ridge.

It was a decent question. If Jake managed to fell a tree, the spiders would climb over it. He didn't have fire, or any means to start one. Even if he did, there wouldn't be enough time. The spiders were advancing. Lumpen nut browns and tans, soft as suede, covered in fine hairs that sparkled like sharp glass slivers as they threaded through patches of sunlight. Their legs rising and falling like mechanized twigs. The combined effect of their movement made him think his eyes were playing tricks on him. A jittery mass proceeding as if it were controlled by a single intelligence, and a malevolent one. They made no sound. If he'd had his back to them, they'd have been on top of him before he knew anything was wrong. An army of spiders burying him alive. Biting him, injecting their venom. A single stinging bite from a tarantula wasn't typically fatal. But dozens of fangs sinking into your flesh? Sheer panic might be enough to induce a heart attack. What if they filled your mouth and eyes? You'd swell like a poison-filled pumpkin. There were more dangerous species in the mix. Jake didn't have a chance to identify all his pursuers. The onslaught marched ahead with a dogged, terrible consistency.

Fear made him cancel his plans for slowing the surging torrent of arachnids.

Fear propelled him toward the plantation.

The rifle banged against his side as he ran. He tossed it into the roofless main building.

Maude splashed through the flooded rail trackway ahead. Andy was right behind her.

Then Jake noticed the forest moving on both sides of them. Plants laying down as if unseen hands pushed them. Bushes quivered. Grasses flattened. The narrow limbs of young trees bent over until they bowed and finally touched the ground. Vines swaying like clock pendulums.

Every one of them covered in spiders. Overrun. Infested.

They weren't only coming up the river trail. Spiders surrounded the abandoned plantation. Had they always been out there? This whole time waiting for a signal. A call to attack.

Jake hit the muddied waters between the rails. Boots pummeling the stagnant pool. His ankle twisted. He fell hard. Fetid brown water gushed into his stunned open mouth, choking him. It tasted like metal and sulfur. He spit it out. His hands sunk past the wrists in the sucking mud at the bottom. He yanked his right fist out, only to have his left arm push deeper down in the muck.

"Gah."

He shook his head to clear the slime from his eyes. His hands, once freed, flung away the sludge. But it was as if he wore a pair of heavy, sticky, waste-covered gloves. On his knees in the water, gasping, he was able to see well enough to observe the spiders on either side closing ranks, like a pair of hairy brown pincers. They'd cut him off from the others.

From the shelter of the Spider Queen's shrine.

He saw them now in the treetops.

Dropping down on threads of silk. Lowering themselves methodically. Above him, their numbers were too great to count. At his back, they crested the slope, spreading out.

Quick as a wildfire.

Silent and lethal.

He got to his feet.

And fell.

A breath-stealing jolt of pain. His twisted ankle. Sprained. Maybe broken. He couldn't put any weight on it. He rolled off the submerged rail line, an iron bar digging into his spine. He began crawling on his knees and elbows. Spiders hit the ground around him. *Tap-tap-tap.* Soft, grass-cushioned thumps, like ripe fruit falling. He tried not to look. Keeping his eyes low. Fixed. Focused straight ahead of him. Where the pincers closed. The fastest skitterers already meeting up. Spiders swinging on glassy cords they spun, wiggling ornaments descending, descending…

A tickle on his neck. Gentle pressure, like baby fingers, pressing at the back of his shirt. He reached around and felt the investigative *pit-pat* of two poking, hairy legs. He flicked the spider off. A tarantula. He saw it land on its back in the grass. Squirming. They were riding on the backs of his legs now. He didn't need to see. It was enough to feel them. Inching along.

No one back home will ever believe it, he thought. Giddy with adrenaline. Past his fear. Not feeling anything like acceptance of his own fate, at least not yet. But knowing his death was in the offing. His brain caught in a kind of limbo, some light-headed state between the realization he was going to die and the event itself. A man on a precipice, already falling over the edge.

His heart was like a spider now, skipping inside his chest.

Who am I kidding? No one back home will ever hear what happened to me. I'll be a skeleton picked clean on the jungle floor.

My bones overgrown, washed in the rains, eaten by the mud. Earth-devoured.

Jake shut his eyes. Waiting for it.

But he kept crawling too.

A small spider raced across his forehead. Another – bigger – sat contented on his cheek.

He'd crawl until they forced him to stop.

Maybe he'd die quickly. Shock. Venom overload. Soon he'd know. It wouldn't be good.

"Jake! Here. Take this."

Jake looked up. The fat spider on his cheek stretched a furry leg across his eye socket.

But in his other eye he saw the end of a stick.

A striped walking staff.

He grasped it. "I can't stand. My ankle's sprained," he said.

Galton carefully lifted the spider off his face and placed it on the ground. He helped Jake into an upright position. Tenderly, smoothly, he removed the spiders, one by one, from Jake's body. Then he threw Jake's arm over his shoulder, taking the weight off Jake's twisted foot.

They walked together.

Jake was amazed to see the sea of spiders dividing ahead of them, wandering nimbly off the trail, making a clear path for them leading to the shrine.

"Here we go," Galton said.

He was deceptively strong. Wiry. His muscles felt hard as steel as he guided Jake briskly up the steps of the shrine. Maude and Andy were already there. The devotees sat around them in a circle. The cultists joined hands; their knees touching. Making a circuit. They were humming, chanting in a low, buzzing tone. Their faces relaxed. Expressions as blank as if they slept.

Galton boosted Jake off his feet and into the circle. Stepping with him to the center. He lowered Jake between Andy and Maude.

Then he joined the circle of his fellow followers. Maude left the center, sat beside him.

Iris was humming on his other side. Her eyelids partly opened; pale half-moons exposed.

The webs that covered the shrine weren't thin and lacy now.

They were dark. Filled with spiders.

Spiders replaced all the missing gaps where stones used to be. Brick of spiders molded together, linking themselves, turning their bodies into building materials. The roof closed. They dropped threads and began to spin new walls made of web. Great swags of bunting. Silk drapes.

Andy and Jake sat there without speaking. Mesmerized by the activities.

It was wondrous to watch the spiders work.

49
Company of Puppets

When the night came, the devotees lit the lamps they'd brought up from the camp and put them at marked intervals on the tiles, making a star-like configuration. The spiders were still there. They hadn't moved. At some point the devotees' chanting ceased. They set a table inside the temple. A procession of food and drink, more lamps. A few old notebooks: their sacred texts – all penned by Galton, Andy was informed – books like the one Iris carried in her bag. He flipped through pages of cramped handwriting he couldn't decipher.

The crisis had passed. The mood of the cult was celebratory. They welcomed the spiders.

If Andy didn't feel at ease, he at least felt out of immediate danger. He was allowed to leave the center of the circle. That wasn't certain to him at first. But he told one of the people closest to him, the gruff Englishman, Bradley, that he had to use the bathroom.

Bradley pointed to a slab hut outside of the shrine.

"The bog's over there," he said. "Dug the pit myself, I did."

Andy was afraid the man meant an actual bog, which he had no intention of visiting in the pitch darkness. Bradley laughed.

"An outhouse," the man corrected himself. "Just don't fall in. The trench runs down to a cliff out the back." Bradley walked Andy over to it and assured him he would be safe. "The smell's the only thing might kill you in there. Be mindful of the snakes, though." He gave Andy a lamp. "I'll wait out here until you're finished." Bradley snorted some homemade snuff he pinched from a pouch on a leather cord around his neck. "Go on."

He waved Andy in.

The lamp filled the enclave with twitchy yellow light. Andy was about to step in when a bat flew at him, blowing his hair as it flapped nightward into the canopy. He drew a quick breath and wished he hadn't. The toilet was a gap in the stone cut in the shape of a keyhole. The long part led under the back wall of the hut. Andy set the lamp on a shelf. There was no door. The darkness outside the shrine was complete. Between the clouds and the canopy, the lack of any moon or stars in the sky, it was a perfectly solid black rectangle. You felt you might touch it.

Or it might touch you.

He listened to the Englishman taking another snort, and sneezing. A short cough.

Sweat-soaked and feeling claustrophobic, Andy finished his business.

When he came out, he gulped a few cleansing lungfuls of fresh night air. To his surprise, Bradley was gone. Probably back to the shrine, which was where Andy headed. Rain pattered.

Jogging to the confines of the shrine, amused with himself for feeling better inside the network of webs stocked with more spiders than he'd seen in his lifetime, he marveled at how quickly we humans adapt. Strangely, Bradley wasn't in the shrine either.

Andy found Jake suffering, in obvious pain. His ankle had swollen, doubled in size. In the lamplight, the tight skin glowed a mottled purple. Maude hadn't spoken to them since they fled the spiders. She kept herself at a distance, avoiding even a casual glance in their direction, as if she didn't know them and hadn't been discussing the possibility of escape earlier.

Iris was meditating. Or sleeping while sitting with her legs crisscrossed. Gold relic ring glittering. Who knew what was up with her? She'd grown more peculiar since they'd gotten lost in the canoes.

Galton came over to inquire about Jake's condition. His staff tapping the tiles.

"I can give you something for the pain," he said.

"No," Jake said. "I'll wrap it. I'm fine." He gingerly propped his foot on his pack.

When Galton withdrew as if insulted, Jake added, "Thank you for saving me."

"You were never in danger," Galton said dismissively.

"It didn't seem that way to me," Jake said. "Anyway, I owe you one."

"Panic is what hurt you. A failure of understanding. The spiders are our partners here. As you can plainly see." Galton gestured to the web cathedral, mostly hidden now in the darkness. Flames from the lamps illuminated the occasional cluster of bejeweled, unblinking eyes. Spider bodies, woody or soil-colored, arranged in their gauzy homespun hammocks, resembling nothing so much as a hothouse of withered, rotten flowers – a jumble of dark buds, stalks, and filaments – which suddenly might turn, organize themselves, and crawl away. Andy had to stop himself from starting at every juddering shadow, every curly wisp of lamp smoke, thinking it was creeping inexorably toward him. The spiders, for whatever reason, liked it here. They'd found a sanctuary.

Rain dripped from the webs. Jake laid on the tiles, exhausted, letting the drops land on him. He elevated his foot, throwing an arm over his face to rest. He hadn't mentioned Ursula.

It was almost time to eat.

Federico and one of the Frenchmen were chopping away, tossing unidentifiable chunks into an iron cauldron squatting on the tiles by the table. *Plip plop.* They had a fire blazing. The spiders fashioned a hole in the roof for the smoke. A funnel of rain fell through the vent, slickening the tiles around the cauldron. But it did not put out the fire. The coals hissed and sputtered, popping little puffs of ash. The hot iron dried puddles as rapidly as they formed. Despite everything that had happened – and might happen still – Andy was hungry.

His stomach gurgled. He hadn't had a real meal since they left Marcos's boat.

Whatever they were cooking smelled … edible.

He'd attended enough church cookouts to recognize a festive atmosphere brewing in the temple tonight. People gathered in good cheer. There were about a dozen, a smaller group than he first thought. Chipping in with tasks, chatting over cups of jungle tea, and commenting on the parade their spider brethren put on, or ruminating on the wise words Galton constantly uttered.

Andy decided to mingle. He had questions. If he was stuck here, he'd try to get a few answers. He found a pair of Americans, Cole and Forsythe, former rubber company employees.

"What's for dinner?" he asked them.

"The usual vittles," Cole said.

The devotees were a scrawny lot, not exactly unhealthy, but hungry looking, as if they wouldn't turn down a sandwich if you offered. Water boiled in the iron cauldron. Andy waved his hand in the steam, smelling it. Nothing. Hot water and wet leaves. He dipped a long wooden spoon, stirred, and saw a kind of porridge sticking to it. Federico and the Frenchman wiped their knives and counted out bowls and spoons.

"Where's Bradley?" Federico said.

The Frenchman shrugged.

"Is this manioc?" Andy asked the Frenchman.

"Hmm?"

"The stew. Is it manioc?"

"No," the Frenchman said, the corners of his mouth turned down.

"What is it?"

"A local root. Dull but nutritious. We add spices. There's fruit if you'd prefer."

Andy smiled. "I'll have what you're having. I'm simply curious, that's all."

"The inquisitive are rewarded in ways their passive counterparts will never experience."

I'll bet, Andy thought.

"How did you get here?" he asked the four men without any preamble.

"We are delightfully trapped in the web of the Queen," Cole said. Although he was a thin man, he carried himself like a very fat one. Swaybacked and deliberate. His skin hung loose.

"Sure, I understand," Andy said. "But I'm talking about literally. How'd you get here?"

"Oh," Cole said. He sipped his murky tea. His breath smelled vaguely cod-liver-fishy.

"We are called to in our dreams." Forsythe stepped up to bat for him. "A summoning. We found our way through the dark to her. We all worked in the jungle. Cole and I did the books for the plantation. They were shutting down. Everybody knew. We stayed on to make sure nothing got stolen at the end. Bills and wages paid out. Collections made. From over the entire globe, we all came here to find our destiny, to make our fortunes. Seeking adventure and a life well lived. We are seekers by nature. She seeks the seekers, our Queen. Cole and I missed the last boat out."

"You missed it?" Andy didn't bother with his notepad. He wasn't going to forget this.

Nods. Smiles. From all four men. Federico and the Frenchman must've heard the story before. "We walked off and hid. Watched them looking for us, like a couple of schoolboys playing hooky," Cole said. "They had to leave us. I think they imagined we'd been murdered."

"Where'd you get the courage to stay? Weren't you afraid?" Andy asked.

He was missing something. But what?

A Portuguese man with a single black eyebrow like a caterpillar joined their conversation. "You ask how we were drawn to our fates. How are most people? It is a mystery. To them, to their loved ones. People go where they are meant to go. The Dreamlands is where the Queen found us first. That is the gateway."

Cole and Forsythe were quick to agree.

Federico asked again after Bradley. But no one had seen him.

Andy hadn't after the bog. But he didn't bother telling. The man would turn up.

"I'm unfamiliar with the Dreamlands. Are they around here someplace?" Andy said.

Laughter from the group, boisterous this time. Tears of laughter running down grinning faces. Andy assumed these were signs of amusement, of whimsical joy, but if he'd been told these same men milling in the shrine were suffering from unspeakable anguish – looking at them, their contorted expressions and rigidly awkward postures – he'd have believed that too.

"You go to the Dreamlands every night, silly boy," the cooking Frenchman said. He poured pink powder from a bamboo tube into the cauldron. "They are as close as your pillow."

"Closer still," said Federico slyly.

The Italian leaned forward and tapped Andy on the forehead. One, twice, thrice.

"They are here. For your pleasure. Your excitement. They are infinite and boundless."

Federico picked up a stack of bowls and passed one to the Frenchman for filling.

"You mean our dreams," Andy said. "The ones we have when we sleep? You dream about the Spider Queen, or you have visions of her while you're dreaming. That's it?"

Galton appeared behind Andy, putting his hand on him.

"*It* is vast," he said. "Vaster than the known universe. Fantastic and fabulous. Do not underestimate the depths that are contained within you, young Andy. Within us all. The Queen knows our inner world as well as the outer playground she explores." He took the first portion they'd scooped into a bowl. He slurped the steaming broth and ate with his fingers.

"I was lucky Galton found me in the Dreamlands," Cole said.

"He found me there as well," said the man with the caterpillar eyebrow. "Good man."

The talk around the firepit showed that Galton had found everyone there. It wasn't the Queen who recruited them while they slept. It was Galton Reed. But hadn't they rescued him?

Did he come to them in their dreams before they found him in the waking world?

Or was it the other way around? Andy's head was spinning as he sampled the stew. It was like nothing he'd eaten before. Salty, and it had a kick at the end. His lips tingled.

Iris was awake. Andy watched as she materialized from the gloom. Unfolded from her lotus position, finished with the long meditation or whatever had occupied her mind. She curled up against Galton. Running her fingers through his hair. "And I thought I was special," she said.

"You are special. I rediscovered you. Rescued you from the decay of the cities, the universities and their humdrum drudgery, those insular clubbish claustrophobic coffins of pseudo-intellect. I broke you out of a cemetery of dead ideas. And guided you here, instead."

Was Iris harder to find because she started so far away, in New England? Andy was struggling with the logistics. But he was tired, too. The day's excitement had taken a toll. He needed to rest like Jake. A good night's sleep after dinner. He had trouble following the devotees' explanations. When he tried to pin Galton down, to get him to state the physics of the Dreamlands, he got tongue-tied. Words flowed around him. But he couldn't soak them in.

"Space is not the same in the Dreamlands. Our rules don't apply. Ever flown like a bird in your dreams? Disappeared from one place and reappeared in another instantly? Kingdoms exist there and nowhere else. Creatures beyond all imagination. The realm has its own history. Separate from ours but underlying it. Time differs there as well. How long is a dream measured against the dull clocks we set in the waking world? You can live an entire lifetime in a minute."

Andy nodded, not really understanding any of it. His jaw felt numb. He rubbed it.

"What about morals?" Jake asked. He was laid out on the floor with his head propped up.

"What about them?" Galton said with a bite to his words. "I don't understand."

"Are we bound to follow laws of conduct and thought? Are we judged for our acts?"

"We are freer in the Dreamlands. That dimension is more malleable and balanced."

"Are there no consequences, then for, say, murder, or theft, or corruption of the spirit?"

Galton's wizard features appeared more haughty than wise. He tossed his hair, pointed with his staff. "You are welcome to do whatever you can imagine. As for consequences? The worst consequence I can think of would be waking up to this world. Its maddening inhabitants."

"I like this world. My friends live here. Exploring with my friends is what I love."

Galton sneered. "Every bug eats according to its taste. It can do no better."

Jake had no reply to that. He drank from his canteen and told them he wasn't hungry.

Andy sat down where he was standing. His bowl spilled, but he didn't bother with it.

The longer the group of men talked, the more Andy experienced a growth of perception, and an aura of unease. Sensations expanded faster than he could follow. But he tried to glean the essence of meaning. Here was the crux of the matter. Except for Jake and the two women, it was as if one person were speaking all night through different faces, using alternate bodies but the same gestures, the exact mannerisms and patterns of speech. Not simply like a family with their private glossary of common household discourse, tailored meanings shaped by years of living together in a limited space. This was more explicit. Despite the various countries of their origin and heritage, not to mention subtleties of language and cultural nuance, it was like being in a roomful of ventriloquist dummies. Who was the ventriloquist?

Galton seemed the most obvious choice. But he too had an essence of fakery about him. As if he were merely the biggest doll in the company of puppets, and the master lurked offstage, making individual mouths open and close, limbs jump on invisible wires – that gliding swerve of a jerky head and a body controlled from afar – but the other, the superior influence, could not mask its own voice. It leaked through.

50
Falls

"Every master is a servant to another master. Only the gods are unbound. Count yourself lucky if they only steal your labor and not the meat off your bones. We use each other and in turn are used. The universe, every universe, works on this principle. It is not right. But it is all there is." The merchant unfolded a silk screen and stepped behind it. Not even his head was visible. "If my travels have taught me one thing, it is this. No one looks out for you, except you. Do you agree?"

"No, I don't," Ursula said. "But you're not interested in what I think. Only hearing yourself."

"That is not true." The merchant peeked around the corner of the screen. An unseen attendant had delivered a change of clothes for her host. Evening wear. An elaborate golden tiara and a garment with shiny gold buttons and a glimmering sash to match. Apparently, this cabin was the merchant's own, and he had nowhere else to dress. The screen had been stowed behind a false panel in the wall, which opened to reveal a closet. On the inside of the door hung a mirror.

Ursula was growing impatient with the merchant's lecture.

She had to find a way back on deck. But the merchant was

unwilling to leave after their ship rammed the paddleboat. He did relish his nightcap under the stars, and Ursula was hoping to persuade him to take her topside to contemplate them. For this reason alone, she kept up the conversation. If it didn't yield results soon, she planned to use her knife. And get radical.

"Will you tell me who my masters are to be?" she asked.

Rolls of fine silk appeared at the top of the screen as the merchant hung up his daywear.

"No. But answer me this. Have you ever wished you might visit the moon?"

The moon? What was he getting at?

"Who hasn't?" she said. "If only I could see the moon tonight, I would feel happy."

A soft chuckle. He kicked off his oddly stout slippers, and she heard them drop.

"That might be arranged. My bosses live in a place with excellent lunar views."

Enough of this talk, Ursula thought. She unsnapped her knife and drew it partially free.

The merchant's pudgy hand emerged.

And she startled.

But he was only reaching for his new clothes, the sash, and tiara. As Ursula tipped back, thinking at first the merchant was coming around the bend for her, she noticed she had a view in the mirror on the closet's still open door. She could spy a sliver of the space behind the screen.

It repulsed her to think what she might glimpse. But fascination soon replaced disgust.

Atop the merchant's naked head stood two goatish horns. So, they were the reason for the peculiar double mound of head wrappings. His forehead was broad, tall, and flat. It tilted back at an acute angle which his turban had concealed. A ridge of shaggy black hair ran between the horns. She watched as he wrapped his new headdress around the horns, pushing the ruby-studded tiara down like a crown. He cinched up his robes, draping himself in the extravagant gilded sash.

What was he? Obviously, something inhuman. Yet he talked and reasoned like men do.

Ursula thought the shocks were finished, but then she saw him snugging on his evening slippers. His feet were hooves! That explained their shape. More questions arose, but this much she knew for certain: she was getting off this ship. The merchant was no man at all. Her poisoner was a satyr-like creature, as outlandish as the monsters she and Iris witnessed fighting in the flooded zone. If she had not seen it with her own eyes, she never would've believed it possible.

Who was this monster's master?

Who would her master be?

Could it be they were one and the same?

"I have never asked you your name," the merchant said, still behind the screen. "Nor have you asked me for mine. Let's share names and a drink. A second taste is not so potent. You may find it quite pleasing. Under the stars." As he stepped out, he reached for his ruby bottle.

Ursula held the point of her blade against the side of his thick neck. She felt his pulse.

"I will kill you."

"I don't doubt it," he said. His fresh wardrobe smelled of musky perfumes, but they could not hide the odor of fear he released as surely as a skunk does when threatened by a wolf. The last time she drew a knife he had defended himself. With a knife to his throat, the odds changed.

"Answer me truthfully. Or your lies will be your last. Who is the master of this ship?"

"The moon-beasts," he said.

"Are they my new masters?"

He tried to nod, and a bead of blood ran down the knife's edge. "Yes."

"Where is the galley headed?"

"To the moon."

She pushed the tip of the blade.

"It's true," the merchant said, hurriedly. "We travel through the Dreamlands to the moon. I am but a poor slave too. A noble Man of Leng forced into servitude–"

"Leng? I've heard the name before. Your homeland is rumored to lie hidden near Tibet. Or as far away as Antarctica." If circumstances had been different, she might've quizzed him more about his people and their kingdom, which evaded discovery but spawned many tales.

"Through the Dreamlands is how we go. You cannot reach there any other way."

"Get me off this ship, or you will die."

The merchant swallowed. He knew she meant it.

"Follow me. I make no guarantees. The galley will slow, briefly, when we spill over the edge of the waterfall. That is when we depart this waking world and launch into the heavens."

"If you lie…"

"It will be my last. I know."

Ursula lowered the knife, repositioning it in the small of the satyr-like creature's back.

Outside the door, the passage was empty and dimly lit. They proceeded up the steps. An appalling smell of roasted fat and charry smoke rose from the gloomy hollows trapped below.

In the night air, Ursula felt her chance at freedom was close at hand, as near as a leap into the water speeding past. Looking down caused a rush of dizziness. The impact would break her.

"You may drown," the merchant cautioned as they pressed against the bow railing.

"I'd rather drown than meet the fate you described." Still, she was not feeling suicidal.

"See ahead! The sprays make a silvery cloud. That is the falls. If you go over…"

"Don't worry about me," Ursula said. She sheathed her knife. The merchant wouldn't try to stop her. If he did, she'd tip him over the side into the river. He'd feed a lot of hungry fish.

"How do you cross from the Dreamlands to this world?" Ursula asked.

If the galley was slowing, she hadn't noticed it yet. Her hair blew back from her face.

"I don't know."

"Don't make me take my knife out."

"I don't. Not really. There is a gap. An aperture between dimensions. It opens and closes like an… orifice, a mouth… or an eye. The portal shape is like an eye, but it's ironically hard to see inside it because the light is a strong bluish white. When it is wide enough, we pass through."

"Where is the eye?"

"It moves. Sometimes it is back in the lagoon. Other times it is here over the falls."

Perhaps their speed diminished a mile or two per hour. The deck grew slick with river spray. She and the merchant were soaked. His fine silks darkened and sagged unflatteringly.

"You take your chances going over the falls, hoping the portal will be there," she said.

"I'm told that if you hit it hard enough it opens. Like a piece of silk, it tears apart. But I am neither a sorcerer nor a man of science. I only trade in rubies, gold, and others like me."

If he wanted pity from her, he'd be disappointed.

They were slowing now. The black water of the river changed from a blur to glossy waves. Using the merchant's shoulder, Ursula boosted herself onto the rail, nearly slipping.

Beyond the falls was emptiness. The thunderous rumble of churning water crashed.

Through the clouds, the moon appeared. That magic rock, one couldn't help but stare.

A spot of sky quivered.

Was that the eye preparing to open? The portal. Or was it mist in the moonlight?

"Get ready to jump," the merchant shouted over the noise.

A queer whistled sounded.

The galley lurched, and as the earth fell away, she sailed into space. Nothing under her.

If the portal opened to receive the vessel, Ursula didn't see it.

She was too busy falling. How high were these falls? How deep was the pool at the bottom? How sharp and numerous the rocks lying in wait like a giant's chipped, ragged teeth?

It didn't matter.

She'd meet them soon enough.

51
What If... ?

Andy Van Nortwick felt drunk. He'd never been drunk in his life. But if he had been drunk, it would definitely feel like this. He was floaty and carefree. Everybody he saw, he loved. The spiders too. He loved them, the little guys and dolls, working on their creeping, spinning their nets, not nets... webs... spinning their webs and eating bugs that were dumb enough to crawl in.

He saw Iris watching him in the smoky lamplight.

"I'd kill for a butt," he said. He slumped against a pillar carved with flames and webs.

She came closer. Sat down beside him. Where was Jake anyway?

"Luckily, you don't need to be so dramatic." Iris opened her gold case and held it out.

Andy squinted and poked his finger inside the case, hunting for a smoke.

"Here, let me help you. I've only got two left. One for you, and one for moi," she said.

Andy put the cigarette between his lips.

Iris pulled over a lamp, and they tipped their heads together in the flame, puffing.

"Ahh, that's glorious," Andy said. He picked a speck of tobacco off his tongue.

Iris leaned back on her elbows. Knees up. Collar unbuttoned. Moths fluttering about her.

"Are you feeling fine?" she asked, smiling at him. The moths were like rose petals.

"I'm drunk," Andy said. "The kid is drunk. Let the record show. Print it."

"How? Hopkins drained the last of my whiskey. Galton says the camp is dry."

"I'm drunk on stew." He hiccupped. Moving to cover his mouth, he scorched his hand on the cigarette's red tip. "Yeow! That smarts. I've gone out now. Poor me." He bent over the lamp.

Iris laughed, a loud cackling. Her golden locks tossed about in the shadowy flickers.

"You may be something, Mr Van Nortwick. But drunk you are not."

Andy smiled around his smoldering butt. His eyes felt heavy and irritated. He rubbed them and saw splotches of vivid color. "I'm seeing things. That much is true. Hearing them too. Just now, I heard a whatchacallit… a ghast coughing in the bush… right there. So damned dark."

Iris didn't want to talk about ghasts. But she did want to talk.

"You like to think about things…" she began.

"I do. I do."

"What if the spiders aren't real? What if the other people here aren't real either?"

Andy slapped the tiles. "OH MY GOD."

Iris put her finger to his lips. She glared at him but smiled.

When she took her finger away, he said, "Oh my God. I was thinking the exact same thing. Only, somehow, I'd forgotten it until you reminded me just now. They're phonies."

He frowned and studied the glowing end of his cigarette. How it made squiggly trails.

"It's all Galton," Iris said. "His magic or illusions. Maybe delusions. That's what I'm thinking. What if he's making us believe something's true when it's not? How would we know?"

"Yes. Like a magician. What you said. When I was boy, I went to the boardwalk and there was a magician set up there with his dog. I can't remember if the dog was stuffed or not. But the magician would ask for volunteers. They all do that. Get those that want to believe to identify themselves. He'd perform the same tricks, over and over. I'd fall for them every time."

Andy thought Iris looked sad after he said that. He was a boy then, and he didn't feel sad.

"I knew he was alive. The rest of you didn't, but I did. In my heart," Iris said.

"But how could you?" Andy said.

"He came to me in my dreams. I knew, though. I'd never had dreams like those before. Too real. I was lying to myself thinking they were only dreams. He was there in my mind."

"It isn't your fault. Don't blame yourself for wanting your husband to be alive."

She looked at him kindly. But the sadness lingered. It's permanent, he thought.

"You're not drunk, Andy. However, you might be drugged."

"Is that what's wrong with the dev-o-tees," he broke the word up into pieces. "I thought they were bewitched. That tea they're sipping. The way they never blink. Have you noticed?"

"Galton used to have trouble sleeping. For years. He'd get desperate and drink himself to sleep with beer or cheap wine. He smoked opium for a while. When we traveled, he asked the locals their homemade remedies for sleeplessness. He'd try anything. Tinctures and drops. Warm milk and brandy. Nothing did the job until we got here. He extracted venom from spiders. Tiny little droplets that he dried on a leaf. He'd lick the leaf. I told him not to. The people living here thought he was crazy. People get sick and die in the jungle from venoms. Frogs and centipedes. Snakes. Bullet ants. Spiders too. Galton would lick the leaf and go to sleep. He started mixing his nightly sleep ritual with magic. Recitations he'd found in books. Words he dreamt. Phrases that just popped in his head. He called his dreams *night jaunts*. I said, one day you'll take too much or milk the wrong spider, and you'll jaunt your way into a grave. That didn't scare him, though."

"Galton put venom in the stew?" Andy's brain felt stuck in molasses.

Iris shrugged. "I don't know if he did. But I know he *would*. No rules with Galton."

"What's wrong with him?"

"He wants to talk to the gods. He'd rather be with them than with me, I guess."

"What if Galton isn't Galton? What if something else is playing with him – with all of them – like toys? One of those gods he was trying to contact. What if this is an experiment?"

Iris looked at him for a long time. The lights were changing. Her image flickered like the end of a film reel. Flashes and shadows. Andy didn't know if the lights were only in his head.

She stabilized. A radiance glowed behind her, almost too bright. Her face grew serious.

Later, Andy wasn't sure if she said what he remembered her saying. He might've made it up. Or maybe he was dreaming. Everything got mixed up for him that night in the shrine.

But what he recalled her saying to him was this: "In the moldy gothic novels of old, hauntings occur in crumbly castles, or drafty half-abandoned houses that sit beside stagnant lakes out in the middle of nowhere. What if the planet is a giant haunted house? And no one ever escapes. Phantoms, gods, and monsters – we're trapped together. Dreaming. What then, Andy?"

He didn't think he answered her. He was tired. His stomach hurt as if he'd been punched. He turned his head and was sick on the tiles. He was so thirsty for a cold drink of water.

A blank space came next, an erasure.

Something bad was happening. Screams in the jungle.

He had blood on him. His arms were dripping red past the elbows.

The screams were his.

Then he was running through the forest. He wanted to find Jake. Where was Jake?

52
Spit

The pool at the foot of the falls was deep and black. Ursula never touched bottom. After smacking the water, she plunged down and down, losing momentum until she could kick her way back to the surface. Her lungs burned. She forced her mouth shut, then when she couldn't, she released her air slowly and followed the trail of bubbles rising like spheres of moonlit glass.

There, there was the moon. Bright and globular. Staring down impassively. Into the world of air from the world of water, she rejoiced as she coughed and swam. Side-stroking through the mists, she saw a sleek black shadow slice past the stony disk. It had many legs.

Was it the black galley with her load of slaves? Were the legs their oars?

She couldn't swear to it.

In the shallows, she stood and breathed, hands on her hips, bent over. Alive.

Nothing broken. She still had her knife. I'll make it, she told herself. I always do.

Ursula looked up the wall of falling water. A craggy rock cliff ran along one side, its opposite was trees and heavy brush. She'd take the rocks once she had her wind back. Climb. She walked through the water. Careful to test first with a stick she found. Don't fall in a hole. The ascent was slippery, but clean. The holds were plenty. She found a crack and went slowly.

At the top, she paused.

The black galley had traveled a tributary she wasn't familiar with, and the idea of making any progress through the dark jungle was moot. She found a spit of land and hunkered out there for protection. She'd see predators coming. There'd be no sleep. Building a fire would be a challenge. Everything was wet, herself included. But the forest was moonlit and warm. She'd be drier by morning. This was a time for thinking. Ursula had to go back to the lagoon. No question.

That's where she left her party. Jake would be searching for her. He'd keep the others safe. She wrung out her clothes, and in her pocket found a good surprise. Her map. By moonlight she oriented herself. The falls were a clear landmark. Upstream, she thought she could see a fork. It wasn't far. Faint lines. It was too dark for reading. Maybe the fork went to Manaus.

A light.

She thought she was imagining things at first.

Then she saw it again.

Up at the fork, or where she thought there might be a fork, the light was moving. Above the water, then she saw the darker, blocky form around the light take shape. The moon traced it in pencil lead. A steamboat. With its paddle turning. Floated up to the falls, but in control, back paddling to slow its progress. The one light became two. She calculated her odds.

Were they friend or foe?

Ursula gambled.

She jumped up and down and started yelling.

The paddleboat didn't alter its speed. But it was getting closer. The lights growing bigger.

They turned on a searchlight. Fanned it across the water. The beam picked out the edge of the falls. She saw figures moving on the deck. Heard voices. They were pointing. At the falls.

At her.

The searchlight beam hit the spit of land and illuminated it. Ursula was out at the end.

The light blinded her.

The voices were louder.

"Jake? Jake, is that you? It's me. Ursula. Jake?"

The boat stopped coming.

That's when she saw the canoe. She shielded her eyes from the beam. It stayed on her.

The canoe pulled up to the spit of land.

It was Thiago. Behind him sat a man she didn't recognize. He had something white stuck in his mouth. A cigarette? No. A toothpick. And he had a rifle pointed at Thiago's back.

But there was a third passenger. Smaller than the other two men. She hadn't seen him at first, because he'd ducked right behind Thiago. Now he leaned out to the side and waved.

"Well, well, if it isn't the Damned Miss Downs," Ashley Lott said.

53
Freakish Lights

"Am I awake or am I dreaming?"

"Does it matter?"

"Yes. It does," she said.

"Soon it won't." Galton stroked Iris's hair. He'd found her in the temple of the Spider Queen after she'd finished talking with Andy. The reporter had crawled off into a corner, huddled up in a feverish sweat, murmuring a disjointed narrative of his own nightmares. Galton helped her to her feet. They passed by Jake splayed on the tiles, legs akimbo, like a boxcar hobo.

"You put something in their food?" Iris asked. "To make them sleep."

Galton's face twitched. She felt him squeezing her hand tightly. Pain. He was still suffering lingering effects from the spider bite five long years ago. But he accepted suffering as the necessary price for special knowledge. To be set apart. She never agreed with him on that.

"They are taken care of. I need them pliant. We're visiting the Queen at the mine. Maude's going to film us. Isn't that grand? I'll be a film star. Did you ever imagine yourself married to a hero of the silver screen?"

"You were my hero. Always," she said. "Even before this." Why did she feel like she getting ready to say goodbye to him again? This time it felt different, though. She was choosing.

He carried a lamp. They walked down the deteriorated steps, toward the path that led to the mine and the camp the devotees had pitched there. The devotees were busy. Putting candles on the ground to mark their descent. Bowls of incense smoldered, deterring the mosquitos and adding a heady aroma of long buried temples in ancient broken forgotten lands. The detritus of the forest lay in heaps along the sides of the pathway, forming mounds on either side that snaked with each bend of the trail, a pair of serpentine guardians. The moon split from the clouds.

Fat and cold. It stared down like a diseased eye, blind to this world but open to another.

Iris shivered despite the cloying heat. It reminded her of her husband's eye.

"You really did something here, Galton. I wish I'd been with you. You sent me away."

"The jungle is not easy, darling. Life in the jungle is not easy... Life... is not easy."

She touched his arm. He was cold too. It was like touching a cemetery statue.

"Tell me what happened after I left that day in the jungle."

He patted her hand. "You don't need to know that."

"I want to," she said. "I'm your wife."

Galton dug his staff into the loose earth and helped her balance. "Careful here."

They reached level ground at last. The encampment. So many torches! Maude was there setting up her camera. Pointing her lens at the mouth of the old goldmine. She ignored them.

Galton escorted his wife to a pair of old stumps at the edge of the trees.

Bats flitted overhead. Cries and howls echoed from the river valley. Meepings and coughs. Gibbering. More bats flying. Big ones. Larger than any birds she knew that lived there.

They only seem big because it's so dark. Those sounds? Monkeys, she told herself.

Galton sat and brushed a twig from the stump beside him. "Sit, sit."

"How did you open a gate for the Queen? I want to know your story in the Dreamlands."

"My story? I'll tell you a better one. Long ago, but not too long, a young man, about the age of your friend Andy, had been wandering from his village. Farther than he should have ventured. That's like your friend too. But this young man discovered something in his rambles. Maybe it lay on the ground. Or lodged against the shallow ledge of a stream, snuggled in the mud. Where he found it isn't important. What's important is he picked it up. A relic. It must've looked special to him. Powerful. So, he cleaned it off, warming it between his sweaty palms. He breathed his young man's breath on it. And the relic came to life. It opened a gateway, a portal, to the Dreamlands.

"After feeling the danger of what he'd done, he panicked. He wanted to close the gate. But how? He didn't even understand what had happened. There was a slit between dimensions. Full of planets and stars. Freakish lights. He went up to it. Curious, as curious boys are. And he gazed in and saw an eye! Who was watching him from the other side of that beyond? Why, a small spider. It was tiny enough to slip inside the crack between worlds.

"This spider was no ordinary interdimensional spider. She was the Spider Queen, who had shrunk herself to fit into this peculiar gap because it was unfamiliar to her, and she had a very inquisitive, most adventurous spirit. She was eager to explore a new world. To hunt in it. Always clever, she learned to cross back and forth between dimensions, following a thread she spun behind herself, so she never lost her way home. The door may have first opened in the Underworld, inside the Vaults of Zin, before passing through the well in the monastery on the Plateau of Leng. No one knows.

"Think of the portal as an eye. It blinks, narrows, but never shuts completely. Sometimes the floating eye sees Leng. A cold waste. Other times it gazes at the Underworld. Today, with my magic, I can open the eye. Where it opens is… imprecise. Oh, the worlds I see, Iris. Visions you cannot imagine. Cities and wonders. Sometimes in the gap things slide past. Quick things."

He laughed softly. He tickled her knee and ran his bony fingers up her thigh.

Iris did not know the names of all the places he'd mentioned. *The Vaults of Zin.* Which Underworld? The one from Greek mythology, or another? She had a more important question.

"Were you that young man, Galton? Is your tale really about you?"

He shook his head as if her suggestion were absurd. Unworthy of an outright denial.

"Everything I've ever tried to do ended in failure." His eyes cut away from the far-off lands he had been staring into as he told his tale. They went to her instead. She felt him then, the old Galton, returning. Showing up like a ghost at a window for one last wave goodbye. She felt sorrow for him. For them. For both their wrecked marriage and professional partnership. "Alas, life is chaos. Death is at least orderly. The day you left I had reached my end. Then I saw something looking at me when I opened the portal with magic. So, I asked a favor of whatever was watching me from that interdimensional crevice I'd pried apart. I said, *'Take me'*. I was ready, willing to accept any offer on the table. Oblivion. Or some other thing, anything else…"

"What did you get, Galton? In the end?"

"I got power. Atlach-Nacha is a goddess. Greater than I, yes. But my magic for now is like a leash looped around her. She is weak from crossing dimensions. I can confuse her. I lured her into the mine. That day I wanted anything. This day I demand a bargain. I will set her free. If she allows me a morsel. Atlach-Nacha is building a bridge between dimensions. When she finishes, the waking world ends. The Dreamlands become all. Give me a kingdom, I asked. Not the biggest. A small kingdom of my own. Where I rule. You, my dear Iris, may sit at my side."

Iris could hardly bear to look at him. His needs were so raw. He was like an open wound.

"What was her answer?" she said.

He grimaced in pain. "She hasn't answered." He gripped his head in his trembling hands.

The pain passed. His breathing was ragged. Sour sweat covered his pale white skin.

"She will answer me tonight, and I will set her free. Maude is going to film it. Did I already tell you that?" His cheek twitched spasmodically. His blind eye glared from its socket.

"You told me."

Galton nodded, stood up, and ducked under one of the tarps. When he came out again, he was wearing his old costume robe, with its torn red lining, the cheap and crookedly sewn silver magic symbols, as if they'd been designed by a child's hand. Iris forced herself not to cringe.

"How do I look?" he asked, turning.

"Splendid," she said, holding back her tears.

He grinned and clapped his hands.

54
Empty Spoons

Cole and Forsythe approached Jake with caution. Cole crouched down and held a lamp over the explorer's damaged foot. "Swelled up like a sausage. Looks like if you poked it, it'd burst."

Forsythe made an unpleasant face.

"Squeamish?" Cole asked him, amused.

"I don't like to dwell on the gory details," he said. "I have a weak stomach."

"Then you'd better bring a blindfold for later," Cole snickered. "Help me get him up."

Forsythe was wary. He kicked at Jake's boot. The one on his good foot.

"He out?"

"He's out," Cole said. "Trust me."

Jake was not out but quite awake. Alert. He had a chunk of limestone wedged in his pocket if he needed it. But he'd decided to play possum. His ankle was bad. The pain had gotten worse. There was no way he could walk. So, if they were willing to carry him to the action, he'd play his part and act the ragdoll. Cole shoved his hands under Jake's armpits. Forsythe took his legs. His ravaged ankle was left swinging in the wind as they transported him.

It took all his concentration and willpower not to scream.

"He's sweaty," Forsythe said. "Looks slippery as a fish off the hook."

"The Queen's potion will do that to a first-timer. You remember, don't you?"

Forsythe was walking backwards, checking over his shoulder for the best route. "I don't remember those days. I was sick as a dog. The euphoria was nice, though. Head in the clouds."

"We're two good floaty boys now," Cole said. He was puffing from exertion.

"Galton wants us to lug him the whole way down the hill to the mine? We're going to drop him, you know? My back can't handle it." Forsythe grunted and squeezed Jake's legs.

"Hey, I know," Cole said. "Where's the wheelbarrow? We can use that."

"You're a genius," Forsythe said.

They laid Jake on the ground. Forsythe watched after him while Cole fetched the cart.

Jake slitted his eyes. Forsythe wore smudgy glasses. He was cleaning them poorly with his shirttail. Cole had taken the lantern. He'd been dangling it from the crook of his elbow.

Forsythe and Jake waited in the semi-dark. The honeyed glow of the temple spilled out behind them. Webs glistened like spun sugar. The lamps from the shrine cast a syrupy radiance on the complex. At the back, the obelisks stood. Jake hadn't investigated there yet. But the devotees were busy staking torches in the ground. Waiting for the rain to stop to light them.

Jake was awake because Maude helped him. He suspected the stew was poisoned. He didn't think Galton would be killing everyone, but he wasn't about to eat it. He hadn't gotten a chance to warn Andy. When Maude walked by as he reclined on the tiles, Jake reached for her.

"Don't," she said. "They're watching us."

"The food isn't safe. Is it?"

"It has spider venom in it. Mushrooms from the forest. Galton's private tea. It keeps the followers numb and suggestible." She checked his ankle, propped it up higher, shoving a chunk of stone under his pack. "Your ankle is ugly. The swelling's worse, and it's turning purple."

"I know," Jake said.

"The stew will make the pain go away," she said.

"Are you suggesting I drug myself?"

"No… I only… It will help… if you want to go to sleep. The devotees are sleepwalkers."

"No, thank you. I prefer to stay awake when people are plotting to knock me out."

"Galton won't forget about you. He'll only try something else. He's clever."

"What mickey did he slip you?" Jake asked. "Aren't you a volunteer sleepwalker too?"

"Stop. You're being unfair."

"Am I?" Jake's bowl of uneaten stew lay on the tile beside him. Maude picked it up and began to spoon it into his mouth. But the spoons were empty.

"Why are you still here? If he needs to control everything, he wouldn't let you run free. You're too smart. That's a threat. From what I can tell, Galton doesn't appreciate threats."

"He wants me to make a movie about him. His Cult of the Spider Queen epic. He needs me lucid. And you forget something." She poured most of the stew down in a crack between the tiles, using her leg to block the view of spies in the shrine. She kept feeding him empty spoons.

"What's that?" he asked.

"I'm an actor. A good one, too. Convincing. Galton believes what I show him."

Jake said, "What's Galton planning? Is the Spider Queen real?"

"She's real all right. He's got her boarded up in the goldmine. For now. He wants her to be his co-star. Atlach-Nacha, that's her name. She's a goddess from the Dreamlands. Don't ask me for details. Galton spins yarns about the Dreamlands. I've heard them for more than a year, and my head is dizzy. I don't know what's true and what's his fantasy. Luckily, I'm used to that."

"Where'd you learn about fantasies?"

"Hollywood."

Jake sat up.

"I saw a giant spider kill Hopkins. If the spider is caged in the mine, what did I see?"

She pushed him back. "I don't know. Maybe there's more than–"

"Sshhh… he's coming." Jake leaned back and started to close his eyes.

Maude turned her head. "Oh, hello. I was just telling Jake here that it's going to be a wonderful night. The rain is almost finished. I feel things cooling off. Are you getting excited?"

Galton loomed over them. He didn't answer her. He was assessing Jake's current status.

Jake fluttered his eyes. Yawned. He hoped he wasn't heaping it on too thick.

"How was your meal?" Galton asked.

"Good. I'm tired though. My leg's killing me."

"You should've let me give you something," Galton said.

Maude showed him the empty stew bowl.

"It's going to be perfect for shooting," she said. "Full moon. The light will be good."

"Excellent, excellent." Galton tapped his staff on Jake's good leg. "I'll have two of my men transfer you to more comfortable surroundings. There's going to be a show tonight."

"A sh… shooow?" Jake slurred his words. He licked his lips. Let his mouth hang open.

"You're in it," Galton said with a guffaw. "Maude, I'm going to speak to my wife. Make certain everything is set for our filming. We'll have one take. So, if you need more lamps…"

"It's all taken care of. I'm handling it," she said. "And I'm the best."

Cole returned with the wheelbarrow. He and Forsythe loaded Jake inside and headed to the mine.

As they rolled him downhill, he wondered how insane Galton was. Isolated out here and leading a group delusion. Juiced up on spider toxins and fungal tea. Was Maude any less crazy?

Or was she just the better actor?

55
One Boot

Ursula had no choice but to climb into the canoe. Ashley was strangely silent as a stoic Thiago paddled them back to the steamship. Thiago wouldn't look at her. The third man was a soldier, with a soldier's curtness. His hunter's eyes scanned the darkness like any nighttime predator.

"Any trouble, I'll put a bullet in you," he said. "Understand?"

"I'm no trouble," Ursula said.

Ashley snorted.

"Let's go," the soldier said.

As they neared the ship, Ursula recognized Marcos's rusty hulk. But the none of the half-dozen men she counted on deck were Marcos. Or Thiago's brother, Davi. She decided not to ask.

Wait and see, she told herself. Asking too many questions was a risk she couldn't afford.

The lanterns on deck revealed streaks of blood staining the boards. One of the soldiers wore Marcos's black captain's hat. All the men were filthy, and some had injuries.

"Did you find your El Dorado, eh?" Ashley asked her. He had a black eye. A cut across the bridge of his nose. His suit was muddy and ripped to shreds. He tried to maintain his aplomb.

And failed.

"Shuddup," the soldier with the toothpick said. He shoved Ashley in the back with the butt of his rifle. "Over there. Sit. Another word and you're piranha pickings."

Ashley did as he was told.

Ursula noticed he was only wearing one boot. All the other men had a pair.

"We saw the black galley go down that fork," the toothpick soldier said. "How'd you get off before it went over?"

"I jumped," Ursula said. So, they think the galley went over the falls. She tucked it away.

"Where are the others? The ones who rammed us?"

She shrugged.

"Dead. That's good. Here's our problem. We work for a Mr Oscar Hurley. He hired us to follow you. Bring back any treasure you discovered. Mark the location on a map. The idiot who lost his boot was supposed to catalogue any rare finds. He was *supposed* to tell us where to go."

"I tried to, Toothpick," Ashley said. "Who expected that boat to attack–"

Toothpick aimed the rifle at him.

Ashley put his hands up and his head down.

"Now, we got two problems," Toothpick said. "One. No map. Idiot lost it. Two. We got no treasure. No money to get home. Most of my men are missing or dead. The ones still here need to be paid. The Indian can run the boat, but we're lost. Mr Hurley is not going to be happy."

Ursula perked up. "I can help you."

"How?"

If Ursula wanted answers, now was the time to ask.

"Tell me, where is Marcos?" she said. "And where's that man's brother?"

She pointed to Thiago.

"We commandeered the ship. Needed one to run the boat. The other two we put ashore."

"Alive?" Ursula asked.

"More or less. Now give me a reason to keep *you* alive," Toothpick said.

"I'll give you two. First, I know where the treasure is. The shrine of the Spider Queen." She waited for the soldiers' reaction. They were a stony bunch. Not predisposed to believing strangers, particularly archaeologists. If Ashley was the only archaeologist they knew, she couldn't blame them. Mercenaries wouldn't have been her choice to return her to the lagoon. But she was lying to them. She had no idea if the shrine was there. But if they could find her team, then good, she'd come up with an excuse to make it back to Manaus. Andy could talk to Hurley.

"What's two?" Toothpick asked.

Ursula went to her pocket.

One of the mercenaries aimed a pistol at her head. He cocked the hammer.

"Go slow," Toothpick suggested to her.

She removed the map. Unfolded it. As the lantern shone through the paper, the tributaries stood out like blood vessels. They carried life. Life meant treasure and a way home.

The toothpick fell from the soldier's lips when he grinned.

56
Silent Movie

The entire scene is one continuous take without any cuts. That's how it was discovered, later, after the disaster. No one edited it. Towards the end of the reel, shadows took over. A black screen. No sound, of course. Only the images remained to tell the story.

It begins with atmosphere. The opening shot is the sealed entrance of an abandoned goldmine. Torches lit. Lamps set out. Moonlight shines through the trees. On the ground are tailings: drilled-out core samples from the miners. They looked everywhere for treasure. Found traces. No motherlode.

Galton Reed stands at the mouth of the mine. Dressed in a magician's velvet cape.

He's reciting words from a book. The language isn't English. Or any other known language, according to experts who have examined the footage. His followers, the devotees – the Cult of the Spider Queen – gather at his feet. His wife, Iris Bennett Reed, stands off to the side, neither with her husband nor the group. Maude Brion filmed the event. She's behind the camera.

You can't see him yet, but the explorer Jake Williams is in a wheelbarrow parked at the back of the crowd. He isn't moving. Andy Van Nortwick, a reporter for the *Arkham Advertiser*, was also in attendance. Although at this point in the film his whereabouts are still unknown.

Galton Reed raises his arms. Several boulders behind him, blocking the mine, begin to shake. Slowly, they roll away into the jungle. A few appear to levitate. It is suspected an earthquake occurred at this time. Fortunately, none of rocks collided with the people in attendance. Iris Bennett Reed staggers. She appears the most shocked by the earthquake.

Six of the cult members rise and begin prying boards loose from the blockade.

Galton beckons to his wife. But she remains on the other side of the cult activities.

Upon removing the last board, the devotees return to their seats. Everyone waits.

A bat flies out of the mine.

Soon other bats emerge, a large colony, apparently trapped when the mine was shut.

Galton steps into the mouth of the mine. He is shouting. Agitated, he throws his book.

He calls to the group, and two men retrieve the wheelbarrow containing Jake Williams. They push it into the mine. The camera tilts, angling to view the top of the plateau out of which the mine has been dug. Galton gestures to the camera operator to come forward.

Maude Brion moves the camera in for a closer look. Torches are brought forward.

Several are cast into the mine. The camera steadies. Re-focuses.

Jake Williams is now visible, attempting to climb out of the wheelbarrow.

Galton clubs him several times with his walking stick. He is particularly determined, hitting the explorer's legs. Iris attempts to intervene. A final blow to the head knocks Jake unconscious. Cultists approach Iris, at first seemingly trying to calm her, then forcefully chasing her as she tries to flee. Galton swings his staff at the devotees, driving them back, away from his wife. Iris is clearly terrified. She picks up one of the discarded boards, studded with nails, and brandishes it. Who is she afraid of? The devotees? Clearly. Her husband? Perhaps. Galton drops his staff. He waves his arms at her in a repeated pattern, slashing lines and smooth, looping whirls. He speaks indecipherable words. Iris returns to him, waiting in front of the mine.

Nothing happens.

Then there is a sudden spray of water from off screen. A gush of liquid pools around the devotees. They are knocked over by the force of it. Dripping wet, they stare to the left. Galton and Iris turn together. The camera is caught in the deluge. The lens is dripping wet. Subsequent images are distorted. Maude Brion picks up the camera, moving back to her original position.

A huge, blurred form lunges into the center of the group. Bodies fly.

Experts suggest an explosion may have occurred. Possibly from gases trapped inside the goldmine and released by its reopening. Because of its exposure to moisture, the functions of the camera may have been impaired. The speed of the film is erratic, the picture jumps, slips out of focus, making it difficult to interpret, or trust, what one thinks one might be seeing on the screen.

Several devotees lay motionless on the ground until they are dragged away by – it is unclear – something in the blurred shadows affecting the film. The picture comes into better focus for a brief interval. Galton is seen fleeing offscreen. Iris remains frozen in place. The blur moves above her. She turns to observe it. The weight of whatever is inside the blurred image triggers a rockslide.

Large rocks fall across the entrance of the mine, burying Iris. The blur disappears. The image becomes crisper. Maude Brion enters the mine, pushing out the cart with Jake Williams in it. Then she returns to examine the rockpile on top of Iris. She crouches and picks an object off the ground. [It is not known who is cranking the camera and filming here.] Maude places the object – maybe Galton's book? – in the wheelbarrow with Jake. She moves out of picture. The filming continues. Shadows flood the screen, until it becomes solid black. End.

57

The Part That Andy Forgot

Andy had wandered away from the shrine after getting sick. Nobody was paying attention to him. Nothing new there, he thought, hiccupping. He still wasn't feeling good *at all*. He stopped and laid his head against a tree trunk. So dizzy. He heaved and felt a little better. Where was he?

How awful would it be to make it this far and get lost? He had to look for the lights.

Where were they?

There. Gold flashes through the mazy leaves. Tongue of flames. Green fires burning on the edges of the yellow. Something wasn't right with his head. His vision was screwy. Too many colors. Streaks in the air, trails flagging on everything like long flowing banners. Blisters of color exploding out of nothing. It was pretty. But damn if it didn't make it hard to walk in the jungle.

He stepped in something sloppy.

More mud most likely. Andy looked up and saw the slab hut where he'd relieved himself. The bog. Is that what the Englishman called it? What was his name? Bartleby?

No. That wasn't right.

Bradley. The gruff snuff sniffer. He dug the trench behind the bog. The outhouse.

Oh God, Andy hoped he wasn't standing in that trench. He lifted his boots to inspect.

How'd the slop get all the way up his shirt? He was covered in it. Like a bucket poured over him. It didn't smell like it came from an outhouse. Slaughterhouse was more like it.

Metal smell. Like a butcher shop. Like that taste when you bite your lip. Metal and meat.

The rain was sticky. He touched his legs: more stickiness. And now his arms were coated with it. What the hell? Andy looked up at the sky where the sticky rain was drizzling on him.

He saw a human face.

Two human faces, in fact. One he recognized. It was Bradley.

"Hey, Bradley, what're you doing up in that tree? It's kind of late for a climb, ain't it?"

Andy was lucky. If it hadn't been for a slice of moonlight carving through the canopy, he wouldn't have seen Bradley at all. Hanging upside-down like a goof. All silver and satiny black.

"Who's that with you, Bradley? Do I know them?"

Though he didn't know why, Andy felt fear rushing up from his gut. He stepped, traipsing under the moon, trying for a better view at what was hanging from the trees. "Bradley?"

That thing up there with Bradley was much bigger than he first thought. Gigantic. Its body was like a black hot air balloon caught under the canopy. A wave of dizziness overtook him as he stared. He looked down at his hands. Squeezed them shut. His head was spinning from the stew, from whatever they'd put in it. He couldn't tell what was real from what wasn't. Panic burst inside him. Nothing he could do slowed the flood. Unable to resist, he gazed up again.

Bradley's face didn't move at all. That surprised expression of his wouldn't quit.

But the other face turned to contemplate Andy. Blankly, coldly.

Then it went back to eating Bradley.

Rubbery strands swayed from its chin. It slurped them up like noodles. Black globules fell, hitting Andy's cheeks. Not black, only black in the moonlight. In the sun, they'd be red.

Andy ran.

58
For the Record

Whether it was fate or chance, Andy would never know. For it would have been far more likely that he stumbled lost in the forest until he collapsed, succumbing one day soon to thirst, starvation, predation, or disease. He was a babe in the woods – a cub – or like Red Phelan condescendingly called him, a "kiddo" . He didn't run toward the flaming lamps of the shrine as he fled the monster coolly consuming Bradley's entrails. Fear made him mindless. He wanted only to hide, to flee, to be lost – if being lost meant losing that morbid creature and his memory of it. Gravity saved him, perhaps, because Andy tumbled downhill, tearing up greenery as he went. Somersaulting, slashing at the darkness, he emerged on his knees with a candle in his face. It was the devotees' trail. Lit for the ceremony. He inched forward, sticking his head and torso through the leaves. Candles and lamps irradiated the path to the encampment. He saw the saggy rooftops of the tarps spread below, holding cups of rain in their swollen bellies. Moths and bats flitted. Tiny flying bugs like bits of ash and snow. Galton's voice filled the cavity of this niche. Booming. A language Andy didn't know. And he didn't want to know. He crawled onto the path. Where was Jake?

Maude? Even catching sight of Iris would've provided an anchor to his sanity and kept him from drifting, drifting, out into an endless ocean of monsters and magic. Rituals.

Realms unfamiliar and bleak threatened to take him in their elongated maws.

He stood up. The sound of a waterfall off to his left. He smelled water. Tasted sour mist.

Slowly he went, farther along.

I'm covered in blood, he thought. How must I look?

I don't care.

If I can find people like me. Not sorcerers. No more cultists. I want to go home now.

Where was Jake? And Ursula.

We should've gone the other way and never come to this accursed site.

Ursula would know what to do. She'd protect us.

But she isn't here, Andy, he told himself. You are.

Talking to yourself is a sign of madness.

That's what his mother told him when he was a little boy.

There was a heavy vibration in the ground. Earthquake? He watched rocks the size of beer kegs rolling loose in the mud, landing with a squishy thud against a tree or in a soggy ditch.

They were having a revival meeting – the cultists.

Galton delivered unto them a sermon of gibberish.

Then Andy saw the camera, and Maude standing by it.

Her arm cranking, making a movie. She was dedicated, he'd give her that. Obsessed.

With what? Lunatics in the moonlight. What if he and Iris were right about them? What if they weren't even real? If he grabbed one by the arm and yanked hard, would the limb break off, a stuffing of sawdust and dry beans come pouring out? Were they mannequins?

Toys of a bored god? He heard the shriek of nails being pulled; the hollow claps of wood tossed on wood.

I must talk to Maude. I'll ask her about Jake. How's his ankle? Will you go with us now?

Two men pushed a wheelbarrow. Inside, he saw a head pop forward. Somebody was sitting in the pan. It was Jake. His face gaunt and yellow in the torchlight. A waxy, haunted stare.

No, no, no…

Andy crept behind a tree where he might observe the proceedings in secret. The sudden urge to laugh, to giggle, bubbled up inside him. I need to remain silent. He covered his mouth.

They've poisoned me. I'm probably dying already. Doomed to a jungle grave.

No, stop it, Andy. Hold it together. If only he could have some water, a few hours' sleep.

Sleep? No, sleep was what got us into this.

Sleep and a lonely man playing with relics and old books. Talking to himself in the dark.

They put Jake in the mine. Galton was angry. Iris looked like she wanted to die.

Maybe she'd get her wish. Maybe they'd all be dead by morning.

Don't think like that, Andy, he told himself. He was fighting battles outside and within.

Maude moved with her camera. Replanting it, the tripod spread apart at the cave mouth.

Galton was beating Jake. Andy came around the tree, fists clenched. He had to stop this. But how? He was outnumbered. Outplayed by Galton and his superior knowledge, his occultism.

Andy retreated. He could see the blood on Jake's face. His crooked, shattered legs. But Andy looked very carefully for a specific sign. There it was. Jake's chest pumped up and down.

He was alive. Breathing. It wasn't too late. Was it?

When the giant spider came out of the water, Andy fell to the ground, trembling. It was such an awful, stomach-turning sight. Like a bull, it rushed the devotees, but not like a bull, too. It had a clockwork grace. As if it were an exquisitely designed piece of oiled machinery, it advanced. The model of efficiency. There was nothing like it in this world he'd ever seen before.

Except the other spider.

The one up in the canopy munching away on Bradley's guts.

That one was bigger. That one had a human face. At least he had thought so then.

The giant spider that launched itself from under the waterfall had a monster's face. Hideous as it was, terrifying and alien, it did not cause the perverse revulsion of the eater in the tree. However, it was no doubt a killer. It speared a man through his chest. And trampled two more underfoot. With fangs it snip-snipped apart bodies like a pair of mad garden shears.

He didn't know it was almost over when he went to Maude. Iris was dead. He saw the rocks crush her. She could've moved. That would always bother him. Seeing how she had time. The spider wasn't paying attention to her. It saw her. But it only paused at the arch above the mine entrance. Iris stood there and said something he couldn't hear. She was talking to the Spider Queen. Not screaming like her husband. No, these were quiet words. Iris looked like she was making a request. Asking politely. The spider gave her its sparkling, eight-eyed stare. Iris held up her hand. She was showing her gold relic ring to the Queen, as she asked for a favor. Andy swore he saw her lips form the words "Take me" . The Queen shifted. No clumsiness. No slippage on that craggy rock face. Her leg flicked once. The avalanche fell on Iris. Right on her.

A direct hit.

Andy had no time to think about what he'd witnessed. He needed a document for later. So he might make sense of things if he lived. He didn't think he would. But he might have a story to tell. That's when he walked over to Maude and took over camera duties. For the record.

So she could save Jake from the pit.

And snatch up Galton's spell book from the blood-soaked, suety mud.

59
Night Attack

Ursula had Toothpick scoping the far riverbank, while she scanned the beach where she'd last seen her team. There was nothing there now. Only remnants of their old fire. She swore and wondered how she'd persuade the soldiers of fortune to conduct a closer examination of the land, when he called out urgently. She switched over to the other side of the bow. Binocs in hand.

"I've got something," Toothpick said.

"Where?" she said, surprised, heart beating faster. Her team?

"There," he pointed with his rifle. "A stone marker. I see a canoe in the brush."

Ursula aimed her binoculars. It was the oblong stone from Maude's film reel. Or it looked enough like it to warrant a closer investigation. And the dugout canoe, it might be theirs.

It had to be.

She had gone out and gotten kidnapped by the Men of Leng, and they'd crossed the lagoon and discovered the location of the shrine. Maude Brion was up there, dead or alive.

Ursula felt it in her bones. They were there, Jake and the others. Up at the lost shrine.

"Get your men ready to go ashore," she said to Toothpick.

The paddleboat angled for the white stone, using it as a beacon, as if it was calling to them, had always been calling to them, since they reached the docks of Manaus. Waving them in.

60
Offering Web

After they wheeled Jake up the path to the shrine complex, Andy and Maude stopped to survey the scene. No giant spiders. The shrine appeared as honey-lit and golden as it had earlier in the night. The devotees – the half-dozen or so who hadn't run off into the forest – regrouped at the foot of the obelisks. They lit torches. Hoping the fire would keep the spider away. Andy wasn't sure it would. Torches were meager insurance against a foe as adroit and formidable as the two he'd witnessed. There were two, he reminded himself. I know what I saw. Two spiders.

"Where do you think you're going?" Galton pointed a heavy American pistol at them.

"Galton?" Maude said. "I'm so glad to see you. We thought you might've been taken."

"Taken?" He acted as if she'd said something entertaining. "I should be so privileged for Atlach-Nacha to collect me to her bosom. I am her servant. We share that eternal bond."

"But she killed those people down there," Andy said. "She killed Iris. Your wife is dead."

"That was not Atlach-Nacha!" Incensed, Galton cracked his staff over his knee and nearly dropped the pistol. "That was a Grey

Weaver. A servant of the goddess. An automaton. The goddess
rules her. But the goddess must be elsewhere. I should've known
I couldn't fool a goddess so easily. I've been dealing with servants
instead of masters. My negotiations are with the master. I demand
that she see me at once!" He fired his pistol into the sky. "I am an
adept of the Dreamlands. No commoner. How dare she ignore me
and send a servant in her place."

"What will you do?" Maude asked. Andy couldn't believe her
courage to speak. Galton might shoot her, might shoot anyone, for
any reason at all. He didn't need a reason. Only rage.

"Offer sacrifices, of course. As I have before. I gave her pick of
the litter. I've been feeding her for years. Minds and bodies. And for
what? She must acknowledge me. I will not be denied my audience.
I alone kept the gateway open. When do I get the respect due me?
When?"

"You should have it now, Galton. I agree totally." Maude started
off toward the shrine.

"Where are you going?" He raised the gun.

"To get more film. I have one reel left. My camera's still down by
the mine. Andy can fetch that. We must save this for posterity. This
is the culmination of your work." Maude smiled a beautiful smile
that warmed Andy's heart and made him afraid too. Because she
was either telling the truth – in which case he was doomed – or she
was lying to Galton, and she'd managed to fool Andy too. He didn't
know what to believe. Was Maude a follower of the Spider Queen?

Jake moaned. He flailed one arm out toward Galton. Andy lifted
the wheelbarrow legs.

"Bring him to the Offering Web," Galton said.

"What?" Andy said.

"He means the obelisks," Maude said. "We call the netting at the
top the Offering Web."

Andy searched in her gaze for a clue that she was on his side. He found brown eyes.

Galton stepped forward and pressed the gun to his back. "Do it. Go."

"Andy, don't let them start the offering until I get back with my camera and film."

"I won't," Andy muttered, as Galton led him away at gunpoint.

The cultists welcomed them to their circle. Andy stared up at the obelisks. Two tapering stone towers, shaped like a pair of hands. A spiderweb stretched between the fingers. In the film Hopkins sent to Arkham, there'd been a giant spider up there. A Grey Weaver, apparently. And not the Spider Queen Galton was hoping for. A devotee hauled at a rope coiled on the ground. The mousy *squeak, squeak* of a pulley sounded above them. A string of lanterns rose steadily between the obelisks, illuminated the web. Which wasn't a web, but an old fishing net lashed to the stone fingers. Mushrooms proliferated under the obelisks. Hundreds. Of all shapes and sizes.

"Fungi grow where sacrifices are made to the gods." It was the Frenchman speaking.

Andy didn't know what to say to him. His clothes were damp with pink diluted blood.

"Put this around his waist," Galton tossed another looped rope to Andy. "Quickly."

Andy bent Jake forward and cinched the rope around his middle. Then Galton began hoisting Jake into the net. The Offering Web. It was sickening. It reminded him of Bradley. But what could he do? He hoped Maude had a plan. He felt like man in a trance, out of control.

"She'll come now," Galton said. "She's heard my wrath. My complaints. I'm right."

Jake's body reached the net, swaying. Galton tied the end of the rope he was holding to a stake in the ground. There was a second stake, another rope attached to a pulley in the web.

"What's that one for?" Andy pondered the halo of lamps around Jake. The second pulley.

"It's for you, kiddo," Galton said.

He cracked the butt of his gun into the back of Andy's skull.

The light in Andy's eyes went out.

61
Maude's Photoplay

Maude raced through the shrine, grabbing a lamp off the floor as she passed. Down the lane of the old railway tracks. Into the rubber plantation. The abandoned huts where the executives had slept. Where they dreamed their dreams of riches, of railroads through jungles, of land stripped of trees claimed by men from across the ocean who came sporting linen suits, Panama hats, khakis and rifles, smoking cigars on the decks of paddleboats, sipping whiskey, flashing gold rings. In the biggest of these decayed huts, she stored all her reels, the ones she and Hopkins shot and those she'd finished on her own. A table with scattered camera parts. She swept them away.

Where was it?

She put her lamp down and hunted.

It had to be here. Had to. She'd left it here, in case one day she got curious enough to try.

At last, she found what she was searching for under an old *Photoplay* magazine with her picture on the cover. Maude's dark curly hair bobbed, wearing a silver tiara. The next big thing. That was what she was going to be. But it wasn't what she wanted. Not then, not now. She threw it aside and seized the film canister underneath. Her last film can. She looked at all the others stacked rotting in the wet heat. Celluloid was as good as gasoline. She kept the film away from the camp, the shrine. If you weren't careful, you'd burn the whole forest.

Maude knew what she had to do. She pulled over the only office chair left in the camp.

She took out the wavy, waterlogged notebook in her back pocket. She peeled apart pages.

Galton's spells. His guide to the Dreamlands. He always tried to show her. She never wanted to go. Not his way, with the venom on his tongue and a mission to destroy all the people and the places he hated so deeply. His grudges all repaid. She'd absorbed enough knowledge – at least she hoped she had. She opened the film canister. There wasn't any film in it. She'd used all that was left back at the mine. The can contained a single glass vial. She unscrewed the vial and shook out a single brown leaf. It looked like nothing. A dried-up insect. She licked it. The taste was bitter. She shivered as she swallowed her saliva. There were two dried mushroom buttons rattling in the canister. She chewed them up. Unclipped the canteen on her belt. It was filled with broth from the stew. She drank it. Maude started reading the crabbed lines of Galton's journal. His recipe for dreaming. This was the only way. She couldn't do it alone. She needed to go where she was most afraid to go. She read aloud, using his weird cadences. Touching the page so she didn't lose her place. Twisted words like gnarled black vines. She climbed on them with her fingers and her voice. Recitations of a dead language, alien utterances that didn't fit inside a living human mouth. She did her best. Is anything happening? she wondered. Am I failing?

Her chair fell backward with a bang. The back of her head slammed on the floor.

She grumbled in pain. Then her muscles locked. Limbs gone rigid.

Mouth-eyes-ears unshut. Opening. Expanding.

She was convulsing. Her heels beating *rat-a-tat-tat* on the boards. Then they stopped.

Maude had arrived with no ticket – her trip unscheduled – in the Dreamlands.

Houses with no windows. Fields of white mushrooms. A viscous, oily sea. This is not Earth. Wharves. A port. Beings on the docks, inhuman. Grotesque. Eyeless toads hopping, loading and unloading ships. Pink snouts sprouting tentacles that wiggled like a fist of worms. Sensing. A stench of charred meats, inedible to humans, repulsive. She gagged at the smell. Then she saw them. The ones she was looking for. She knew she was being watched. But she went ahead.

Maude awoke with a gasp. She sat up in the hut. Her lamp was burning low. How long had she been unconscious? She didn't know. She'd found the ones she sought out.

But then… another…

She couldn't remember. She tried and tried. But nothing came. It was as if the answer slipped from her grasp, couldn't be grasped, a handful of smoke… that stench… then later…

A face. Human seeming.

It saw her, and it did not move. She knew it saw her. Eight legs. Poised. Unmoving.

Was that vision in the Dreamlands, or was it here in the Brazilian Amazon?

Maude thought she saw her in both places.

A human face… but wrong. The body of a spider.

The Spider Queen. This was she who spun the web between dimensions.

Maude needed to get back to Andy. To tell him what she saw. She was certain Galton planned to kill Andy. To offer up Jake, and everyone but himself, to the Spider Queen. She had to tell Andy what she did. No person who purposefully sees a god can live among humans.

Galton told her that.

Maude tried to stand. She fell back, landing hard on her side.

Her arm stayed pinned to the floor. *Her hand.* Where was it? Lost in a crevice of bluish white light. She tried to free herself. This was insane. How could she be stuck? Like a magnet, an invisible energy was pulling at her. Tugging her down. It hurt her eyes to gaze into the light.

Maude gritted her teeth, and with all her strength she withdrew her limb from that place.

The resistance gave way, and she was free.

Her hand wrapped around the end of a white cord, a woven cable, thicker than her wrist. She inspected it. A connection to the other dimension. Vibrations flowed through the cord into her. She felt that energy reaching into her mind, thrumming her like a musical string. It didn't hurt. It felt wonderful. Ecstatic.

Maude tried to take more of the cord. It slid without friction now. Free and gliding.

Taking it with her, she left the hut.

62
The Strand

"Is this really necessary? Do you need to tie me? I'm not going to go anywhere," Ashley said.

A muffled impact. Followed by an intake of breath. Ursula didn't need to see what was happening belowdecks. She could imagine. Ashley didn't say anything after that. Toothpick's men tied Thiago. Leaving both men bound.

"Let's go," Toothpick said.

The soldiers had lights but didn't use them. Comfortable in the night, they moved when the breeze blew, stealthy, using the dark. The moonlight was adequate for navigation. She walked in front with Toothpick. They found the trailhead. Climbed. Cautious but swift. When they reached the plantation, things went slower. They split their number. Checking buildings, one by one. It was deserted. At the final hut, bigger than the rest, a luminescent strand stretched along the ground. The men dropped low. Crabbing along. Fingers on triggers. Eyes wide.

"What's that?" Toothpick whispered to her.

"I don't know," Ursula said. "I've never–"

A scream cut her off.

Close by. One of Toothpick's men. The last in line. He'd worn black gloves, a slouch hat.

He was gone. His hat lay in the grass. One glove. With a hand still in it, twitching.

Toothpick turned. Spoke through gritted teeth. "What happened to him, Sullivan?"

A shadow-face shook its head. "I didn't see. He was right next–"

The next time it came, Ursula saw it. A flick of motion. Blacker than black.

Shadow-face Sullivan didn't have a face anymore. Or a head. His body was dragged through the grasses into the tree line. Nothing was taking him there. A quick, fuzzy blur. The soldiers started shooting. Flashes from gun barrels. Gunsmoke hovered. The shots deafened her.

Toothpick lifted his hand.

"Wait! Wait!"

"There's his head, cap. Sullivan's head," a soldier said in disbelief.

"Quiet," Toothpick said.

Clip-clopping. From the final hut, the glowing strand stretched on the ground. A blinding blue-white flash of light. The afterimage marred her vision. But she made out forms. There were men running on it. Ursula couldn't believe what she was seeing. They had wrappings mounded in two heaps on their heads. They wobbled as they walked. She didn't need to see them drinking from rubies to recognize them. The Men of Leng were here. Making a night raid of some kind.

Toothpick raised his rifle and picked out one of the Men.

Ursula didn't get a chance to stop him. *They aren't the ones killing your men, Toothpick.*

Before he could fire a bullet, Toothpick dropped his rifle. And for the second time tonight, he dropped his toothpick. A furry paw, that's what it looked like at close range – a paw with a black claw curving out of the tip. Toothpick's beating heart stuck to the end of it.

He crumpled to the ground.

Ursula sprinted for the strand. She never turned back to see if the giant spider was pursuing her. When she got to the strand, the Men of Leng were gone, splashing down a flooded lane hacked into the bush. Their hunched shadows bobbed up and down as they ran.

She followed the strand the other way. Into the ramshackle ruins of the hut.

Cans of film stacked against the wall. But no Maude Brion. No Jake, Andy, or Iris.

A soft crackle of movement outside the doorway.

Everything is afraid of fire, she thought.

Ursula got an idea.

She opened cans as fast as she could. She was building a nest of celluloid.

63
It Kills

It went up above the trees where it felt safe. Not as safe as in the ground. But in the ground was bad and good. Trapped in the ground was bad. It had its little ones coming soon. It needed food.

From the waterfall, it took the food left on the ground and packed it in the trees. Later, it would put little ones in the trees and sit with them. A web across the trees in the moonlight is beautiful.

Smoke in the trees. It crawled, looked down in the fish web. Here was fire. Here was food. At the bottom, small on the ground was the man with the voice it hated. He pressed on its head from inside. He was forcing her. It crawled onto the fish web wanting to kill the man. Two meals were snagged there. One smelled like blood and his legs were broken. The other was waking up and saw it coming. The man it hated could wait. It crept and crept toward the food.

The waking one thrashed as if it could fly. It tasted the other one. It took a broken leg, tore it, and ate it. The thrashing one beat fists into the huntress. Then the man it hated screamed into its head. *Where is Atlach-Nacha? Where is she?*

The goddess goes where she wants to go.

No more waiting. It stopped eating food and went down to kill the magic man.

It chased down the stone trees and bit the man in two. Her fangs sawed him slowly.

He squirmed like a bug. While he was squirming, she collected other food around her.

At the edge of the fire circle, she saw Men from the Dreamlands. From Leng. They didn't come close but watched her collecting her food. Did they want this too? They looked jealous.

Take it. Here, Men.

Try and take it from me.

They had one or two smaller meals bundled up on threads. Leading them along.

What is this? The radiant cord! The thread of Atlach-Nacha in this waking world? How? The thread of silk glowed on the ground. She took that to be a summons from her goddess, her mighty Queen. Praise her. It walked the thread home. Home to her Queen. It took its little ones inside it home, to be born.

Home.

64
A Spider's Thread

"The spider ate his leg," Andy said. "It ate Jake's leg. I think he's dead. He's not moving. Get him down. Get him down. Fast." Andy loosened the rope around his torso and helped Ursula lower Jake's body to the ground. Jake was white as paper. Limp. But breathing.

She put her ear to his chest.

"His heart sounds erratic. Give me your belt. I need to tourniquet his leg above the knee."

Below that point the limb was missing. Ursula did her work quickly, methodically.

"Who are those men wearing the turbans?" Andy asked.

"They're the ones from the galley. The Men of Leng. I don't know how they got here."

"I brought them," Maude said. She emerged from the shrine. "I didn't know what else to do. I went to the Dreamlands and brought them here. They wanted to raid the cult for the moon-beasts. They only got one or two of us. Everyone else is..."

She waved her arm at the circle that resembled a medieval battleground.

Ursula stared hard at Maude. "You're Maude Brion. I've seen your films."

"Oh, thank you." The actor and director clutched at her shirt front. It was ludicrous.

"The ones up at the plantation, I mean. I saw where you kept them. Where this otherworldly cable leads? Into that hut with the equipment. I was there."

"It's a spider's thread. From Atlach-Nacha... I think." Maude faltered, teetering over to the obelisk, using it to keep herself from falling over.

"Are you injured?" Ursula asked.

She said, "I'm dizzy. My legs feel weak." She yawned. "Are you real?"

"What?" Ursula said.

"Is this a dream?" Maude leaned her back into the obelisk, sliding down into a crouch.

"Andy, see if she has any injuries."

Andy, covered in blood, none of it his own, stooped over the visionary picture director.

"She looks fine," he said.

"We need to build a stretcher. Get Jake to the boat. Marcos has medicine on board."

"Marcos is here?" Andy said, a hint of hope in his voice.

"No. He's somewhere in the jungle. So's Davi. Thiago is tied up in the cabin with Ashley Lott. There's no time for discussion." Ursula pulled back on her hair, sighing. "We have a boat. Let's get going."

Andy nodded. "At the bottom of this hill is an encampment. I'll find something to wrap Jake in. A tarp. We can use it to carry him down to the river."

"Good man. Fetch it."

Andy took several steps toward the path to the mine, then paused.

"Where's the Spider Queen?"

"She walked off on that cord," Ursula said. "She's returning to the Dreamlands."

"What about the other one? The one with the human face?" he asked.

Maude lifted her head but said nothing. She yawned again and closed her eyes, smiling.

"There's only one Spider Queen, Andy," Ursula said.

"I don't think so…"

"We need that stretcher. Now go."

Andy picked up Galton's pistol from the grass and jogged down to the camp by the mine.

"She does have a human face. It's lovely," Maude said to Ursula when Andy was gone.

Ursula suspected that Maude had taken something stronger than liquor. Pills? She was anesthetized in some way. There were jungle plants that had this sort of effect. Fungi. Toxins.

Delirious. The woman was having visions. Her reports were untrustworthy.

Jake moaned and turned his head. His eyes opened briefly. Shut them again.

"I'm here, Jake. It's Ursula. We're taking you to the boat. Marcos's boat. You're going to be fine. Do you understand me? You'll live, Jake." She wiped the blood from him.

He was out again. Still breathing. The worst of the bleeding slowed. His trouser leg was empty below the knee. His other leg was broken. A deep, ugly gash matted the hair on his head.

She wanted him to make it. But she knew the odds. She had to get him to the boat.

•••

Ursula and Andy carried Jake in a sling made from a camping roll. Maude trailed behind them; she was holding a torch to light their way, her other arm wrapped around her body as if she were freezing. She was silent as she followed. The sky was turning milky white. Morning.

They walked beside the thread glimmering on the ground, careful not to step on it.

"You sure you saw the spider go this way?" Andy asked.

"Yes," Ursula said. "The Men of Leng took their slaves down here. They probably went right after her. There's a portal open inside that hut, leading to the Dreamlands. But it may close."

"This is insane." Andy shook his head. "How can I write this? No one will believe me."

They splashed along the rusted tracks that were thrust up like devil's prongs from the underworld. The thread veered left, off to the hut. The trail to the river went right.

"We need to reach the river, then get back to Manaus. One step at a time," Ursula said.

Andy stopped. He was holding the corners of his end of the roll.

"Where's Maude going?" he said.

Her torch swerved left.

Ursula set Jake down. "Stay with him. If I can't convince her to come with me, we're leaving her. I'll be gone one minute."

Andy looked worried. The last thing he wanted was for Ursula to go.

"One minute," she said.

65
Torchlight

Ursula saw the torchlight flickering in the doorway to the hut. Maude was trying to get back there. Back to the Dreamlands. Well, I'll let her go, she thought. Jake's not dying while I argue with her. Ursula rushed over the threshold, keeping off the pulsing, luminescent thread.

"Stop," Maude whispered to her as she entered. "Look."

Ursula turned her head toward the far end of the narrow hut. A hulking form filled up the space. Too big to fit, part of its body pushed up high against the wall, mashed into the upper corner. The rest disappeared down through the shattered floor of the hut.

It was so much bigger than what she'd witnessed climbing down the obelisk.

Slurping and chewing, if it knew they were there, it didn't care.

It was feasting.

Maude put her fingers to her own lips. "She must've been angry to do that. Or very hungry." She gave a little laugh. "Her own servant. That is nasty business. Even for a queen."

The noises stopped.

A vague shape that must've been the true Spider Queen turned in the torchlight. A masklike human face flashed momentarily toward them. What was that? The face – if it was a face – vanished. Ursula couldn't tell what she was seeing. The room was cramped. So dark. The torch smoked. The smoke burned her eyes. She blinked and looked, but nothing became clearer.

The huge thing oriented as if considering them. Then it was difficult to tell what was happening. More noises. Something was prodding and nuzzling into the split-open abdomen of the Grey Weaver from the obelisk, consuming it. The walls dripped with splattered amber fluid.

"Give me the torch," Ursula said.

"Why? What're you doing?" Maude backed away. But there was nowhere to go. Half the room was spiders. The other half was unrolled reels of celluloid – the nest Ursula had made.

Ursula snatched the torch from Maude and hurled it into the nest.

"No, wait!" Maude yelled. "What did you do?"

Heat rushed at them.

Ursula dragged Maude from the inferno.

"What did you do? What did you do?"

66
Pale Yellow

Manaus appeared on the horizon. Thiago was at the helm, steering them past other boats, fishermen and travelers. Businessmen. He told Ursula he was sure his brother could make a dugout and would return soon with Marcos. But he would go looking.

Andy sat beside Jake. He hadn't regained consciousness, but he was alive. Of course he'd never walk the way he had in the past. Ursula said he'd make it if there was no infection. Ashley sat in the bow under the shade of a tarp.

"You came back with nothing to show?" he asked Ursula for the umpteenth time.

"I came back with my team," she said. "I consider that a success."

She sat on the other side of Jake.

"What about her?" Ashley said, tipping his chin. "Is she a success too?"

Andy turned to look at Maude who was leaning over the stern, watching their wake.

Maude hadn't spoken since Ursula ran aboard with her. Their clothing was singed. Ursula's hands were red and blistered. Andy carried Jake the rest of the way down on his own. He didn't know how, but he did it.

"No one will believe you. You know that?" Ashley delighted in the misfortune of others.

"I don't know about that," Andy said. "I'm going to write a book."

"You have no proof," Ashley said, scoffing. "Another tall tale from the Amazon."

Andy had kept a secret from them. A surprise more than a secret, because it was good news and he was ready to tell them now, right before they arrived back in so-called civilization.

He slid the film canister from his satchel. He tapped on it. He'd prove Ashley wrong.

"What's that?" Ashley said, sitting up. He poked his head into the hot sunlight.

"It's footage Maude and I filmed that night. Shows a giant spider."

He was surprised he didn't get a reaction from Maude. She hadn't budged. But she wasn't right in the head since she came back. He hoped she'd get better. She needed help. She'd been through more than any of them. Except for Jake. But his wounds were physical.

"Let me see that." Ashley came over.

"Nothing to see," Andy said. "Not yet. I grabbed it when I went to look for a stretcher for Jake. It's all there. I'm giving it to the *Advertiser* when we get back. If Maude doesn't mind…"

"It's her picture," Ursula said. "She made it."

They all looked at Maude. She was slouched over, resting her cheek on the rail.

Ashley grabbed the can and pried it apart.

"Don't open it," Andy said. He lunged at the archaeologist.

Ashley dropped both halves of the canister on the deck.

"It's empty," he said. "You're a phony. A conman. A carnival barker."

"How could that be?" Andy said, astonished. He guarded it like a watchdog. Today was the first time he had the reel out from under his hammock. He lit a cigarette he'd found left behind by one of the soldiers of fortune and wandered despondently to the stern where Maude brooded. That film was the proof he needed for his story.

There was something in the water. Trailing behind the boat.

Andy stepped to the rail.

Maude had her film cradled in her arm. She was peeling off loops, tossing them to the waves. Her face had a dreamy quality. Her eyes were soft-focused, staring out at nothing.

"Hey! No, don't do that. Maude, that's our evidence we're telling the truth."

Andy gripped what was left of the reel. She let him have it. As he pulled her arm back, he noticed a scar on the inside of her wrist. It looked like a white spider. Had she done that to herself, he wondered. He let go of her and wound up the drowned reel. "It's ruined," he said.

"Maybe some of it can be saved," Ursula said.

Andy walked off in a huff.

Maude said, "Look! Look at the waves. The way the sun is hitting them. It's like golden spiders crawling on the surface. Can you see them?"

A small spider crept along the rail. She lifted it carefully onto her fingers, letting it crawl on her. Finger to finger. It was pale yellow and translucent. She studied it as if her life depended on it. As if it were the only thing that mattered.

ABOUT THE AUTHOR

S A SIDOR is the author of four dark crime thrillers and more recently two splendid supernatural-pulp adventures, *Fury From the Tomb* and *The Beast of Nightfall Lodge*. He lives near Chicago with his family.

sasidor.com // twitter.com/sa_sidor

WORLD EXPANDING FICTION

Do you have them all?

ARKHAM HORROR
- ☐ *Wrath of N'kai* by Josh Reynolds
- ☐ *The Last Ritual* by S A Sidor
- ☐ *Mask of Silver* by Rosemary Jones
- ☐ *Litany of Dreams* by Ari Marmell
- ☐ *The Devourer Below* ed Charlotte Llewelyn-Wells
- ☐ *Dark Origins, The Collected Novellas Vol 1*
- ☑ *Cult of the Spider Queen* by S A Sidor
- ☐ *The Deadly Grimoire* by Rosemary Jones
  (coming soon)

DESCENT
- ☐ *The Doom of Fallowhearth* by Robbie MacNiven
- ☐ *The Shield of Daqan* by David Guymer
- ☐ *The Gates of Thelgrim* by Robbie MacNiven
- ☐ *Zachareth* by Robbie MacNiven *(coming soon)*

KEYFORGE
- ☐ *Tales from the Crucible* ed Charlotte Llewelyn-Wells
- ☐ *The Qubit Zirconium* by M Darusha Wehm

LEGEND OF THE FIVE RINGS
- ☐ *Curse of Honor* by David Annandale
- ☐ *Poison River* by Josh Reynolds
- ☐ *The Night Parade of 100 Demons*
  by Marie Brennan
- ☐ *Death's Kiss* by Josh Reynolds
- ☐ *The Great Clans of Rokugan, The Collected Novellas Vol 1*
- ☐ *To Chart the Clouds* by Evan Dicken
  (coming soon)

PANDEMIC
- ☐ *Patient Zero* by Amanda Bridgeman

TERRAFORMING MARS
- ☐ *In the Shadow of Deimos* by Jane Killick

TWILIGHT IMPERIUM
- ☐ *The Fractured Void* by Tim Pratt
- ☐ *The Necropolis Empire* by Tim Pratt

ZOMBICIDE
- ☐ *Last Resort* by Josh Reynolds
- ☐ *Planet Havoc* by Tim Waggoner *(coming soon)*